The critics love

BLACK DUST MAMBO

"Phoenix is a beautiful storyteller—her prose flows like poetry . . . an extraordinarily entertaining novel that is addictively readable."

—Explorations: The BN SciFi and Fantasy Blog

"Phoenix creates characters and worlds so vivid that the reader feels as though they are taking part in the story rather than just observing the action. . . . The author excels at characterization, and her talents are once again evident here . . . a fascinating story that belongs on the shelves and in the hands of all urban fantasy readers."

—Bitten By Books

"*Black Dust Mambo* started with a bang and kept on going with intrigue, family secrets, double lives, mystery, murder, and a little bit of romance. This book was packed from cover to cover that kept me turning the pages and craving more. . . . Adrian Phoenix brings it to the reader with a punch!"

—Fresh Fiction

"Something new set in the sexy, supernatural city of New Orleans. Voodoo, hoodoo, and magic abound in this crazy tale about hexes and curses, nomads, vessels, and root doctors. . . . Magic, sex, mystery, murder, and hot guys abound in this book."

—Fang-tastic Books

the Ma

Black Heart Loa

BENEATH THE SKIN

"Adrian Phoenix has done it again! Complex, lyrical, and beautifully written . . . another unique and compulsive page-turner."

—Jenna Black, author of *Speak of the Devil*

"This violent, wrenching tale is something special."

—*Affaire de Coeur*

"Lush, sexy, and thrilling . . . darkly addictive."

—*New York Times* bestselling author Jeaniene Frost

"This darkly dramatic tale is one wild ride in a series that only promises to get better."

—*Romantic Times*

IN THE BLOOD

"Phoenix trips the dark fantastic in this wild, bloody sequel. . . . She keeps the plot thick and the tension high."

—*Publishers Weekly*

"Filled with twisting plots, shadowy government agencies, conspiracies, and betrayals . . . this dark urban fantasy is not only action-packed from beginning to end but, at its core, it is also a story of hope and love."

—*ParaNormal Romance*

"The atmosphere is dark, and treachery abounds, making this story white-knuckle reading in the extreme."

—*Romantic Times*

A RUSH OF WINGS

"Hard-charging action sequences, steamy sex scenes, and a surprising government conspiracy make this debut, the first in a series, engrossingly fun."

—*Entertainment Weekly*

"Phoenix's lively debut has it all. . . . Phoenix alternates romantic homages to gothdom and steamy blood-drinking threesomes with enough terse, fast-paced thriller scenes to satisfy even the most jaded fan."

—*Publishers Weekly*

"Sharp, wicked, and hot as sin."

—*New York Times* bestselling author Marjorie M. Liu

"A thrilling tale of lust and murder that will keep you turning the pages to see what happens next."

—*Gothic Beauty*

"This one pulled me in from the first page. Heather and Dante are among those rare characters readers so often look for and seldom find."

—*New York Times* bestselling author Barb Hendee

"A fast-paced ride, its New Orleans setting appropriately rich and gothic, its characters both real and surprising."

—*New York Times* bestselling author Kristine Kathryn Rusch

BLACK HEART LOA

ADRIAN PHOENIX

POCKET BOOKS

New York   London   Toronto   Sydney

Pocket Books
A Division of Simon & Schuster, Inc.
1230 Avenue of the Americas
New York, NY 10020

First Pocket Books paperback edition July 2011

POCKET and colophon are registered trademarks of Simon & Schuster, Inc.

For information about special discounts for bulk purchases, please contact Simon & Schuster Special Sales at 1-866-506-1949 or business@simonandschuster.com.

The Simon & Schuster Speakers Bureau can bring authors to your live event. For more information or to book an event contact the Simon & Schuster Speakers Bureau at 1-866-248-3049 or visit our website at www.simonspeakers.com.

Text design by Jacquelynne Hudson
Cover design by John Vairo Jr.
Cover illustration by Steve Stone

Manufactured in the United States of America

10 9 8 7 6 5 4 3 2 1

ISBN 978-1-4391-6792-2
ISBN 978-1-4391-6794-6 (ebook)

*Dedicated to
my wonderful sons, Sebastian and Matt.
Thanks for believing in my dream and cheering me
on every step of the way. I love you both!*

ACKNOWLEDGMENTS

Thanks, as always, to my editor, Jennifer Heddle, for her amazing insight and for helping me shape the best possible story—each and every time. You won't find a better editor anywhere. Ain't possible. And to my agent, Matt Bialer, for his unflagging support and encouragement. You always lift my spirits. (And to Lindsay Ribar for all the *Supernatural* chats.)

Tons of hugs and kisses to all the folks at Pocket Books who poured their time, energy, and love into this book: Renee Huff, Erica Feldon, Stephanie DeLuca, and Anne Cherry—among others.

Thanks so much to Steve Stone for the truly stunning covers and for bringing Kallie and her world to life.

Special hugs and kisses to all my readers. I can't thank you enough for picking up this book. If this is your first Kallie adventure, *bienvenue*! If this is your second trip into the bayou with Kallie, *merci beaucoup* and welcome back!

And, as always, thanks to my friends and family for making this all possible: Sherri Lyons, Jen Phoenix, Kylah, and Liam—I love you all! Karen Abrahamson, D. T. Steiner, Lynn Adams, Marty and Sharon Embertson—I couldn't do it without you!

BLACK HEART LOA

ONE

FIVE OF SPADES

The goddamned nightmare hadn't ended, after all.

Kallie Rivière shuffled the blue Bicycle cards she used for divination, their worn edges flipping against her palms. Drawing in a steadying breath, she closed her eyes and focused on her cousin Jackson Bonaparte, desperately hoping that the last words he'd said to her wouldn't become his last words, period.

"Gotta go. See you on Sunday. Love ya."

After not seeing his pickup in the driveway, Kallie had assumed Jackson had tossed his Siberian husky into the bed of his Dodge Ram and driven into town for a couple of beers—despite the fact that she'd asked him to stay put, to keep him safe from the man stalking their family.

Then she'd discovered Jackson's protective mojo bag in the grass in front of their *ti-tante*'s house—its leather cord torn as though it had been ripped from around his neck—along with the baseball bat he kept beside the back door in case of trouble.

As Kallie picked up the mojo bag from the grass, the woodsy scents of sandalwood and dog rose wafting up from its red flannel, dread had dropped like stones into her belly. She'd *known*. Felt it down to the marrow.

Jackson *hadn't* driven to the Hair of the Dog Tavern. He was missing.

"An eye for an eye is never enough," Doctor Heron whispers.

And the long nightmare Kallie thought had just ended—one she had barely survived—was still very much in play and had just swept over her cousin.

A nightmare that had begun damned near twenty-four hours earlier in her blood-soaked bed at the Prestige Hotel in New Orleans and had ended on the banks of the bayou behind her *tante* Divinity's house in Bayou Cyprés Noir.

All because her hoodoo aunt had stolen the identity of another conjurer and had, therefore, brought revenge-seeking, soul-killing Jean-Julien St. Cyr—Doctor Heron—the bogeyman of hoodoo, into their lives.

And had nearly cost Kallie her own—body and soul. Or would've if she *had* a soul—and that was another goddamned matter altogether. Another matter for another time. Right now, she needed to find her cousin.

Kallie shuffled the cards, Jackson's words looping through her mind like a mantra, a fervent prayer.

Gotta go. See you on Sunday. Love ya.

She pictured Jackson as the cards ricocheted against her palms—eyes the color of heated honey and brimming with laughter, slightly tilted like her own; sun-bronzed skin; coffee-dark hair brushing against his muscle-corded shoulders in thick waves; lips slanted into a pirate's wicked smirk; he stood just a whisper under a lean-muscled six feet.

He was the same age as she, twenty-three, but just a

couple of months ahead of her. And in love with the restless sea he had once called—in a rum-sodden moment—his briny bride.

Kallie saturated her cousin's image with her desire to find him. Alive. Intact.

Love ya back, and I'm goddamned holding you to Sunday, Jacks.

She'd finished shuffling the cards, and Kallie's fingers stilled on top of the blue deck. She opened her eyes. Her pulse raced through her veins. Her heart kicked hard against her CPR-compression-injured and aching ribs. She felt the weight of each set of eyes settling like anxious doves along her shoulders.

Her *tante* and hoodoo teacher, Divinity, stood behind her along with the woman whose identity Divinity had stolen, a woman Kallie had met only an hour or so ago—Gabrielle LaRue.

Kallie didn't know whether Gabrielle was a rootworker like her and her aunt or a voodoo mambo. But it was Gabrielle LaRue who Doctor Heron had blamed for his time in prison; Gabrielle LaRue he'd blamed for poisoning his clients and leaving him to take the blame.

"An eye for an eye is never enough," Doctor Heron whispers.

But the bastard had gone after the wrong woman, the wrong family, because of that goddamned stolen identity. Kallie's throat tightened. Several people had died because of that mistake, more than one in her place. Gage had been the first.

He lies on his belly, his face turned to the side. Blood masks his fine features, glitters in his black curls. All color has drained from his espresso-brown skin, leaving his blue-inked clan tattoos stark on his muscular back, ass, and thighs.

The sexy conjurer from one of the freewheeling nomad clans—a pagan blend of biker and Gypsy—had died body and soul upon her hex-poisoned hotel bed in New Orleans after a night of sweaty, bendy, hot-blooded play, while she'd been in the bathroom sick on too much champagne.

Then Lord Basil Augustine, the leader of the Hecatean Alliance—a fraternity of magicians, conjurers, and rootworkers—had taken a bullet meant for Kallie, a bullet fired in desperation by Doctor Heron's doomed, crazed daughter, Rosette.

Rough hands latch onto Kallie's shoulders and spin her away. Augustine's suit jacket whispers against her robe as he twists his body past hers. Thunder cracks through the room. Augustine grunts. He stumbles against Kallie . . .

And Dallas. Kallie drew upon a deep well of relief when she thought of the hard-drinking root doctor and how he'd survived Doctor Heron's murderous attack—a knife across the throat—thanks to the skill of the Hecatean Alliance surgeons and healers who'd saved his life. He was currently hospitalized at the medical center on the twentieth floor of the Prestige, fresh out of surgery, and hopefully drugged to the gills.

Oh, and let's not forget Belladonna—poppet-bound and kidnapped.

And speaking of whom . . .

Belladonna Brown, mambo-in-training and Kallie's best friend, sat straight-backed on the floral-patterned sofa Kallie was kneeling beside, her face with its flawless chocolate-colored skin composed despite the worry flickering in her startling hazel eyes.

"You okay, Shug?" Belladonna asked. "You look like you're about to start throwing punches."

"Not a bad idea," Kallie said. "Just wish I had someone to throw them *at*."

"Mmm-hmm," Belladonna sympathized.

She'd been snoozing on the sofa after the night's events when Kallie had awakened her with a frantic shake of her shoulder.

It's Jacks. And his ass is in the fire, for true.

Hellfire. Then we gotta pull his fine ass out.

Goddamned straight.

"Take a deep breath, Shug, before you turn over that card," Belladonna murmured. "I can see the pulse pounding in your throat. Try to relax."

"Focus on yo' cousin, you," Divinity urged.

Kallie gritted her teeth against the urge to tell them both, *No goddamned shit. Now shut the hell up and let me do what I know how to do already.*

Closing her eyes, Kallie drew in a deep breath of air scented with beeswax, the perfume of her aunt's side-yard roses drifting in through the screen door, and the earthy odors of patchouli and frankincense from the herb- and root-cluttered worktable, and drew them deep into her lungs, ignoring the pain twinging through her sternum.

Her pulse eased off the throttle. She brushed her fingers across the deck's slick back, then cut the deck into three stacks on the sofa cushion beside Belladonna.

Kallie flipped over the first card on the first stack.

She wasn't surprised when she saw the king of spades—bad luck coming from a man or with men. Okay, then. Was the late Doctor Heron responsible for Jackson's disappearance or had a posse of unhappy outlaws decided to put a stop to her cousin's Robin Hood–style bayou thefts of illegal goods?

Jackson had been skating on thin luck for some time now.

Grasping the sharp edge of the first card on the second stack, Kallie turned it over. Her blood chilled. The goddamned queen of spades. Bad luck coming from a woman or with women.

"Hellfire," Belladonna breathed. "Both the king and queen. Jackson's in deep."

"*Beaucoup* deep, Bell," Kallie said. "Deep enough to drown."

"We ain't gonna allow dat, girl," Divinity said, voice tight. "Boy ain't gonna drown, no. Now turn over de next damned card."

Kallie touched the back of the top card on the third stack, drew in a deep breath of sandalwood- and sage-fragrant air, then flipped it over. Her heart sank. The five of spades.

"Sweet Jesus, dey all be spades."

"At least we haven't seen the ace of spades," Gabrielle soothed.

"True dat," Divinity agreed. "*Mauvaise partance, bonne arrivée.*"

A *bad beginning brings a good ending.* Kallie mentally crossed her fingers, wishing those words true.

"Delays, setbacks, maybe defeat," Belladonna said. She shook her head, her black and midnight-blue curls shivering like a flower in the breeze. "Maybe," she added hopefully, "that's meant for whoever *took* Jacks and not for those of us *looking* for Jacks."

Kallie blew out a breath and nodded, even though

she thought the prospect unlikely. She gathered up the three piles and merged them into one stack again. She was just about to lay down the first row of six cards, when the *whang* of the porch door slamming against the house jolted her up onto her feet and spun her around.

Wondering why Cielo hadn't barked a warning, Kallie remembered with a sudden pang that Jackson's Siberian husky was also missing.

Two men wearing black ski masks, jeans, and black T-shirts dashed into the living room, shotguns in their black-gloved hands. The ominous *shuh-shunk* of rounds being pumped into place echoed throughout the room.

Kallie's heart launched into overdrive, racking a round of adrenaline into her veins. She eyed the cards still clutched in her hands. *Welcome to a setback. Hello, delay.* Goddamned five of spades.

TWO

HOUSE FULL O' HOODOOS

"Don't none of y'all make a fucking move!" The taller of the two men yelled as he halted beside the coffee table, his shotgun swinging between Kallie and Belladonna on the sofa and Divinity and Gabrielle at the cherrywood rockers opposite. Kallie noticed the back end of a blond mullet poking out of his ski mask. "Or I'll blow your fucking brains out!"

"Cash, man, tone it down a little," his partner said, voice low and uneasy. "I ain't real comfortable with that kinda language around women."

"What the *hell* have I fucking *said* about using my *name* on jobs, asswipe?" Cash grated through clenched teeth. "How many goddamned times do I hafta tell you, *Kerry*? There. How does it feel, Kerry-Kerry-goddamned-fucking-Kerry?"

"You don't hafta to be such a dick about it," Kerry muttered.

Belladonna made an odd snorting sound, like she was choking. Kallie risked a quick glance and confirmed that her friend had clasped both hands over her mouth, trying to trap the laughter inside.

"Cash and Kerry?" Kallie questioned, speaking for them all. "Y'all kidding?"

"Shut the hell up," Cash snarled, pointing the shotgun's dark mouth at her. "And sit your ass down."

Kerry glanced at Divinity and said, "Apologies for the language, ma'am. My mama always told me to be respectful around womenfolk."

Divinity's hands dropped to her lavender-skirted hips as she drew herself up to her magically looming five-seven and lifted her chin, the expression on her light cocoa-colored face forbidding.

"Yo' apologies ain't accepted, boy," she said. "Breaking into a house is a sight more disrespectful dan de language. And I'm sure yo' mama would agree dat aiming shotguns at de people inside dat house be even *more* disrespectful. And dis ain't just a house full o' women. Dis be a house full o' hoodoos."

"And mambos," Gabrielle added, folding her arms underneath the bustline of her carnation-red blouse and giving a curt nod of her red-scarfed head for emphasis.

Kallie glanced at her. Well, one question answered.

Kerry's ski-mask-encircled eyes widened. "Hoodoos? Mambos?"

Cash snorted. "Hoodoos and mambos. Different names for the same thing—con artists. Kerry-man, if brains were leather, you wouldn't have enough to saddle a damned june bug."

"Ain't true," Kerry protested, shaking his head. "I ain't the stupid one here. At least I know that hoodoos handle juju and potions and medicines and mambos are like voodoo priestesses—all about the religion and the *loas* and shit. *You're* the one who ain't got enough brains to saddle a june bug."

Kallie offered Kerry a sweet-as-pecan-pie smile and held up the deck of cards. "And y'all happened to interrupt a reading."

"I don't think the *loa* are gonna care much for that, you messing with their *gris-gris,*" Belladonna said, her voice a soft, velvety purr—a sound as ominous as shotgun shells being chambered. "Especially since you didn't bring a gift."

Kerry's entire body twitched. His gaze squirrel-skittered around the room, darting from ceiling to dark corners as though he expected the spirits to drop on him like a weighted net or a nest of tree-dwelling snakes, and finally coming to rest on Divinity's herb- and root-cluttered table. His pupils expanded as he took in the jars and bottles, the candles and empty mojo bags, the half-finished poppet with purple button eyes.

"Jesus," he whispered. And backed up a pace.

"I don't believe in that juju bullshit," Cash declared. But his uneasy stance and shifting feet made a liar of him—or at least a partial liar. His fingers white-knuckled around the shotgun's grip and gleaming steel barrel. "So y'all just shut your fucking mouths and tell me where the hell that bastard Bonaparte hid our shit."

Belladonna snorted. "Outlaw, please. Which is it? Shut up or talk? Because you sure as sin can't have both."

"He's sounding like an eat-his-cake-and-have-it-too kinda guy," Kallie said, switching the cards to her left hand and leaving her right empty. If he got close enough for her to throw a punch, she wanted to hit him with her strongest. She might not get a second shot.

Belladonna's curls bobbed. "Mmm-hmm. That he is."

"Christ," Cash muttered. "I got a feeling *Shut up* is

beyond y'all." He raised the shotgun to chest level and aimed the barrel between Kallie's breasts. His old-sweat-and-tobacco odor deepened. "You're that fucking thief's hot little cousin, ain'tcha?"

"Sounds like you got all the goddamned answers," Kallie replied, lifting her chin. "Why don't *you* tell *me*?"

Cash's gaze, burning with a fire stoked by a self-righteous wrath, scorched a path from the top of her head to just past her cutoffs and back up along her snug black tank to her face. A smirk tugged up one corner of his ski-mask-framed lips.

"A pretty little thing with that long, dark hair and them purple eyes, ain'tcha? Yeah, you're Bonaparte's cousin, all right." His smirk vanished. "So sit your pretty little ass down and tell me where the hell the sonuvabitch stashed our shit."

Kallie narrowed her eyes. "What makes you think I'd know?"

"Ain't playing games here, sugar," Cash said, glancing pointedly at the shotgun in his hands. "Y'all live in the same house. Can't be many secrets."

"Oh, you'd be surprised," Kallie muttered, lancing a dark look at her aunt.

Keeping her attention on Cash's nervous ceiling-scanning buddy, Divinity tsked and shook her head. "Stop yo' pouting, ungrateful child. I did what had to be done and dat's de end of it."

"No, that ain't the end of it, goddammit," Kallie said, knotting her right hand into a fist. "We're just getting started. But later, I mean. Not now."

Thunder boomed through the house, ricocheting off the walls and Kallie's eardrums. She winced in pain.

Chunks of plaster from the ceiling exploded against the hardwood floor. The pungent scent of cordite peppered the air.

"We are now officially back to SHUT! THE! FUCK! UP!" Cash screamed, neck tendons cording. Smoke curled from the shotgun's barrel. "If anyone makes a fucking peep, except to tell me where that goddamned Jackson Bonaparte hides all the shit he steals, I ain't gonna be blowing holes in the ceiling! Y'all got that?"

"Jesus Christ, Cash!" Kerry yelled, hands over his ears. "You trying to make us all deaf?"

"You can shut the fuck up too," Cash snarled. "You ain't been no kind of help, you fucking superstitious mama's boy."

"Hey," Kerry protested, yelling, an injured expression on his face. "Ain't no call to be like that. I'm watching your back, ain't I?"

"I don't know—are you?"

"I got a stake in this too, dammit! I just don't wanna get my ass hexed, that's all."

Kallie felt the tap of fingers against her calf. Glancing over her shoulder, she saw Belladonna nod at the floor as she mouthed: *Look*, the urgency in her hazel eyes directing Kallie's gaze down.

The eight of clubs rested on the hardwood floor between the sofa and the beer bottle and candle-cluttered coffee table, bits of white plaster sprinkled across its surface. It'd slipped free from the deck in her hand. Her heart thumped against her chest.

Go ahead with the situation or person. Take the chance.

From over Cash's tension-taut shoulders, Kallie noticed her aunt sliding a hand into the pocket of her long, Gypsy-style skirt, her fingers no doubt seeking a powder or potion she'd tucked inside. Anything would work on twitching Kerry. Hell, baby powder would probably scare the man into a dead run out the front door.

Eight of clubs. Take the chance.

Kallie looked up. Kerry stood on the other side of the table, close to her aunt and Gabrielle, while Cash stood on Kallie's side of the coffee table, his smoking-barreled shotgun once more aimed dead center at Kallie's chest now that he and his partner were done quibbling.

"You'd better pipe up with something useful, darlin'!" Cash shouted. "I'm all out of goddamned patience!"

Needing to lure Cash into right-hook range, Kallie decided to go for demure and helpless. She lowered her eyes, then bit her lower lip. "I don't know anything about my cousin's doings," she lied, speaking in a whisper and hoping his ears were ringing as badly as her own. "His business is his own. But . . . he *does* have a storage unit."

"What?" The floor boards creaked as Cash took a step closer. His battered cowboy boots came into Kallie's downcast view. "Repeat that. He's got a what?"

Kallie lifted her gaze. "A cousin who ain't gonna put up with this shit."

She flipped the deck of cards in her left hand at Cash while simultaneously swinging her adrenaline-cocked right fist into the bastard's ski-masked nose as he flinched away from the hailstorm of sharp-edged cards. Bone crunched beneath her knuckles.

Kallie grabbed the shotgun barrel, wrenching it free from Cash's grip despite the pain rippling through her chest from her injured ribs, and aimed it at him as he staggered backward, both gloved hands cupped over his broken nose.

"Fuck!" he screamed.

From the other side of the coffee table, Divinity yelled, "You put dat shotgun down, boy, or I'll be hexing you and yo' future offspring down to the seventh generation!"

Kallie heard the clunk of metal against wood as Kerry wordlessly—as far as she could tell with all the god-damned ringing in her ears—rested the shotgun on the floor. Followed a heartbeat later by a jarring thud.

Divinity tsked in disapproval. "Dey don't make men like dey used to."

THREE

GATOR CHOW

Not willing to risk looking away from Cash for even a split second, Kallie asked, "Did Kerry just faint?"

"More like a swoon, actually!" Belladonna shouted. "Only thing missing was the hand to the forehead and a gentleman to catch him on his way down!"

"Ain't no gentlemen here, no," Divinity grumbled. Kallie could picture her glowering down at the unconscious home invasion terrorist, hands on her curvaceous hips.

"Do you have rope to tie this boy up with?" Gabrielle yelled.

"In the garage!" Belladonna shouted in reply.

Kallie heard the clack of Gabrielle's sandals against the floor, followed by the *thunk* of the screen door as she hurried outside.

"We oughta give him to the gators," Divinity declared. "Boy t'inks he can break into my home, then just waltz away? Well, he can't. T'inks he can just wave a shotgun around and get what he wants? No, he cannot. He got some hard lessons comin', him."

"What the hell is wrong with you people?" Cash

hollered, his narrowed and furious gaze still fixed on Kallie. He yanked off his ski mask, revealing a sweat-damp and ruffled mullet and a face that might've been good-looking if not for all the bruises, swelling, and blood. "Y'all can't do that!"

"Sure we can," Kallie said. "Did anyone else know that your plans for the morning involved terrorizing a household of women with guns and threats of violence?"

Pressing his wadded-up ski mask against his bleeding nose, Cash barked out a rough laugh. "*Terrorize?* That's a laugh. I couldn't even get y'all to shut up. The only person terrorized here is that fucking douchebag, Kerry."

Belladonna yelled, "Granted, the man's a bit of a delicate flower, but at least no one pointed a shotgun at *him!*"

Kallie felt a smile twitch across her lips. Still keeping her eyes on Cash, she said, "You can use your inside voice, Bell. I think we're all hearing just fine again."

"Oh? Oh. I mean—I knew that. I was only yelling in case Mr. Hard-Ass there had delivered some concussive damage to his eardrums with that shotgun blast."

"'Concussive damage'? Seriously? How much time *do* you spend on WebMD?"

"I don't think you'll be asking that question, Shug, when the time I've spent perusing winds up saving your fanny."

"Enough nonsense," Divinity snapped. "Are we gonna tie dem boys up or feed dem to de damned gators? I vote for de gators, me."

"I'm pretty sure that would be considered murder, ma'am," Belladonna said, then added thoughtfully, "but only if they're actually discovered in said gator tummies."

Only Cash's tensed muscles and the dark patches

underneath the arms of his T-shirt betrayed his nervousness. His gaze remained on Kallie, colder than an ice storm in July. "That ain't funny," he muttered.

"You see anyone laughing, boy?" Divinity replied quietly.

"Just hold your damned horses for a moment," Kallie said. She wasn't sure if Cash and his swooning buddy Kerry had anything to do with Jackson's disappearance or not, but their timing made her suspicious. They hadn't asked about Jackson's whereabouts, hadn't seemed surprised at his absence—or even concerned by it.

And that scared her.

Maybe they'd noticed that his truck wasn't in the driveway. Or maybe they'd had every reason to believe he wouldn't be home.

Pumping a fresh round into the shotgun, Kallie curled her finger around the trigger and aimed the barrel at the crotch of Cash's jeans.

Cash blinked and swung his hands down from his nose to form a protective, albeit useless, barrier in front of his manhood.

A cold sweat beaded Kallie's forehead as the past iced her from the inside out.

Mama pulls the gun's trigger and the side of Papa's head explodes in a spray of blood and bone. He slumps down in his chair, a bottle of Abita still in his hand.

Mama turns and faces her, aims the gun carefully between her shaking hands. Her hands shake, but her face is still, resigned.

"Sorry, baby, I ain't got a choice."

Mama pulls the trigger once more.

Queasiness knotted Kallie's gut. She thought of Basil

Augustine stumbling against her as he took a bullet intended for her. Remembered him dying as she desperately tried to stop the bleeding, tried to fill him with healing light.

Pull it together, girl. If this snake of a bastard sees you wavering, he's gonna strike. It's just a gun. A tool. That's all. And it ain't currently aimed at you. So goddamned pull it together.

Just as Kallie clenched her jaw and tightened her sweat-slick grip on the shotgun, she caught a faint whiff of patchouli, then a velvet-soft voice murmured from beside her right shoulder, "Let me, Shug."

Kallie glanced up, surprised. Belladonna's gaze was fixed on Cash, her plump lips curved into a cat's smile. She held her hand out for the shotgun. "I'm a much better shot than you are," she purred.

"Hard to miss with a shotgun. Especially at this range."

"Don't spoil my fun, Shug."

Relieved and grateful—she had no doubt as to why Belladonna had stepped in—Kallie handed the shotgun to the voodooienne, then stepped aside. Belladonna swung the barrel back into place, aimed at Cash's hand-protected crotch.

Belladonna tsked. "Tiny target."

"That the best y'all can do?" Cash said, blood oozing from his swollen nose. The skin beneath his eyes was just starting to bruise and puff up. "Small-dick jokes?"

"Nope," Kallie replied, drawing Cash's attention back to herself. "We can *gris-gris* that small dick into reality. Lay a shrivel package trick on you. How about that?"

Belladonna's cat smile deepened. "Mmm-hmm," she agreed.

"I figure you and your partner are the reason my cousin's missing," Kallie said, holding Cash's contemptuous gaze. "And I also figure Jacks wouldn't tell you what you wanted to know, so you decided to give us a try." She paused, her heart pounding as the full implications of that statement—*Jacks wouldn't tell you*—sank in.

Inhaling, she resumed speaking, voice taut. "If you plan to avoid becoming gator chow and walking outta here a functioning male, you'd better goddamned tell me where my goddamned cousin is."

Amusement glittered like frost in Cash's eyes. He lifted a hand and wiped at his nose with his ski mask. "Well, you got *part* of that right. We ain't the reason Jackson's missing, but we knew he was gone, for true. We was about to pay Jackson a little social call, when someone else beat us to the doorstep."

A cold finger trailed ice along Kallie's spine. So maybe St. Cyr *had* been responsible, after all. He'd designed a soul-killing hex for her, and maybe he'd crafted something equally evil for Jackson.

"Who?" Kallie asked. "Who got to Jackson before you did?"

Cash shrugged. "Hell if I know. Two black, one white. And it took all three of them to wrestle that slippery little bastard down, but not before he'd put that baseball bat of his to work. And his damned dog." Turning his head, he spat blood on the floor.

A muscle flexed in Kallie's jaw. Right then, she'd have been happy to dish out a few lessons via baseball bat too. She sucked in a deep breath, tried to cool the fire searing her control.

One Mississippi. Two Mississippi. Three . . .

FOUR

JUJU BOOMERANG

Cash's words swept the house clear of sound, like water being sucked back into the sea, before being released again in a surf-pounding rush—a tide of stunned voices.

"Hellfire. That can't be true. It can't!"

"Sounds like Jean-Julien's doing. He lived in Chacahoula."

"Uhhh . . . Where am I? Cash?"

"Sweet Jesus. Dey *buried* de boy? You saying Jackson be *dead*?"

Kallie stared at Cash, blood roaring in her ears. "You're fulla shit," she snarled, hoping the bastard was just fucking with her, but she saw truth, malicious and raw, in his eyes, his smug half-smile.

Kallie caught a flash of peripheral movement as Belladonna shifted her aim, the shotgun barrel sighting on Cash's sweat-gleaming forehead.

"*Is* he?" Belladonna asked, voice strained. "Dead?"

"Let's put it this way," Cash replied. "Jackson was still breathing when they planted him. But," he shrugged, "it's been hours, so . . ."

Dread punched a cold knife into Kallie's heart and stole her breath away.

Jacks had been buried *alive*, and this bastard had just sat back and watched as dirt had been shoveled over his head. Hell, he'd probably even had himself a nice cold beer as he took in the show. Then he and his good ol' buddy Kerry had left Jackson there, alive in his makeshift grave.

Hours ago.

"Gotta go. See you on Sunday. Love ya."

Red stained Kallie's vision as she leveled her gaze on Cash. All the dark mirth drained from his face at whatever he saw in her eyes. He straightened, muscles bunching along his shoulders.

"Hey, it ain't like *we* fucking buried him," he protested.

Kallie was moving before her brain caught up with her actions. Jerking the shotgun from Belladonna's grasp, Kallie shoved past her startled friend and jammed the barrel hard underneath Cash's chin, the muzzle imprinting itself onto his whiskered flesh.

"An eye for an eye is never enough," Doctor Heron whispers.

Alarmed shouts arrowed through the air, hitting their target, but missing the bull's-eye—the words meant nothing to Kallie, didn't apply to her.

"Don't kill him, girl! Not yet!"

"Easy now, Shug."

"Jesus Christ! Oh, holy Mary! She's gonna kill Cash! Stop her!"

Kallie's heart drummed a fierce, primal rhythm. Her finger twitched against the trigger. Cash's breath caught rough in his throat and he squeezed his eyes shut. Sweat beaded his forehead. She could see each whisker on his face, each smear of blood from his swelling nose. He reeked, ripe with sweat and sour fear and copper tang.

"You left him there in the ground, you *fi' de garce*," Kallie rasped from a throat almost too tight for speech. "You *left* him."

"She's gonna blow Cash's brains out," Kerry groaned. "Oh, Jesus—"

"Hush, you," Divinity snapped. "How dare you call on holy names after you done left my boy alive in a grave. You got nerve, you. Jesus gonna come down and kick yo' sorry ass if you call on him one mo' time. And if he don't, I *surely* will."

"When was Jacks buried, exactly?" Kallie asked, shoving the shotgun's muzzle deeper into the underside of Cash's chin, forcing his head up and back. "How long ago?"

Cash swallowed hard, then opened his eyes. He wrapped one gloved hand around the shotgun's barrel as though he could stop a shell with his touch, his curled fingers a prayer for mercy, or as though he were adjusting Kallie's aim:

Here. Please make sure you do it right so I don't end up a vegetable waiting for someone to have enough guts to unplug me from the respirator.

"Think you can yank it away before I pull the goddamned trigger?" Kallie said. "Try it, if the last thing you ever want to see in this life is my face."

"Kallie . . . Shug . . ." Belladonna's voice was low, uncertain. Kallie ignored it.

Cash's pupils contracted to pinpoints. His fingers remained locked around the barrel, leather glove creaking, his arm taut, muscles corded.

"When was Jacks buried? How fucking long ago?"

"Ain't sure, exactly," Cash grated. "They grabbed him shortly after dark."

"It's an hour's drive to Chacahoula," Gabrielle said, her words spreading through the silent room like raindrops ripple across a still pond.

No one wanted to be the first to say what they were all thinking—what Kallie knew *she* was thinking: Jackson had been in the ground at least seven or eight hours. How long would his oxygen—if any at all had been trapped with him—have lasted?

"Hellfire," Belladonna whispered.

King of spades. Queen of spades. Five of spades.

Bad luck. Delays. Setbacks. Defeat.

No. She refused to lose Jackson. She refused to believe he'd survived the hurricane that had killed his parents and sisters nine years ago—the same year her mama had murdered her papa, and nearly killed Kallie as well—only to suffocate to death inside the earth because a vengeance-fueled hoodoo man had mistaken her aunt for another woman.

Besides, she'd made a promise. *Love ya back, and I'm goddamned holding you to Sunday, Jacks.*

Cash's figure—knotted and wary-eyed—blurred in Kallie's vision and she blinked her stinging eyes until the sonuvabitch was in focus once more. "I say we give him to the gators. Alive."

Cash's eyes widened. His gloved hand flexed around the shotgun barrel. "Look," he said, desperation edging his voice, "your cousin brought this on himself. It's just the consequences of his own actions finally catching up to him, and y'all are blaming *us*. And that ain't right."

"I have every right to blame you for breaking into my

aunt's house and for leaving my cousin in a grave," Kallie said. "And I don't think what happened to Jacks had anything to do with his . . . work."

Cash snorted. "*Work*. Ain't that a sweet word for stealing."

Kallie shoved the muzzle of the shotgun harder into Cash's chin. "Well, ain't that the pot calling the kettle black? What's *your* line of work? Dope dealer? Art thief? Identity hacker? Pimp? Home invasion specialist?"

"Not that last one," Belladonna said. "He kinda sucks at it."

Kallie nodded. "That he does."

Divinity's fragrance of lavender and sandalwood announced her aunt's presence even before she spoke. "Step aside, Kallie-girl. I got a few words for dis dirt-grubbing worm, me."

Blowing out a breath, Kallie reluctantly eased the shotgun muzzle from Cash's flesh and stepped back as Divinity planted herself in front of the man. Looking at the gun in her white-knuckled hands, Kallie felt sick.

I woulda done it. Woulda pulled the trigger. Just like Mama.

"Maybe you'd better hold this," she said, fighting to keep the muscles in her arms from shaking as she extended the shotgun to Belladonna.

"That's what he said," Belladonna said with a wink, accepting the weapon. "But since you ruined one of my nails when you yanked that damned gun out of my hands, you owe me a manicure, Shug. And dessert of my choice at Mama's House of Cake."

"The manicure, sure," Kallie agreed, wiping her palms against her cutoffs. "But cake?"

"Mmm-hmm. For pain and suffering."

Kallie rolled her eyes. "Fine. Cake it is."

"Now," Belladonna said, slipping to the side and aiming the shotgun at Cash's temple, all teasing amusement gone from her face. "Let's bring Jackson home."

Kallie's throat constricted, and she nodded, not trusting her voice, clenching her hands into fists, not trusting her body to keep still either as her aunt looked Cash up and down, then shook her head in disgust.

"No, dey sure as hell don't make men like dey used to. You're gonna stop with de nonsense and show us where Jackson be," Divinity declared, emphasizing each word with a poke of her finger into Cash's chest. "You don't tell us de truth, I'm gonna hand-feed you to de gators, starting with yo' tender bits."

The defiance drained out of Cash like coolant from a bad radiator. He looked away, jaw working, then said, "Fine, I'll draw y'all a map, but I don't know what good it'll do. He's been in—"

Divinity stopped his words with another hard-fingered poke against his chest. "You say it and I'm gonna trick yo' insides up with snakes."

Cash's face paled. "I told you. I don't believe in that juju bullshit."

Another poke. "You don't need to believe in it, *boy*, for it to work. We be talking hoodoo, not wishing yo'self and yo' little dog home to Kansas with yo' ruby slippers."

"Forget drawing us a goddamned map," Kallie cut in, earning Cash's glowering gaze. "You're gonna guide us out there, *tout de suite*."

"*Oui, c'est une bonne idée*, girl," Divinity said, her voice tight. She gave Cash's chest another poke. "And

you ain't gonna waste one more second since de trip over
dere will mean anudder hour in de ground for my boy."
She glanced at Kallie from over her shoulder. "De sand's
almost run through for Jackson." She looked away, blinking, and Kallie knew what she was thinking: *If it hasn't
already.*

Kallie's heart contracted, a hard pulse of pain. She
wished they could rocket to Chacahoula at warp speed or
teleport themselves à la *Star Trek*. She thought of Layne
Valin, the gorgeous nomad with the waist-length honey-
blond dreads and lean, sexy body, redlining it back to New
Orleans on his Harley. It hadn't been that long since he'd
left the house—he might not be too far away.

"Layne could get me to Chacahoula in less than an
hour," Kallie said. "I can call him and—"

Divinity gave a soft sigh, one laced with regret. "No,
Kallie-girl, let dat boy be. Let him return to his clan. He's
got burdens enough, him. We don't need to be adding to
dem." She shook her head. "Been years and years since I
met a Vessel for de dead. Even longer since I met one who
had all o' his cups in de cupboard."

A Vessel for the dead. Layne was a living, breathing
spirit cabinet and, at the moment, he was carrying a ghost
inside as passenger and copilot—the shade of the murdered Lord Basil Augustine, the man who'd taken a bullet
intended for *her*.

And who'd forced his spirit upon Layne while the
nomad was still reeling from the loss of his best friend,
Gage, to a hex meant for Kallie.

A sharp pang of guilt knifed her. All of Layne's burdens
and grief were due to her and as much as she liked Layne
and hungered to get to know him better—much, *much*

better—she knew her *tante* was right. Layne Valin would be safer the farther away from her he traveled.

Divinity poked her finger into Cash's chest once more. "Let's get movin', boy. You gonna show us exactly where Jackson be."

"I ain't going nowhere with that little hellcat," Cash declared, the old defiance flaring in his eyes and making an encore performance as he glared at Kallie. "She broke my fucking nose."

Kallie folded her arms under her breasts and shifted her weight onto one hip. "So says the man who barged into *our* house in a ski mask waving a shotgun around. So wah-fucking-wah, you big baby."

Belladonna snorted. Cash's eyes narrowed to slits. His jaw tightened, but he wisely elected to keep any more comments to himself.

"I'll show you where your nephew is, ma'am," Kerry said quietly, his voice coming from floor level. "Ain't no need to give nobody to the gators or throw around any nasty tricks. I'll do it if you promise to let us go afterwards."

"Deal," Kallie said before Divinity could even open her mouth, then turned around to see Gabrielle kneeling behind Kerry, her red-scarfed head bowed as she finished binding his wrists with a length of rough rope—Jackson's rope. That felt more than a little karmic.

"But," Kallie continued, "you gotta give your word that neither of you will come near Jackson or any of us again."

Gabrielle had yanked off Kerry's ski mask and his short brown hair stuck up in sweat-gelled spikes all around his head. He looked scared and younger than the twenty-five or so Kallie pegged him at. He nodded. "Deal," he agreed.

Cash shook his head in disgust. "They ain't gonna let

us go, asswipe. We're gonna end up taking Bonaparte's place in that grave."

"Dat's it," Divinity declared. "My patience be at an end with you, boy. I've had just about enough of yo' bitter and angry words." Dipping a hand into a pocket of her Gypsy-style skirt, she pulled out a small blue glass bottle. "You ain't gonna cooperate, den I t'ink it be time you took a little nap. Maybe dat will sweeten up yo' disposition."

"Hey!" Kerry cried. "No juju. Y'all promised!"

"*Kallie* made de promise, boy, not me. 'Sides, dis ain't no hex, just a simple sleep trick. Now *tais-toi*, you."

The mingled scents of frankincense, roses, the citrus tang of bergamot oil, and licorice wafted into the air as Divinity tapped a pale brown powder into the palm of her hand.

"Hey, now," Cash said, putting his back against the wall, his body stretching up and away as though he were standing on tiptoe despite the fact that his boot soles were planted flat on the floor. His dark eyes locked onto the hand Divinity was lifting to her mouth.

"Awww. Looks like Mr. Don't-Believe-in-Juju has had a change of heart," Belladonna commented. "Funny how that happens when a man finds himself facing a pissed-off hoodoo with a palmful of dust."

"Whatever you're thinking of doing—don't," Cash said, all cockiness gone. "Ain't no need to poison me. Just tie me up like—"

Divinity blew the powder into Cash's sweat-beaded face. The back of his head thumped against the wall as he flinched away, coughing, eyes squeezed shut, and wiping frantically at his face with his gloved hands.

"Sweet dreams, nightie-night," Divinity chanted.

"Close yo' eyes and curl up tight. No need to fret, no need for prayers. Just close yo' eyes and forget yo' cares. Sweet dreams, nightie-night. Everyt'ing'll be all right . . ."

A sharp pain pierced Kallie's solar plexus. Wincing, she pressed her fingertips against her bruised breastbone. Black spots peppered her vision and for a split second, she thought she tasted licorice and bergamot.

Christ, did I breathe in some of Divinity's potion?

But instead of trick-induced sleepiness pouring through her like sun-heated honey, Kallie felt something within her pull taut, a hard inward pulse, like a cocked fist, then release. Her breath caught in her throat. Power pealed through the room like the strike of a bell, a deep chiming that vibrated into Kallie's bones, through the floor, ceiling, and walls of the house, then *out*. The hair lifted on her arms.

"Sweet dreams, nightie-night," Divinity repeated a final time. "Everyt'ing'll be all right."

Kallie blinked until the black spots faded from her vision. The licorice taste faded.

"Well, dat be dat." Yawning, Divinity stepped back a few paces from Cash's trembling and coughing form and dusted off her palms. Her eyelids drooped as she cast a lover's yearning glance at the sofa. "Lord. I be too old to be staying up all night an' be dealing with nonsense like dis. I t'ink I need a little nap."

Kallie stared at her aunt, all manner of internal alarms and klaxons blaring. "Old? You ain't even fifty! And a nap? What about Jackson?"

Divinity gave a sleepy snort and flapped a hand at Kallie. "Boy be fine. He always is, him. Knows how to take care of himself. Everyt'ing'll be all right. You'll see." She plopped onto the sofa, plumped a pillow, then lay down. Curled up. Closed her eyes—with a happy, contented sigh.

"*Fine?* Fine *how*? He's in a goddamned grave!"

Divinity's soft snores buzzed into the air in reply.

"Hellfire," Belladonna said. "What just happened? Did y'all feel that?"

Kallie nodded. "One hell of a goddamned magic surge. Like a downed power line."

Cash's coughing stopped. He quit scrubbing at his face and cautiously opened one eye and looked around the room.

"I think your aunt's trick boomeranged and hit her instead," Gabrielle said, her island-spiced words slow and incredulous.

Kallie blinked. "Is that even possible?"

The red-scarfed mambo shook her head, then waved a hand at Divinity sprawled on the sofa. "How else would you explain it?"

"I don't know . . ." Kallie's words trailed off as her thoughts flicked back to the pain and vision spots, the faint taste of bergamot haunting the back of her throat. She raked a hand through her hair. Had she *felt* her aunt's trick backfire?

"Maybe he's wearing some kind of protection," Belladonna said, fixing powder-freckled Cash with a Class One Death Glare. She jerked the shotgun barrel up, encouraging a confession.

Cash laughed—relief curling like Christmas ribbon through his voice. "Protection from what? A household of deluded women who've had a couple of sixers of Abita too many and think they're badass hoodoos?" His gaze shifted past Belladonna to his buddy sitting cross-legged and tied up on the floor. "You're an idiot, man."

Fury coiled hot around Kallie's spine. She wanted nothing more than to teach this jerk a lesson, but they didn't have the time. Not now, anyway. But as for later . . . "We'll see who's deluded," she said, marching past her snoring aunt to the woman's worktable cluttered with roots, herbs, and candles.

Kallie spotted the scissors resting beside a half-finished purple button-eyed poppet—*that's supposed to be me*—and a muscle in her jaw flexed as her *ti-tante*'s words, spoken just an hour ago, rippled through her memory.

"*When you were born to yo' mama and papa, yo' soul was removed to make room for de* loa *placed inside yo' infant body. Dere ain't nothing I wouldn't do to help you, Kalindra Sophia. Teach you. Guide you. Lie to you. Bind you, if it be necessary. Because a big wrong's been done to you.*"

Shoving the memory aside, Kallie snatched up the scissors, whirled, and stormed back to where Cash stood, contemptuous smirk on his powdered face. Without a word, she reached up and snipped a lock from his blond mullet.

He jerked his head away—too late—thumping it against the wall again. "Hey! What the fuck!" He grabbed for Kallie's hand as she stepped back, his hair tucked against her palm.

The shotgun barrel appeared against his temple. Pressed a divot into his skin. "Ah, ah, ah. Hands to yourself if you want to keep what few brains you have," Belladonna said.

Cash lowered his hand, knotting it into a fist. "What you gonna do with that?"

"What do you care? We're all deluded, right?" Kallie slipped the damp lock of hair into the right pocket of her cutoffs, then tossed the scissors onto the coffee table. She offered Cash a smile. "Guess you'll just hafta find out."

"You can't do nothing to me," Cash challenged. "'Cuz I don't believe—"

Kallie cut him off. "Yeah, yeah, we know, Mr. Don't-Believe-in-Juju. No need to repeat yourself."

She went into the kitchen and rummaged through the junk drawer until she found a roll of duct tape, then she turned around to fetch one of the wood chairs from the table. Her heart constricted when she saw the box of Trix sitting on the table, the shoved-back chair, and the purple glass mixing bowl sitting on the floor.

Looks like Jacks had cereal for dinner, then put the bowl down so Cielo could lap up the milk. For a dog, she's always had a cat's sensibilities. Then they came for him—whoever the hell they are—before he could even pick up after himself.

No way a bowl of goddamned Trix is gonna be Jacks's last meal. Ain't gonna let it happen.

Kallie strode back into the living room and thumped the chair down in the middle of the floor. She looked at Cash. "You're gonna sit your ass down in that chair and I'm gonna tie you up. You put up a fight and we'll do an old-fashioned sleep trick, one involving a shotgun butt and your skull. Your choice."

Cash studied Kallie for a long moment before walking over—Belladonna right behind him, shotgun aimed at his back—and planting said ass in the chair as requested. "I ain't forgetting you, darlin'," he said, his dark gaze promising things much worse than a kitchen chair, rope, and duct tape.

"You might wanna rethink that, *darlin'*," Kallie drawled as she took the lengths of rope Gabrielle extended to her and draped them over her shoulder. "You cause me or mine one more lick of grief, I'll put that lock of hair to work." She tore a strip free from the roll of duct tape, the sound ripping through the room—nearly silent but for her aunt's snoring.

"And she can use it in any number of ways: potion, poppet, hex," Belladonna helpfully pointed out. "She could have you dancing naked but for a tutu in the parking lot of the Z & M truck stop with the words *Kick my ass, pretty pretty please* painted on your scrawny chest."

"You ain't scaring me," Cash said, gaze fixed on Kallie. "I don't give a rat's ass about that fucking piece of hair."

"Duly noted," Kallie replied, slapping the piece of duct tape over his mouth. She bent and tied Cash to the chair, wrists and ankles, knotting the rope tight enough to earn more than one grunt from him.

"What about your aunt, Shug?" Belladonna asked, lowering the shotgun to her side and nodding her head in Divinity's direction. "You think it's safe to leave her alone? We could always lock this asshole in the garage until we get back."

"I'll be staying here, so don't worry about her."

Kallie straightened, then turned to face the mambo, meeting Gabrielle's dark and steady gaze. Worry flickered candle-bright in her eyes. But given that the woman had never met Jackson, Kallie couldn't imagine that her concern was solely for a man she didn't even know.

"Is there something else we should be aware of?" Kallie asked.

Gabrielle considered, a crease etching the smooth

dark skin between her brows, her fingers gently tapping her lips. "Don't know yet. But your aunt's trick boomeranging like that? Worries me. I don't know if it's something to do with your aunt or this place or because of what happened with Doctor Heron, but be careful, hear?"

"Double careful," Belladonna agreed.

Kallie suddenly remembered something the mambo had said earlier, something that had given her pause, since it didn't match the information she already possessed. "You said that Doctor Heron has a place in Chacahoula. But I found an address for him in Delacroix."

Gabrielle nodded. "Delacroix is where his daughter moved after her mama died. Chacahoula is where Jean-Julien and Babette lived before he was sent away to prison. But I don't know if he kept the place or sold it."

"I have a feeling he mighta found a way to keep it," Kallie said.

"He might've at that," Gabrielle said. She inclined her head at Kerry. "You girls grab this one and get going. Time is against us, so while you're driving to Chacahoula, I plan on asking the *Gédé* to intercede on your cousin's behalf." She looked at Kallie. "I plan to summon Baron Samedi. If anyone can save your cousin, turn him away from death, the Baron can."

Hope pulsed through Kallie. The *Gédé*—the *loas* of the dead and keepers of ancestral knowledge—were skilled healers able to keep a soul from entering death's realm before its time. And presiding over the *Gédé* was Baron Samedi, *loa* of death and resurrection, gatekeeper to the world of the dead.

Kallie's fingers automatically reached up to curl around the Saint Bernadette medallion hanging around her throat, the metal cool against her skin. She missed the smooth feel of the little coffin pendant—representing Baron Samedi—that she'd worn at Divinity's insistence for nine years. She'd given the pendant to Layne as a gift to burn with Gage's body in the crematorium in New Orleans.

Gabrielle was right. If anyone could help Jackson, the Baron could.

"I appreciate that," Kallie said quietly, throat tightening. "*Merci bien.*"

"No need to thank me, child. I'm a priestess and I think your cousin needs all the help he can get."

"Do you need help with the invocation?" Belladonna asked. "I'm in training to be a mambo, so I know the rites for invoking the spirits of the dead."

Kallie nodded. "If you need her, keep her. I don't need help handling Kerry." She bent, hooked a hand around Kerry's hard biceps, and helped him haul himself up to his feet. Straightening, she looked at the rope-bound outlaw and arched an eyebrow. "Do I?"

Kerry kept his attention on the floor and his dusty boots and shook his head mournfully. "No, ma'am."

"Thanks for the offer, girl," Gabrielle replied, smiling at Belladonna, "but you go with your friend. I been doing these invocations for years."

"Let's go, Bell," Kallie said, steering Kerry toward the screen door. "Jacks is waiting. Grab your mambo scout bag and let's keep the shotgun too. Just in case."

"Right behind you, Shug."

Kallie stepped out onto the porch and looked up into the darkening sky. Even though dawn was still fresh on the horizon and dew beaded the grass and the petals of her aunt's rosebushes, gray swollen-bellied clouds bruised the sky, stealing the morning's brightness along with its flush of peach and apricot pink.

Humidity thick with the smell of roses, impending rain, and decaying vegetation from the banks of the bayou behind the house drenched the air. Sweat sprang up along her hairline.

Goddamned five of spades. Enough with the setbacks, already!

"Storm's coming, Bell," she said, chest tight. As she propelled Kerry down the porch steps, she thought of Jackson in his grave, the weight of rain-churned mud squeezing the last bit of air from his lungs. "And we gotta beat it to Chacahoula."

Belladonna paused in the doorway, her gaze on the sky. "Hellfire."

FIVE

KINDRED SOULS

Panting, tongue lolling and flecked with foam, Cielo follows her nose down the dirt road, inhaling scent and information with each whiff of air. The damp dirt is ripe with moldering green leaves, sour bugs, cool grass, but the scent she cares about, the scent she follows—the stinky exhaust from Daddy's Get-in-the-Truck and hot rubber from its round paws—is fading.

Other scents from the still water beyond the road's sawgrass and vine-choked edge entice her, make her nose twitch: stinky dead things caught in the cattails. And even though she loves stinky dead things, she doesn't slow or pause. Not even for a drink. Daddy's energy is nearly gone, his voice a fading whisper cupped within her inner ears.

Here, girl. Here.

Her paws throb, prickling with owies from running along the highway all night. But she didn't run it alone. Sometime during her run, she became aware that fleet shapes raced alongside her, paralleling her on either side of the highway, black shadows slipping in and out among the moss- and lichen-draped trees on graceful paws. Radiating curiosity. Play.

But Cielo has no time for play.

She remembers the pungent smell of Daddy's blood as the men knocked him down in the yard, then threw him into his Get-in-the-Truck. She also remembers the smell and taste of their blood, and their musky, fur-spiking scent.

She growls low in her throat. She will *always* remember.

Cielo pads, limping, beneath the low, grass-sweeping branches of a tree pungent with the smell of spring sap, and into an overgrown yard. A people-den sits quiet in the morning shade, the porch and its swing empty, the windows closed.

She lifts her muzzle and sniffs for threat, for the stink of the men who'd grabbed Daddy. But all she smells is decayed wood, mildew, and termites, and the thunder-and-rain odor of a shadow woman.

Shadow people often drift through *Tante's* den, wisping through and away like bits of early morning mist.

Dey be traveling, dog, so leave dem be, hear? No growling or barking. No howling or whooing. Deir journey be a long one, for true. Dey don't need none o' yo' foolishness, so be a good dog, you.

Since *Tante* is alpha female of the den, Cielo listens. Mostly. She is, after all, a *very* good dog.

The shadow woman, threadbare body shafted through with sunlight and edged with wagging tails of thick, black night, stands in the driveway just beyond the porch, her gaze on a low pile of fresh-turned dirt. And beyond the pile of dirt, Cielo sees a Get-in-the-Truck parked beside the empty den.

Daddy's Get-in-the-Truck.

Cielo's blood sings, her heart leaps, and, despite the bad energy crackling around the shadow woman, she races across the yard, aimed for the Get-in-the-Truck. But she slows to a stop beside the pile of dirt, muzzle lifted as she sniffs the air. The mingled odors of roots and green things, slugs and wriggling worms, decaying vegetation, and the cold metal tang of a shovel blade dance into her nostrils.

Cielo goes still. Inhales deeply.

She catches a whiff of the pungent sweat and adrenaline from the bad men. And Daddy. She breathes in blood-smell, and not just Daddy's. Breathes in sweaty, heart-pounding desperation.

Here, girl.

Like words from a shadow person now, threadbare and shot through with light.

Cielo stares at the pile of dark, moist dirt. Tilts her head. The bad men buried Daddy like he was a yummie to be hidden and savored, like a treasured squeaka, or a squirrel that quit moving. (*No, Cielo-girl, no. Squirrels are not squeakas. You can't squeak 'em and expect them to keep breathin'.*)

But Daddy wasn't a yummie or a squeaka or a non-moving squirrel and he didn't belong in the ground. Cielo bolts to the long pile of dirt, nuzzles it with her nose. She *whoo-whoo*s.

Daddy?

Here . . . Like a final squirrel-squeaka breath.

Cielo starts digging.

<Dog! What you doing? Stop that. Shoo! Get out of here. Shoo! Boy's planted too deep for you anyhow.>

Cielo ignores the shadow woman and digs faster, dirt flinging out from under her paws. The thunder and rain scent intensifies and, for a moment, drowns out Daddy's scent in her nostrils. A cold hand sinks into her fur.

<You're not digging up that boy. He belongs to me and my husband now. Go away. Get out of here!>

Cielo pauses and growls low in her throat, a deep, warning rumble. The hand vanishes from her fur, but the cold lingers. She resumes digging.

<Even if you reach him, dog, it won't matter. He's gone.> The shadow woman laughs as she drifts away, but the sound is chewed-up butterfly-bitter, not full of warmth and humor like Daddy's.

Cielo burrows deep into the pile, dark earth flying into the air by the double pawful, but it seems like she's no closer to digging Daddy out of the ground than when she began. When she sends her inner voice to him, she hears nothing in return. She redoubles her efforts. Blood and foam fleck the soil.

She hears soft padding behind her and her hackles rise. Dark shapes slip out from around the trees. She smells heated fur and musk, the reek of wolf and something other, something she doesn't recognize.

A howl rakes the morning, a morning that has steadily darkened as Cielo's paws tore through the dirt.

Just as she whirls around, forelegs planted in the dirt, muzzle lowered and lips wrinkled up, revealing her fangs, thunder cracks along the horizon. Her fierce warning growl rumbles to a stop in her throat at what she sees.

Three wolves, one black, the others rain-cloud gray,

SIX

*L*OA OF *D*EATH AND *R*ESURRECTION

Gabrielle watched through the porch door's screen as Belladonna steered her age-weathered Dodge Dart down the rutted dirt driveway, her tied-up and nervous guide strapped into the passenger seat, while Kallie sat in the back behind him, his shotgun lying across her bare thighs, her cousin's red flannel mojo bag tucked into her pocket.

"Lord have mercy," Gabrielle prayed. "Christ have mercy, *ago-ago yé*. Saint Expédite, pray and intercede for that poor boy buried in the ground, and grant his cousin speed and perfect timing. His life is in the hands of Bon Dieu."

As the lime green vehicle bounced out of view in a wake of pale dust, Gabrielle added, "And in the Baron's." She could only hope that it wasn't already too late.

Closing the front door, she twisted the simple lock into place. No dead bolts here, no security chains or bars on doors or windows. Most folks would never dream of crossing a conjurer's threshold uninvited.

Well, not the locals, anyway. As for those who don't know better . . . Gabrielle glanced at the sullen expression above Cash's duct-taped mouth. A smile brushed her lips.

A fist-throwing, shotgun-grabbing niece will do the job just as nicely.

And as for unseen and otherworldly danger, a hoodoo's wards usually guarded the home quite handily, but the tingle Gabrielle had felt—the warm spiderweb touch of protective *gris-gris* against evil—as she'd stepped into Divinity's cozy, frankincense- and rose-fragrant home a few hours earlier was now inexplicably missing.

Gabrielle walked into the living room, her gaze skipping from that chair-bound fool Cash to Divinity's softly snoring form on the sofa. The woman's face was untroubled, her light cocoa-colored skin uncreased by worry, fear, or doubt. And Gabrielle had seen every one of those emotions chase across the rootworker's face that morning since she'd learned of her nephew's dire situation.

How in the name of Bon Dieu and all the saints and angels had Divinity's spell backfired? How was such a thing even possible?

Power peals through the room in a deep, bone-thrumming vibration and Gabrielle's heart stutters.

A cold hand trailed ice down Gabrielle's spine—and not for the first time that morning either. Something was *very* wrong, something that traveled deeper than backfiring spells and suddenly missing house wards.

Maybe it was more of Jean-Julien's—*no, make that Doctor Heron, the Jean-Julien she'd once loved had disappeared the day he was arrested for murder*—dark work, a hex laid down before Kallie and her handsome dreadlocked nomad had ended his dark work forever.

Maybe it was due to the fact that Kallie carried a *loa* inside of her instead of a soul—a fact her aunt had hidden from the girl until just an hour or so ago.

Yo' soul—yo' Gros Bon Ange—was removed to make room for de loa placed inside you. De same loa dat your mama tried to awaken with blood and darkness by murdering yo' papa and shooting you.

But why was a loa put inside me? Who did it? How? And why the hell would Mama want to awaken it? And where's my soul?

Well, see, dat be de problem. We don't know. Your mama was de last one who had it, and she ain't talking.

Gabrielle shook her head, still amazed. She'd never heard of such a thing. A child's—no, an *infant's*—soul stolen, the emptiness inside filled with a sleeping *loa*—one that apparently craved violence.

Which explained—somewhat—what Gabrielle had seen Kallie do as Jean-Julien's soul had escaped his dying, knife-savaged body.

The black dust coating Jean-Julien's soul ripples, then flows backward and down into Kallie's waiting palm. The root doctor's spirit unravels inch by inch, molecule by molecule, until the air is empty.

Gabrielle's fingers plucked at the edges of her scarf, then she mentally shooed away the image of her former lover's ultimate death. Just who or what resided inside of Kallie Rivière? And why? Questions asked by the girl herself, questions that remained unanswered—so far.

A surge of anger stiffened Gabrielle's spine. Stealing identities. Costing innocent folks their lives. Lying to her niece—even if to protect her from her mother's inexplicable and reprehensible actions.

Divinity Santiago has a helluva lot of explaining to do and much to answer for. A shame her niece and nephew are paying for her foolishness. And thinking of that poor boy . . .

Maybe, just maybe, there was still time for Gabrielle to help Kallie rescue her cousin from the fate Jean-Julien had no doubt spun into motion even before he'd attempted to kill Kallie body and soul—and would've succeeded, if not for her missing soul.

Gabrielle quickly cleared the coffee table of empty Abita bottles, a blue glass vase full of white roses with peach-rimmed petals, magazines—*Boat World, Star Magazine, Louisiana Cookin'*—and a slim, well-thumbed copy of *The Complete Poems of John Keats*.

Makeshift altar clean and empty, Gabrielle hurried to Divinity's worktable for a couple of blessed candles, some holy water, and an incense brazier. Digging through the woman's collection of roots and herbs, she also scooped up a handful of tobacco leaf, a chunk of frankincense resin, and a little bottle of dragon's blood ink.

A small wood carving of a penis nestled in among the brightly painted saint statues caught her attention. *Just the thing for the randy* loa *of the dead.* Smiling, she added it to her little pile of goodies.

From the kitchen, she fetched a couple of slices of sourdough bread, grumbling at the lack of peanuts—one of the Baron's favorites—then poured a cup of cold coffee from the carafe on the counter. She discovered a bottle of Captain Morgan spiced rum in the cupboard above the quietly humming refrigerator and was surprised, but pleased, to see hot peppers floating inside.

A quick count revealed the hot pepper tally as twenty-one, a perfect offering for Baron Samedi, gatekeeper to the world of the dead.

And given the hot-peppered rum, it seemed that although Divinity was a hoodoo rootworker and not a

Vodou mambo or even a voodoo priestess, the woman was, if nothing else, a hoodoo prepared for a client's any request.

Satisfied with her plunder, Gabrielle returned to the living room, knelt in front of the coffee table, and dumped her offerings onto its polished mahogany surface. With the ease and sure-handedness of decades of practice, she laid out the offerings—bread, black coffee, and rum. Although she wished she were working at her own altar with its *vévé*-and-cross-etched spirit pot, she had no choice but to make do with what she had.

A life hangs in the balance.

Rising to her feet, Gabrielle unstoppered the small blue bottle of holy water, then dipped her fingers into the consecrated fluid. She walked the room, murmuring a protection spell—*Where this sacred water is cast, no thing of darkness or evil can last or can endure this water pure*—and flicking holy water into the corners, and on the thresholds of the doors and windows.

She paused to sprinkle both a scowling Cash and the sweet-dreaming Divinity, before anointing the items on the altar and then replaced the cork stopper on the bottle of holy water.

Kneeling once more, Gabrielle lit the mingled frankincense and tobacco piled on a charcoal round in the brazier with a wood match, then touched the flame to each of the three candles in turn. The pungent aroma of sweet leaf tobacco and musky incense wafted into the air.

Grabbing one of the magazines from where she'd placed them on the hardwood floor, Gabrielle placed it on the coffee table beside the upright carved wood dick. Then, dipping her finger into the red, cinnamon-scented ink, she drew a cross and a coffin outline on one of the magazines' back page.

With the Baron's symbols—cross, coffin, and phallus—etched on paper, Gabrielle twisted open the bottle of Captain Morgan. The eye-watering odor of peppered rum curled into the air and, blinking, she fanned a hand in front of her face.

Cash emitted a duct-tape muffled complaint—lip-smushed words that sounded something like: *Jesus Christ! I can even smell that shit over here.*

"Hush, boy," she said. "This rum ain't for you—or any mortal man. It's a gift to the Baron. Now keep quiet while I work." She nodded in satisfaction as Cash rolled his eyes, but otherwise remained silent.

Divinity snored, oblivious.

After voicing the Litany of the Saints and the Lord's Prayer, Gabrielle crossed herself, murmuring, "*Au nom du Père, le Fils, et le Saint Esprit,* I call upon you, oh mighty Baron Samedi, all-knowing *loa* of death and resurrection, gatekeeper to the world of the dead, to humbly ask for a young man's life to be spared."

As she spilled a little of the peppered rum onto the bread, her skin rose in goose bumps, suddenly chilled. The energy charging the room's atmosphere wasn't the tranquil and hushed sense of the sacred that usually followed a blessing or protection spell and invocation. No. *This* energy was dense and dark and coiled like a python around a twisted oak branch, waiting.

And very, *very* wrong.

Heart thudding, Gabrielle lowered the bottle of rum to the table and carefully scanned the room, but saw nothing out of place, nothing amiss. Except . . .

As her gaze returned to the makeshift altar, she noticed that the smoke from the brazier had thickened, spreading throughout the room like a roiling nicotine- and frankincense-scented thundercloud. The hair lifted on the back of her neck.

"I believe in God, the Father Almighty," she prayed, grabbing the bottle of holy water and rising to her feet, "Creator of heaven and earth."

"Dat nice and all, but I t'ink He be too busy stroking Hisself to pay much mind to yo' prayers," a nasal, masculine voice said, then a night-skinned man wearing a black fedora with a purple band, sunglasses, and a purple shirt beneath what looked like a well-tailored black Armani suit stepped from the thundercloud of smoke. "A cock dat large—an eternal fucking cock—needs *beaucoup* attention, *ma belle femme*."

Standing in front of the sofa and the sleeping Divinity, Baron Samedi thrust his silver-handled walking stick between his legs as a visual aid. Waggled it up and down, in and out.

"Mmmph-*mmft*!" Cash exclaimed.

Gabrielle somewhat agreed with the young outlaw's *Holy shit* assessment.

Despite the *loa*'s requested presence, everything still felt very wrong to Gabrielle, dangerously off-kilter. From outside, she heard the low rumble of distant thunder. She carefully unstoppered the bottle of holy water, keeping her attention fixed on the Baron and his hip-thrusting pantomime.

"Thank you for answering my call and listening to my petition," she said. "A young man named—" Gabrielle's words withered in her throat as the Baron moved with striking cobra swiftness to stand in front of Cash.

Mr. I-Don't-Believe-in-Juju's eyes widened. His eyebrows disappeared into his sweaty hairline. He hopped his chair back across the hardwood, but the Baron remained right in front of him as though the toes of his black leather dress shoes were duct-taped to the chair legs.

"Mmmph!"

A grin split the Baron's lips. He tapped his walking stick against the top of Cash's blond mullet, then the *loa* vanished. Cash stiffened, his eyes rolling up white in his head. He slumped in his chair, the ropes knotted around his ankles and wrists keeping him more or less upright.

Before Gabrielle could say a word, Cash straightened up in the chair, yanking free as though the ropes binding him had been braided out of butter, then rose to his feet. He ripped the duct-tape from his mouth and dropped the wilted gray strip to the floor.

Holding out his hands, he wriggled his fingers, then lowered his arms. "Pasty," he declared. "But a fine *cheval* all de fucking same." His nostrils flared. "Ah, I smell de rum."

"Here," Gabrielle said, lifting the opened bottle. She hadn't expected the Baron to possess Cash, but then, she hadn't expected him to actually manifest for an invocation of mercy either. "I humbly ask for a life, a young man named—"

The Baron laughed. "Let me drink first, woman." He strode over to the coffee-table altar and snatched up the bottle of rum from Gabrielle's hands. With a lewd wink, he tipped the bottle back and poured the hot-peppered rum down his gullet in one long, throat-stretching swallow. The peppers' sharp smell spiced the air.

Rum gone, the Baron saluted Gabrielle with the emptied bottle. "T'anks fo' de drink," he said, his silver-handled walking stick shimmering into his right hand. "And if I wasn't married to my beautiful Maman Brigitte, I would fuck yo' sweet pussy till you begged fo' mercy." Another lewd wink, then a sigh. "But I be married and I got motherfucking work to do."

"My petition . . ."

"Ah, *oui*. Since Jackson Bonaparte already be in his grave, I t'ink it best to keep him dere." The Baron laughed again, but the humorous warmth was missing this time. This time the *loa*'s laughter cut through the air like a razor-edged shovel. "The sonuvabitch had it coming," he said, sounding in that moment exactly like Cash.

But that was impossible. A possessed *cheval* remained that way until released by the *loa*. They had no voice of their own, no say, no—

"And you were right about that rum not being for any mortal man," the Baron continued in Cash's voice. "Hoo-ee! It was hot enough to set my throat on fire and burn my gut to ash. Good thing I ain't mortal no more, huh?"

Gabrielle stared, mouth dry, heart pounding.

Scooping up the bread and cup of coffee from the altar, Baron Samedi sauntered back into the smoke, then smoke, *loa*, and the man he rode vanished as thunder cracked overhead.

Oh, Bon Dieu! *How was this possible?*

Feeling faint, Gabrielle pressed her fisted hands

SEVEN

A DESPERATE AND BRUTAL FIGHT

Found you, Daddy.

An image of Cielo flared behind Jackson's eyes—ears pricked forward, intelligence and concern in her eyes (one blue, one brown), her muzzle lifted as though sniffing the air—and prodded him from the half-dreaming twilight he'd tumbled into, poked at his awareness until he was no longer dreaming.

Here, girl . . .

He woke up. Unable to breathe. Unable to see. Unable to move.

Panic writhed through Jackson, wriggling like worms underneath the skin, then memory flared like heat lightning across a summer-scorched sky, and he remembered the whole damned nightmare.

The desperate and brutal fight in the yard with three men he's never seen before—two black, one white, all deadly—wondering who hired them even as he swings the baseball bat at their heads.

Being forced out of his own goddamned pickup, wrists bound, and marched in front of a freshly dug grave, a cold sweat bathing his body.

Falling to his knees as his feet are kicked out from under him. Pain ripples along his scalp as someone grabs a handful of hair, jerks his head back, and pours a potion down his throat—a dark liquid smelling of graveyards, oranges, and decay. Jackson gags, struggles to pull free. Fails.

Refusing to look at him, to meet his eyes, the white dude slices at Jackson with a pocketknife—arms, thighs, chest, belly, scalp. Blood pours, stinging, into his eyes. Slicks his skin. Soaks his shirt, his jeans. Warm and wet and sticky.

"Careful, asshole! He's supposed to bleed out slow."

A numbing cold curls through his veins, crackles across his thoughts, slows his heart. And even before they kick him into the grave, Jackson knows he is beyond fucked.

The earth weighed down on Jackson like a lead-lined blanket, pushing him further toward its dark, moist heart, slowly crushing from his aching lungs what little air he'd managed to keep. Dirt clogged his nostrils, clung to his lips, and coated his tongue despite the arms he'd managed to crisscross protectively over his face as the bastards had shoveled soil on top of him.

All business, those sons of bitches. No laughing. No teasing final words. Just the solid *schunk* of shovel blades into the ground, followed by the cascade of dirt on flesh and denim.

Hell, he could understand that—why waste breath on a tricked-up dead man? But who the fuck would go to so much trouble? None of the crews or dealers he liberated goods from dealt with hoodoo or voodoo—as far as he knew—they'd just plug two into the back of his skull, then dump his body into the bayou.

Another image of Cielo filled Jackson's thoughts. He smelled sunshine warm in her fur.

Daddy. Digging.

A tendril of hope rooted itself in Jackson's heart. *Good girl, you.*

Six feet above, he heard howling—a sudden blow-down, maybe, or Cielo singing as she worked. His body itched and burned and spasmed, his thoughts spinning like a steering wheel ripping a three-sixty turn.

Panting for air, Jackson slipped underneath the surface of dreams again and plummeted into a cold and endless twilight. And remembered another day, another savage storm.

"The wind is scaring me, Jacks!" Jeanette yells, locking her arms tight around Jackson's neck as he carries her across the yard to the Dodge pickup. Her long dark pigtails, rain-soaked and thick, whip against his face.

"Moi aussi! But I'm glad I've got you to keep me safe, p'tite peu," Jackson teases, despite the tension knotting his belly. "Do you think we could stop and change places? You carry me to the truck?"

"No, silly." Jeanette tightens her stranglehold around his neck. For a split second he feels like he can't breathe, but the sensation vanishes when his sister giggles into his ear. "And don't call me 'little bit' no more. I'm turning seven tomorrow, so I'm big now."

"Big enough to carry me?"

"Uh-huh. I just hafta shrink you with a backwards magnifying glass, then tuck you into my pocket."

"Got that backwards magnifying glass with you?"

"Nuh-uh."

"Looks like I'm gonna hafta keep carrying you, then, bebelle."

"Okay."

Jackson loads his baby sister into the pickup, rain soaking him to the skin despite the dark blue slicker and rubber fishing boots he wears. The wind slams into him, a bully's hard, ruthless shove, and he plants his feet wide in the driveway as he fights to keep his balance. Gulf-warm water needles his face, stings his eyes, sucks at his breath.

"Get your butt in the truck, Jacks!" his mama yells over the wind's ever-increasing shriek as she struggles to open the driver's door and climb in behind the wheel. Her cinnamon curls, café au lait skin, and green slicker glisten with rain. "We need to get the hell outta here before it's too late."

Jackson gets in, and pulls Jeanette onto his lap. Shivering, she wraps her cold, wet arms around his neck. Ten-year-old Junalee sits next to Mama, her dark hair rain-soaked, wet tendrils plastered against her face and neck. She glances at Jackson, and he sees his own fear and doubt reflected in her amber eyes. Sees it validated in the worry furrowing Mama's brow.

It's already too late to leave.

At fourteen, Jackson's weathered a handful of hurricanes—some in Houma, before his folks split, the rest in Morgan City—and he feels like an old hand. But not today.

Today butterflies whip up a storm inside his gut and his body thrums with the need to run, to hunker down and hide.

Hurricane Gaspard was supposed to make landfall in Texas at Corpus Christi. Morgan City only expected heavy rain and wind, and Jackson helped Mama make sure they had plenty of canned goods and bottled water on hand. Made sure the generator was primed and that bottled propane was at hand in case something went wrong with the generator.

By the time the weather service realizes that Gaspard has no intention of making landfall at Corpus Christi and has changed its course with unheard-of speed, arrowing for the Cajun coast instead, Jackson barely has time to nail plywood up over the house's windows before the wind's intensity makes it impossible for him to wield a hammer, let alone remain on a ladder.

Papa calls just before the landline goes out. "Get out of there. A monster's on the way. Tell your mama to head north, cher. I'm heading your way, me. I'll meet y'all on the road and follow until I'm sure—"

The line crackled, then fell silent.

Jackson passed Papa's instructions to his mother, but instead of the usual argument—Dat man. Still be t'inking he can tell me what to do—she just nodded, face grim, and told the girls to get into their rain gear.

The truck rocks in the wind like a boat bobbing on rough water as Mama steers it down the driveway for the road. The windshield wipers are useless and would only be stripped from their housing if turned on, so Mama peers through the water and leafy debris sheeting the windshield, interpreting the shapes and shadows beyond it with an unerring confidence that eases a little of the tension in Jackson's knotted muscles.

Jackson locks his arms around Jeanette, squeezing her tight against his chest, when a shrieking gust of wind catches the truck's underside and tips it for a moment before dropping it back onto all four tires. Just as his pulse is throttling back down, another fierce gust broadsides the truck and flips it onto its side.

Jackson's head and shoulder smack into the passenger window and then his breath explodes from his lungs when weight—Mama and Junalee—slams into him. Jeanette squeaks.

The wind shrieks in a powerful and eerie rise and fall cadence, the sound as loud as a freight train hurtling at high speed toward disaster. Jackson feels his heart pounding but doesn't hear it even internally. The hurricane has drowned out all other sound.

Hurricane Gaspard now composes their universe. Nothing else exists.

Lightning fills Jackson's vision with eye-slitting white brilliance. A door slams, the sound quickly swallowed by the howling wind. Maybe headlights, not lightning?

He hears Papa's voice, screaming his mother's name, "Lucia!"

Jackson struggles to suck in a breath of air and . . .

. . . and choked as dirt poured into his windpipe.

Jackson tried to cough, but his empty lungs spasmed, sucked in more dirt. Suffocating. Pain seared every inch of skin as though his body were a cushion for thousands of burning pins. White stars and black flecks danced behind his closed eyes. But even as his mind and lungs craved and struggled for air, his body remained still, his heart untroubled. And dread burrowed deep inside of him.

Maybe I'm already dead.

A familiar and frantic *whoo-whoo* bounced against his dirt-muffled ears. Hands or maybe paws brushed at his face. And light glimmered against his eyelids. Hands hooked around his shoulders—hot palms, a bruising steel grip. Hauled him out and up into buckets of rain, the dirt—no, mud now—making a wet, sucking sound as he was yanked out of the grave.

"Breathe, you," a rough male voice insisted, accompanied by more *whoo-whoo*s. "C'mon, boy. Breathe. Open yo' eyes."

"Smell that?" a female voice asked. "Sulfur and piss and anise? Black juju."

It took every bit of Jackson's strength to inhale a lungful of fresh, sweet air, to force his mud-caked eyelids open. He winced as gray morning light shafted into his eyes.

Cielo, ears pricked up, gaze intense, stared at him from behind two crouching, mud-streaked, and *beaucoup* nude people, one guy and one gal with wild and wind-twisted hair. Both studied him with gleaming silver-frosted eyes.

Well, hell, maybe I ain't been rescued after all.

A firestorm raged inside his skull, ashing each thought as it raced through his mind. Jackson struggled to make sense of what he was seeing. Ghosts? Fellow zombies-to-be fresh from their own graves to welcome him into his new undead life? *Welcome to the Zombie Corps, maggot.*

Something nagged at Jackson, something he knew he should know, something about the mud-streaked and crouching pair's gleaming silver eyes, but the pain in his head stomped all recollections flat.

"Hey, girl," he tried to say to Cielo, but all that came out was a dirt-rough croak.

"Hoo-eee, look at his eyes, Jubilee," the guy said. "He be in a world of hurt, him."

The crouching feral gal's nostrils—*Jubilee?*—flared.

"For true," she agreed. "And he looks and smells like he's just about done bleeding out, too."

As Jackson's vision narrowed to a single point of gray, rain-streaked light, he heard Jubilee add, "Might be too late for this little *chien de maison*, so let's haul ass."

House dog? Jackson wondered as pain chewed into him with sharp and splintered teeth, then darkness swallowed him once more.

EIGHT

BLOOD PRICE

One more stop before Gage is truly avenged and Kallie truly safe. A quick visit to the vengeful spirit of Doctor Heron's long-dead and bitter wife.

Dead or not, she does not get to walk away from this.

Layne Valin arrowed his Harley along US 90 East toward Chacahoula, the engine a deep, steady rumble beneath him, the pavement rain-slick and gleaming as the early morning downpour continued. Though getting soaked to the skin in a storm while speeding down the road was nothing new, Layne was grateful that at least the rain was warm.

Rain beaded up on his goggles, rolled along the sleeves of his leather jacket, and plastered his soaked dreads to his back and shoulders. He smelled ozone, rain, and heated engine oil with each moist breath he drew in.

He felt his cell phone, tucked into a pocket of his leather jacket, vibrating against his hip. Another call from McKenna, no doubt. He ignored it, already knowing what the conversation-slash-argument would entail—and all of their conversations seemed to be arguments lately, especially where Kallie Rivière was concerned. He opened up the bike's throttle.

Cool air slipstreamed over him, a thief plucking at his breath. But, argument or not, it had been his ex-wife's earlier call that had cemented his decision to swing his bike away from I-10 and New Orleans and head for the nearest of two addresses he'd Googled for the freshly deceased Doctor Heron—Chacahoula—though he planned to check the Delacroix address as well if necessary.

According to McKenna, Rosette St. Cyr had been murdered by one of the Hecatean Alliance guards just as she was about to be handed over to the nomads to face clan law—*Daoine shena liri*—for Gage's death. Rosette and her cold-blooded bastard of a father had been responsible for the hex that had killed Gage and destroyed his soul, so she was about to face a similar fate.

Or would've, if not for the guard's unexpected interference.

Layne pictures McKenna as her soft brogue rolls into his ear—large, dark doe eyes, black bird vee for clan Raven inked beneath the right, her hair a cap of nearly black anime-character spiked hair, laugh lines bracketing her eyes and generous mouth; she has the will, power, and strength of a doomed Spartan army packed into her curvy five-foot frame.

"St. Cyr's daughter is dead, luv. One of the guards put a bullet into her, then blew his own brains out. Avenging ol' Basil, some think."

"Jesus Christ. If the guard was avenging Augustine, then why kill himself too? And why didn't he just let our clan carry out Rosette's sentence?"

"Yer asking the same questions me and Basil's Bond-babe assistant asked, and we both believe the guard musta been compelled."

"But who would . . . Shit. Christ on a Ritz cracker.

You're thinking St. Cyr *somehow controlled the guard and offed his own* daughter?"

"To keep her soul intact? Aye, I do. Know what this means, don'tcha, luv?"

"Dammit, yeah, I do. Kallie might still be in danger."

"Bloody hell. No. Yer being man-stupid. Again," McKenna growls, her Scottish accent giving her tone of disgust a lilting and lyrical quality. "Tha' woman *is* the sodding danger. No, with Rosette dead, yer promise to let him stay in yer body long enough to see the woman get much-deserved justice no longer applies. This means you can finally boot Augustine's spirit arse out. The clan and yer mum are wondering where you are. Have ye forgotten Gage's funeral?"

"You should *fucking* know better than that, buttercup." Even Layne hears the icicles slivering his voice. "I'll be there—after I've finished what I gotta do."

"Layne, lad, wait—"

But he hadn't waited. Hadn't listened to another word. He'd ended the call, then had slipped the cell back into his pocket and, jaw tight, had ignored each bumblebee buzz against his hip ever since.

Layne rubbed his knuckles against his chest as if easing a kink, but the grief and pain plugging the hole Gage's loss had punched into his heart refused to come loose.

Gage, clan-brother, best friend, his *draíocht-brúthair* in the world of magic.

Layne's throat tightened, ached. Accidental or not, Gage had given up his life and soul for Kallie Rivière, the dark-haired swamp beauty, the hoodoo with mysterious purple eyes, heart-stopping curves, and—Layne winced, remembering—rib-cracking CPR skills.

Gage died in Kallie Rivière's place and paid for her life with his own, and now it's my duty to make sure she stays alive, to make sure that no one succeeds in closing her violet eyes forever. It's the only way I can give his death some kind of meaning.

Ain't the only reason, though. The woman fought for my life with all she had when the hex that killed Gage nearly aced me too—body and soul.

Downshifting automatically, Layne steered the Harley off the wet highway and onto an oak-lined side road. He gunned it through the rain-dripping tree shadows, searching for street signs.

Hey, how about being completely honest, bro? Saving your life, giving Gage's death a purpose, that ain't the whole story, yeah? What about how Kallie's lips, all soft and heated, felt beneath yours, or how she smells—hyacinths and white honey—or the pulse-pounding connection you feel arcing between you like uncontained and wild electricity whenever you lay eyes on her for the first time?

Nope, ain't going there. Not now. She's the last woman Gage kissed, the last woman Gage loved between the sheets, the last person he ever spoke to.

A brilliant fork of lightning split the sky, quickly followed by a rolling boom of thunder. Layne's path was taking him at 70+ mph into the heart of the storm as he steered his bike for St. Cyr's Chacahoula home, guided by Kallie's blood divination from the night before.

"*Who am I looking at?*" Layne asks, studying the photo of a pretty, black-haired, brown-eyed woman with toffee-colored skin.

"*Babette St. Cyr,*" Kallie answers. "*Rosette's mama. The photo's from her obituary.*"

"*If she's dead, then she can't be the third person involved in this, yeah?*"

"*I think she is. When I did the blood divination, it showed me a heron for Rosette's papa, Doctor Heron, and that made total sense. I'm sure he's the goddamned bastard who slashed Dallas's throat. But then it showed me a woman standing in front of a house. Babette.*"

Dead or not, Babette St. Cyr owed Layne and his clan a blood price, one he intended to collect.

Cars and pickup trucks traveling the opposite way whooshed past Layne, tires shushing along the wet pavement, windshield wipers clocking back and forth. Lightning strobed in multiple and soundless strikes from the bruised bellies of the clouds to the ground, dazzling Layne's vision with orange and white starbursts. Thunder cracked and boomed as the storm intensified.

Rain sheeted down, making it damned near impossible to see the road. Layne eased up on the throttle.

Clang! Clang! Clang!

Layne winced as the internal bell's sharp clanging reverberated along the inside of his skull. Lord Basil Augustine's—aka the stowaway—annoying and headache-inducing signal. Seemed the ghost in the cargo hold wanted to have a little chat.

Or wanted to take charge of the driver's seat for a while again. Nope. As far as Layne was concerned, the illusionist's steering time was all used up.

And in that, their situation was more than a little unique. Even though Augustine had sieved into Layne while one of his Alliance guards had ensured Layne's cooperation by holding a gun to McKenna's head, the bastard had figured out a way for them to take turns at the helm, allowing Layne to resume control of his own ghost-possessed body—something Layne had never been able to accomplish on his own before.

Most Vessels lost control of their bodies whenever a ghost slipped inside, becoming little more than gagged and bound stowaways shanghaied by ethereal, uncrossed-over body pirates hoping to say good-bye to loved ones, to seek revenge for their murder, to finish a final task, or simply clinging to flesh out of denial or fear of the unknown.

Grief awakened like a hibernating bear.

To say good-bye to loved ones . . .

Layne had offered himself to his murdered sister so she could say the good-byes stolen from her along with her life when squatters had beaten her to death in a Winn-Dixie parking lot. They'd nearly killed Layne too and, unfortunately for them, had believed they'd done just that.

When he'd healed enough to walk out of the hospital, he'd gone looking for the bastards. And had found them. One by one.

Layne sweeps one blade across the inside of the squatter's raised wrist, slicing through flesh, muscles, and tendons. The blade's edge scrapes against bone. Blood streams from the wound, threads the smell of copper into the air.

Layne drew in a deep breath. None of the blood he'd spilled had brought Poesy back. Nor had it subtracted from the pain of her loss or knowing that it'd been his screwup that had caused it.

But at least the fuckers who'd killed her would never draw in another breath, let alone enjoy another day.

Layne never had the chance to say good-bye to his sister. And knowing it would be too dangerous for him while she was still inside, Poesy hadn't tried. To keep from spiraling into madness, to keep their personalities from blending and meshing, ghost and Vessel couldn't interact.

Instead, she'd given Gage a message to pass along to Layne.

It wasn't your fault, you couldn't have known. Gage has orders to kick your ass on my behalf whenever he catches you blaming yourself. Kick your ass hard. I love you, little brother. I wish I could stay, but I can't.

"Love you too," Layne whispered into the wind.

Layne had learned over the years to create his own Fortress of Solitude within his mind and had managed to keep his sanity intact. He sure as hell couldn't say the same of his memories. A possession's most deadly moment occurred when the departing passenger, accidentally or otherwise, ran the risk of hooking into a Vessel's memories and unthreading a few as they vacated the premises.

"No one wants to tell you, because they love you, bro," Gage says, *"and don't want to see you hurt, but it's happened again."*

"Shit. What did I lose this time?"

"See that woman over there? The yummy little brunette?"

"Yeah, man. You kidding? That's McKenna, our gorgeous shuvani."

"Yeeaahh. And she's your wife too, bro."

"Fuck me. My wife?"

His and McKenna's relationship had never truly recovered from that loss. So even though he'd learned to love her once more, he'd forced himself to walk away before he broke her heart again.

You deserve a man who will always remember you, buttercup.

Most Vessels plummeted into despair and madness by their late teens or early twenties and ended their lives in messy and desperate ways.

Layne was twenty-five. He knew the odds were stacking up mile-high against him.

Clang! Clang! Clang!

Seemed like the Hecatean master—or *former* master, actually, since the Brit was technically dead—refused to be ignored.

Layne tightened his wet-fingered hold on the handlebar's rubber grips, then focused his attention inward to the bubble of static encircling Augustine, keeping them both safe from any accidental memory/personality merging.

Huh. Wonder if mental conversations fall under the texting/talking on cell phone no-no category while driving?

Deciding that they probably did, Layne compromised with his stunted sense of caution and reduced the Harley's speed, reluctant to pull over to the roadside.

<Why the hell are you clanging that goddamned bell?> Layne sent.

An image of Augustine as he'd appeared in life formed in Layne's mind. Tall and lean, with penetrating, deepset gray eyes and an unruly shock of nut-brown hair that kept tumbling over them, the Brit was aristocratic and elegant—or had been, anyway—in a tailored pale gray suit and French blue shirt, a cigarette held carelessly between two long fingers.

<I heard about Ms. St. Cyr. I imagine your clan is quite unhappy with her easy escape.>

Even inside Layne's head, the illusionist "spoke" with a lofty British accent. *<"Heard," huh? I think* eavesdropped *is the word you're actually looking for.>*

<I rather prefer heard.>

<Oh, I'm sure you do. But I'll bet you weren't clanging that fricking bell just to discuss semantics. In any case, now that Rosette's dead, once we're done in Chacahoula and back in New Orleans, you need to pack up and split and go into the light. Again, man, my condolences.>

A blazing flash of white light freeze-framed the gray sky, then thunder cracked directly overhead. Layne's heart catapulted into his throat. "Christ!"

Ozone saturated the air. Layne felt the hair rise on the back of his neck. His skin prickled. *Too fucking close.* Blinking away retinal ghosts from his vision, he peered through the curtain of heavy rain, trying to make out the street signs.

<Go into the light. Of course. Once we've returned to New Orleans, we can discuss my departure.>

<Wait. No. Ain't gonna be a discussion. You—>

<Since you're sending us full steam ahead into the territory of the no doubt furious and grieving Babette St. Cyr,> Augustine interrupted, *<I thought I'd inquire as to your plan. You can't use your knives on her like you did on her husband.>*

<No shit, Sherlock.>

<Ah, yet another fine display of those legendary nomad manners. So tell me, Valin, do you know how to banish a vengeful spirit?>

<If I did, would you be here?>

<Unfair. I'm hardly vengeful. And I rather thought we worked well as a team.>

Lightning illuminated another upcoming street sign. Rain beaded the letters: COTTONWOOD ROAD.

Bingo. Almost there. St. Cyr's place branched off from

Cottonwood—a dirt driveway snaking down from the road.

Layne turned the Harley right onto Cottonwood, the pavement giving way to gravel. Reducing his speed to 30 mph, he shifted his attention back to Augustine.

<A team? You kidding me? You entered me in a wet boxers contest and stripped me down in front of a crowd.>

<Teamwork at its finest. And the crowd loved our performance. May I point out that you won? Quite handily?>

<Christ in a pecan shell. Can we keep on subject? As for banishing spirits, I know a trick or two. But they don't always work.>

<Ah. "Don't always work." Bravo. Very helpful that, Valin.> Augustine's sending was dry as a river in the Sahara.

<Kiss my kickstand, Basil.>

<Mmm. Tempting,> Augustine murmured, and Layne had the uneasy feeling he meant it. *<But we need to keep on the subject—as you put it. I happen to know a banishing ritual or two, but in order for the magic to work, I'll need to be at the controls.>*

A mental snort. *<Imagine that. Why ain't I surprised?>* Layne felt a wry smile pull at his lips. *<And the answer's no. If I can't—>*

Layne's thought died unfinished as a vehicle blurred out from a side road at high speed less than twenty-five yards in front of him. Layne swerved and felt the Harley's tires stutter across the rain-puddled gravel, then slide. Felt the bike going down as the road rushed up. Sound faded, drowned out by his drumming heart.

Fuck.

Time stretched out, slow and elastic, while the truck

swung wide in an effort to miss him, a scowl of concentration on the driver's face as he spun the steering wheel. Caught in the slo-mo of imminent disaster, Layne realized that if he wanted to avoid a collision between his head and the Dodge Ram's looming steel bumper with the trailer hitch jutting like a sword pommel behind it, he had to move. *Now.*

Layne kicked his legs free of the bike and rolled.

Time snapped back in on itself.

He hit the road hard, shoulder first. He heard a loud crack as his helmet smacked into something. Blue light flashed like jet engine flame through his mind. Pain stunned him, stole his breath, as he bounced and somersaulted across the gravel road and into a tree trunk or post or rock wall.

Stars lit up his vision like a Disneyland fireworks display.

Just before the fireworks display went dark and he was shuffled off to Night-Nightland, Layne thought he saw a Siberian husky and what looked like a pair of wolves staring at him from the back of the fishtailing Dodge Ram.

Musta hit the son-of-a-bitching bumper after all.

Then all thought winked out.

NINE

QUEEN OF SPADES

Augustine felt the nomad's consciousness switch off, even through his protective bubble of static. Neurons pulsed and flashed in the darkness, a ferocious lightning storm of pain—which he, fortunately, couldn't feel. But if he abandoned his bubble and climbed into the driver's seat, he *would*, and he might very well black out, just as Valin had.

Of course, attempting to replace Valin at the controls without his cooperation and without their precise little avoidance dance could lead to some very ugly consequences—the meshing and/or unthreading of their personalities.

The images he'd caught from Valin—a rain-blurred truck, an anxious-looking Siberian husky, the sliding Harley, lambent-eyed wolves—told Augustine that they'd been in an accident. And, given the dubious presence of the animals in Valin's vision, that the nomad had thumped his thick skull dangerously hard.

Several questions pinged through Augustine's mind in rapid succession: How serious were Valin's injuries? Had the driver of the truck stopped to render assistance? And if he/she hadn't, how could help be summoned? Only one way to find out on all accounts—he would have to leave Valin's body and assess the situation.

Augustine hesitated, a conversation nearly twenty-four hours old swirling through his mind, a conversation between a just-murdered man and an unoccupied (and determined to stay that way) Vessel.

Permission isn't required, and Vessels aren't supposed to be capable of resisting. At least, that's always been my understanding.

Most can't. But I've learned how, and you ain't getting in.

I believe you're bluffing. You're a Vessel for a reason, Valin. You are a natural and needed resource. And, since I don't believe in coincidences, your arrival here when you were needed most shouldn't be wasted.

But in the end, a gun strategically placed against the head of Valin's fierce pixie of an ex-wife had produced the result that Augustine's calm, rational arguments hadn't—Valin had stopped resisting.

While it was a shame the gun had been necessary, Augustine had no regrets. The nomad hadn't been harmed and their arrangement was only temporary.

However, given what he now understood about the nomad's strength and force of will, Augustine suspected that Valin *hadn't* been bluffing when he'd claimed that he'd learned how to keep from getting shanghaied by desperate ghosts.

So what if Valin awoke while he was outside of his body and refused to let him back in? What then?

Augustine thinned his static bubble, then erased it entirely. A risk he'd simply have to take. Valin's injuries could be critical. He could even be dying. Of course, if that *was* the case, he didn't really know what he could do to help. But he had to try.

Which presented another very important question: How *does* one leave a body? Wish upon a star? Snap one's fingers three times? Click one's heels?

Ghosting into the nomad had been like pulling on a crisp new shirt, a cool and irresistible glide into silken flesh and rippling muscle. Valin's presence had radiated a magnetic, magical quality, like a human ley line, like a curved *Hey, sailor* finger, and even if Augustine *had* decided to cross over after his unexpected murder, he would've been quite helpless against the nomad's allure.

Would that magnetic lure make it difficult to free himself from Valin's unconscious body? Only one way to find out.

Drawing in a breath—a figurative one, anyway, a mental girding of the (also figurative) loins—Augustine visualized sieving out of Layne Valin's body, imagined streaming out of his pores, mouth, and nostrils, in countless curls of pale mist.

Or smoke, he amended, thinking of his much-missed cigarettes and yearning for the taste of vanilla-spiced dark tobacco.

Right. Here we go, then.

Augustine snapped his fingers three times, then tossed in "Olly, olly, oxen free" just for good measure.

A Velcro ripping sound, then Augustine felt himself peeling away from the nomad's familiar and comfortable flesh. He blinked. He was *out* and standing in a mud-puddled dirt road in a pouring rain he couldn't feel as anything more than a generalized cold sensation.

Well, that was bloody easy.

Had it been the visualization, the finger snaps, or the childhood chant? All three? A puzzle to ponder another time, he reminded himself. *Otherwise you and Valin both might be without bodies and utterly homeless.*

Augustine looked down. Valin lay crumpled on his left side, his long, thick dreads snaking across the rain-soaked ground like honey-colored vines. His body rested beneath a rain-dripping palmetto bush beside a canted and dented mailbox.

Augustine noted that a crack split the back side of the nomad's matte black shorty-style helmet and wondered if he'd smacked his head against the mailbox's wooden post.

Dammit, Valin. Not good.

Kneeling, Augustine examined the nomad closer. Breathing. Small trickle of blood from his mouth and one nostril. None from his ears—good sign, that.

He tried to remove Valin's rain-beaded goggles so he could lift one eyelid to take a peek at the pupil, but even though his fingers gripped the protective gear, nothing happened. They didn't move. At all.

Hmmm. Apparently I lack what it takes to be a poltergeist. A shame. Hurling things and moving objects might've come in handy.

Abandoning the pupil-gazing attempt as lost, Augustine slid his hands along the nomad's limbs, feeling for broken bones, but succeeding only in sinking elbow-deep into the handsome and tattooed Valin's oh-so-comfy flesh as his ghostly body responded to the nomad's magical pull.

I'll bet if Valin weren't a Vessel, I could feel him up without any bother.

His ghostly body responded in another way entirely at the memory of his/Valin's heated hands exploring the nomad's freshly possessed body.

Mmm. Dear God, yes. But no. No. Not now.

With a sigh of frustration, Augustine gave up his search for injuries and patted Valin down, fingers seeking his cell phone. It wasn't tucked into a pocket of the nomad's storm-drenched jeans. Nor in his leather jacket.

Blast.

Rising to his feet, Augustine automatically brushed at the knees of his gray trousers and scanned the wet grass, palmetto bushes, and scrub for any sign of the phone, not sure what he planned to do with it even if he located it. If he couldn't lift an unconscious man's eyelid, odds were against his being able to use a cell phone.

But one never knew until one tried.

A searing flash of lightning painted the sky blue-white and Augustine froze. He'd *felt* that. A prickling, pins-and-needles sensation surged through his body—essence, spirit, whatever you wished to call it—an energizing and electric energy.

Thunder grumbled and boomed. Augustine looked up, excitement curling through him. Hadn't he read something once about how ghosts drained energy from objects and the living in order to communicate or manifest?

Maybe if he drank in enough energy from the storm, he *would* be able to pick up and use Valin's cell phone. Provided he found it, that was.

Augustine studied the angle of Valin's body against the post and visualized possible trajectories for items bounced free from his pockets by the force of impact. His gaze traveled beyond the fractured, listing mailbox.

A rutted dirt driveway wound past oaks and elms to a house with a wraparound porch shaded by palm trees. The uncurtained windows looked like dark, empty eyes, and seen through the rain, the house looked weathered, desolate.

Augustine frowned. The place seemed familiar even though he was positive he'd never seen it before. He mentally thumbed through his recall, seeking the reason for the unsettling familiarity—had he seen a photo? Read/ heard a description?

Then Kallie Rivière's voice, low and grim, sounded through his memory.

There's another woman involved as well.

Another? Do you know who?

No. But I have some ideas I need to research online.

A deep unease curled along Augustine's spine. It seemed Valin had found the home of Doctor Heron and his long-dead bride, Babette St. Cyr, after all.

So who had been driving the truck that had blasted out of the driveway as though fueled by an illicit tank of nitrous oxide—or chased by a ghost? And why hadn't they stopped after Valin bit the road?

More important, where was Babette St. Cyr?

Energy prickled through Augustine as lightning flared overhead in a strobing series of strikes, temporarily bleaching the ground; and glinting in the rain beside a clump of yellow dandelions, he spotted what looked like a cell phone.

A crash of heart-stopping thunder rolled for several long seconds across the storm-bruised sky.

Glancing at Valin's motionless form, Augustine sent a thought to his unconscious mind. *<Hold on. Keep breathing. I'll be back in a moment.>*

When Augustine returned his attention to the driveway, his figurative heart kicked against his ribs. A darkhaired woman wearing a black and flowing gown was bending over the little clump of dandelions. When the late Mrs. St. Cyr straightened, she held the cell phone in her hand, a smile glacier-cold on her lips. Straightened black hair swept to her shoulders and framed a toffeebrown face. Her eyes were nearly iridescent with captured storm-energy.

"Finders keepers, dead man," she said.

"Good morning, Mrs. St. Cyr," Augustine said, casually tucking one hand into his trouser pocket. He nodded at the cell phone. "If you're hoping to call your husband to check in on the progress of your various murderous schemes, I'm afraid I have sad news for you. Jean-Julien is dead."

Babette stared at him, her smile dying upon her lips. "When?"

"Just a few hours ago. He received what he was so busy dishing out, I might add."

"That man's been a corpse in my heart for over two decades now. Ever since he took up with that harlot, that witch, Gabrielle. I quit mourning him a long time ago."

"Your daughter is dead also," Augustine said quietly.

Grief crackled like frost across Babette's face and she closed her luminous eyes. She touched her fingers to her breast, above her heart. "I felt my baby cross over," she whispered. "Jean-Julien's fault. He couldn't be a man and take care of things on his own. No. He used Rosette to do his dirty work at the hotel. And he cost my baby—my only child—her life."

Augustine shook his head, unmoved. "I believe your

daughter's death is as much your fault as your husband's—perhaps even more so."

"How dare you? I had *nothing* to do with Rosette's death, dead man."

"Oh, I disagree, Mrs. St. Cyr." Drawing upon the conversation he'd "heard" between Layne and Kallie last night—*eavesdropped* is such an ugly word—Augustine took a gamble.

"You poisoned your husband's clients after you learned of his affair, didn't you? Then you allowed him to take the fall and be sent to prison, knowing he was innocent of the crimes he was charged with. You let him think Gabrielle had betrayed him. Let your daughter believe the same, poisoning her heart and soul with your lies. Even on your deathbed."

Fury rippled like oil across Babette's face. "Of all the things Jean-Julien was, he was *never* innocent," she spat. "Who are you, dead man, to speak to me this way?"

"I'm a man your daughter murdered by mistake," Augustine replied.

"By mistake?" Babette glided forward, the hem of her black dress a spill of ink trailing the muddy road. Her body flowed and undulated, her shape suddenly fluid.

Augustine felt a moment of uncertainty. Babette St. Cyr had been dead for ten years, he for less than twenty-four hours. Ten years removed from life and humanity. He had no idea what she was capable of.

She halted in front of Augustine. A lightless corona danced and flickered like black flame around her body, crowned her lovely head. "How did my Rosie kill you by mistake?" Her hand lifted for his face, tiny sparks of incandescent energy arcing between her fingertips.

Augustine took a controlled and, hopefully, nonchalant step backward, placing himself out of touching range. "I got between Rosette and the woman she intended to shoot."

Babette frowned. "*Shoot?* Rosette didn't have a gun — only spells and tricks that Jean-Julien taught her."

"Trust me," Augustine said dryly, "she found a gun when her hex failed. Oh. Wait. It *didn't* fail. She killed an innocent with her hex as . . ." His words trailed off when Babette blinked away.

Where did she — His heart leapt into his throat. *Valin.*

Whirling around, Augustine saw Babette standing beside the splintered mailbox post and Valin's body. Wonder thawed the ice from her expression. Energy danced from her fingertips in electric Frankenstein flickers as she reached a hand toward the nomad.

"He feels like sanctuary, like an invitation," she breathed. "Like a hearth-warmed home after a long wandering in dark and icy woods." Turning her head, she lifted her gleaming gaze to Augustine. "He your Vessel?"

Not wishing to startle Babette into action—by sliding into the nomad's body, for instance—Augustine suppressed his intense desire to sprint, and forced himself to amble over to Valin's crumpled form.

"Yes. But he's injured and unconscious. An accident with the truck that barreled out of your driveway."

Babette snorted in irritation, then waved a hand. "Foolish creatures and a doomed boy, but I expected more from the dog."

Augustine blinked. Maybe Valin truly *had* seen a Siberian husky and a pair of wolves in the back of the speeding hit-and-run truck. "It was my hope to use the cell phone to summon help for him," he said.

"The dog?"

"Yes, absolutely, the dog and I chat on a regular basis." Augustine flipped his hair out of his eyes with a flick of his fingers. "No. The nomad bleeding on the ground."

"Won't do you no good. You don't have enough juice in you to use this phone, dead man," she said, tossing it into the palmetto bush.

"Name's Lord Augustine, not *dead man*. Although it *does* have a certain cachet."

Babette snorted. "How does *Lord* Dead Man suit you?"

"I could do far worse, Lady Murderess."

"Think you're smart, think you're clever," Babette murmured, returning her gaze to the nomad. "Think you're all manner of fine things, don't you, dead man?"

"I try not to blow my own horn."

Lightning licked across the sky, a jagged white snake's tongue. Augustine felt his body suck up the residual energy charging the air and crackling like static electricity along his body, but it wasn't enough. Not yet.

Her eyes brimming with radiant storm light, Babette slid a coquettish look Augustine's way as she bent over the nomad once more and said, "Finders keepers." She lowered her hand to Valin's face.

Knowing that a Vessel could carry only one ghost at a time, Augustine hurled himself at Valin.

TEN

FIXED BUT GOOD

"Hellfire!"

Belladonna slammed on the brakes and Kallie grabbed the back of Kerry's seat to brace herself, her other hand locking around the shotgun. The Dodge Dart stuttered to a halt, gravel scrunching beneath its tires and pinging against its undercarriage.

"Jesus. Is that a motorcycle?" Kerry asked, leaning forward and trying to peer past the rain and the furiously tocking windshield wipers.

Unease snaked along Kallie's spine. The black-and-chrome object lying in the road like a kissing-game bottle that had been spun, then abandoned, was a motorcycle. And it looked like Layne's Harley.

"Sure is," Belladonna affirmed.

And crumpled at the road's edge beside a damaged mailbox post, a helmeted and leather-jacketed figure. "Layne," Kallie whispered.

"Shit," Belladonna breathed.

Fumbling with her seat belt, Kallie pushed at the back of Belladonna's seat. "Let me out." But her best friend was already swinging the door open and ducking into the rain.

Kallie shoved the driver's seat against the steering wheel, then climbed from the car, shotgun in hand. Sucking in a breath of air thick with the smell of wet greenery and gravel, she ran to the side of the road and the man lying so still at its edge, the rain soaking her to the skin in the brief time it took her to reach him.

With a wordless glance at Belladonna, Kallie handed the mambo-in-training the rain-slicked shotgun, then dropped to her knees beside Layne. She touched her fingers to his throat, seeking his pulse.

His heart beat, slow and steady, beneath her fingertips.

Kallie sighed, relief draining the tension from her body like a tossed-back shot of premium whiskey. What the hell was Layne doing in Chacahoula anyway? When he'd left her place, he'd been headed for New Orleans and Gage's cremation. Given the driveway he'd ended up in—the same one Kerry had directed her and Belladonna to—a dark suspicion simmered at the back of her mind.

I told him Doctor Heron's dead wife was involved in the attack that killed Gage by mistake. What do you wanna bet he decided to go looking for her? And what do you wanna bet it's no coincidence that we ended up at the same place?

"He still breathing?" Belladonna asked, crouching down beside her. Glimmers of rain jeweled her blue and black curls.

Kallie nodded. "So far."

Belladonna tsked. "Saving his sexy nomad ass is starting to become a habit, Shug. Not that I object," she amended, eyeing his unconscious length. "Not at all. But this just underscores the point I was making the other night."

"Which point was that?" Kallie unstrapped Layne's cracked helmet and removed it with slow, easy care, trying not to aggravate any injuries he might have. She hoped the helmet had spared him from anything more serious than a temporary loss of consciousness.

"Oh, you know, the one about how helpless men as a species are," Belladonna replied. "Falling into pits. Knocking their thick skulls against, from, on, or off all manner of hard-ass things. Hurling themselves out of objects moving at high rates of speed and/or altitudes. Poking sticks at things they shouldn't." Bottles clinked as she searched through her bag. She tsked. "Without us . . ."

"They'd be in a pretty pickle," Kallie agreed, easing Layne's goggles up to his forehead. "But I know women guilty of the things you just listed too, so it ain't only the men."

"By *women* do you mean *woman*, as in Kallie Rivière?"

"I've *never* hurled myself out of anything or—"

Layne moaned softly, but his eyes remained closed. Kallie trailed the back of one finger along the stiletto-thin sideburn curving along the line of his jaw, then touched the stylized fox black-inked beneath his right eye, naming his clan. Even though she wanted to stay with him, she couldn't.

Layne was still breathing, yes, but Jackson might not be.

She slid her fingers along the rain-chilled chain of the Saint Bernadette medallion around her throat, then up to unfasten the clasp. Bending, she looped the chain around Layne's neck, clicked the clasp shut. She straightened the medallion as it dipped and nestled in the hollow of his throat and rested her fingers against both—cool silver and warm, taut flesh—as rain continued to pour.

Heal him, O Glorious and Blessed Lady. Soothe and mend his hurts. Keep him intact. Amen.

Kallie lifted her hand. "Stay with him, Bell, and check him over." She tossed Layne's helmet into the grass as she rose to her feet. "I'm going to fetch Jacks." She held her hand out for the shotgun.

Belladonna arched an eyebrow as she relinquished the weapon. Her drenched tunic hugged the curves of her breasts and hips. "You're gonna need help digging him free, Shug."

"I know," Kallie replied, striding to the car and crossing to the passenger side. She opened the door.

Kerry looked at the shotgun, then up at her, his dark eyes uncertain. "Hey, hey, now. I brought you to the place your cousin is buried, just like you asked—"

"Yup, and I might need your help working a shovel," Kallie said, tucking the shotgun's stock under her arm. "I'm gonna untie you, but if you try to run . . ."

Kerry winced as she plucked a single dark hair from his head. Twirling the hair between her thumb and forefinger and making sure he got a good look, she said, "I'll fix you but good."

The color drained from Kerry's face. "Ain't no call for that. I'll help and I ain't running. To be honest, I never felt good about leaving your cousin behind like that in the first place." He shook his head, looked away. "Man, I told Cash this whole thing about hitting Bonaparte's house was a fucking . . . excuse my French . . . bad idea."

"A goddamned shame the bastard—excuse my English—didn't fucking listen to you." Kallie slipped the hair into a pocket of her cutoffs. "You'll get that back as soon as we have my cousin out of the ground. Now, lean forward."

Kerry complied and Kallie quickly unknotted the rope Gabrielle had tied around his wrists, then tucked the rope into her hip pocket. *Just in case.*

Leaving Kerry rubbing his freed wrists, Kallie raced around to the other side of the Dodge Dart. She shoved the driver's seat back into place, hopped in behind the wheel, slammed the car into gear, and turned into the driveway marked by the broken mailbox post.

She drove up the rutted and bumpy drive, feeling a bone-deep chill as she recognized the house and its sheltering palm trees from her blood divination.

Doctor Heron's home.

As she'd suspected, Layne's presence *wasn't* a coincidence. And that ended any remaining mystery as to who had ordered Jacks snatched from their home and put into the ground.

Icy fingers locked around Kallie's heart. If the twisted and vengeance-seeking root doctor had ordered Jackson buried alive, there'd been a goddamned good reason for it. Fear pulsed through her like blood.

She could think of any number of dark and nasty potions that could've—and most likely had—been forced down her cousin's throat before he'd been tossed into his grave.

Potions of command and compelling. Potions of brutal transformation. Enslaving potions. Potions that extended pain and suffering.

A muscle jumped in Kallie's jaw. As if slowly suffocating to death weren't bad enough . . .

She eased her foot off the gas as she reached the end of the driveway, then hit the brakes. A flash of lightning strobed across a grave-size hole in the side-yard beside a pile of mud and dirt. Several mud-smeared shovels rested in the grass at strange angles, as though flung aside.

Kallie thought of Layne and wondered if by some weird quirk of fate he'd somehow stumbled upon Jackson's burial site before the accident happened and had dug him up. But if he had, where was her cousin? The yard was empty, no sign of anyone around, living, ghost, or otherwise.

"You sure this is the right driveway?" Kallie asked, even as her mind tossed back: *Hello, even if it ain't, just how many homes along this stretch of road have people buried in their yards? A neighborhood zombie garden?*

"Yeah, positive. This is the driveway and the house," Kerry replied. "And that there's where they buried your cousin. But," he added, voice puzzled, "looks like he ain't buried no more. Maybe they-all just wanted to scare him."

"Maybe." But given this was Doctor Heron's house, she doubted just scaring Jackson was the intention, even as she hoped Kerry's words were true. Her CPR-aching ribs and sternum gave testimony to the dead root doctor's true intentions.

Switching off the engine, Kallie slipped out of the car, shotgun in hand, and raced through thinning rain across the wet, slippery yard to the grave. She pressed a protective hand against her bruised breastbone, felt the rapid drumming of her heart as she halted at the hole's foot.

She wanted to look, but an image of Jackson lying broken and pale and lifeless at the grave's muddy bottom stole her strength.

Ah, Jacks, please. You can't. You just can't. You may have been born my cousin, but Hurricane Gaspard and my mama made us siblings. I ain't about to lose the only brother I've ever had.

Kallie closed her eyes and, as she drew in breath to voice a prayer, lines from a Keats poem she'd heard Jackson quote from time and again, always with his wicked drawl, played through her memory and slipped from her lips instead, like a prayer, a summons.

"'Give me women, wine and snuff / Until I cry out "hold, enough!" You may do so sans objection / Till the day of resurrection: / For, bless my beard, they aye shall be / My beloved Trinity.'" Kallie opened her eyes. "You ain't said 'enough' to anything yet, Jackson."

Drawing in a deep and steadying breath of air laced with the smells of wet wood and leaves, of muddy ground, she stepped forward; but just as she was about to look down, she caught a nose-crinkling whiff of pungent cigar smoke and booze and something spicy like . . .

Kallie's blood chilled.

. . . hot peppers.

"I too be fucking fond of de women and wine, but give me a big ol' cigar over snuff any day," said a jovial but nasal voice from behind her.

Not being a practitioner like Belladonna and Gabrielle, Kallie had never attended a voodoo ceremony, had never watched as the *loa* had ridden their human *chevaux*, had never heard the *loa* speak.

But she *was* a hoodoo rootworker, taught by one of the best, and she knew the hell out of her saints and *loas* and the proper offerings when asking for favors.

Hot-peppered rum was a favorite of Baron Samedi — the all-knowing *loa* of death. And if the Baron was *here*, that meant . . .

No. No. No. Jackson, no.

Needing to know the truth before she turned to

confront the presence behind her, Kallie looked down into the open grave. Empty. Nothing but glistening mud and muck and groundwater. No sign of Jackson—alive or dead.

Intense relief sapped the last of the strength from her muscles and when Kallie tried to spin around to face the Baron, her legs gave and she fell to her knees instead, the cold mud oozing against her bare skin. She heard a soft thud as the shotgun slipped from her nerveless grasp and into the mud.

"Now, that's the perfect place for you," said a voice behind her. A different voice. No longer jovial or nasal and impossibly familiar. "On your knees."

No goddamned way.

Kallie swiveled around on her knees, her fingers searching the slick mud for the shotgun, then froze when she saw who stood behind her, a shovel leveled casually across his shoulder, a smoldering cigar jutting from between his teeth.

Goddamned Cash. More or less, anyway.

The home-invasion amateur's face was painted as a skull, his eyes hidden behind shades, his nose circled and hollowed out with black paint, a lipless grimace painted onto his mouth. Black fedora, purple shirt, and tailored black suit completed his *loa*-possessed ensemble.

How the holy loving hell is this possible? And when did the Baron switch from top hat and tuxedo to a goddamned fedora and suit?

He grinned—giving him a double set of teeth, one real, one painted—then said, "Toldja I wouldn't be forgetting you, darlin'."

Cash kicked out with his right leg, and before Kallie

could jump to her feet or grab the shotgun or twitch away to the side, the pointed toe of his scuffed-up cowboy boot caught her square in the gut.

The force of the kick knocked Kallie backward. Gasping for air and struggling for balance, she felt the wet, muddy ground edging the grave give way. Then she felt only empty air beneath her.

Kallie fell, Cash's mocking laughter kiting above like a vulture.

ELEVEN

SPIRIT BOX

Hoping against hope that Kallie would reach Jackson in time, Belladonna eased Layne onto his back and resumed searching him for damage, her trained healer's hands listening to his body as she felt his limbs and skimmed her fingers over his skin.

Mmm-mmm-mmm. A shame the man's unconscious. Well. And injured.

So far, she'd only discovered bruises, along with pebble- and dirt-filled road rash. No broken bones. Now, as for internal injury or brain damage, a more experienced healer or maybe a CT scan at a hospital would be able to tell for sure. She pushed up his black Inferno T-shirt.

Blue-inked tattoos curled across his lean-muscled chest and flat, belly-fluttering six-pack abs in flowing Celtic designs—detailed knotwork beneath his hard pecs curved around to his back; concentric circles looped around his nipples; shamrocks, spirals, stylized and fanciful beasts, decorated his skin in flowing patterns—each tat signifying, as far as she understood, nomad rites of passage.

She thought of the tattoo—a dragon's knotwork tail— she'd glimpsed disappearing into his waistband during the wet-boxers contest at the May Madness Carnival, and wondered where it ended and what rite *that* particular tat signified.

Maybe once he and Kallie finally spend a little well-deserved playtime together—instead of just trying to keep each other alive—I can persuade her to share a few details over beignets and hot cocoa, a little girl talk.

Relieved at the lack of bruising on Layne's torso, Belladonna took her time smoothing his T-shirt back down over his belly. *Oops. A wrinkle. Can't have that. Oh, look, another. What a shame. Let's get that taken care of too.*

But even with the lack of bruising, she knew Layne could have internal injuries that hadn't revealed themselves yet. And that worried her. He could be bleeding out even now, and she wouldn't necessarily know it. She mentally thumbed through a list of WebMD cautions regarding internal injuries. SEEK IMMEDIATE EMERGENCY CARE was the most popular response. She sighed. Well. Duh.

She reached into her bag for her bottle of healing oil and uncapped it, tilted the bottle against her finger. She anointed Layne, touching her oil-beaded fingertip to the center of his forehead, then to each temple. The spiky scents of rosemary, sage, and bitter wormwood prickled into the humid air.

Just as Belladonna parted her lips to murmur a prayer to Saint Joseph, Layne opened his eyes. His pupils were dilated, expanding into the pine-green irises but not swallowing them.

"Hey, you," she greeted. "Welcome back. How's that thick nomad skull of yours feeling?"

Wincing in the storm-grayed daylight, Layne blinked several times, struggling to focus. His dazed, pained expression gave way to confusion, his mouth opened and closed several times before he finally managed to whisper, "Oh, Bon Dieu, my aching head. Boy musta rung his bell damned hard."

Belladonna blinked. Was Layne speaking of himself in the third person? It couldn't be Augustine piloting the nomad's body, since he spoke in a posh British accent, so it *had* to be Layne, but his rhythm, even his word choice, felt wrong.

An icy curl of dread twisted through her belly. This was beginning to feel a lot more serious than a concussion. Maybe Layne had fractured his skull and his brain was swelling.

"Who the hell are you, girl?" Layne said, squinting at her.

Hoo-boy. Not good.

"Belladonna. I'm Belladonna, Layne. You just keep still, okay—"

"Get away from me, dead man," Layne hissed, his gaze shifting inward. "I beat you fair and—" His eyes suddenly rolled up white in his head, then the nomad passed out again.

"Dead man"?

Layne's eyes flicked open again. His face paled. "Dear God," he said in a familiar British accent. "My head." He swallowed hard several times, as if trying to keep from puking, then focused on Belladonna. "I can't stay long, Ms. Brown, I need to protect Valin. So I need you to—" His eyes shuttered again, long honey-blond lashes sweeping up, as he passed out once more.

"Hellfire," Belladonna breathed.

A chill that had nothing to do with sitting in the rain in

sopping-wet clothes shuddered along the length of Bella-donna's spine. She shivered convulsively. Either Layne had suffered serious damage to his noggin or he was carrying someone else inside of him—someone *besides* Augustine.

"Hellfire," Belladonna repeated, realizing what a trea-sure trove Layne's unconscious and helpless body would be for any ghosts just wandering about, seeking something to haunt.

Belladonna's knowledge about Vessels was scant, and she didn't know if multiple ghost takeovers of one body was even possible, but if it was—and if Augustine and the stranger(s) were warring over possession of Layne's body—someone was going to get hurt, and that someone was most likely Layne.

Can't have that. She started digging through her bag for a knock-'em-out potion.

Layne shuddered, then his eyes flew open. Again. "Help me up, girl," he demanded, lifting a shaking, gravel-abraded hand.

"Ghost, please," Belladonna scoffed. "Given that you don't belong in there, I don't think so. And you need to scoot your spirit butt out of there. No vacancies." Finding the potion, she yanked it from her bag just in time to see the nomad turn his head to the side, retch into the grass, then pass out. Yet again.

"Boy's like a spirit box full of ghostly jumping beans. Y'all need to leave him be," she said, directing her words to the ghosts tussling inside Layne, "before you do him some permanent damage."

Belladonna twisted the cap from the potion, releasing the faint scent of poppies and 150-proof homemade white lightning moonshine into the air.

Layne groaned, then his eyelids fluttered open. "Ms. Brown," he began in a British accent, then all color drained from his face.

Rolling onto his side, Augustine puked Layne's guts out—or tried to, anyway. From where Belladonna was sitting, it looked like the nomad hadn't eaten in a while.

And, right now, that's a good thing.

"Gah. Yuck." Belladonna clapped a hand over her mouth. She scooted back a couple of feet, trying hard not to puke herself.

Layne-Augustine flopped back onto his back, breathing hard, eyes closed. Sweat beaded his face. "Ms. Brown," he gasped. "Unless you know how to perform an exorcism on a Vessel, you need to call Valin's ex-wife. I seem to have my hands full at the moment with Babette St. Cyr."

Hoping she'd heard wrong, Belladonna lowered her hands. "You sure?"

"About having my hands full?"

"No, the other thing."

"About calling Valin's ex-wife?"

"No," Belladonna grated. "The other, other thing—about Babette. You sure?"

"Ah. Oh, yes. Quite."

During their drive to Chacahoula, Kallie had filled Belladonna in on what she'd seen in her blood divination in New Orleans and her suspicions about the late Babette St. Cyr.

"I believe that she set her husband up for murder by poisoning the potions he gave his clients, then allowed him and their daughter to believe that Gabrielle LaRue was the person responsible for sending him to prison for twenty-five years."

"*Just because he had an affair with Gabrielle? That's one cold-hearted woman.*"

"*You gotta have a heart first, Bell, for it to be cold. I don't think Babette qualifies, heartwise.*"

"Hellfire. If I potion up Layne, will that help?"

"I believe so, yes." Retching again, Layne-Augustine rolled onto his side, his body racked with dry heaves. He sounded like he was trying to turn himself inside out and Belladonna's gut knotted in queasy sympathy.

When he finished, he whispered, "If Valin's body is drugged, none of us will be able to use it— Get *away* from here, you harpy! He's mine!"

"Excuse me?" Belladonna said indignantly, then realized that the Brit was speaking to Babette. But before the illusionist could say another word, his eyes rolled up white once more and he lost consciousness.

"Shit, Layne," Belladonna murmured. "I can't even imagine how much all of this must suck from your end."

The fingers on Layne's right hand twitched. Belladonna's eyes narrowed. Had he—or someone else inside— just tried to flip her off?

Crawling back to the nomad's side, Belladonna slipped a careful hand under Layne's head and lifted it enough so he could swallow without choking to death. She tipped the green bottle against his lips, then hesitated.

The memory of Divinity blowing powder into Cash's face, then curling up on the sofa for a snooze, played through Belladonna's mind. How the hell had Kallie's aunt's spell backfired? And why?

Had Doctor Heron tricked the house somehow? Had Cash been wearing some kind of protective mojo bag or *paquet*? Power had exploded through the house, hitting

Belladonna in the solar plexus—her magical center—like a hard-knuckled punch. She'd never felt anything like it before—unbalanced, cold, and hungry.

There was no reason to think that the same kind of magical misfire would happen out here, but . . .

Belladonna studied Layne's pale, sweat-glistening face. She couldn't chance it. The potion itself was strong enough to knock him out and keep him that way for a while without her magically enhancing or lengthening its effect.

Better safe than sorry, definitely.

Belladonna swallowed back the spell she'd been about to chant and instead murmured, "Sleep well, Layne. You too, Augustine."

She poured the potion into the nomad's mouth and he swallowed convulsively, drinking it down. "That's it," she encouraged. "There you go." The eye-watering smell of moonshine stung her nostrils. She fed Layne until half the bottle had been emptied.

With a soft sigh, his body relaxed, tension drained from his muscles, and his fingers uncurled from his palms. She gently lowered his head back onto the wet grass, then rolled him onto his side in case he started puking again.

Screwing the cap back on the half-empty bottle of knock-'em-out, Belladonna returned the potion to her bag. She rose to her feet, brushing at her sodden leggings. *Ruined*, she mourned.

She tossed a glance down the long, rutted driveway, wondering how Kallie was doing, wondering if she'd found Jackson, wondering if she needed any help. But the sight that greeted her gaze froze her to the spot.

Kallie knelt in front of the *loa* of death and

resurrection—Baron Samedi. She stared at the fedora-capped man in front of her, her expression one of shock. As Belladonna watched, the Baron kicked Kallie, knocking her backward.

She vanished from sight and Belladonna's heart leapt into her throat.

Mocking laughter drifted into the air. Familiar laughter, but Belladonna couldn't quite place it. Standing beside the opened passenger door of her Dodge Dart, Kerry crumpled to the ground in a boneless swoon.

Again? Was the man wearing a corset under his T-shirt?

"Hellfire." Belladonna spun, bent over Layne, and searched inside his leather jacket for his gun. Her fingers whispered past his sheathed blades and she plucked one free before grabbing his Glock.

Belladonna was pretty damned sure that the asshole who'd just kicked Kallie into the grave had to be a blond-mulleted Baron imposter, possibly someone hired by Doctor Heron to mess with Jackson's mind before tossing him into the grave, and who happened to still be hanging around, maybe waiting for his boss to return.

Because the real Baron would either be lifting Jackson up out of the grave or filling it in, but in either case, he'd never strike or kick a living woman.

A knife in one hand, gun in the other, Belladonna raced down the driveway.

TWELVE

CHAINED HEART

Kallie hit the bottom of the grave with a thud that knocked what little air still remained in her lungs out between her lips in an explosive *whoof*. For a split second, the image of a heart bound in chains made of pale bones and fenced in by black X's flared behind her eyes—then vanished.

Wait. I've seen that before. From my dying dream . . . a horse and a chained heart.

Her aunt's voice whispered through her memory: *No dream, girl.*

Trouble for another time. You've got other things to worry about. Like finding Jackson. Oh, and surviving a loa *possessed by a mullet-wearing guy with a huge grudge.*

Black spots whirling through her vision, her heart trip-hammering against her bruised ribs, Kallie struggled to catch her breath.

What the hell just happened? Baron Samedi and Cash? How . . .

Words spoken at the house just before she and Belladonna had split to find Jackson rolled through Kallie's memory, a promise from Mambo Gabrielle.

Time is against us, so while you're driving to Chaca-

houla, I plan on asking the Gédé to intercede on your cousin's behalf. I plan to summon Baron Samedi. If anyone can save your cousin, turn him away from death, the Baron can.

Lightning fractured the empty gray sky above her, followed by a low mutter of thunder. A grim possibility unfolded within Kallie's mind. What if Gabrielle's plea to the Baron had gone full pedal-to-the-metal south just like Divinity's sleep trick had?

Jesus Christ. That would be all kinds of bad.

Kallie shoved the heels of her hands into the cold mud and pushed herself up into a sitting position. Mud coated her skin, her clothes, coiled her hair into mud-dreads. Lungs finally cooperating again, she drew in a breath of air reeking of decaying plants and swamp-muck as she gauged the grave's depth.

Six feet. Higher than me. I'm gonna need help getting out.

The mud made sucking sounds as Kallie climbed to her feet. Intending to call Belladonna, she fumbled her cell phone from the pocket of her cutoffs, but her finger stilled on the send button when something half-buried in the mud caught her eye.

A boot.

Kallie took a squelching step over to it and tugged it free. A square-toed Dingo she was pretty damned sure was Jackson's. Hope radiated through her, warm as summer sunshine on pavement.

Maybe he climbed out or someone pulled him out and the mud claimed his boot as a graveside trophy, but if so, then Jackson's probably alive.

"Question be, for how much longer?" a nasal voice

asked. "I t'ink I smell yo' cousin's lifeblood mixed up in de earth."

And then, as if the *loa*'s words had heightened her sense of smell or had woven an olfactory illusion, Kallie smelled it too, ever so slightly—the coppery tang of blood.

Everything inside her stilled. She stared at the boot clutched in her hand, refusing to let go of her hope. Maybe it wasn't blood she smelled. Maybe it was some kind of mineral deposit or metal ore in the ground or . . .

"Oh, it's blood all right. And it belongs to your mother-fucking cousin."

Kallie's jaw tightened. Goddamned Cash-in-Charge again. *This day keeps getting better and better. Wonder if I should pick up a goddamned lottery ticket?*

A black fedora encircled with a purple band drifted down into the grave like a bouquet of dead violets, see-sawing to a gentle stop in the mud beside Kallie's feet. She drew back her booted foot to kick it aside, then hesitated.

Disrespecting Cash was one thing. But disrespecting a *loa*? The *loa* of death, the gatekeeper between worlds, no less? Not to mention someone who could hold a grudge both in this world *and* the next if he wanted to?

That wasna't something she cared to risk at the moment.

Kallie lowered her foot back into the mud. Without thinking, she reached for the little coffin pendant she wore, the Baron's symbol, a gift of protection from her aunt, and remembered placing it into Layne's palm as a crematorium gift for Gage. Fingers curling shut over her empty palm, she dropped her hand to her side.

"Blood ain't de only t'ing I smell here. I caughts me a big ol' stinky whiff of wet dog and . . . wolves. No, *not* wolves. *Loups-garous.*"

"*Loups-garous?*" she questioned, lifting her gaze. "*Werewolves?* Seriously?"

The memory of a dream-vision tugged at Kallie—*her gaze seeks the shadow flitting among the live oaks and cypress on the bayou's other side, a man-shaped shadow that drops from upright to all fours*—but she shook it off.

No time for weird-ass dreams or bullshit. No matter how much they might nudge at the corners of her mind, trying to remind her of something just beyond the ragged edge of her recall. A child's voice.

Wanna know a secret? But you gotta promise never to tell . . .

Baron Samedi-Cash lounged against the dirt wall, one shoulder braced against the grave's mouth, but untouched or unstained by mud, his skeletal double grin fixed on Kallie. He blew a cloud of tobacco-fragrant cigar smoke in her direction.

"Smells cheap," Kallie commented. "Sure ain't Cuban."

"Maybe I like cheap." The Baron looked her up and down and Kallie saw her reflection in the lenses of his shades—wet and muddy, her hair hanging in long soaked strands over her face with mud-twisted dreads down her back.

Great. I look like a swamp rat for true.

The Baron winked. "I loves me a woman who can roll in de mud and get dirty."

His grin vanished as if switched off. He lifted a middle

finger and extended it, and Kallie knew she was now looking at Cash again.

None of this made sense. The Baron could possess a
human, ride him like a horse—any *loa* could. But the *cheval*'s personality and mannerisms disappeared, submerged
beneath the *loa*'s more forceful and powerful personality.

Or so Kallie had been told.

She'd also heard a few people describe a possession as
channeling a *loa*, but Belladonna had disagreed, stating
that complete possession was far more accurate.

Regardless of how the Baron had discovered Cash—
and Kallie had a strong suspicion she was right that
Gabrielle's invocation to the Baron had misfired—the hot-
tempered outlaw's personality should've been swallowed
up by the *loa*'s.

Samedi-Cash tilted his head. "Perhaps you be right,
girl," he said. "I t'ink dat's how it's always been." He puffed
on his cigar, painted face thoughtful. "But not today."

"Do you know why?" Kallie asked, pushing her bedrag-
gled hair back from her face and wondering if the *loa*
would confirm that Doctor Heron had placed a hex on
her aunt's house.

The Baron shrugged. "Maybe it just be time for
somet'ing different."

"Hey, Shug, you all right down there?" A soft and dangerous velvet purr.

Kallie glanced up. Then blinked.

Belladonna knelt at the grave's lip with a pistol that
looked like Layne's held tight in both hands and aimed at
the Baron, cold outrage on her rain-beaded face. As she
leaned forward, Kallie caught a metallic glint at her waist.

Girl is strapped and *she has one of Layne's knives*

tucked into her belt too. I don't think she learned that on WebMD. If she did, I need to log on.

"I'm okay, Bell." She held up her cell phone for a second before tucking it back into her pocket. "I was just about to call you."

"So who's the religion-dissing asshole with the mullet? The one kicking women into graves while dressed up as Baron Samedi?" Belladonna asked, her voice still a velvety purr. "Though he's done a poor-ass job, since the Baron wears a top hot and a tuxedo."

"Bell . . . it's the Baron for true," Kallie said. "I think Gabrielle's invocation for help went wrong and . . . . well . . ." She gestured at the tall Armani-suited form in front of her. "He claimed Cash as his *cheval.*"

A long silence; then: "How hard did you hit your head when you fell, Shug? You know, it ain't been all that long since you smacked your noggin in New Orleans and maybe you're—"

"She didn't hit her head," the Baron said, shoving away from the wall and looking up. He blew a plume of cigar smoke into the air. "Well. At least, not *dis* time. *Bonjour,* Belladonna Brown."

Belladonna's eyes widened as she recognized the man beneath the paint, the human carrying the *loa.* "Hellfire," she breathed. "Mr. I-Don't-Believe-in-Juju Cash." Her gaze flicked over to Kallie, skimmed the boot in her hand. Fear glimmered in the depths of her eyes. "And Jacks?"

Kallie shook her head. "Not here."

"No, he ain't, and this is where the sonuvabitch belongs," Cash tossed in, his voice low and feral. "But I'm gonna find him. He can't hide from death."

"Looks like he's doing a damned fine job so far," Kallie retorted.

Belladonna blinked. "Um . . . that sounds like Cash is—"

"In charge of the Baron," Kallie finished. "Yeah. Impossible, I know. But there it is. They've been switching off like Augustine and Layne." Her heart gave a hard, painful pulse. *Layne.*

"Don't worry," Belladonna said, either reading Kallie's expression or just working a little best-friend telepathy mojo. "Layne's potioned up and out cold, but he needs medical attention as soon as possible."

"Maybe I'll take you with me," Cash said, eyeing Kallie and drawing in on the cigar. "That way you can watch when I finally catch up with your motherfucking cousin."

"Try it and I'll empty this clip into your sorry ass," Belladonna promised.

Cash cast a contemptuous glance at her. "Go ahead. As long as the Baron's still inside of me, I'll keep breathing. But Bonaparte won't."

Kallie's hands knuckled into fists at her sides. "What the hell did Jacks steal from you, anyway? Your meth lab? Your girlfriend? Your hidden bank account? A goddamned *kiss*? What the hell did he take that's so goddamned important that you'd risk your goddamned life and everyone else's to get it back?"

"It ain't *what* he took, it's the fact that he took it from *me*."

"And who the hell are you supposed to be? Some big drug lord? Some big pimp-pornographer? *What?*"

"His fucking *friend*, his drinking buddy," Cash snarled. "That fucking Cajun bastard betrayed my trust and stabbed me in the goddamned back without even a *Sorry, podna, I had no choice and I hate myself for doing this.*"

Kallie stared at Cash, stunned. She couldn't imagine her cousin hanging out, let alone hitting the taverns, with Cash. But she couldn't deny the raw emotion behind his words either. He was telling the truth.

Kallie had thought she knew all of her cousin's friends—bayou pirates, outlaws, poets, fellow fishermen, and regular Joes. Now she wondered how many others Jackson had, friends on the seriously wrong side of the law, whom he hid from her and their *tante.*

What else had Jackson kept hidden? Even though the question left Kallie feeling gut-punched, she clung to her belief that whatever he hid, he did so to protect them.

"No," Kallie said finally. "Jackson would never betray or steal from a friend. Maybe someone set him up, spread a few lies around, knowing you'd go after him. Maybe someone—"

"Nobody had to set him up or spread lies," Cash said quietly. "I caught the bastard dead to rights. I caught him in the act. And then he tried to kill me."

THIRTEEN

UNNAMED AND UNTAMED

"No," Kallie said, shaking her head. "I don't believe that. Jacks might be a thief, but he's no goddamned killer."

Cash laughed and tossed his cigar into the mud. It went out with a hiss and a curl of smoke. "*Might* be a thief? You're kidding, right?" Shadows undulated across the painted-skull landscape of his face, negative ghosts in a bleached night. "The only reason I'm still alive is because I jumped overboard while your cousin was busy puncturing the air with high-velocity lead."

Kallie felt like she'd just taken another gut punch. But before she could say anything more to Cash—to refute his words, to question what he'd seen and, more important, who he'd thought he'd seen shooting at him—he stepped forward and pinioned her shoulders with fingers as hard and as cold as marble tombstones. Squeezed. She felt the bones in her shoulders and collarbone shift. She gritted her teeth against the pain.

"Ah, but you'd know all about goddamned killers, now, wouldn't you, *ma jeune belle*?" The Baron's nostrils flared. He dipped his head, brushed his cheek against Kallie's. His breath, cold as dry ice and pungent with peppered rum, fluttered her hair. "You be drenched in death and murder. I smell it all over you like sweat and heated musk, like a lover just rolled offa your luscious body."

She's bloody death in cutoffs and a tank top.

Words spoken by Layne's ex-wife, McKenna, during the long and dreadful night that had ended only a few hours ago; words that pricked Kallie with their bitter truth.

"Sounds like I need to switch perfumes," Kallie said, wishing she felt as confident as her words. Pinpricks needled her hands and fingers as the Baron's hard grip cut off her circulation.

The Baron laughed, sounding genuinely amused. "A woman with sass be a beautiful thing, for true. But you ain't *just* a woman, ain't dat so?"

"Hey, granted, I look more like a drowned swamp rat at the moment, but of *course* I'm just a woman. I'm—"

"More," the Baron interjected. "Different." His winter-hard hands slid down Kallie's shoulders to her biceps, trailing frost and a strange, skin-tingling heat in their wake. "What you hiding, Kallie Rivière? Hmmm, *ma belle*? Somet'ing don't feel right here."

Kallie stiffened beneath the *loa*'s unrelenting grip, her pulse drumming at her temples. "I ain't hiding nothing."

"Den dere be no harm in looking," the Baron declared.

Kallie wasn't so sure about that. She wasn't hiding anything, no, but according to Divinity, an unnamed *loa* had been secreted inside her, a *loa* her mama had tried to awaken with bullets and blood and cold murder.

Sorry, baby. I ain't got a choice.

An awakening her aunt was determined to prevent, no matter the cost.

"Dere ain't nothing I wouldn't do to help you, Kalindra

Sophia. Teach you. Guide you. Lie to you. Bind you, if it be necessary. Because a big wrong's been done to you."

Right now, facing Baron Samedi, a little guidance would be pure gold. Especially given the question circling her mind: Who was her mama hiding the *loa from?*

"Look at me, little hoodoo."

A dark, powerful energy radiated from the Baron, spiking out like deadly icicles in shades of coldest midnight and purple, icing Kallie to the bone, pricking against her soul. Or would've if she'd still possessed one.

She held no doubt that she was truly in the presence of Baron Samedi, lord of the *Gédé loa,* and not Cash. Her reflection flickered like flame in his shades—long cinnamon curls, café-au-lait skin, summer green eyes.

A pang of fear pierced Kallie to her core. *That's not me.* An image shaped itself behind her eyes—a heart bound in chains of pale bones—and a memory, a dying dream, unwrapped itself like a gift.

The jarring thud of hooves against the ground vibrates along Kallie's spine, jolts her body with each ground-swallowing gallop. Rough hair rubs against her cheek, twists around her fingers. She smells horse musk and, underneath her thighs, feels the powerful flex of muscles.

<Hold on, m'âme-soeur, *and ride.>*

Soul sister.

The reflection glimmering on the lenses of the Baron's night-deep shades guttered like the flame it resembled, then vanished as another image flared to life and tugged Kallie's vision inward.

Drums pound in time with the throbbing in Kallie's skull, the rhythm fast and primal and hungry. Shadows ripple at the edges of her vision. Cold frosts her veins. And still the black dust pours from her into St. Cyr—mouth, nose, ears, and eyes—in a violent rush of power that scrapes against her heart and threatens to yank her under.

"By Bon Dieu's holy cock!"

Kallie's memory wisped away at the Baron's abrupt words and she nearly stumbled when his icy fingers disappeared from her arms with all the frantic speed of a man jumping away from a downed and wriggling power line. The Baron stepped back, Cash's cowboy boots squelching in the mud, his tensed body language both wary and predatory.

"I don't know de how or de why of it, since it ain't riding you like a *cheval*, but a wild *loa* be hiding inside of yo' curvy body. And bristling with pure darkness. And dat just won't do. It don't belong dere."

Kallie blinked, caught off guard. She'd expected/feared that he'd find the *loa* harbored inside her body and had a bone-deep feeling, a wordless intuition, that if he did, it would be bad news all around. But *this* . . .

"Hellfire." Low and heartfelt from above. Belladonna.

Kallie's heart beat against her ribs like a caged and feral thing seeking release. "Okay. I agree. *Dat* most definitely won't do," she said, pleased her voice remained level. "And I figure it'll take more than a regular cleansing to get rid of it. So what do I do?"

"Well, now, dat depends on de unnamed and untamed *loa* you got coiled up in yo' soul's place. It be up to *her* which road we take, *ma belle*. Her choice—hard or easy."

And there it was. Her goddamned secret—one forced upon her as an infant and one she didn't have any answers for, only tons of questions—was no longer hidden. At least, not to the eyes of the *loa* of death. But instead of feeling relief, Kallie felt only hollow dread and a sense of wrongness.

Kallie knew that without this nameless *loa*, she'd be well and truly dead—body and soul—at the hands of that bastard Doctor Heron. Just like Gage. And without the nameless *loa*, she might not be able to get her locked-up mama to reveal the location of her missing soul.

If the *loa* was important enough for Mama to murder her own husband in cold blood and important enough to steal away her only child's soul, then the *loa* ought to make one damned fine bargaining chip.

Looking into the Baron's shades and relieved to see only her own reflection in the lenses this time, Kallie asked, "What if I want to keep the *loa* for the time being?"

"Dat ain't an option, girl. Dat t'ing inside you be wild and willful, shaped outta slivers of moonless nights and Halloween shadows and ill intentions. And she's fattening herself up on darkness and violence like a tick." The Baron shook his head, then sighed. "Normally, I loves me a woman—be she *loa* or human—with a round and sassy ass, but dis be a whole 'nudder t'ing."

"Will it hurt Kallie?" Belladonna asked. "When you take the *loa* from her?"

And yet another reason she's my best friend—asking all the hard questions.

Laughing, the Baron tipped his face up to look at Belladonna. "No, *ma jolie*, don't worry. De girl won't feel one lick o' pain—as long as de *loa* takes de easy road, dat is." Returning his attention to Kallie, he added, "But de hard road—now, dat will hurt like a motherfucker."

"Fantastic," Kallie muttered. "Sounds like Christmas just came early."

"Sure," Belladonna agreed, her voice light, but sympathetic. "If by *Christmas* you mean *hell*."

"Yup, you got it." Sudden pain throbbed at Kallie's temples—*in anticipation of the hard road?*—and scraped at her concentration. Made it hard to think. White sparks flitted across her vision.

Exhaustion must be catching up with me. And at the worst goddamned moment possible.

"And the best part about all of this bullshit?" the Baron said, his voice slipping into Cash's mocking cadence. "You die no matter which road your *loa* takes. But don't worry none. You won't be lonely. I'll be sending your cousin to join you."

An electric jolt surged through Kallie, short-circuiting and disconnecting her thoughts. Images whirled behind her eyes against a backdrop of white sparks: *Pale bones. A chained heart. A black horse. A ruby red skeleton key. A woman with cinnamon curls.*

"Well, then," she heard herself say, her voice coming from far away, "in that case, I guess I'm taking the goddamned hard road." Then she felt herself step forward, swinging a wicked right hook at the Baron's painted nose just as a gunshot cracked through the air.

The gun jumped hard in Belladonna's hand, smoke curling up from the muzzle, and she nearly dropped the damned thing. She sucked in air reeking of cordite as Kallie's powerhouse punch missed the lord of the dead—just as the bullet had—breezing past where his skull-decorated face *would've* been—if he hadn't vanished, his mouth shaping an O of surprise.

"Jesus Christ," Belladonna whispered, tightening her

grip on Layne's Glock, and wondering who to pray to in a situation like this. Praying *against* a *loa* or asking another to intercede would be like refusing one parent's ruling and running to another for a different, more favorable answer.

You die no matter which road your loa *takes.*

Belladonna refused to accept that. Baron Samedi tended to view death in a favorable light, so maybe he was just biased. There had to be another way. One that led to life and not to the graveyard.

Her determined face framed by her wet, muddy locks, Kallie spun around on her heels, Jackson's boot still clutched in the fingers of her left hand, her right fist cocked and loaded.

Belladonna sighted the gun around the grave, waiting for the Baron's return too, pulse pounding through her veins.

Now that she knew she wasn't dealing with a Baron Samedi imposter but the real deal in a weird, unnatural amalgam of dual and fluctuating control, Belladonna figured a bullet fired into Cash's body wouldn't do much more than distract the Baron from Kallie, but maybe that would be distraction enough to get the girl out of that grave and into the car.

Like we can speed away from death.

Worth a try, girl. Otherwise . . .

Lifting one hand from the gun to wipe rain from her eyes, Belladonna refused to finish the thought.

Given that she often served the *Gédé loa* and the Barons that ruled them in religious ceremonies at the *hounfor* where she studied to be a mambo, the thought of working against one—even to save her best friend's life—left her guts tied in knots and her heart cold.

But the thought of losing Kallie iced Belladonna to the soul, steadied her aim.

The Baron blip-appeared behind Kallie in the spot he'd just vacated, instead of where she'd clearly antici- pated him.

Just as Belladonna was about to yell a warning to Kallie and squeeze off another careful round, the distinct and unnerving *shu-schunk* of a shotgun shell being cham- bered launched her heart into her throat, and her words died unvoiced. She caught a peripheral glimpse of rain- glistening, mud-streaked, *familiar* sneakers.

Thunder growled overhead, moving away.

Hellfire. Guess who's roused from his damned swoon and discovered that his balls have finally dropped?

"Don't move, y'hear?" Kerry said, his voice unusually calm and steady. *Well. Maybe not calm, per se, just less panicky.* "Now toss the gun."

"We had this conversation back at the house," Bella- donna replied, sitting back on heels, her gaze remaining on the action in the grave. Kallie whirled to face the *loa* just as the Baron lifted a hand and traced a symbol of some kind in the air.

Pain tightened Kallie's features, darkened her eyes.

Hoo-boy. Not good. Could be a banishing or compel command.

"I can't do both," Belladonna continued, sparing Kerry a quick glance. His hands white-knuckled the shotgun, his lips a thin, determined line. "Now, which is it? Don't move, or toss the gun?"

Kerry blew out a frustrated breath. "Toss the gun, dam- mit. And technically, y'all had that particular conversation with Cash, not me."

"Oh. Well. That makes all the difference in the world," Belladonna said. "It's not like you were in the same room standing right next to each other or anything."

Power undulated up from the grave and through the air, and it seemed, for a heartbeat, that even the rain rippled like a breeze-pushed, water-pearled curtain. The hair lifted on the back of Belladonna's neck. An icy hand trailed her spine.

The surge of dark and unbalanced energy felt like a countdown timer on a suicide vest packed full of C-4 bricks.

Wow. Great analogy there, imagination. Thanks for that mental image.

Kallie swung at the Baron again, and the *loa* danced away, still etching symbols in the air, clearly reluctant to make physical contact with Kallie until he'd finished laying down his trick. Until he'd finished binding her. Entrapping her.

"Look, you gonna toss the gun or what? I'd hate to hurt a woman, I truly would, but I will if I hafta."

Belladonna snorted. "Redneck, please. I could turn you into a stewpot chicken before you could get off a single round."

"Ain't no call for that. *Redneck*. That's just plain hurtful."

"You like *stewpot chicken* better?"

The blood drained from Kerry's face and gravel scrunched beneath his sneakers as he shuffled his feet, his reptilian survival brain contemplating a hasty retreat. "Didn't I help y'all?" he said, reproach edging his voice. "Didn't I show y'all where Bonaparte was buried?"

"Yup, you did. But"—Belladonna paused to nod

at the grave and the bizarre action taking place in its depths—"I don't think you appreciate the gravity of this situation."

Kerry looked down, pursed his lips, tightened his fingers around the shotgun.

The Baron crafted his spell as he dodged more sight-blurring punches from Kallie—*and when the hell had she started moving so fast?*—intoning in a deep and nasal voice: "I command you, nameless one, I compel you. Hear my voice, the voice of Baron Samedi, a voice impossible to deny or resist. Come to me. I command you, compel you."

The *loa* of death and resurrection's words rumbled like long-rolling thunder, like the distant boom of storm-driven waves against rock, the sound echoing from the grave's muddy walls and vibrating up through the ground beneath Belladonna's knees and into her bones. Goose bumps tingled as power skittered electric along her skin.

"I command you, nameless spirit, flesh-hidden and unbound . . ."

"Okay," Kerry admitted, "maybe things *are* a little weird—"

Belladonna arched an eyebrow. "A *little*? Please."

"Okay, maybe a lot weird, but it's you who ain't appreciating the situation," Kerry insisted, returning his gaze to Belladonna. "I don't pretend to know how Cash got here or what the hell he's doing, but I'm getting us out. Me and Cash, we're gonna take your car and split. Now, toss the gun!"

"Hear my voice, nameless and untamed *loa*. Yo' lord, Baron Samedi, commands and compels you to leave de girl's warm flesh. Yo' master, Baron Samedi, unthreads you from her being with each word, every command. Come to me."

Belladonna's muscles cabled tight across her shoulders. She couldn't let the Baron finish laying his trick, couldn't risk his killing Kallie with his commands. Maybe the *loa*'s magic would backfire. *Maybe.* But she refused to gamble with her friend's life.

"That's not Cash down there, not exactly," Belladonna said, shifting her gaze from Kerry to skull-painted Cash in the grave. "But fine, have it your way."

Narrowing her eyes, Belladonna sighted in on her target and hurled the Glock. The gun bounced off the back of the Baron's head with a loud *thok*, then pinwheeled into the mud.

The chanting stopped. The Baron looked up at Belladonna, wagged a *Naughty, naughty, you've got a spanking coming, girl* finger at her, then returned his attention to Kallie just in time to backpedal away from her rocketing fist.

"Yo' lord, Baron Samedi, commands you, wild *loa*, unnamed spirit . . ."

Kerry took a step closer to the edge of the grave. "Cash! C'mon, man, forget about her. I've got the car and the shotgun and—"

His words cut off abruptly as Belladonna reached up, yanked the shotgun from his rain-slick grasp, twirling the weapon around so that its muzzle was aimed at him. "Wrong on both counts," Belladonna purred. She tsked. "Y'all really don't know how to hold on to a shotgun, do you?"

Kerry buried his face in his hands. "Fuck," he groaned. No apology for his "French" was offered; the manners his mama had taught him apparently worn thin.

"Compelled. Commanded. Come to me, wild one!" the Baron shouted.

Fear stabbed a cold blade into Belladonna. Just as she thought, *That sounds like a finished trick*, and flashed an anxious glance at Kallie, a hard blast of power pulsed up from the grave and out, knocking Belladonna onto her ass in a rush of heated air reeking of brimstone and ozone and prickling with *wrongness*.

Her teeth clicked together, narrowly missing her tongue, as her hind end hit the wet ground. She heard Kerry cry out in confused terror, followed by a soft thud. Knocked to his ass too. Or swooned. She'd lay odds on swooned. She also thought she heard a chicken clucking in an unhappy way.

Stewpot?

Belladonna crawled back to the grave's muddy edge and peered down. Then blinked. Kallie was also on her ass in the muck, a dazed expression on her face. And in front of her . . .

"Where'd the chicken come from?" Kerry asked. "And where the hell's Cash?"

FOURTEEN

HISTORY REPEATS ITSELF

"You feeling any better?" Gabrielle asked. "Has the potion finally worn off?"

"I'm awake, me," Divinity replied. She paused her teacup at her lips, and its aroma, redolent of black tea, honey, and ripe cherries, curled into her nostrils. "But feeling better? After what you told me? Hell, no."

She studied the makeshift altar on her coffee table, thought of the words Gabrielle had spoken as soon as Divinity awakened from her oh-so-restful damned snooze.

"Baron Samedi is hunting your nephew. And it's my fault."

"So de Baron just vanished? After saying Jackson was getting what he deserved?"

"In a puff of smoke, no less. And taking his new *cheval* with him too." Gabrielle shook her head, her eyes pools of disbelief. "Never seen nothing like that before."

Divinity could imagine.

But what she *couldn't* imagine was how an invocation for help had managed to go so wrong, downgrading her nephew's situation from bad to Sweet-Jesus-it-can't-get-much-worse.

Gabrielle looked genuinely troubled, but any hoodoo or mambo worth her salt knew how to *act* when it was necessary to show a client or student or worshipper what they needed to see when it mattered most.

"So, den," Divinity said, leaning forward and resting her teacup on the table, her gaze on Gabrielle, "I be safe in t'inking what happened with yo' invocation had nothing to do with my borrowing of yo' identity?"

Gabrielle's cup of tea froze in midair. She stiffened in her rocker and shot a barbed look at Divinity. "You can't *borrow* an identity," she stated, her tone level, yet hot enough to weld iron. "But you can obviously *steal* one. The problem between us has *nothing* to do with what happened. Unlike Jean-Julien St. Cyr, I'd never harm an innocent over a crime committed by someone else."

"Never thought you would, you," Divinity lied, meeting the other woman glare for glare. "Just stating facts. Don't get so riled up."

"Mmm-hmm." Dubious. Gabrielle's cup resumed its journey to her lips. "I got no reason to wish ill on your nephew or your niece." She sipped at her tea. "Now, *you*, however . . ."

"Don't worry, you'll get yo' chance, you. We'll hash all dat out later. *After* Jackson and Kallie are safe."

Gabrielle eyed Divinity from over the rim of the delicate rose-patterned cup. "After," she agreed. "But until then, I'd like an explanation to tide me over. You owe me that much."

Divinity nodded. "True, dat. But it's gonna need to be de Reader's Digest condensed version. We ain't got de time to waste on de past just now."

"We don't. Agreed. So let's hear it."

Clutching her cup and taking a sip of the cooling tea, Divinity gathered her thoughts for a moment, picking and choosing, saving others for a later date. "When I figured out what Sophie had done, I knew de day would come when I'd need to steal Kallie away and hide her. I just didn't know when dat day would be. So I prepared.

"I knew dat you'd gone to Haiti just a year or two before Kallie'd been born—after Jean-Julien had gone to prison—and I didn't figure you'd be back, so I buried my name and gave new life to yours. I wanted to be sure no one could link Gabrielle LaRue to Sophie Rivière."

"But why? Didn't you say your sister's locked up?"

"*Oui.* In Saint Dymphna's for de criminally insane. But," Divinity said, holding up a finger and capturing the mambo's gaze, "I also knew dat my sister couldn't've done dat evil t'ing to her daughter—her own flesh and blood— alone. It had to've been a group effort."

"A group effort," Gabrielle repeated, stunned realization widening her eyes. "So that's who you're hiding the girl from."

"Dat I be. I be hiding her from her mama too. If Sophie knew where Kallie is, she might pass de word along."

The mambo's brow furrowed. "Doesn't she know Kallie's with you?"

"No. De authorities done kept dat knowledge from Sophie, since dey still consider her a threat to Kallie."

"Bon Dieu. Do you know who the others are?"

Divinity shook her head, a familiar knot of anxiety twisting around her heart. "Dat I don't. And it worries me for true. But enough of dat. We got udder t'ings to figure out—like how my sleep potion and yo' incantation went so wrong."

Gabrielle eyed her for a moment before nodding and

saying, "All right. But this matter between us is far from finished."

"*Ça c'est bon*," Divinity agreed. "Once t'ings be settled, we'll get back to it, us. Now, tell me again what happened when I laid down dat sleep trick and don't skip a detail. We need to straighten dis mess out."

Gabrielle leaned back into her rocker and started speaking.

Divinity took another sip of the black cherry tea Gabrielle had brewed for her, but its honey-sweetened warmth was incapable of melting the cold lump of dread—growing colder and heavier with each word from the red-scarfed mambo's lips—icing her belly ever since she'd awakened from a refreshing nap on the sofa to the sound of rain drumming against the roof.

And that was another thing, that. An unexpected and shocking awakening, given that her last memory had been of laying a go-to-sleep trick on that foul-tempered, ornery boy who'd broken into her house.

The same foul-tempered and ornery boy who now housed the *loa* of death, and who'd stood by and watched as Jackson was buried alive . . . Divinity shook the bleak thought away.

No. Dat boy—my sea-roaming, Robin Hood–faring man—still be alive. I won't have it no other way. Our Kallie-girl will find him and bring him home again.

Divinity felt a sharp pang of guilt.

After all dat poor girl's endured in de last twenty-four hours? After all she's learned? You lay another burden on her and with no rest.

Divinity realized she was no longer certain who she chastised—the Lord, the *loa* and the saints, or herself.

Sweet Jesus, my girl died *last night and she's only alive now because de t'ing dat I tried to hide from her all dese years, tried to keep from awakening within her, kept her missing soul safe. Looks like her mama did her an unintended favor.*

All because of one man's misdirected need for vengeance.

With a soft sigh, Divinity lifted her cup to her lips again, but this time the cherries-and-honey aroma only made her belly clench.

Dat ain't de whole truth, now, be it? One man's misdirected need for vengeance and yo' desire to keep dem children safe. But you grabbed de wrong identity, you.

Gabrielle halted her recounting of the invocation gone wrong. "Want me to stop? You're looking awful grim," she commented from her rocker.

Divinity snorted. "Dat be de pot calling de kettle black."

And that was the absolute truth. The trim mambo in her red blouse and tan cords seemed to have aged since Divinity had sleep-tricked herself onto the sofa. Lines had deepened beside the woman's mouth, creased her forehead; worry and regret haunted her dark eyes.

No wonder. Her invocation to Baron Samedi hadn't fared any better than Divinity's go-to-sleep potion had on Cash, and the *loa* of death had poured himself into Cash's pride- and hate-poisoned heart. Now both, man and *loa*, hunted her nephew.

Divinity shook her head. As if being buried in the deep, dark ground weren't bad enough.

Her troubled thoughts returned to the magic backfires—her potion and Gabrielle's invocation. Had they been due to a hex placed on the house by Doctor Heron? Or something else entirely? Something darker and deadlier than a final shard of bitter laughter from a dead man?

And dat would be . . . ?

Nothing useful popped into mind, but a deep sense of unease glided through her like a partially submerged gator and her gaze slid over to her worktable and the poppet with the violet button eyes and brown yarn hair.

No, de loa still be sleeping. Dat much I'm sure of. Awake, it would take over de girl, maybe even destroy her mind, force her to do evil t'ings. She sure as hell wouldn't be searching for Jackson. Awake, de loa would eventually cast her body aside, a ruptured cocoon. No, de loa still be sleeping, for true.

Yet her unease threaded dark roots into her heart and anchored itself deep.

Divinity set her cup of tea aside on the coffee table, next to the flame-snuffed remains of a white candle. The faint odor of rum, tobacco smoke, and hot peppers still spiced the air.

"How long's it been since de girls left?" Divinity asked, rising to her feet and walking to the front window. The old oak floor creaked comfortably beneath her feet, familiar and solid.

Rain streaked the double-paned glass, the beads of water rippling with the deep green of the weeping willows and oaks and lawn beyond. Thunder muttered, but the storm seemed to be passing.

Divinity's heart gave a hard and painful pulse. Had the girls reached Jackson before the storm?

"Nearly two hours," Gabrielle replied. "They could be on their way back."

But what neither of them voiced lingered in the air nonetheless, like black smoke heavy with tension and dark possibilities: *Then why haven't they called to let us know one way or another?*

Divinity unlatched the window and pushed it up. The mingled rain-fresh scents of roses and tree bark and rich, wet soil flowed into the room. She studied the empty driveway—no Dodge Ram truck, no Siberian husky chasing squirrels, no niece or nephew arguing or blasting music—and felt just as empty inside.

"I'm gonna give Kallie a call, see if everyt'ing be okay," she said. "Den we need to cleanse dis house of dat man's evil, top to bottom, inside and out, and break his damned hex."

"Agreed," Gabrielle said, then paused, a troubled expression shadowing her face. She set her teacup on the candle-cluttered end table between the cherrywood rockers, then leaned forward, holding Divinity's gaze. "But we need to consider one very important thing before we begin."

"And dat very important t'ing would be?"

"What if a cleansing backfires just like the tricks did and we end up inviting *more* evil in?"

Sweet Jesus. Divinity hadn't even considered that possibility. *Refused* to consider it. "We'll use holy water first. Ain't no way dat can backfire."

"I used holy water during my invocation," Gabrielle said, casting a pointed glance at the makeshift altar on the coffee table.

Tapping a finger against her lips, Divinity mulled over the problem, perusing the sad altar and its remnants—candles, brazier, cup of coffee, small wood penis, symbols etched in dragon's blood ink on the back of a magazine.

Were prayers of the same weave as spells, a novena and

offering the same as laying a trick? She hated to think about what a backfiring *prayer* might cost a person . . . or their soul.

"You be a priestess," Divinity said finally, shifting her attention back to Gabrielle's watchful face. "Do prayers use de same kind o' magic as hoodoo tricks?"

The mambo leaned back in her chair, frowning and tugging absentmindedly at the edge of her carnation-red scarf. "I think it has more to do with power, with inner energy, than magic, but—" The phone's sudden ringing stopped Gabrielle's words.

Kallie, praise de Lord! Relief flooded Divinity.

Holding up a *Just a second* finger, she whirled and hurried into the kitchen. She snagged the cream-colored wall phone's handset and pressed it to her ear. "Tell me what be happening, girl," she said just a trifle breathlessly into the receiver. "You okay? You find yo' cousin?"

"Umm . . . no," a female voice decidedly not Kallie's, but familiar all the same, replied, and disappointment scratched thorn-sharp through Divinity. "This ain't your niece, Miz LaRue. It's Addie Thompson in Crowley. And we've got *beaucoup* big trouble over here."

Miz LaRue. Hmmm. Dis could get awkward now that de real Gabrielle LaRue is back in Louisiana.

"Talk fast, Addie, I be expecting an important call from Kallie. What be de problem over dere?"

As Divinity listened to the Crowley-based hoodoo spill eye-widening news, the dread coiled ever tighter around her spine, showing no sign of letting go or slithering away anytime soon. No sooner had Addie finished speaking in a breathless rush than Divinity heard the double click on the line that indicated a call waiting.

Putting the Crowley hoodoo on hold, Divinity

switched over to the incoming call, but again, it wasn't Kallie or even Belladonna.

"Woman, you ain't gonna believe what's been happening here the last hour or so," a deep and currently very tense masculine voice proclaimed—a root doctor in Jeanerette known as Doctor Coyote.

The call-waiting double click sounded again. And again.

A strong sense of urgency quivered in Divinity's muscles and pooled in her chest as she listened to every hoodoo and root doctor she knew—no, wait, only those she knew in *Louisiana*—recite a litany of magic gone suddenly awry.

And the thought that filled her mind was: An eye for an eye is never enough.

What kinda evil crossing did dat man lay down? And how did we set it off? More important, how do we uncross it?

She tried to imagine the power it would take to lay down a crossing that, when triggered, rippled outward in all directions, shredding magic like deadly shrapnel from a massive bomb.

And sniffing along behind those thoughts came another: *Doctor Heron's own power? Maybe he hadn't acted alone, after all. Or maybe he'd made some dark crossroads deal in de event of his sudden demise . . .*

When the flood of stunned and frantic voices finally ran dry and the phone quit ringing, Divinity fetched two bottles of Abita from the fridge, then returned slowly to the living room, the phone's handset tucked into a pocket of her purple skirt.

Alarm flashed across Gabrielle's face. She perched at the rocker's end. "Divinity?" she asked.

Wordlessly handing the mambo one of the cold bottles of beer, Divinity plopped down onto the sofa across from the other woman. She leaned back into its cushions with a weary sigh. "We be in deep shit," she said, twisting off the beer's cap, then meeting and holding Gabrielle's eyes.

"How deep?"

Divinity took a long drink of the cold amber pale brew, then told her what the rattled hoodoos and root doctors had funneled into her ear.

"A silence-the-witness trick I performed for a client to help him win his court case ended up with the fool confessing to a bunch of crimes he didn't even commit."

"You ain't gonna believe . . . I don't even know where to begin . . . but the short of it is, a client wants to marry a gator instead of the woman I fixed to fall in love with him. And the gator seems agreeable."

Spontaneously combusting mojo bags.

Poppets that stitch together companion poppets to run away with, taking sewing needles and thread with them.

Some of the backfiring tricks had landed on the good side of wonderful, others had decidedly not, and still others had landed squarely in the bizarre and inexplicable category—gators in love and runaway poppets.

"Jesus Christ," Gabrielle breathed. She took a long, throat-stretching pull from the Abita. When she lowered the bottle again, she asked, "What in Bon Dieu's name is going on? Could this have anything to do with Doctor Heron's death? With what your niece . . . did . . . to him?"

Divinity's gaze slid almost unwillingly to her worktable at the room's end and the unfinished poppet with the purple button eyes. "I t'ink de *loa* inside Kallie had more to do with dat man's soul unraveling dan Kallie herself did," she said, a hint of defensiveness threading through her voice—even to her own ears. "Man killed her, after all. Girl ain't got dat kind o' power on her own. De *loa* mighta roused long enough to teach de *fi' de garce* a well-deserved lesson."

"And then went back to sleep?" Gabrielle questioned dubiously, one eyebrow arched. "Does this *loa* have a name? A purpose?"

Just as Divinity opened her mouth to answer, the phone rang again, the shrill sound grating against already touchy nerves. She yanked the handset out of her pocket and thumbed the talk button.

"Addie," she murmured, "I still be waiting to hear from Kallie—"

"Just called to tell you one more thing. Turn your TV to the Weather Channel."

Divinity frowned. "Why?"

"You been keeping up with that tropical storm in the Caribbean? Evelyn?"

"*Oui*, of course, but it ain't aimed at us. Dem poor folks in de Honduras and Belize are de ones in de storm's path."

"Evelyn's grown up," Addie said. "And more."

Spotting the remote on the floor beside the coffee table, Divinity grabbed it and powered on the flat-screen TV Jackson had given her a couple of years ago, then flipped through the channels until she found the one Addie mentioned.

"You see what I'm talking about?" Addie asked.

"Yup, but—" Then Divinity saw it scrolling across the bottom of the screen in bold letters over and over. HURRI-CANE WATCH. "Sweet Jesus."

Gabrielle swiveled around in her chair to look at the TV screen, then her brow furrowed in a frown. "May's early for a blowdown, but not unheard-of."

"True, dat," Divinity said, voice grim. She thumbed up the TV's volume, then wished she hadn't, the talking head's somber words frosting her from the inside out.

"I repeat, Tropical Storm Evelyn is now a category two hurricane and her projected trajectory has changed. Landfall is no longer expected in Belize. The hurricane's sudden shift in direction will take it into the Gulf of Mexico."

Divinity listened as the forecaster talked about Evelyn's record low pressure system and her ever-increasing wind speeds. Grim excitement vibrated through his voice as he speculated on how Hurricane Evelyn was shaping up to be a monster storm as she powered her way toward the Gulf of Mexico.

"And this storm is still picking up steam, Jim. If it keeps up at this rate, I predict Evelyn will be bigger than Katrina and more powerful than Gaspard."

"You see?" Addie repeated. "And it's headed into the Gulf."

"But it don't mean de storm be headed *here*," Divinity said. "If it comes dis far, it could still blow into Mexico or Texas. Hell, it could blow itself out over de sea or loop back for de Honduras. And even if it do get over dis way, we be safe. We got de wards guarding Louzeann. So take a deep breath and calm yo'self down, woman."

After the devastation, loss of life, and heartbreak wreaked by Katrina, the local conjurers had joined forces to create a protective network, a magical levee system and shield that spanned the entire Louisiana coastline, protecting people, land, and cities—including the land's music-steeped heart, New Orleans—from a hurricane's worst. In all the years that had followed, the wards had failed only once.

Hurricane Gaspard.

"About that," Addie said, her voice graveyard grim. "I've got even worse news."

"I t'ought you just wanted to tell me *one* more t'ing," Divinity grumped.

"Well, it's really more of a two-parter, but still just one thing."

A dark and chilling possibility occurred to Divinity. She desperately hoped she was wrong. "I be betting you're gonna tell me dat wit' all de trouble with magic today, de damned wards have fallen."

"No. Not fallen. Much worse." Something in Addie's tone, choked and scared, a child watching a closet door slowly open on its own, made Divinity pause.

"I be listening," she said quietly.

"The wards are still in place, but their feel—the energy and juju fueling them—has . . . changed." Addie stopped talking and Divinity heard her swallow before continuing. "Some of us are a little worried that, given Evelyn's change in course, maybe instead of *protecting* from hurricanes, the wards are drawing the storm in. *Summoning* it."

"Sweet Jesus," Divinity breathed. "You sure?"

"No. No, we're not—not one hundred percent—but that's the word from the hoodoos maintaining the protection system."

"Dey need to undo de wards," Divinity said. "If de wards no longer exist, den dey can't summon anyt'ing."

"Yup, I agree. But a couple of New Orleans hoodoos

are arguing that we wait until we're positive the wards are malfunctioning before undoing them."

"And?"

"The ward hoodoos aren't going to wait," Addie replied. "No one wants to chance *bringing* a hurricane to Louisiana."

"Dat good. Keep me posted, y'hear?" Divinity said.

"Will do. Talk to you soon." Addie ended the call.

Divinity looked at the TV screen, at the Doppler radar image of the rapidly growing storm. If it shaped itself into an unstoppable monster like Hurricane Gaspard, then the Louisiana coastline along with all of its cities, towns, and fragile ecosystems would be virtually defenseless. If tainted, the wards would guarantee catastrophic destruction.

History be repeating itself. Sweet Jesus.

But, unlike the last time nine years ago, at least Divinity knew why. Or thought she did, anyway.

An eye for an eye is never enough. Never, never, never.

Those words had set everything into motion—a murdered nomad, Kallie's death and resurrection and, more than likely, Jackson's disappearance and burial, the twisted magic. Words given to Kallie by Doctor Heron's daughter and passed on to Divinity.

An eye for an eye is never enough.

Could a man hate so much that it transformed his very soul into a bitter and poisoned pool? One that *warped* everything he touched, everything he thought, every word spoken—including spells? And imbued his hexes with a dark and seething power beyond imagining?

Sweet Jesus and Holy Mary.

Divinity glanced at the unfinished purple-eyed poppet on her worktable. Her uneasiness intensified.

What if I be wrong and dis ain't due to a hex laid down by Doctor Heron? What if de loa be awake after all, just more subtle dan I ever imagined and working tru Kallie instead of just using de girl up?

All my work. All my careful training and guidance. Useless in de end.

No. Not possible. I'd know.

Her gaze on the TV and the banner rolling along the bottom of its screen, Divinity punched in Kallie's cell phone number with a numb but steady finger.

FIFTEEN

HOODOO LOVE TRICKS

*B*elladonna Brown struts into Dallas Brûler's hoodoo shop and into his dreams, a black leather catsuit just like the one that had clung to Halle Berry's mouthwatering curves in Catwoman hugging her own. The catsuit squeaks and creaks enticingly as she crosses to his powder-dusted and herb-sprinkled worktable in spike-heeled boots, her luscious boobs shimmying with each step.

Watching her slinky, jiggly, squeaky approach, all Dallas can think is: Mmm-mmm-mmm. Lucky catsuit.

Standing on the opposite side of the worktable, he sets down the candle he's busy dressing with van van oil, then wipes his lemon-scented fingertips against his jeans. He feels the heat of Belladonna's autumn-dappled gaze as she looks him up and down, literally stripping him to his . . .

A quick glance down reveals a surprising pair of black boxer-briefs instead of his usual boxers and Dallas frowns, wondering if his subconscious is trying to tell him something.

But he has a few words of his own for his subconscious: Dreams like this? Skip the damned boxers, podna, and go for buck-ass naked.

"We need something from you, Doctor Snake," Belladonna purrs.

"Of course you do, darlin'." Dallas quirks up one eyebrow. "'We'?"

A gorgeous woman with strawberry blonde locks teased into a sixties sex-kitten bouffant sashays through the door to stand beside Belladonna. She looks like a Bond babe, a double-oh-seven bedroom treat in her tight paisley blouse, black miniskirt, and thigh-high boots.

Belladonna and Felicity Fields. Dallas applauds his subconscious.

"We indeed, Doctor Snake," she affirms in a British-spiced accent. It thrills Dallas to notice that her blouse is unbuttoned enough to reveal ample cleavage dewed with perspiration.

"Well, hell, ladies. I'm sure Doctor Snake can accommodate you both."

"I'm sure you can," Felicity breathes, putting additional strain on the buttons valiantly struggling to keep her blouse closed. "One bottle of your legendary love potion, please."

"A big bottle," Belladonna adds with a slow wink.

"Oh, I've got all manner of big, darlin'," Dallas promises.

Felicity draws in a breath and, much to his delight, a button pops from her shirt, exposing another inch of bra-cupped, freckled breasts.

"My, my, my," she murmurs, glancing down at her blouse. "Another one gone. How embarrassing." But no blush of embarrassment rosies her cheeks.

"Hey, no apologies necessary," Dallas says as he walks around his worktable to the compact refrigerator parked beside it. "Not with a view that fine," he adds, bending over and pulling a corked blue bottle out of the fridge.

"Mmm. Speaking of fine views," Belladonna and Felicity say in sultry unison.

"Just a word of caution, ladies," Dallas says, straightening—to soft, feminine sounds of disappointment—and turning around, chilled bottle in hand. "This potion's potent as all hell. So don't be giving it to anyone you don't plan on spending a lot of intimate time with."

Both women exchange a lingering look, their gazes sliding over each other. "Oh, we won't," Belladonna says. "We promise."

"Oh." Dallas stares, his heart using his ribs for a xylophone, his boxer-briefs suddenly too tight. "Um . . . Y'all need someone to film this intimate event?" he asks, drymouthed. "Give you a little artistic direction? Keep you company?"

Felicity glances at him from beneath dark lashes. "Possibly."

Dallas thanks his subconscious, swears never to question it again.

"What do we owe you?" Belladonna's fingers wriggle into the cup of her crisscross leather bra and Dallas's pulse does a steam whistle blast through his veins. A look of dismay flashes across her face as she gropes herself. "Damn. I can't find my cash."

"I'll be glad to help search, sugar," Dallas volunteers, joining them and handing the blue bottle to Felicity. Her scent is heady and all woman—an enticing blend of musk, light sweat, and rose petals.

"What other forms of payment do you accept, Doctor Snake?" Felicity asks.

Dallas leans against the table, hands braced on its edge behind him—noticing as he does that his boxer-briefs have mysteriously been replaced with his blue-striped boxers— and allows his gaze to take a slow pleasure cruise along Felicity's curve-blessed form. He nods at the sign posted on the wall behind her.

CURRENCY ACCEPTED: LOCAL CHECKS WITH ID, MAJOR CREDIT CARDS, CASH, TOP-GRADE BOURBON, FRENCH KISSES.

"French kisses it is, then," Felicity says.

"I second that choice," Belladonna tosses in, her hand no longer in her bra—to Dallas's disappointment. "They don't need to be confined to the mouth, do they?"

More steam whistle blasts. Dallas feels himself grow hard. Feels his boxers tent.

"Feel free to warm up on each other," Dallas encourages. "Maybe y'all ought to take a sip or two of that potion first."

"Maybe," Felicity concurs. Her fingers lift to the next button on her paisley blouse. Linger. "But first, any other warnings about the potion?"

"Only that it's a lot like me, sugar. Very intense. Long-lasting. Difficult to control. Whoever you give it to will want nothing but your sweet body, will crave only your lips. And they won't take no for an answer. They'll ravish you, eat you up, and leave you hollering for more."

"Oh," Felicity breathes, her heaving chest threatening another button. "My."

"Until you can't holler no more," Dallas adds, a smile sliding slow across his lips.

The button zings across the room as though fired from a catapult. A thrill courses through Dallas, heating his skin, simmering his blood.

Unhooking one of the few remaining buttons, Felicity pushes the blouse's silky material aside to reveal the bottom edge of her black lace bra and the pale, rounded flesh curving above it. Her stiff nipples jut against the black lace—as if begging for his warm, wet mouth.

No need to beg, my mouth is all yours, baby doll.

Then Dallas imagines Belladonna's lips nuzzling Felicity's perky nipples. His mouth dries. And he believes his boxers have nearly exceeded maximum tenting allowance.

"My, my, my," *Felicity murmurs, her gaze dropping to his crotch. A coy smile plays across her glossy red lips before she lifts her gaze again.* "Wouldn't you say that it's time we rendered payment to Doctor Snake, Belladonna-luv?"

"Mmm-hmm. Oh, definitely."

Felicity presses in on Dallas from the left, Belladonna from the right, and he finds himself surrounded by firm, rounded flesh—white and freckled on one side and black and smooth on the other. Lips like ripe cherries. Lips like succulent plums.

Dallas feels delirious. And happy. Very, very happy.

"What's in the potion, anyway?" *Felicity whispers, her lips grazing the edge of his mouth.*

"You're asking trade secrets, baby doll," *he replies.* "But, hell, for you . . . Wine, basil leaves, red rose petals, cloves and apple seeds, vanilla extract, strawberry and apple juices, and ginseng root. But the magic comes in with the measurements, the timing, and the spell fixed upon it."

"Mmm. I bet you know how to fix things real good."

"That I do, darlin'."

He catches a whiff of sweet red wine, cloves, and strawberries from the bottle. A deep breath and, just as Dallas imagined/hoped it would, Felicity's bra bursts at the seams and her tits jiggle free and into his waiting hands.

His boxers rip apart and go the way of her bra.

"Oh!" Felicity gasps, fumbling the bottle onto the table as Dallas lowers his head, his mouth closing hungrily around one hard pink pearl of a nipple. He hears the slide of cloth as her skirt and panties mysteriously tumble to the floor.

"Oh. Oh. I see how you be, Dallas Brûler." A fist knuckles into his shoulder, staggering him back against the table's edge. "Trying to stick yo' dick into any bit of female flesh dat catches yo' eye. Pretending like I don't even exist."

Her British accent, all posh and cream, is gone, replaced with musical Creole pepper. Her new voice is strangely familiar.

And disconcerting.

Dallas jerks his head up, the off-balance sense of a suddenly shifting dream swirling through his awareness. Felicity stands in front of him, hands on her bare hips, her nipples aimed at him, accusing nubs, fury in her hazel eyes—eyes that darken to a deep brown as he watches.

Disappointment curls through Dallas as he realizes that Belladonna has vanished.

"Is dis what you want? Women fawning over yo' sorry ass?" She gestures with one hand at her very naked and very luscious body, a look of disgust rippling across her face. "Dis pale, red-headed bit o' fluff?"

Dallas grins, thinking, Well, yes, ma'am, at the moment, very much, *but before he can utter those words, alarm Klaxons blare through his mind:* Danger! Danger! Danger!

*As he pauses to reconsider his answer—*I want you as

you are, baby doll, or, You did something different with your hair, didn'tcha? I love it—*she starts to change.*

Her strawberry blonde tresses shift to black ringlets. Color deepens her skin to a sun-warmed caramel. Her curves become even more lush and bountiful; dark curls shadow the juncture between her legs. She smells of magnolias and dying leaves.

And around her throat, a pendant hangs—a vévé depicting a heart pierced with a knife.

Dallas goes cold. Waking memory nudges at him— surface, surface, surface! But his dream isn't quite ready to let go of him yet. And neither is his swollen dick.

Erzulie, the loa of love, passion, and sex, locks her hand tight around Dallas's dick and, despite his dream's sudden twist into the dark, the damned thing remains hard, hoping things will still work out—nightmare or no.

"I tole you when I found you bleeding yo' life blood out on de floor," Erzulie whispers into his ear, her stroking fingers encouraging his dick's delusions, "you be mine, Dallas Brûler. And mine alone. You ain't never gonna betray another woman, 'cuz dis t'ing in my hand? It belongs to me now."

SIXTEEN

TEMPORARY SHELTER

Dallas jerked awake on the strings created by the *loa's* words: *Bleeding yo' life blood out on de floor.* He stared at a white-tiled ceiling, blinking in the daylight gloom, his heart trying to punch its way free of his rib cage.

Memory unspooled like old-fashioned film through a vintage projector, looping images onto the floor of his mind. He remembered following the man he suspected of stalking Kallie from the May Madness Carnival and into the hotel. And losing him somewhere on the sixth floor near Belladonna's room.

But in truth, he hadn't lost the sonuvabitch at all.

A steel-muscled arm around Dallas's shoulders. A stranger's pale green eyes, cold and amused. "You ain't worth wasting magic on, boy."

Three quick, breath-stealing punches. Dallas stares at the blood-smeared knife in the stranger's hand. He presses a hand against his belly, feels something warm and sticky soaking his shirt.

Street light slants along the knife's bloodied length as it slashes across Dallas's throat. He hears his own blood gushing from the wound, smells it thick and cloying in his nostrils.

Dallas squeezed his eyes shut and stopped the flow of memories. *Enough, goddammit.* A cold sweat popped up on his forehead. He swallowed hard. Pain prickled across his throat. Reaching up, he gingerly traced shaking fingers across the gauze bandaged from one side of his throat to the other.

Unbidden, the vision he'd had—a dying dream— while sprawled in a warm pool of his own blood played itself out behind his eyes.

A black-veiled woman—woman, hell, make that a loa— in a scarlet dress rides into the room astride a wild-maned white horse with embered eyes, a pendant etched with a vévé of a dagger-pierced heart resting against the brown skin of her throat.

"You be mine, Dallas Brûler. And mine alone."

And even as darkness enfolds Dallas, as cold seeps into his bones and skates across the frozen wasteland of his soul, Erzulie lays claim to him.

Opening his eyes, Dallas studied the ceiling above him—institutional ceiling tiles, no brown outlines of water stains—as his trembling hands traveled from his throat to the bandages taped across his belly.

Looks like it wasn't *a dying dream, podna. And if that's the case, if what you experienced wasn't just a blood-deprived hallucination, then a certain curvaceous and fierce loa has you by the balls. Literally.*

The steady, quiet beep of the equipment monitoring his vitals, the nostril-stinging scent of antiseptic and pine in the air, the bustling activity he sensed in the halls beyond his room, confirmed his diagnosis of being alive.

Not sure how he had survived, but more than a little grateful, Dallas relaxed back into his pillows. What surprised him was how good he felt—oh, not just good because he was motherfucking alive—but *good* as in rested, clearheaded, with strength surging through his muscles. What pain he felt, and that was only slight, came with movement.

He eyed his IV bags, zeroing in on the one with a little button/pump attached to the line so he could feed himself more pain-numbing meds. *Whatever's in that bag, it's working miracles.*

"My, my, my. I wasn't expecting you to be awake yet, Mr. Brûler."

Hazel eyes. A sleek and shining fall of strawberry blonde hair. A sprinkle of freckles across the bridge of her nose. A Bondalicious babe of a woman in a tight purple blouse and black pencil skirt. And the recent subject of his lust-fueled dreams.

Disappointment curled through him when he noticed that not only was her blouse completely fastened, none of the little pearl buttons appeared to be in any danger of popping loose. As she stepped closer, he caught a trace of her scent, natural and clean—roses warmed by the sun.

Mmm. All woman.

A voice whispered into his ear. *You be mine, Dallas Brûler.*

Pain burned through his abdominal muscles as Dallas bolted upright in the bed and swept a frantic look around the room. Empty. Except for the woman standing beside his bed, her head tilted to one side, curiosity in her eyes.

"You looking for someone?" she asked. "A nurse, perhaps?" She reached for the call button.

Dallas shook his head, pain twinging across his throat with the movement, then stopped her hand with his own.

Her skin felt warm and rose-petal soft beneath his. "No, darlin', I'm fine," he rasped from a dry throat, just as her name returned to him—Felicity Fields, assistant to the Hecatean Alliance head honcho, Augustine, the man who'd taken a bullet meant for Kallie, and died doing so.

Just as he himself had nearly done.

Words spoken by the knife-wielding stranger with the pale green eyes uncoiled through Dallas's memory: *You're the lucky one. You'll get to keep your soul. Kallie and her cousin won't be so fortunate.*

Fear flashed through Dallas, icing his marrow. "Holy shit. Kallie—is she all right? That bastard didn't find her, did he?"

"Yes," Felicity replied.

"Yes? To which part of my goddamned question?"

"To both."

Lifting her hand free of his, Felicity smoothed her skirt, then sat down in the bedside chair. With an elegant shift of her legs, she crossed one slim ankle behind the other.

"Ms. Rivière is all right and Doctor Heron—the afore-mentioned bastard, the same bastard who tried to kill you—did indeed find her. Though I'm not sure he had time to regret doing so."

"You saying he's dead? Not that I'm complaining."

"I am."

"And that the bastard was the infamous Doctor Heron—Jean-Julien St. Cyr?"

"Again, I am."

Dallas frowned, trying to make sense of her words. Why would a root doctor sent to prison for poisoning and killing a few clients—what, twenty-five plus years ago?—be seeking soul-killing revenge on Kallie and her family?

His memory kicked up a chilling response, more words spoken to him by the stranger that he now knew to be Doctor Heron: *You've got your teacher Gabrielle to thank for this, Dallas Brûler. You're gonna die because of things she did long before you ever knew her.*

From outside, Dallas heard the low mutter of thunder and the click of rain against glass. He glanced at the windows, but thick curtains hid the storm from view.

Shifting his gaze back to Felicity, Dallas croaked, "Gabrielle? She okay too? And Jackson—the sick sonuvabitch threatened Kallie's cousin too."

Felicity picked up a small pitcher with a crinkly straw protruding from its lid from the bedside table, then leaned over and handed it to Dallas. "Ice water," she informed him.

Dallas accepted it gratefully, and sucked down several strawfuls of cold, soothing water. As he drank, Felicity brushed a smooth wing of hair back from her face and studied him, her cool and assessing gaze traveling his length several times.

"Fascinating," she mused. "For a man who's just had his throat ruthlessly cut, in addition to being stabbed three times, you look incredibly well, Mr. Brûler. A little pale, yes, but nothing like a man who nearly bled to death only twelve hours ago."

"Thanks for reminding me," Dallas muttered. "Appreciate it."

"You're quite welcome, and given your questions, it seems we need to bring you up to speed on a few things, Mr. Brûler."

"You can call me Dallas, darlin'. No need for the 'Mr. Brûler' bullshit."

An impish smile dimpled Felicity's cheeks. "All right, Dallas *darling*, if you insist. The first thing you need to know is that your mentor is *not* Gabrielle LaRue."

As Dallas listened, stunned, to Felicity's recital of recent events and revelations—the true identity of his hoodoo mentor, another woman's stolen years ago leading to a fatal case of mistaken identity; the removal of Kallie's soul by her own mother to make room for a sleeping *loa*—his disbelief crumbled beneath a growing sense of outrage.

His throat had been cut by motherfucking *mistake*.

"Jesus Christ." Dallas flopped back onto his pillows, ignoring the tiny jabs of pain from his abdomen, his hand clutching the plastic pitcher of water. The fingers of his other hand twisted into the sheets as he stared at the ceiling.

I knew it. I fucking knew she wasn't telling me something.

Dallas remembered his last conversation with his mentor, recalled her profound silence after he'd passed along the *An eye for an eye is never enough* comment from Rosette St. Cyr, and realized that Gabrielle—*dammit, Divinity*—must've known or at least suspected who had been behind all the death and violence.

She'd never said a word.

And damned near got all of us—me, Kallie, and Belladonna—killed because she kept her goddamned secrets. Just told me to keep watching Kallie, to make sure she was safe. But how the hell could I do that when I never had the truth—not even about what was inside Kallie?

"What I don't get," Dallas said, "is this—with Kallie's

mama locked up, who the hell is she hiding Kallie from? That's why she stole that Gabrielle LaRue's identity, right? So she could hide Kallie."

"From what I understand, yes. But it's an unanswered question at this point."

"Jesus Christ," Dallas repeated, voice rough. "How's Kallie holding up?"

"I wouldn't know," Felicity replied. "Lord Augustine's report came via Mr. Valin after they left Bayou Cyprés Noir. But from what I understand, Ms. Rivière was tired and planned to sleep."

Dallas looked at Felicity in amazement. "After all that? I woulda been as pissed as a dozen rain-soaked cats in that girl's place. Pissed as *hell*. I wouldn't've stayed one more minute under that roof."

Felicity shrugged. "And perhaps she won't—after a bit of rest."

"Maybe," Dallas allowed. Lifting the pitcher to his mouth, he sipped more cold water through the straw.

"I can't help but wonder how it was done, though."

Dallas looked at Felicity. Raised his eyebrows.

"The soul removal," she clarified. "How, exactly, would one do it?"

"Why you wanna know? You got some kinda home-work assignment?"

"Perhaps."

Dallas shook his head. "Ain't information to toss out there like chicken feed."

A smile brushed Felicity's lips—not cherry red, her lips, like in his dream, but a deep and glossy peach. She rose to her feet in one smooth motion and crossed to the bed. Her soap and roses scent laced around him.

"Of course it isn't," she said. "I understand that. Which is why I would keep it secret."

Dallas looked into Felicity's eyes, speckled green and golden-brown, and sudden heat tingled beneath his skin. "Sorry, sugar. You ain't hoodoo or voodoo, so no can do." The disappointment shadowing her face made him add, "Why you wanna know, anyway?"

Curling her fingers around the bedrail, Felicity glanced at the floor as if gathering her thoughts. When she lifted her gaze and looked at Dallas again, her expression was stark.

"What would you do if someone you cared for very much, someone you'd shared a large and important portion of your life with, was murdered? Their life stolen. But instead of crossing over and leaving forever, this someone found shelter inside a Vessel—temporary shelter that they would soon have to vacate?"

"I would do my best to find this someone I cared about a permanent home," Dallas replied, voice low. "But you're talking about some serious shit here, darlin'. You can't just yank out someone's soul and stuff Augustine's into the body."

"But it *can* be done? A nonnative soul inserted into a live body?"

"Yeah," Dallas sighed. "It can. Kallie's obvious proof of that. But note that it was done *without* her permission. I can't imagine that you're gonna have volunteers lining up for the honor of housing your boss's soul."

"True," Felicity said. "Unless they happen to be death row inmates whose time has just run out."

Light flared behind the curtains. Thunder boomed.

Dallas stared at her. Even though he was pretty

damned sure he'd understood her just fine, he still heard himself asking, "Say what?"

"I've also considered the possibility of using the body of a Vessel who has checked out mentally," Felicity said. "Of course, in that scenario, a catatonic, nonviolent type of insanity would be best. Lord Augustine could surround what remains of the Vessel's mind with static and take control of the body."

"But . . . they wouldn't be capable of giving consent."

"Regrettable, I agree," Felicity replied, without an ounce of regret in her voice. "But a wasted body, otherwise. However, I *do* prefer the first option."

"Look," Dallas said softly, "as hard as it is to accept, Augustine *died*. Maybe you need to let him go. Encourage him to complete his journey or crossing or whatever."

"Never." Felicity pinned Dallas in place with a fierce, almost savage look. He could see her pulse pounding in her pale throat.

Dallas held her gaze. "Not even if he *wanted* you to let go?"

She lifted her chin. "He doesn't. He loves life."

"Who the hell doesn't, darlin'? But we all gotta go sometime. Look, I get it. I understand—"

Felicity shook her head. "I doubt that. From what I understand, Dallas darling, you're an expert on leaving. Not sticking around."

"And you would know that how?"

"From the long and obvious trail of rumpled beds, broken hearts, and wrecked marriages you've left behind you, Mr. Brûler."

Ouch.

Dallas opened his mouth, mentally thumbing through

his repertoire of snarky witticisms and finding them all sadly lacking. He closed his mouth, deciding silence the better option—especially since the damned woman was right.

He *was* an expert at leaving.

Not a fact that made him proud.

Expression smoothing into its usual calm, Felicity murmured, "Excuse me," then touched a finger to the purple-skinned Bluetooth hooked around her ear. She stepped back from the bed, then turned around.

Dallas's pulse picked up speed as he drank in the sight of her tight skirt lovingly outlining her heart-shaped ass. Like a pencil skirt valentine. *Mmm-mmm-mmm. Lucky skirt.* He sighed. *Too bad she's crazy in a mad scientist kinda way.*

"No, that won't do," Felicity said. "I don't care if the hamster *is* piloting the model plane with amazing skill, all live animal spells are to be . . ." She frowned, listening. "It was supposed to a top hat full of daffodils, *not* a hamster-piloted plane? I see. *Another* mistake. My, my, my. Well, until the spell-caster can figure out what went wrong, see if you can shoo the hamster outside onto the carnival grounds. Hotel guests don't appreciate being buzzed by rodents."

Dallas silently agreed with that assessment.

Finished with her call, Felicity swiveled around to face Dallas looking just a little harried. "Seems we're having a rash of mysterious magical mishaps this morning, a matter I need to tend to, Mr. Brû—Dallas darling, so I'll leave you to the capable care of our medical staff. If you need anything—"

"My cell phone. I need to have a little chat with Gab—Divinity, dammit."

A smile brushed Felicity's lips. "You can use the bedside phone. Interstate calls are allowed. Just dial nine first."

"Gotcha. Good luck with your magical mishaps."

Felicity started for the door, the heels of her black pumps clicking against the floor tiles, then she stopped and turned back around. She regarded him thoughtfully. "I'm still intrigued by how well you're doing considering the severe—no, make that *critical*—nature of your injuries."

"Like you said, capable medical staff."

"I wonder." Felicity tapped a rose-lacquered nail against her chin. "Your surgery was magically enhanced. Perhaps whatever's causing the mishaps is responsible for your amazing recovery as well."

Dallas shrugged. "Your guess is as good as mine, darlin'." But he suspected another source as the smell of dying leaves and magnolias curled through his memory, Erzulie's words embedded in her earthy scent.

"You be mine, Dallas Brûler. And mine alone."

"A mystery worth investigation," Felicity said. Touching a finger to her Bluetooth again, she mouthed *Goodbye*, then click-clickety-clicked from the room, giving Dallas another supreme view of her ass.

He was reaching for the phone, wondering who he would call first, wondering if his anger with Divinity would win out over his concern for Kallie, when the TV mounted on the wall suddenly blared to life.

Dallas's body spasmed in alarm and he winced as pain burned through his abdomen. The TV flickered through its channels in rapid succession as though a ghostly butt had parked itself on the remote—but given that said remote was tucked into its bedrail holster, that seemed unlikely.

A faint whiff of brimstone drifting in from the hall along with the echo of multiple TVs flipping through the channels suggested to Dallas that someone's spell had gone awry—another so-called magical mishap.

"Crap!" someone confirmed from the hall.

Dallas yanked the remote from its holster, then aimed it at the TV, intending to turn the damned thing off. But before he could, it finally settled on a channel. Dallas's heart started pounding hard as the words sliding across the bottom of the screen sank in.

HURRICANE WATCH FOR THE GULF COAST. EVELYN NEARS CATEGORY THREE.

The remote dropped into Dallas's lap.

SEVENTEEN

AND THE WORLD WILL WEEP AND MOAN

"May I fetch you anything, ma'am?" asked the anxious-to-please Hecatean Alliance receptionist—Robert—in his neat gray suit and stylish horn-rimmed glasses as he opened the door, then politely stood aside. "We have tea, coffee, juice, and water. It's a tad early for champagne, but for a member of the board, anything could be arranged."

"No, thank you," Helena Diamond said, sweeping into the room in a swish of navy blue silk and peach blossom perfume.

The late Lord Basil Augustine's New Orleans office smelled of black tea, vanilla, and dark tobacco, a warm and inviting aroma, masculine. A masculine space as well, Helena judged, one dominating a sizable portion of the Prestige Hotel's fifteenth floor.

"Please make sure that no one uses magic until the source of its malfunction can be discovered and taken care of," Helena instructed. "We don't need housekeeping accidentally conjuring any more goats, carpet-eating or otherwise."

"Yes, ma'am," Robert murmured. "Lord Augustine's

assistant, Mrs. Fields, has already placed a temporary injunction against magic use."

"Good."

"Will there be anything else, ma'am?"

"No, Robert, thank you." Helena dismissed the receptionist with a slight incline of her head along with a tight smile. And although Robert nodded, acknowledging the dismissal, the bastard lingered.

"I'd be happy to summon Mrs. Fields," Robert volunteered cheerfully. "I believe she might still be visiting the medical clinic." His eyes widened behind his glasses. "But not for herself," he quickly amended, tongue tripping over his words. "I mean, she's well, ma'am. She's merely checking on someone in the clinic." His voice slipped a few octaves into a confidential tone. "Nasty business, that. A near murder. Blood everywhere. Well, not *literally* everywhere, of course, but—"

"I think you'd do well to shut your mouth and leave, if you hope to keep your job," Helena said, swiveling around and pinning the openmouthed receptionist in place with a glare cold enough to flash-freeze a mammoth. "You're discussing matters way above your pay grade, young man. And we can leave Lord Augustine's assistant to her business. I'll wait for her to return. Now shoo." She flapped an impatient hand. "Shoo."

Robert closed his mouth and swallowed hard. Embarrassment rouging his cheeks, he whirled and fled the office. The door snicked shut behind him.

Man seems to be a bit of a gossip. Might need to discuss that with his supervisor.

Helena rested her back against the door and surveyed the room, her gaze absorbing details in the rainy daylight filtering through the floor-to-ceiling windows composing the back wall.

A large mahogany desk. Leather captain's chair. Two plush visitor's chairs artfully angled in front, tea service and cart tucked into a corner. A smaller desk against the east wall with lumbar-correct chair behind it—an assistant's workstation. A vase bursting with bright flowers, sunny daffodils and blushing pink carnations and baby's breath perfuming the air.

Lovely. The assistant's touch, no doubt.

But what truly interested Helena were the HP computers with their little green telltales winking in the rainy gloom and the curious plastic crate resting on the polished surface of Augustine's desk.

Anticipation surged through her. Her breathing quickened. If the report the Hecatean Alliance board of directors had received was correct—and Helena had no reason to doubt that it was, since it had been sent by Lord Augustine himself—a nine-year-old mystery might soon be unraveled . . .

"A series of dangerous events has taken place during the carnival, centered around one Kallie Rivière, and which has resulted, regrettably, in my own death."

. . . the whereabouts of Sophie Rivière's daughter and the *loa* hidden inside her.

And, at long last, a chance to finish what I started all those years ago.

Helena pushed away from the door and crossed to Lord Augustine's orderly desk, the cream-colored carpet swallowing all sound from her pumps. As she stepped behind the desk, she caught a pungent whiff of frankincense and cloves and juniper wafting up from the depths of the plastic crate on its surface. A smile curled along her lips as she peered inside.

Since it takes one to know one . . . looks like hoodoo.

Cloth, sticks, needles, thread—for making poppets. Oils and powders and mojo bags. Nails, candles, small jars of dirt—graveyard, most likely. Gnarled roots. Saint votives. Various religious statues. Musky incense.

A couple of weathered manila folders tucked against the crate's interior goosed Helena's pulse. *Holy bingo.* Pulling them free, she sank into the captain's chair, the leather creaking underneath her and smelling of fragrant Turkish tobacco. She opened the first folder.

A cold thrill of excitement rushed through Helena as she studied the photo on top—from a newspaper called the *Bayou Cyprés Noir Gazette*—of two youths, a female and a male who looked enough alike to be related, standing on a wharf in front of a blue-trimmed white boat named *Bright Star*, arms around each other's shoulders. A man in sunglasses and a woven-straw cowboy hat stood next to them, just a foot or so away.

It was the young woman who captured all of Helena's attention, fascinated her. Dressed in jeans and a short-sleeved red blouse, she squinted in the sunshine, her long, espresso-brown locks trailing across her face in a camera-stilled breeze.

She looks a bit like Sophie, a beauty, but vulnerable and far less calculating . . .

Helena flipped the photo over and confirmed what she already suspected. Scrawled on the back in what looked like black Sharpie: *With Dallas Brûler and her cousin Jackson Bonaparte at the launch of his boat . . .*

Dallas Brûler—the red-haired root doctor in the

shades and cowboy hat—was the near murder whose blood had been not quite literally everywhere as Robert had so thoughtlessly stated—but close.

As Helena could well imagine. *A cut throat tends to be messy.*

She also imagined that Lord Augustine's assistant, Felicity Fields, was doing a bit of PR work on behalf of the Prestige and the Hecatean Alliance by visiting Brûler in the twentieth-floor medical clinic.

And the handsome boy in the photo with the roguish grin, his CAJUN HOT RODS T-shirt clinging to his tight-muscled chest, had to be Jackson Bonaparte, Sophie's nephew.

Sophie's pathetic attempt to spare the baby in her ever-swelling womb by removing her newborn nephew's soul—alone!—and seeding his body with the *loa* while her exhausted sister slept in a potioned slumber had failed for reasons unknown.

A flaw in the boy, perhaps. An unsuitable host. More likely Sophie simply lacked sufficient power. Foolish woman.

And even though the young woman with the espresso-brown locks in the photo wasn't named, Helena had no doubt she was Kallie Rivière. Just the fact that Jackson Bonaparte's fingers had been captured in the act of shaping a V above the girl's head suggested a familial relationship, as did their similar looks—eyes, cheekbones, lips.

Helena touched a finger to the girl's photo-pixeled face, traced its contours, thinking tenderly of what lay beneath it.

She'll finally be free. And the world will weep and moan.

With a soft sigh, Helena dropped her hand and

scanned the newspaper article—a community celebration of the launch of Jackson Bonaparte's hand-built boat—and learned exactly where to find Kallie Rivière, or, if she no longer lived with her aunt, at least where to start looking for her.

Bayou Cyprés Noir. Another backwater town I've never heard of.

Returning the folders to the plastic crate, Helena pulled her cell phone from an outside pocket of her black leather purse and quickly snapped shots of the newspaper article and photo. She sent the images to a number she hadn't dialed in years—but still knew by heart—along with a text message.

Wait until after the hurricane to fetch her.

A reply beeped onto her cell's screen a moment later: *Understood.*

Slipping her cell phone back into its pocket, Helena smiled. Bayou Cyprés Noir was about to witness a birth unlike any recorded in the swamp town's history. Or any other town's, for that matter. But she doubted a newspaper article and *fais do-do* would celebrate the event. Screaming and pools of blood seemed much more likely.

A primal tribute to the sharp teeth of darkness.

Easing back into the chair and catching another warm and welcoming whiff of tobacco, vanilla, and oiled leather, Helena swiveled it around to face the windows and the riveting view of the Mississippi and the New Orleans skyline they afforded. Lightning flickered across the sky, a dragon's tongue of white fire—a spine-chilling sight from fifteen floors up.

Her reflection glimmered like a ghost against the backdrop of the bruised sky—black tresses sweeping in hair-spray-lacquered waves to her shoulders, all trace of gray colored away; shadowed eyes, hidden; pale skin looking a good ten years younger than her fifty-four years; rose-stained lips pursed in a thoughtful frown; regal posture—chin up, shoulders back.

Plumper, yes, I've put on weight. But, really, who hasn't?

Lightning flashed and the ghost vanished. From the windows, at least.

But inside, the past had never stopped haunting her.

Rémy's words from that awful night twenty-four years before returned to Helena with lightning-stroke starkness, crackling and electric.

Dey pulled de teeth from magic, cut off its balls. Made caricatures of de loa, turning dem into nothing more den parlor tricks performed by so-called voodoo queens. I tried to show dem de huge fucking mistake dey all was making. But I failed. And now I gotta leave you, chère. Dat's what I be sorriest about, leaving you.

Even though time had blunted the rough and raw edges of Helena's grief, it was summoned from the grave anew, a Frankenstein monster resurrected by wild, white-hot bolts of loss and molten rage.

Her hands clenched into fists, a bitter taste at the back of her throat.

You've nothing to be sorry for, my sweet love. They gave you no other choice. But as for the pricks calling themselves the Hecatean Alliance, they will never *be sorry enough.*

Helena watched the roiling thunderstorm dry-eyed and kept watching even after she heard the door open. Heard someone stride briskly across the carpet, then pause in front of the desk. Breathed in the faint scent of roses.

The late illusionist's enigmatic assistant had arrived.

"Good morning, Mrs. Fields," Helena said. "Quite a storm, wouldn't you say?"

"I would, ma'am," Felicity Fields agreed, her urbane British tones a far cry from the rough-and-tumble Cockney she'd once spoken. "Both mundane *and* magical."

"Any word yet on what has caused magic to warp?"

"Not yet, ma'am. We know it began just after dawn and we've received word that it seems to be statewide, but that's all the information we have at present. Concerns regarding the hurricane traveling toward the Gulf seems to have slowed the flow of information."

"Ah, yes. Of course."

A smile chilled Helena's lips. She'd often hoped that the wards would fail and that the next hurricane would wipe New Orleans off the map and the Hecatean Alliance's current order out of existence. But not yet, not before she finished Rémy's work, unveiled his final masterpiece.

Lightning danced across the horizon, lit up the sky, and dazzled her sight. Thunder quickly followed in a booming shudder.

"I have every faith in you, Mrs. Fields. I know you'll both find and remedy the problem." Helena swiveled around in the captain's chair to face the redhead. "As I would expect from the woman Lord Augustine named as interim master of the Hecatean Alliance."

Felicity stared at her, expression stunned.

EIGHTEEN

CAN'T CHOOSE BLOOD

Compelled. Commanded. Come to me, wild one!

For a brief moment, something within Kallie responded to those words, kicking and screaming in a tantrum of savage denial and desperate refusal, then pain swallowed her whole as she felt herself—or something within her, a part of her—ripping loose from her moorings, her core, like a *loa*-sized piece of Velcro.

A split second—or a bone-twisting eternity—later, a heavy thrumming vibrated into her, ringing her core like a boxer's bell, over and over and over, but without sound, reverberating out from her center in pulsations strong enough to shake dirt into the grave and knock her off balance.

Kallie landed in the mud on her ass, the heels of her hands slamming into the muck in an attempt to break her fall. The rotten-egg stench of sulfur singed her nostrils, mingling uneasily with the dank reek of mud and oozing swamp water.

Compelled. Commanded. Come to me, wild one!

The Baron's words, spoken with utter confidence and force of will, as though the action had already been accomplished, echoed like thunder through Kallie's mind in gradually diminishing rumbles. But the painful pull she'd felt as the Baron had laid down his trick, the unnerving sensation of being plucked loose, of her essence being unthreaded strand by strand, had vanished.

Along with the Baron.

And in his place . . . Kallie frowned.

From above, a man's voice, low and surfing the edge of panic, questioned, "Where'd the chicken come from? And where's Cash?"

Two *great* questions.

"I think you're looking at him," Kallie replied, studying the black-feathered rooster—wait, no comb, no waddle, make that a *hen*—pecking at the mud in a disgruntled fashion in front of her.

The hen regarded her with one accusing black eye, then resumed stabbing her beak into the mud. Kallie blinked. Chicken rage issues?

The one thing she knew it *wasn't* was a pissed-off home invader with a grudge. She'd never heard of a single trick that could actually transform a person into a hungry hen. Or any other kind of animal, hungry or otherwise.

Certain potions could make you *believe* you were an animal and some conferred the temporary ability to look through a chosen animal's eyes, a mind-to-mind linking, but she'd yet to witness an actual transformation. But she saw no need to enlighten Kerry. Not yet, anyway.

"Might look for some chicken feed in the house," Kallie suggested. "It looks like Cash here has worked up an appetite."

"Being *cheval* for a *loa* will do that," Belladonna agreed with a wink.

"Jesus Christ!" Kerry cried. "Y'all gave me your word that you wouldn't use no juju if I helped you and—"

"I know, I know, and you kept your word." At Belladonna's arched *I got an update for you* eyebrow, Kallie added, "Well, mostly, apparently. Look, I'm messing with you. That ain't Cash, it's just a chicken."

Relief flickered across Kerry's drawn features, only to fade as his gaze returned to the hen. "How do I know for sure? How do I know you ain't messing with me by *telling* me that you're just messing with me?"

From where she knelt on the muddy ground beside Kerry, Belladonna did a *White boy, please* eye roll. Kallie paid heed to her friend's tight grip on the shotgun and the fact that its barrel was aimed unwaveringly in Kerry's direction.

Looks like Kerry has managed to put himself on Bell's bad-boy list—and not *the fun and sexy bad-boy list.*

Kallie sighed. "Sometimes a chicken is just a chicken, Kerry. But I really ain't got time to debate the matter."

"Not when Baron Samedi might rally and return," Belladonna murmured.

"Damn straight."

Kallie pushed herself up to her feet, automatically and uselessly brushing off the mud-coated seat of her cutoffs. She gathered Layne's Glock and Jackson's boot out of the mud, then tossed them topside. Both hit the ground with soft thuds. She eyed the hen. The hen eyed her in return. Fluffed her glossy black feathers. Scratched in the mud.

Kallie frowned. Was the chicken actually giving her *attitude*?

She wondered where the hen had been just five minutes before and how far she'd traveled. Wondered if the manner of travel had contributed to the bird's grumpy disposition. Decided, *Hell yes.* Being yanked through the ether against your will would do that to a person. Or a hen. As the case may be.

Then she wondered if the Baron in his Cash suit was now standing in some feed-scattered yard with a bunch of startled chickens, the stink of brimstone and chicken poop filling the air.

Nothing in the image comforted or amused her.

A pissed-off *loa* was *never* a good thing.

Stepping over to Belladonna and Kerry's side of the grave, Kallie hesitated, glanced once more at the hen, then sighed. She couldn't just leave it there. What if it never managed to get out? Chickens could fly, sort of, but not very far and not very high. "Goddammit," she muttered.

Swiveling around, Kallie then spent several sweaty, frustrating minutes chasing the squawking hen around the grave, boots squelching and squishing, before managing to wrap both hands around its soft, feathered body and thrusting it up into the air.

"Take the damned thing!"

Another startled, but irate, squawk, then Kallie's hands were empty. Wiping sweat from her brow with the back of one hand, she stretched up her arms. "Get me outta here."

"You got it, Shug."

Warm hands wrapped tight around Kallie's wrists and hauled her up. Sucking in deep breaths of air untainted by mud or brimstone reek, she flashed Belladonna a grateful smile, then climbed to her feet.

As she did, she noticed paw prints and footprints—bare human feet—in the churned and muddy ground surrounding the grave. Kallie's heart gave a little leap. *Paw prints.* Cielo? Had the husky rounded up Lassie-styled help for Jackson?

The Baron's words snaked through her mind as she studied the human prints: *"Blood ain't de only t'ing I smell here. I caughts me a big ol' stinky whiff of wet dog and . . . wolves. No, not wolves. Loups-garous."*

Her thoughts kaleidoscoped back to a long-ago summer night, the memory as soft and faded and blurry as a child's much-laundered and well-used favorite blankie. A six-year-old's recall.

She and Jacks race through the night-cooled grass and underneath the old oak's thick twisted branches, chasing fireflies and capturing them in one of his mama's—Tante Lucia's—jam jars. When Jacks looks at Kallie, grinning, his mischievous eyes glow with a soft green light. Faerie dust and fireflies and summer moonlight.

"Wanna hear a secret? But you gotta swear never to tell."

A hand squeezed Kallie's shoulder, drawing her back to the present. "You okay, Shug?"

Kallie nodded. "Yeah, but how's Layne doing? How bad is he?"

Belladonna glanced down the long driveway, concern a deep shadow across her face. "Boy hit his head damned hard, no doubt about that. Doesn't seem to be any broken bones, but . . ." Her gaze returned to Kallie and the worry cradled in her friend's hazel eyes iced Kallie to the bone.

"What? What is it?"

"He and the Brit are no longer alone in there," Belladonna said.

A sudden, horrible realization stole the breath from Kallie's lungs, set her heart to kicking against her ribs. She stared at the silent house behind Belladonna. "Babette," she whispered.

Belladonna nodded, her blue and black curls bobbing. "I potioned Layne up, but we need to get him to your aunt's as quick as possible, maybe even to a hospital."

"No," Kallie said, another horrified thought popping into her mind like a flashlight-lit jack-in-the-box. "Hospital personnel might think he's crazy, might try to detain him against his will . . ."

"He's nomad—wouldn't they need clan permission to hold him?"

Kallie shrugged. "I don't know, Bell. Your guess is as good as mine. I ain't too familiar with nomad rights as far as the law's concerned, but if he needs to go to the hospital, then we're gonna hafta contact McKenna—or *someone* in his clan—just in case."

"Okay. I'm betting Felicity would know how to contact the pixie—I mean, McKenna. Meanwhile, what are we going to do with *him*?"

Kallie followed Belladonna's gaze to dark-haired Kerry. He held the hen at arm's length, studying it. The bird seemed to study him in turn, clucking amiably enough. "It seems to like me," he mused.

"Kindred souls," Belladonna muttered under her breath.

Kallie punched her in the shoulder, biting the inside of her lip to keep from laughing. "Well, sure, you ain't chasing it through the mud."

"You say this ain't Cash," Kerry said. Strands of wet hair clung to his forehead, the sides of his whisker-shadowed face. "But how do I know for sure? Cash was in that goddamned grave, now he ain't. So where is he?"

"I honestly don't know," Kallie replied. "He was just gone."

Kerry cradled the surprisingly docile hen against his rain-drenched T-shirt, its black feathers blending in with the material. His gaze lifted to Kallie's, his expression unsettled. "Y'know, I saw it when Cash appeared behind you—out of thin air, like a magic trick, but without any smoke—then kicked you into the grave." He looked away, swallowed hard. "Even with his weird getup, I truly thought it was him. But then his voice kept changing and the things he was saying . . ."

The hen gave a little cluck, a strangely sympathetic sound.

"You *sure* that ain't Cash?" Belladonna whispered.

Kallie tapped her fist into Belladonna's arm again. "Positive."

"Ow, girl. Use words, not knuckles."

"Knuckles are more to the point."

"So's a stick to the eye, Shug, but you don't see me poking anyone."

"Really? Then what's your finger doing in my ribs?"

"Certainly not poking. Or making a point. Just checking for damage."

"Checking? Or creating?"

"Excuse me," Kerry intruded. "But can we get back to Cash for a minute?" He shifted restlessly, floating the warm and mingled scents of wet denim, feathers, and sweat into the air. "He may be an a-hole at times, but he's blood, y'know. He's *my* cousin. But here, today, he wasn't just Cash, was he?"

Kallie looked away from Belladonna and her smug cat-in-the-cream smile and gave her attention to Kerry. "Your *cousin*? That explains a lot."

"Can't choose blood," Belladonna agreed. "But you need to start standing up to Cash before he lands you in prison or"—she glanced at the grave—"worse."

"Yeah," Kerry said with a sigh. "I know."

Kallie debated the wisdom of telling him that his hard-ass cousin had been possessed by the *loa* of death, wondering if she had the time or energy to deal with his swooning and/or potential hysterics, then realized that he had a right to the truth—a truth he seemed to suspect to one degree or another anyway.

"No," she finally said, "he wasn't just Cash."

Kallie explained the situation to Kerry the best she could, with Belladonna affirming her words with gentle ones of her own, and emphasizing the key point—said possession would be temporary. At least, Kallie *hoped* that was still the case.

Kerry's gaze skipped from Kallie to Belladonna, then back, a muscle jumping in his jaw. No swooning. No hysterics. He nodded in tight-lipped acknowledgment.

Black eyes fixed on Kallie, the hen clucked in a very disapproving manner.

"You absolutely sure—" Belladonna began, eyeing the hen.

"Goddamned positive."

"Look, no disrespect or nothing, but I think y'all are jinxes," Kerry said. "Me and Cash've had nothing but bad luck since we ran into y'all."

"Well," Kallie said, parking one fist against her hip, "if you consider storming into someone's house wearing ski masks and waving around loaded shotguns as 'ran into y'all,' then, yes, *beaucoup* bad luck."

"I know we brung it on ourselves," Kerry said, a determined fire kindling in his dark eyes. "I was against raiding your house and I was against leaving your cousin buried underground, but I've done all I can to make up for that. I'm done and I'm splitting."

"How you planning on getting back?" Kallie asked. "It's a long ways back to Bayou Cyprés Noir."

Lightning pulsed across the sky, thunder grumbling in its wake.

"Walk. Hitchhike. Skip. I don't give a good god . . . dang. Just so long as I ain't nowhere near you gals. No offense."

Kallie shrugged. "None taken. And I ain't got a problem with that. How about you, Bell?"

"Nope. I'm fine with that too. I'm tired of aiming this damned shotgun at him. Which I'm keeping, by the way."

"And *I'm* keeping the chicken. Just in case y'all are wrong about Cash."

"Well, if the damned thing starts scratching out messages in the dirt, like 'SOS' or 'Kerry, you're a dumb ass . . .'" Kallie said, holding up a placating hand, before adding, "Not that it will. That hen *ain't* Cash. You know where to find me."

Kerry nodded, face grim. "That I do."

"One thing I want you to remember," Kallie said, stepping forward to make sure she had his attention. "Keep away from me and mine."

"Trust me, that won't be a problem," Kerry replied. "But I can't make no promises where Cash is concerned."

"*You die no matter which road your loa takes. But don't worry none. You won't be lonely. I'll be sending your cousin to join you.*"

Cold traced up Kallie's spine to the base of her skull and she barely suppressed a shudder. Even when the Baron and Cash finally parted ways, one would be hunting her and the other Jackson. Something wound up clock-spring tight in the middle of her gut and stole her breath.

Hurry, hurry, hurry. Time is slipping away.

"I know," she said to Kerry. "I won't hold you accountable for whatever Cash does." Reaching into a pocket of her cutoffs, her fingers sought and found the hair she'd yanked from his head. She handed it to him. "You helped, and I promised."

Surprise flickered in Kerry's eyes. A smile curled across his lips, then vanished. He snatched the hair from Kallie's fingers as if he was afraid there might be a time limit on her generosity, one measured in milliseconds.

"You're welcome," Kallie said, voice dry.

Tucking the hen securely under one arm, Kerry said, "Good luck with your cousin."

"Yeah, same to you," Kallie replied. "Hope we don't meet again."

"Same here." With the hen clucking, Kerry headed down the gravel driveway in long strides, waving one hand in a *So long, kiss my ass* farewell.

"A boy and his chicken," Belladonna murmured with a soft, *Ain't it romantic* sigh. "True love gets me every single time." She paused, tilted her head, then added, "His ass looks pretty good from here, actually."

"Yup. Incorrigible, true-blue, one hundred percent pure evil. That's you."

Belladonna flapped a hand at her. "Stop. You had me at *incorrigible*."

NINETEEN

MAGNETS FOR DISASTER

After Kerry had ducked past the glistening palmettos at the end of the driveway and vanished from view, Kallie spun around in the mud, cupped her hands around her mouth, and yelled, "*Jacks!*"

"Wait. I thought he wasn't here," Belladonna said.

"He got out of that grave, Bell," Kallie replied. "But since the Baron mentioned smelling blood, he could be hurt and holed up somewhere."

"*Jacks!*" Belladonna cried.

Thunder muttered, low and deep, moving away with the storm. The rain slackened, slowed to a stop, leaving the air hanging heavy with the smells of wet earth and ozone.

Kallie circled the silent house, peering in windows and yelling her cousin's name as she went, Belladonna echoing her cries; but as hard as she listened for the sound of his teasing voice—*Over here, p'tite peu. Hey, short stuff, you blind?*—all she heard was the rain dripping from the eaves, the growl of fading thunder, and Belladonna's shouts.

As Kallie came back around to the grave, she noticed

tire tracks in the mud. According to Kerry, the assholes who'd grabbed Jackson had tossed him into his own truck. But the Dodge Ram was no longer here.

Breathing in a thick perfume of wet greenery, moisture-beaded hyacinths, and decaying wood, Kallie allowed her gaze to follow the tire tracks leading to the mouth of the driveway, and a horrible suspicion flashed like cheap neon in her mind.

Jackson had gotten out of his grave and managed to drive away in his abandoned truck, probably tearing up the gravel driveway to the dirt road. Hell, she would've floored the gas pedal in his place.

And he'd peeled out onto the road just as Layne had arrived.

Pushing her wet hair back from her face, Kallie studied the tire tracks. No. Jacks would've stopped if he'd collided with anyone. He never would've left a man lying beside the road, no matter the cost to himself.

Whereas the bastards who'd buried him in the first place probably wouldn't have even slowed down.

So her happy fantasy of Jacks escaping, his faithful dog at his side, and driving home was tossed aside like a losing lottery ticket.

A less happy fantasy, one involving Jackson's original kidnappers returning to dig him up—alive? Near death? Undead?—to take him to another of Doctor Heron's preordered designations left her cold, her hands knotted into fists.

Shit. Goddammit, Jacks. Where are you?

A sudden thought occurred to her, and she fumbled her cell phone from a pocket. Pulse racing, she speed-dialed Jackson's number and held her breath as it began to ring. After the fifth ring, his voice mail message kicked on.

"If y'all meant to reach little ol' *moi*, the good news is—you succeeded. Bad news is—I ain't able to take your call at the moment, but kick back, have a drink, maybe two, and I'll return your call *tout à l'heure*. Y'all know what to do at the beep."

Disappointment seeping like ice water through her veins, Kallie thumbed in a text message—HOLD TIGHT. IM LOOKING 4 U—then hit send. With a sigh, she slipped her cell phone back into her pocket.

Kallie rubbed her face, weariness returning with leaden muscle vengeance. She couldn't go home without her cousin. Didn't *want* to go home without him. But Layne needed medical attention.

And, most likely, an exorcism.

Another quick glance down the driveway confirmed that Layne still hadn't moved or regained consciousness and Kallie didn't know whether to be scared or—given that goddamned Babette had taken up residence—relieved.

Her aunt was a skilled healer; most folks in Bayou Cyprés Noir took their injuries and ailments to her instead of going to the urgent care center at the south end of town, or to any of the local physicians.

But if Layne's injuries required surgery or if his brain was swelling . . . those were things her aunt *couldn't* tend to. Sooner or later, she would need to call McKenna in New Orleans. Hopefully they could put their differences aside long enough to help Layne.

She took one last look at the grave, throat aching.

I'm not giving up on you, Jacks.

Waving Belladonna over, Kallie waited for her shotgun-toting friend to join her, then said, "We gotta go." She nodded at the driveway. "Layne."

"I know." Belladonna's voice was pitched low. "Do you think that maybe Jacks drove himself home?"

Kallie shrugged. And even though she didn't think so, she still hoped. "Maybe. But he didn't answer his cell."

"Maybe he's being a good driver."

"Maybe."

Another fantasy, but one Kallie wanted to keep for the moment and, judging from a glance at Belladonna's shadowed, half-turned-away face, so did her friend. Without another word, Kallie tucked Layne's Glock into the back of her cutoffs, picked up Jackson's soaked Dingo (the left one, she noticed), and started walking over to the Dodge Dart, with its opened passenger door.

Belladonna strode beside her, tall and willowy, the gravel loud beneath the soles of her platform boots. "Y'know," she said, the shotgun crooked over her arm, "all that business in the grave. How is it possible for Cash to be influencing the *loa* of death? And speaking of *loas*, how the *hell* did one end up inside of you, girl? Did I miss something when I was sleeping at your aunt's?"

"Shit, Bell, I'm sorry. I forgot you were busy snoozing when Gabr—dammit, *Divinity*—finally told me the truth—or *part* of it, anyway."

"So spill."

Pushing her wet hair back from her face and trying to finger-comb the thick, mud-snarled tresses into some kind of order, and failing, Kallie quietly told her friend about her *tante*'s dark, disquieting revelation about the long-ago removal of her soul, her *Gros Bon Ange*.

"When you were born to yo' mama and papa, yo' soul was removed to make room for de loa placed inside yo' infant body. De same loa dat yo' mama tried to awaken with blood and darkness by murdering yo' papa and shooting you."

When Kallie finished speaking, she became aware that Belladonna had stopped and was no longer walking beside her. Slowing to a halt, Kallie glanced over her shoulder. Belladonna blinked, then looked away, but not before Kallie saw her expression of horrified disbelief.

"Hellfire," Belladonna whispered. She resumed walking, her pace slow, her stride shortened, catching up with Kallie a few moments later.

"You okay, Bell?"

After a moment, the voodooienne shook her head, then looked at Kallie again. Sympathy softened her features, but anger simmered in her autumn-lit eyes. "Why? Why would your mother do this? And how? And where the hell did she hide your soul?"

"I don't know. On all accounts." Kallie paused at the car's passenger door while Belladonna swung around to the driver's side, then looked at her friend from over the Dart's roof. "But I plan to find out as soon—"

Kallie's cell phone bumblebee-buzzed in her pocket. Slipping the phone free, she noted *Tante* on the caller ID and thumbed the talk button.

"You all right, girl?" her aunt asked. "You find yo' cousin?"

"I found where he was buried, but he's gone." Hearing her aunt's sharp intake of breath, Kallie hastened to add, "I mean *gone* as in *not here*. It looks like someone dug him up before we arrived. And by *arrived*, I mean at Doctor Heron's place."

"So it *was* dat *fi' de garce* that had Jackson grabbed."

"Yup. Looks like. But that's not all." Kallie launched into a condensed version of everything that had happened since they'd screeched to a halt in the road beside Layne's unconscious body with her aunt breathing out *Sweet Jesus* every few moments.

Divinity sighed, a resigned and unhappy sound. "You be doing de right t'ing, Kallie-girl. Given dat de nomad's injured, why don't you meet me at de botanica instead, and I'll look de boy over dere."

"Will do," Kallie replied, relieved. The majority of Divinity's healing herbs and roots and potions, along with her medical supplies, like gauze and needles and thread for suturing, were kept at her botanica in town. She would have easy access to anything she needed to help Layne, and if his injury proved beyond her skills, the urgent care center was just down and over a few streets.

"As for yo' cousin, maybe we can do another reading to find his location. You sure his dog be with him?"

"I saw paw prints, so I'm pretty sure, yeah," Kallie replied. "It's the only thing that makes sense and she *is* gone too."

"Dat good," Divinity breathed in relief. "Dat be real good. At least Jackson won't be alone. Now hurry, child. I t'ink you need to get out o' dere before de Baron returns to finish what he started. I wish to hell Gabrielle had never done her invocation."

"I don't know if running will do any good," Kallie said with a calm her pounding heart didn't emulate. "Baron Samedi can find me anywhere."

"No, he can't," Divinity snapped. "Not if I got any say about it. Don't you talk like dat, girl. I t'ink prayers be a

different kind o' magic, so say yo' Psalms and have Belladonna do a blessing, but don't lay any tricks, hear?"

Remembering how the Baron's voice had slipped into
Cash's hostile and bitter tones instead of his own, Kallie
said, "I hear."

"Den quit yapping and move yo' heinie." A dial tone
signaled the end of the conversation. Her aunt's typical
sign-off.

In the car, Kallie shared her aunt's advice with Belladonna as they drove down the driveway. A sharp pang
pierced her heart at the sight of Layne's motionless body
in the grass.

"I'm not sure about that," Belladonna said, braking
the car to a halt. "Prayers and blessings use energy and
focus just like spells. Except"—she pondered—"prayers
are aimed at an entity instead of a goal. I mean, there's a
goal in the prayer—healing, deliverance from debt, sorrow, trouble, whatever—but the focus is on a saint or *loa*
or Bon Dieu. But since we don't know what's causing the
problem, we don't know what's safe and what's not."

"I think it's me, Bell, I think I might be the cause,"
Kallie said, getting out of the car. "Because of the *loa*.
Maybe when Layne and I killed Doctor Heron, the violence awakened it. Divinity mentioned blood and darkness—that's why my goddamned mother did what she did,
after all."

Sorry, baby. I ain't got a choice.

"I don't know about that," Belladonna replied, yanking
up the emergency brake. "If the *loa* was awake, wouldn't
you be . . . different somehow?"

"I don't know." Kallie paused to recline the passenger
seat as far back as it would go, then hurried around to

Layne and knelt beside his motionless form. The slow rise and fall of his chest reassured her.

Belladonna climbed out from behind the steering wheel of the idling car to join her. "Besides, even if that was true and the *loa* was responsible for the magic glitches, then wouldn't it only affect the tricks that *you* fixed?"

"You would think so, but dunno. Maybe Divinity will have some ideas."

"Or Gabrielle," Belladonna added.

Kallie touched her fingers to Layne's face. He didn't stir. She eyed his lean and hard-muscled six-two length and realized that even with the two of them, hauling his deadweight, luscious ass to the car and hoisting him inside was going to take every bit of strength they had.

"You want to take his head or his feet?" Belladonna asked.

"His head," Kallie replied.

"Guess that means I get to feel up his legs. Mmm-mmm."

"You say that like it's something new," Kallie said dryly, arching a *Fess up* eyebrow. "I'm sure you already felt up everything possible when you checked him for injuries."

"No, but *now* I wish I had, dammit. I'll keep that in mind for next time, Shug."

"Don't make me start talking with my fists again."

Belladonna chuckled.

Swiveling around so she could loop her arms under Layne's and lock them across his leather-jacketed chest, Kallie drew in a deep breath and caught a faint but familiar scent from his dreads—sweet orange and musky sandalwood—and hoped with everything she had that he would be all right. Prayed that Babette would depart without any problems.

Belladonna crouched at Layne's feet, her hands locked onto his jeans-clad calves.

"Ready?" Kallie asked.

Belladonna nodded. "Yup. On three. One. Two. *Three*."

Kallie had been right. By the time she and Belladonna had grunted and cussed and staggered their way over to the idling Dodge Dart, half carrying and half dragging Layne, and had wrestled him more or less into the passenger seat, Kallie was drenched in sweat and utterly drained of strength, her muscles trembling.

She collapsed, panting, against the side of the car. "Goddamn."

"Jesus Christ," Belladonna gasped, folding her arms on the Dodge Dart's roof and leaning against the car. "I never thought I'd complain about a man being long and lean and all muscle, but that was before I had to cart an unconscious nomad around."

Kallie nodded, wishing for a glass or three of cold water. "Sadly, we ain't done yet, Bell," she said, voice thick with exhaustion.

"He's in the car," Belladonna protested. "I think that's mission accomplished."

"His bike. We need to move it out of the road. It's too heavy for me to do by myself. We can park it in the driveway until someone can come get it. Hopefully Layne himself or one of his clan."

"Jesus Christ," Belladonna groaned, then pushed herself away from the car, staggering for the puddled dirt road. "Let's get it done, girl."

Shoving the weight of her wet hair back from her face,

Kallie stumbled after Belladonna, joining her beside the downed Harley. Once they'd battled the heavy machine into an upright position with more grunting, sweating, and cussing, they walked it up the driveway, Belladonna steering the handlebar on the left, Kallie the right.

After carefully easing the gravel-scratched and dinged Harley onto its kickstand in front of the house, Kallie and Belladonna headed back down the driveway to the Dodge Dart.

"Hauling nomads, pushing Harleys, shooting at the *loa* of death," Belladonna grumbled as Kallie climbed into the backseat. "You owe me the biggest margarita ever made, girl. Two," she corrected, sliding in behind the steering wheel and nodding in affirmation. "*Two* big-ass margaritas."

"Two big-ass margaritas and cake," Kallie agreed, scooting closer to Layne and stroking a finger along the wet length of one rain-darkened dread. She frowned as she realized her finger was shaking slightly.

Am I that goddamned tired? And realized yes; yes, she was. Exhaustion had filled her bones with lead and transformed her muscles into unlinked pieces of steel; even sitting upright took everything she had.

Maybe I'll doze on the way back, she thought, but with a glance at Belladonna's weary face, she realized how unfair that was. She needed to keep her friend company and awake during the drive home. Conversation, that was key.

Something easy. Something without any real thought. Something that wouldn't tax the test pattern currently posing as her brain.

"So . . . if you could eat that slice of cake from anyone's six-pack abs, who would it be?"

Belladonna glanced at Kallie in the rearview, hazel eyes glinting. "Ooooh. I like this game." Her gaze shifted, caressed Layne's stretched-out length. "Anyone?"

"Yup. Anyone but Layne."

"Phooey. Spoilsport."

"If anyone's eating cake off his goddamned abs, it's gonna be me."

Belladonna grinned. "I'll be sure to tell him that. I'm betting it'll please him no end."

Kallie narrowed her eyes. "You do and I'll—"

"If you're gonna eat cake off my goddamned abs, I'd prefer red velvet."

Layne's whispered voice whipped Kallie's head around. He watched her from beneath his thick honey-blond lashes, face still drained of color, a faint smile on his lips. "Hey, sunshine."

And that spark, that electric connection she felt every time she looked into his eyes for the first time after a separation, shocked through Kallie once more.

Layne's eyes widened and, hearing the catch in his breath, Kallie had a feeling he'd felt the same skin-tingling shock.

"Hey, you," Kallie breathed. Then heat rushed to her cheeks as she realized what he'd just overheard. "Oh, umm . . . I suppose you *could* have a say in the cake flavor."

Layne's smile deepened, but Kallie saw pain tightening the skin around his dilated pine-green eyes and creasing the small black fox inked beneath his right eye.

"Buttercream for the frosting," he said. "Nah, make it *chocolate* buttercream."

Oh. Yum. Leaning over to grasp his hand, her fingers

folding through his, it was as though his warm lips pressed against hers in a soothing kiss, and all her fears—magic misfires, Jackson, the *loa* inside and the one hunting her—quieted.

Kallie murmured, "Maybe, if you're a good boy."

"And if I'm a bad boy?"

Warm flutters rippled through Kallie's belly. The bumblebee-buzz vibration of her cell phone put the brakes on her budding fantasy. Holding up a *Just a quick minute* finger, Kallie fumbled for her phone. The caller ID let her know it was her aunt again.

Kallie thumbed the talk button. "Is something wrong?" she asked. "Something else, I mean?" Layne's hand went lax in hers and a glance confirmed that he was out again. Reluctantly, she unthreaded her fingers from his.

"*Oui*, girl, just one more t'ing. And it's somet'ing I hate to repeat. It looks like de wards might no longer be protecting de coast. We be worried dat dis weird juju backfire might bring de wards down or have dem acting as magnets for disaster instead."

"Shit. Any way to be sure?" Kallie raked her fingers through her hair. Mud flaked to her thighs and onto the seat.

"De ward hoodoos be looking into it now."

Kallie heard her aunt draw in a slow breath, a careful intake of air just before expelling something painful. She felt tension band across her shoulder muscles as she waited for the other shoe to drop.

"Dere be a hurricane headed for de Gulf, a hurricane named Evelyn, and she's nearing a category three. Dis storm be building with a speed and fury like I ain't seen since Gaspard."

Fear ice-picked Kallie's heart. Memory unspooled. Nine years ago. A month after the shooting. Divinity's low and grief-heavy voice.

"Yo' Tante *Lucia* and Nonc *Nicolas* didn't survive the *blowdown*, hun. Junalee and Jeanette be gone too. But Jackson, he survived, him. I'm going down to what remains of Morgan City and bringing yo' cousin home. We be all he has left."

But the boy Divinity brings home isn't Kallie's cousin, at least not the wild, laughing, reckless cousin she's always known. This boy is silent and still, an amber-eyed shadow who refuses to speak, and Kallie even wonders if he's forgotten how, his speech shocked away by unthinkable loss, a loss he will never be able to give voice to.

But he does, weeks later, standing outside in a thunderstorm, rain lashing his face, his hands clenched into whiteknuckled fists.

A wordless scream of savage and furious grief claws free of his throat and into the wind-lashed night and, for a moment, out-howls the storm.

Kallie stands at the screen door and listens, her pulse pounding at her temples. She wants to join Jackson in the rain. Wants to shriek and yowl like a wild thing fighting its cage. But she's pretty damned sure if she starts, she'll never stop.

Not wanting to end up in the Guinness Book of World Records for longest uninterrupted scream or in a padded room next to her mother's, Kallie remains at the screen door. Listening. Her unvoiced rage piling up in her throat.

"Kallie-girl? You still dere?"

Divinity's voice snapped Kallie back into the present. She swallowed hard. "The wards, the magic, do you think it's because of me? Because of the *loa*?"

"I ain't sure, me," Divinity said, speaking slow. "But I don't t'ink so. Yo' *loa* ain't awake."

Cinnamon curls. Pale bones surrounding a heart. The thunder of hooves.

"How do you know?"

"Because I wouldn't be speaking to *you* if it were and I never woulda let you leave de house if I'd a had any doubts."

Kallie shivered, the quiet certainty in her aunt's voice breathing ice down her spine. She thought of the unfinished poppet on her aunt's worktable.

"*Dere ain't nothing I wouldn't do to help you, Kalindra Sophia. Teach you. Guide you. Lie to you. Bind you . . .*"

"Maybe you should finish it," Kallie said.

"Finish what?"

"The poppet. Maybe you should finish it—in case."

"You let me worry about dat, girl. We gonna get dat *loa* out of you. We'll figure it out. For now, just get over to de botanica. And, Kallie?"

"Yeah?"

"Tell Belladonna to drive dat little rusty bucket o' bolts o' hers careful, y'hear?"

"I hear." Kallie beat her aunt to the punch and ended the call.

Tucking her cell phone back into her pocket, she caught Belladonna's concerned gaze in the rearview. "Divinity called your car a rusty bucket of bolts and hinted that you're a reckless driver doomed to kill your passengers in a fiery crash."

"Aw, she says the *sweetest* things."

"She also said that the goddamned coastal wards might've fallen victim to the magic backfires," Kallie updated, "and they might fall or become goddamned hurricane magnets. And—guess what?—a huge storm's already on the way."

Belladonna's eyes widened. "Hellfire."

"Exactly."

Kallie looked at Layne for a long, lingering moment, hoping once more that he would be okay and wondering if Belladonna's potion had also doped up the ghosts inside him, since all she'd seen in his eyes during the brief moments he'd been conscious had been himself.

With a sigh that she felt down to her toes, Kallie let her head fall back against the seat. She glanced out the side window, not really seeing the greenery blurring past. The soothing quiet Layne had gifted her with unraveled and fell away.

She aimed the rest of her waning focus and energy at her cousin, a final and flaming arrow fired into an endless night as she struggled with the exhaustion trying to weigh down her eyelids.

Goddammit, Jacks, where are you? Give me a sign. Please.

But the road rolled past, silent and utterly lacking in burning bushes.

Jacks . . .

As Kallie lost her battle, the memory of Jackson's furious scream into the storm that long-ago night—*Here I am, you sonuvabitch, come get me!*—morphed into a wolf's soul-scraping howl.

TWENTY

FIRE AND DARKNESS

Two voices—one male, one female—both low and easy, hooked into Jackson's bonfire dreams and slowly reeled him up from the burning darkness like a catfish caught on a line.

"Sounds like he's finally done screaming, him."

"Done screaming or dead, maybe."

"Nah. Ain't dead. He still sucking in air."

The speakers slid into Cajun as easily and naturally as an oar sluicing through water. A comforting murmur that folded around Jackson like his mama's arms had when he was sick.

A man whispered into Jackson's ear, his breath a shock of ice. "*Lâche pas. Lâche pas la patate. Ça va comme ça devrait. Lâche pas.* We're almost dere."

Don't give up. Hang in there. Things are going as they should.

Jackson drifted on a fevered tide, a distant fire licking at his even more distant body with tongues of orange flame. A boat rocked underneath him, his shoulder blades pressing into wood planks. He heard the low drone of a small outboard engine, felt its vibration thrumming deep into his bones.

Somewhere nearby, maybe right beside him, Jackson

heard a steady and comforting panting, and knew he should be able to name her, his Siberian husky with her thick coat of black, white, and gray, her triangular ears and bicolored eyes, but her name pranced away from him. He decided to wait for it to prance on back.

A medley of odors swirled around him, familiar and intimate—lily pads floating on still, green water, the cool silver scent of fish beneath the surface, pungent diesel from the humming engine, fresh sweat slicking bare skin, the musky aroma of wet dog fur, rank mud, and the thick, coppery reek of blood.

"He ain't gonna make it," the woman said, her voice a low swell of silvery sea tones. A name bobbed to the surface of Jackson's dreaming mind—Jubilee. "He's burning up something fierce."

Jackson wanted to disagree, but couldn't remember how. The fire was still raging, sure, but he'd risen high above it like a hot-air balloon, fueled but untouched by the flames beneath him.

"*Tais-toi*, you. You ain't helping. And he's damned well gonna make it."

"Bet you twenty he don't," Jubilee challenged.

"Dat's cold, girl. But you on."

Jackson hot-air balloon drifted away from the bet-laying conversation, thinking he wouldn't mind getting in on a little of the action, but then the desire dropped away like a sandbag cut from its rope.

Daddy?

A wet nose nudged Jackson's hand, so cold, he gasped. Her name made its prancing return across the field of his mind. *Cielo*. He tried to pet her, but couldn't figure out how to lift his hand.

Daddy?

Jackson shivered convulsively as Cielo licked his face, her strangely cold tongue smearing stickiness and the smell of briny fish across his cheek. Seemed someone had been feeding her sardines.

Good girl, you. Which earned him another fish-stinky swipe of the tongue.

He remembered something about a potion, remembered rough hands seizing his hair and yanking his head back and pouring a dark, oily liquid tasting of decay and bitter oranges down his throat.

"Smell that?" a female voice asks. "Sulfur and piss and anise? Black juju."

Jackson felt himself descend with each remembering, felt the bonfire heat below, drawing his skin tight as he sank.

He remembered the *schunk* of shovels into the ground. Remembered the weight of the earth squeezing the air from his lungs.

Dead man.

Skin-searing heat roared against Jackson as consciousness did him a major disservice and returned. He forced his eyes open and caught a glimpse of a cloud-trailing gray sky through the canopy of Spanish-moss-bearded tree branches arching above him and tracing cool shadows across his fevered face.

He was in a boat, maybe a pirogue.

Cielo's head lowered over him, her ears tilted forward, her gaze intent and full of concern. Jackson tried to speak to her, to reassure her, but it hurt even to swallow; his throat was scraped raw and burning with thirst. He tasted the old-penny tang of blood on his tongue, licked it from his lips.

"*Ça va*, boy?" a man asked, and Jackson recognized the voice that had whispered *Lâche pas* in his ear. But he couldn't see past Cielo, lacked the strength to lever himself up.

"Water," he croaked, throat aching. "*D'eau.*"

"Didn't bring none with us," the man said, regret thick in his voice. "But we'll be at *Le Nique* soon. You can drink all you want dere, you."

Le Nique—the den.

Jackson knew that name, but couldn't quite grasp the memory of when or how; it scampered away from him, coy and slippery, playing hard to get.

Then, without warning or preamble, it started again.

The pain.

His eyes snapped shut and his body bowed.

Burning worms writhed underneath Jackson's skin, searing his muscles, ashing the blood in his veins, and melting tunnels through his fevered brain. Charring his thoughts. The edges of reality scorched black and wisping away. The past whispered to him in words of fire.

A monster's on the way. Tell your mama to head north, cher.

Love ya back, Jacks. See you Sunday and keep safe.

Careful, asshole! He's supposed to bleed out slow.

Might be too late for this little chien de maison . . .

Wanna know a secret? But you gotta promise never to tell.

Jackson's worm-riddled thoughts fell apart, curled together again, mismatched and blind. The past and his own mind as incomprehensible as hieroglyphics etched into a desert-dry tomb wall.

Jackson's body twisted again and again, jackknifing,

torquing brutally. He felt like a Ken doll bent backward in a monstrous child's hand. Muscles tore. Ligaments popped. Bones cracked. Blood filled his mouth, hot and metallic.

A long and mournful *whoo* lifted into the air.

"Get dat dog back!"

Someone was screaming, a barely audible and agonized cry wrenched from a hoarse throat. A dispassionate and unriddled part of Jackson's mind politely informed him that *he* was the person screaming.

"Quick, before he tips us all over."

Icy hands touched Jackson's face, others—winter-frosted and hard—held his shoulders, his legs. His blazing body strained against their hands, then suddenly folded up and fell back like a fire-gutted log crumbling onto the grate in a shower of sparks.

Jackson found himself floating again in a heated dream, seeking the darkness.

"*Lâche pas, lâche pas.*" Soft and soothing like a lullaby. "Hold on. *Lâche pas,* you."

"Told you, René," the silvery-toned voice said. The freezing grip on his legs tightened. "He ain't gonna make it. It's come too late for him. We should just give him to the bayou and the gators. Only merciful thing to do."

"He's one of ours, Jubilee. We can't just give up on him. We found him for a reason."

"Dammit, he's been poisoned with bad juju. Hexed. Did you forget that we dug him up from the ground? We should end his misery before he finishes becoming whatever he was spelled to be."

Careful, asshole! He's supposed to bleed out slow.

Smell that? Sulfur and piss and anise? Black juju.

Caught in eddying currents of pain, Jackson thought the woman with the sea's restless voice had a valid point about ending his misery and giving him to the gators and the bayou, even though he had a feeling he'd normally protest a comment like that. With everything he had.

Problem was, he felt gutted and hollowed and scraped dry. Nothing was left.

"Jubilee's right," the other male voice said. "What if he's going zombie right now?" His voice dropped. "Or worse."

"*C'est ça couillon.*" Disgust deepened René's voice. "Fools. Both o' you. Boy's poisoned and Change-sick and dat's all."

"And that's more than enough to kill him," Jubilee said quietly.

Silence descended over the boat, except for Cielo's panting, the rush of water past the boat's prow, and the rapid pounding of Jackson's heart. Pain tiptoed away, a monster seeking a hiding place to pop out from later. *Gotcha!*

Jackson heard the engine cut off, its vibration vanishing from his cindered and broken bones, then he felt a small bump as the boat butted up against a dock or maybe the shore. The boat rocked as people stood and started moving.

His thoughts skimmed away into a deep twilight, still seeking the cool dark. He became aware of cold hands latching around him, lifting him up into air cooled by the rain and savory with the smells of mint and rosemary and frying bacon. Felt himself tossed over a shoulder as easily as a duffel bag.

Feet thumped up a set of stairs and across a wood

porch. Jackson heard the twang of a screen door being pushed open. Heard the click of claws against wood, the jingle of a chain collar.

Daddy. Cielo's nose iced Jackson's face.

Still here, he thought, then made a liar of himself when the darkness he'd been seeking finally rose up, a leviathan from an ice-sheeted abyss, and swallowed him.

TWENTY-ONE

NOMAD BONDS

McKenna Blue's stomach dropped when she saw the matte black shorty-style helmet turtled in the grass beside a badly listing and fractured mailbox.

Bugger all. I was bloody right.

And on one of the rare occasions when she didn't want to be.

McKenna guided her Triumph Speedmaster to a stop on the dirt road's edge and dropped the bike down onto its kickstand. Killing the engine, she swung off, then pelted over to the helmet and picked it up. Her heart drummed so loudly in her chest, she barely heard Maverick and Jude pull in behind her on their bikes—engines rumbling, tires crunching over gravel.

McKenna stared at the helmet in her now numb hands, her worst fears realized as she took in the crack splitting along one side.

Layne.

"Shite," she whispered.

About an hour after her last terse conversation with Layne, she'd felt a profound uneasiness, a deep, intuitive knowing binding McKenna to her ex-husband. Divorced they might be, but some ties could never be severed.

Layne is in trouble. Nocht but darkness and disaster surrounds him. And I'd bet my right tit that sodding swamp witch Kallie Rivière is the reason.

McKenna always heeded her intuition, especially when it concerned Layne.

When she hadn't been able to reach him by phone, McKenna had gone to Augustine's Bondalicious assistant, Felicity Fields, and had learned that Layne had phoned in a report for Augustine.

"Chacahoula? To banish a fooking ghost?"

Felicity tilts her head, her shining curtain of strawberry blonde hair sweeping against her face. "Both Lord Augustine and Mr. Valin believed it best not to leave any loose ends, Ms. Blue. And besides, wasn't it you who invoked Daoine shena liri *in the first place? I believe Mr. Valin is simply doing as that pledge requires."*

Clan law of the People. A nomad blood pledge. A promise to avenge a death, no matter how long it took, or how far, or how many needed to be killed. And aye, she was the one who invoked it following Gage's death.

"But as for banishing it," Felicity continues, "it seems doubtful at the moment. Magic seems to have short-circuited. Perhaps Mr. Valin ran afoul of some spell."

"Give me the address in Chacahoula," McKenna growls.

Address tucked into the hip pocket of her jeans, McKenna had then gone to the Fox clan chieftain, Frost Valin—Layne's mother.

"I'm sending a pair of riders with you as an honor escort and in case you run into trouble," Frost says, her green eyes—as always—cool and steady. "I know Gage's family

will want their son's best friend and the clan shuvani *in attendance at his wake, so I shouldn't have any problem getting them to postpone it until you return.*"

And McKenna notes that there is no doubt in Frost's voice that they will return. The chieftain's already lost one child to unthinkable violence. She refuses to lose her sole remaining child.

"I'll keep ye posted," McKenna promises, throat tight. Unspoken: Neither of us will lose him.

"That Layne's helmet?" Jude asked, her voice tight with concern. She unstrapped her own helmet, ash-blonde locks tumbling free.

Maverick stepped up beside Jude in an earthy swirl of wet leather and patchouli, his red hair rolled into a wind- and helmet-frayed topknot. Rain goggles hid the clan foxes inked beneath their right eyes.

"Aye." McKenna scrutinized the ground around the busted mailbox post and where the helmet had been lying. "Look for anything tha' might tell us where he is."

"You got it, *shuvani*," Maverick replied.

Leather creaked as Jude and Maverick moved away and started searching the area, walking carefully through the wet grass to avoid stepping on anything that might help them figure out what had happened to their clan brother.

McKenna crouched and touched her fingers to the splintered post—impact damage. Question was, had Layne walked away on his own or had he been rushed to the nearest hospital, an ambulance summoned by concerned witnesses to the accident?

"*Shuvani!*" Maverick's voice boomed through the still air.

McKenna straightened, then sprinted up the driveway, her heart skipping a beat when she saw Layne's Harley parked in front of the house bordered by palm trees at the driveway's end. Maverick squatted in front of the motorcycle, his gloved hands skimming the tank.

"Bike's dinged up some," Maverick said as McKenna drew up alongside him. "Looks like Layne mighta dumped it in the road. Maybe whoever lives in the house ran him in for medical aid."

"Aye, right, not bloody likely," McKenna said, shaking her head, voice grim. She placed Layne's helmet on the bike's seat. "Only a ghost lives here—the wife of the fooking bastard who killed our Gage."

McKenna found herself forced to admit that maybe Augustine's presence inside Layne was a good thing in this instance, since it meant that Babette wouldn't be able to claim him.

On the front porch, goggles pushed up on her forehead, Jude rattled the doorknob, then stepped over to the window and peered inside, cupping her hands beside her face. "Don't see anyone and the place is locked up. Want me to kick in the door?" she asked hopefully.

At the Harley, Maverick rolled his eyes and shook his head. "Ever since those tae kwon do lessons in Tampa . . ."

"No need for wanton destruction, lass," McKenna said, suppressing a smile. "Not yet, anyway. Let's get back to searching."

Maverick rose to his feet, unfolding his six-three length with fluid grace, waiting for Jude to trot down the stairs and join him. McKenna headed off to the right, while the two scouts swung left. As she walked the length of the house, she saw what appeared to be a large hole dug into the side yard beyond the porch railing. Dirt was heaped on the ground beside the hole. A chill touched McKenna's spine when she saw shovels lying in the grass.

Always believed tha' I would feel it if Layne died, always believed tha' I would have some instant and immutable knowledge, the fact of his passing emblazoned in fire across my heart.

But what if I'm wrong?

McKenna raced breathlessly to the edge of the mud-rimmed hole and looked down. Empty. She closed her eyes for a moment, waiting for her pulse to slow from a wild gallop. Once it had, she opened her eyes, then called for Maverick. His keen scout's eyes would glean every possible bit of information available embedded in the ground.

Spotting something in the mud, McKenna bent and plucked out a shell casing, a .45, she thought.

A moment later, a whiff of patchouli and leather told McKenna that Maverick had joined her.

"Looks like a grave," he commented. "An unfinished one. And we've got a man's sneaker prints, boot prints topside—two sets, both female—and boot prints down below—male and female—a dog, and what sure as hell looks like wolf prints."

McKenna looked at the crouching Maverick. "*Wolf* prints?"

The broad-shouldered scout nodded. "Yup, they're all jumbled up with the dog's prints, so I ain't sure how many—two or three. And I'm seeing a barefoot print or two also, but again, I ain't sure how many—two, maybe three people. Tire tracks—a pickup, I'm thinking.

Between the rain and the folks who tromped around here mucking the scene up, hard to read the story." He shrugged. "Given the wolf prints and the bare feet, we could have us some werewolves."

"Werewolves, huh?" Jude said, pacing to a stop beside McKenna. "Ain't never seen any, but I'd love to. From a safe distance, that is."

McKenna sighed and raked her fingers through her hair. "Werewolves wouldn't've taken a human, and especially not an injured human. They woulda just left Layne wherever they found him."

"Unless they needed a Vessel for some reason," Jude tossed in quietly.

"No, I don't think so," McKenna said. "Werewolves don't hold to their dead the way humans do. They don't even have cemeteries."

"Looks like a bunch of shit went down here," Maverick mused. "But in all these prints, I ain't seeing any that match Layne's boots. I don't think he was a part of whatever happened here."

"Unless he was carried," Jude said.

"What *are* you?" Maverick asked in a low voice. "The fucking harbinger of doom? Unless this, unless that. Holy shit, woman."

Jude raised her hands palms out, a gesture of peace. "Hey, just listing possibilities so we can rule them out, that's all."

"So who woulda carried him?" McKenna asked. "And where? No' to the grave or he'd be in it. Same for the house. I think Maverick's right, Layne wasnae a part of wha' happened here. He mighta come along *after*."

Jude nodded. "Could've, yeah."

Maverick narrowed his eyes. "I swear to shit that I'm seeing chicken tracks down in the grave. Maybe this was gonna be a BBQ pit or something."

"For barbecuing mastodons, maybe," Jude scoffed.

Maverick glanced up at McKenna. "Nothing here says Layne."

McKenna nodded. Raked her fingers through her hair. Her gaze skipped from one scout to the next. "Keep searching," she told them. "We need to find something that'll lead us to our clan brother."

"*Shuvani*," Maverick murmured, rising to his feet, Jude's quiet acknowledgment heeling his. Both walked away, headed for the opposite side of the yard.

McKenna closed her eyes again, drinking in the quiet and centering herself with deep breaths of air rife with the scents of mud, sharp cedar, and blossoming roses. She listened to the drip-drip-drip of rainwater from the eaves of the house and the branches of the trees.

She mentally traced along the edges of the hard knot of dread and anxiety lodged in her solar plexus. Following it back to the moment when she realized something bad had befallen Layne.

Show me the way.

At the May Madness Carnival in New Orleans, her intuition had raced her through the hotel, taking her unerringly to the room Layne was in—heart-stopped and unbreathing—when she hadn't known he was in a room other than his own.

She called upon that intuitive knowing again.

Give me a path.

An image of Kallie Rivière as McKenna had first seen her shaped itself in the darkness behind her eyes: *Wearing* only a well-filled red lace bra and bikini panties, the dark-haired woman is kneeling beside Layne, her joined hands pressing rhythmically against his chest as she performs CPR on his sprawled body.

And beyond them, Gage lies unmoving on a blood-soaked bed.

McKenna's hands clenched into fists. The image vanished in a furious haze. Her eyes opened and she called for her scouts even as she found herself moving, walking with a determined stride for her Triumph, knowing where she needed to go.

Bayou Cyprés Noir.

TWENTY-TWO

LOUP-GAROU

Hearing the thump of a pirogue against the house dock, Angélique Boudreau put the blackberry-jam-smeared butter knife down on the counter beside the plate of fried cornmeal mush and wiped her hands against her apron.

In their high chairs, the twins were busy with their breakfast. Grease gleamed on their pudgy little fingers as they scooped cut-up bits of *boudin blanc* from the bowls on their trays and stuffed them into their grease-smeared rosebud mouths.

"You eat. Mama be right back," Angélique told them.

Ember smacked her lips happily and wrapped her fingers around her bowl's daisy-etched rim and banged it against the tray. Chance kept poking juicy pieces of sausage into his mouth without pause.

"Chew," Angélique commanded.

"Tew!" Ember shouted, banging her bowl, her nomad father's daughter with her dark curls and caramel skin and bicolored eyes—one brown and one green.

Chance's skin was lighter and red highlights glimmered in his dark curls, his eyes emerald green like his mama's. His cheeks bulged with sausage.

"Chew, *p'tit*," Angélique repeated, hands on her jeans and apron-covered hips. "Your daddy may be from Squirrel clan, but that don't mean you need to store food in your cheeks."

"Tew!" Ember crowed with another bowl bang.

With a sigh, Angélique strode out into the front room in time to see her husband, Merlin Mississippi, swing open the porch door to admit a worried-looking René carrying a limp form over his shoulder.

"*Shuvano*," René greeted Merlin. Then his deep-brown eyes sought and found Angélique. "*Traiteur* Angélique," he murmured respectfully.

"René," she replied with a nod.

Merlin stepped aside as Jubilee, Moss, and a Siberian husky followed René inside the house, the smell of damp fur and clothing breezing in along with them.

Amusement flashed across Merlin's dark brown face, slanted his full lips, and crinkled up the nomad clan tattoo—the slim silhouette of a running squirrel. "When y'all said you were going hunting, René, I assumed you meant deer," he said dryly.

"You and me both," René said.

Jubilee waved a hand at the husky. "We decided to chase her for a while instead. Bad decision, that."

"Hush, you," René growled.

Scowling, Jubilee padded barefoot over to the cold fireplace and leaned one arm against the mantel. Her damp jeans and short-sleeved pale green blouse clung to her curves and her waterfall of silver hair was in disarray. She glared at René for a moment, charcoal brows knitting over cobalt-blue eyes, before folding her arms underneath her breasts and looking away. A muscle ticked in her jaw.

Angélique studied Jubilee's muddied and angry aura, the tension in her body language, and realized that this was something more than just the teasing arguments and quibbling she usually witnessed between the girl and her uncle.

What's going on? What's Jubilee so worked up about?

Jubilee's identical twin, Moss, looked like a very masculine version of his sister, taller and broader, with short ash-gray hair and a clean-shaven face—and, unlike his sister, cheerful. He sniffed the air hungrily, his nostrils no doubt sucking in the spicy aroma wafting from the kitchen.

"Smells good, Angélique," Moss said hopefully.

"I've got fried cornmeal mush and *boudin blanc* in there along with blackberry jam and scrambled eggs. Got buttermilk biscuits and ham too," Angélique said. "You finish feeding the twins and you can eat right along with them."

Moss's blue eyes gleamed. He grinned. Without a word, he scampered off to the kitchen, bare feet whispering against the hardwood planks. Ember's happy shriek greeted him. "Tew!"

Merlin looked at Angélique and winked. They both knew that *she* had come out on the good side of *that* deal.

The dog trotted over to where Angélique stood and started talking in drawn-out and urgent *whoo-whoos,* inflections rising and falling, sounding for all the world like she was giving instructions—or orders—on how to care for her pack member.

Merlin laughed. "She's got all manner of things to say."

"That she does," Angélique agreed. Taking in the

dog's bicolored eyes, amusement curled through her. She looked at her husband. "You never told me that you had Siberian husky in your bloodline."

Merlin regarded her for a moment, his eyes—one a startling and breathtaking sapphire blue, the other deepest brown—glinting. He winked. "You never asked, hun."

Angélique laughed.

"Here, girl," Jubilee said, calling to the dog. "C'mere."

But the Siberian husky ignored her and padded back across the room, nails clicking against the floor, to sit, tongue lolling, at René's bare feet, her intent gaze of blue and brown fixed on the person slung like a bag of potatoes over René's shoulder.

All Angélique could see of that person were mud-smeared jeans and T-shirt and mud-caked boots—no, make that *boot*, since one seemed to be missing. A soiled sock was all that still clung to his left foot.

"So who is he?" Merlin asked, folding his muscle-corded arms over his chest and eyeing René's passenger.

René shook his head. "Never got his name, me. But he be in a bad way."

Angélique's nostrils flared. A subtle olfactory stew of sweat and pheromones and musk marked René's burden as a young adult male. Whoever he was, he was seriously injured. The coppery scent of blood curled thick into her nostrils. And not just blood. She sniffed, drawing in his smell, picking apart his recent history.

Fevered sweat, deep earth, dank mud, wet denim and cotton, the sour stink of a body pushed beyond endurance and shutting down, the musky pheromones of Change.

"That he is." Angélique unknotted her apron ties and tossed the apron into the armchair beside the fireplace.

Pulling a hair tie from the pocket of her jeans, she tied back her long russet hair.

She had a feeling a long day lay ahead of them.

"Take your friend to the back and put him on the table," Angélique instructed, her voice all business and no-nonsense.

"No friend," Jubilee said before René could speak. "We found him planted in the earth just outside o' Chacahoula, and potioned up with bad juju to boot."

Merlin closed the porch door, then glanced over his shoulder at Angélique, his eyes holding hers, his expression grim. "Sounds like black work, hun."

Angélique nodded. "It does. But he's also Change-sick. He reeks of it."

Merlin blinked, startled. "Change-sick? Then that means he's a—"

"Half-'n'-half," Jubilee finished. "And we're all wasting our time. He's too old for the Change. He ain't gonna make it."

"We'll see about that." Angélique pierced Jubilee with a fang-sharp stare.

"*Tais-toi*, girl," René snapped, his gaze also locked on Jubilee.

There was no mistaking the tension in his voice, in his broad, powerful shoulders, and in his brown eyes. Taller than the majority of the pack at six-five, his wild tawny locks curled to the nape of his neck; his sideburns and beard were the same shade as his hair. And right now, his hair was bristling with quiet fury.

Jubilee pushed away from the mantel and met René's gaze. "He's a half blood. Dangerous. Unpredictable. A fucking freak."

Brows knitted together, jaw tight, Merlin started forward, expression furious, but Angélique's reflexes were faster, her speed quicker than her human husband's, and she beat him to Jubilee.

Baring her fangs, Angélique snarled. Her warning was unmistakable: *You have stepped out of place.*

Jubilee dropped down into a crouch, panic flashing across her face as she realized exactly what she had just said, and lowered her head submissively, her gaze aimed at the floor. Her body tensed, muscles quivering.

"I was only talking about the *chien de maison* we dug up," she explained hastily. "I never meant Ember and Chance. Never."

Fingernails morphing into black claws, Angélique dropped down beside Jubilee and grabbed her by the back of the neck, her claw tips pricking the girl's skin. The bright smell of fresh blood floated into the air.

"Say anything like that again," Angélique said in a coiled whisper, "and you will no longer be welcome in my home."

"She ain't welcome right now," Merlin said, his voice cold enough to start another ice age. "Get your ass out of my house, Jubilee Fontaine."

"Merlin, I'm sorry," Jubilee said, her gaze still on the floor, her voice low and contrite. "I wasn't thinking."

"Damn straight you weren't thinking," Merlin agreed. "Now get the hell out."

Angélique slid her claws away from Jubilee's neck, the tips dotted with blood, then stood. She curled her hands into fists, claws biting into her palms, and swallowed back her anger as the younger woman jumped to her feet and bolted from the room.

The porch door slammed behind her.

Angélique's belly knotted. Jubilee wasn't the only *loup-garou* who believed half bloods to be inferior and, worse, dangerous.

She felt Merlin's strong hands on her shoulders, the warmth of his palms through her blouse. She leaned back into him for a moment, drawing strength and calm from his solid, reliable presence, and closed her eyes.

"You okay, hun?" he asked softly.

"Yeah, yeah. I'm okay. Pissed. Exasperated. But okay."

"I'm still with you on the pissed part. And if this closed-minded bullshit ever gets aimed in the twins' direction, we split. We've got options, woman."

A familiar argument-slash-discussion, one they'd been having for the last two years, ever since the twins had been born.

We can join my clan. I refuse to let anyone treat our kids as less, as inferior.

We've got time to educate the pack, show them the flaws in their thinking.

And if we can't? That flawed thinking runs deep, hun. Thousands of years. We ain't got much time before the twins are old enough to realize they are being looked at differently than anyone else in the pack. And why.

We can do it. We have to do it. You've been raised in a human pack—a clan. You know how it is.

Yeah. I do. I understand the ties of kin and clan. I gave up the road for you. Will you give up the pack for our children—if it comes to that?

The pack needs me, Merlin. I'm their traiteur.

Then train another healer and let the pack need them.

Angélique drew in a breath, pulling her husband's warm

and masculine odor—oakmoss and musky amber—deep into her lungs. She opened her eyes. "Later, *cher*. Right now we have someone to take care of," she murmured, sliding out from under his grasp and swiveling around.

"That we do, but remember, we ain't finished with this conversation, woman."

Angélique lifted an eyebrow. "Now you're starting to annoy me," she warned.

"And that's different from every other day, how?" Merlin teased.

"Ask me that in the bedroom tonight, bright boy. And I'll show you."

"Maybe I'll sleep on the couch. Play it safe."

"Oh, it's much too late for that, nomad." Shoving past her grinning husband, Angélique walked over to René and the dog sitting patiently at his feet.

"I apologize for Jubilee," René said with a slight shake of his head. "Somet'ing's bothering dat girl, for true, since I know she t'inks de world of yo' kids."

"*Merci beaucoup*, René, I appreciate that," Angélique replied gently. "But it's a problem for another day, *oui*? Now let's get that boy in back and on the table."

With a nod, René strode from the living room and into the kitchen, the dog right beside him. Ember burbled "Doggie!" then "Tew!" as he passed through, a declaration that Moss echoed in a deep voice: "Tew!"

Giggles and bowl-banging were his applause.

Shaking her head and smiling, Angélique followed René through the sausage-fragrant kitchen, past her laughing grease- and jam-smeared children and a mugging Moss and into the back room, her husband just a pace behind her.

René stopped in front of the first of two hand-carved oak examination tables and eased the unconscious half blood onto its padded surface. The young man's dark hair partially veiled his face in damp tendrils. One mud-streaked hand dangled over the table's side and René gently placed it back on the table, murmuring, "*Lâche pas*, you."

Angélique slipped past and went to the sink beside her worktable with its neat jars, boxes, and bottles full of healing herbs and roots, the room awash in the scents of dill and coriander and frankincense.

Merlin's worktable was opposite hers, a rootworker's version of a partner's desk, and his side was a swirl of clutter and chaos. She usually avoided looking at it. Otherwise her hands would itch with the need to organize it.

"I'll get his clothes off," Merlin said, beelining for the examination table. "Wet and muddy ain't helping. We're gonna need a bowl of warm water and rags to clean him up a bit too, hun."

"Already getting it," Angélique replied, pulling a clear glass bowl down from the cupboard above. She placed it on the sink and twisted on the faucet. As the bowl filled, she gathered clean rags from the drawer.

Bowl brimming with warm water, she carried it and the rags over to the examination table and placed them on the oak instrument tray beside it. The Siberian husky sat on her haunches near the table's head, panting. Her watchful blue-brown gaze was aimed at the young man sprawled on the table.

René lifted the half blood's body up so Merlin could peel his black T-shirt off his lean-muscled torso—or Angélique *supposed* it was black, it might've been a different color before all the mud—revealing dozens of shallow cuts sliced across his chest, belly, and arms.

Merlin whistled low, then said, "Christ. Cut up, potioned, and buried. Somebody truly hated this poor bastard."

"Enough to make him into a true zombie," Angélique agreed, "caught in the twilight between death and life and bound to the will of another. But," she added, casting a quick smile at René, "it looks like the potion didn't work and you saved him from suffocating to death."

Looking grim, René eased the half blood back down on the table. "We was following de dog, us. Playing a game, trying to figure out what she was chasing mile after mile after mile."

"Damned good thing for him," Merlin said.

With the half blood flat on his back again, Angélique moved in with a wet rag to clean his face while Merlin stepped down to tug off his sole remaining boot.

Angélique frowned as she cleaned dried mud and blood away from what was starting to look like a very handsome face underneath all the dirt. A sense of the familiar swirled through her. Something in the angle of his cheekbones, his closed eyes, his lips.

Bending closer, she sniffed delicately, nostrils flaring, seeking a personal scent beneath the blood and fever stench, the sour reek of arrested Change. She caught a faint whiff of rosewood, of brine, and of surf-wet sand, but nothing that insisted, except—*Remember me*—the rosewood. That scent niggled at her memory, nudged.

"What is it?" Merlin asked. "Something wrong? I mean, aside from the obvious."

"I'm not sure. There's something familiar . . ."

Angélique's gaze traveled across the unconscious man's torso to the tattoo inked into his right arm near the shoulder. She wiped away grime and blood to reveal an angel-bordered scroll. Leaning over, she read:

> *Gone, but never forgotten.*
> *Nicolas & Lucia Bonaparte*
> *Junalee & Jeanette, my angels*
> *Je t'aime toujours*

Angélique's breath caught in her throat. Then memory poured through her mind like water through a broken dam.

A boy climbs out of the pirogue and races across the grass yelling her name, but he calls her Ange, since Angélique is too big a mouthful for a four-year-old. He slides to a stop in front of her, his wavy, coffee-brown hair wild, his golden-honey eyes with their slight upward tilt gleaming.

"*Got a baby sister, me!*" *he exclaims.* "*I be a big brudder now!*"

Angélique straightened, heart pounding, and looked at her husband. His hands rested on the half blood's belt buckle, his questioning gaze on hers.

"I know him," she said.

"You do?" Lines creased Merlin's brow. "But how? Who is he?"

Hardly believing her own words, Angélique took another look at the young man on the table to verify the names she'd just read in his tattoo, and her heart leapt into her throat when his eyes opened. Golden-honey eyes, an amber gaze, a slight upward tilt.

All doubt vanished.

This *was* the little boy Angélique had last seen

nineteen years ago, a four-year-old excitedly bragging to his thirteen-year-old aunt about his new baby sister.

"Could you feed my dog?" Jackson Bonaparte whispered, his voice raw and hoarse. His eyes shuttered closed again even as the words slipped from his bitten lips.

"René," Angélique said, surprised at the levelness of her voice while her heart was thundering against her ribs, "I need you to fetch the Alphas."

Looking perplexed, René nodded. "What you want me to tell Ambrose and January when I find dem?"

Angélique drew in a deep breath. "That you've found Ambrose's brother's son."

"Holy shit," Merlin breathed.

TWENTY-THREE

CIRCLE OF PROTECTION

Kallie woke from her doze when Belladonna pulled into the small lot behind Divinity's Circle of Protection botanica and glided the Dodge Dart to a halt in the slot farthest from the trash bin. Aside from Gabrielle's ancient orange VW Bug, the lot was empty.

"Thanks for helping keep me awake during the drive," Belladonna said, looking into the rearview mirror. "Without your constant and unladylike snoring keeping me bright-eyed and bushy-tailed, I probably would've driven us off a cliff."

"A *cliff*? Between Chacahoula and Bayou Cyprés Noir? *Where?*"

"I'm sure there's a cliff *somewhere*. And asleep, I would've found it and driven us to our doom. Guaranteed."

"Well, then. *Ça fait pas rien*, and thanks for not killing us."

Belladonna yawned. "No problem, Shug."

Rubbing a hand over her face, Kallie tried to wipe away her lingering sleepiness and failed. She sat up and unstrapped her seat belt. Her brief sleep had left her feeling more tired than before, her thinking fuzzy, and she wished now that she'd managed to keep her eyes open during the drive back to Bayou Cyprés Noir.

Kallie looked at Layne and confirmed that he was still out, his honey-blond dreads coiling onto the backseat and floorboard. His breathing was low and easy, and his face—blond whiskers indicating his need for a shave—relaxed.

Well, that's one good thing, at least.

The sky beyond the windshield was still gray and ragged with storm clouds, but at least it was no longer raining. Kallie guessed that it was getting close to noon, and on a normal day, she and her *ti-tante* would've opened the botanica at ten.

But this was goddamned *far* from a normal day.

The closed-in air of the car smelled of jasmine, old french fries, leather, and sandalwood. And although the greasy french fry aroma reminded Kallie that she hadn't eaten since early evening the night before, she didn't feel hungry. She actually felt queasy, instead. Too little sleep, too much stress, pure appetite killer.

"After we haul Mr. Sexy Nomad inside, you want to go up to my place and take a shower while your aunt is looking him over?" Belladonna asked. "Give you a chance to catch a second wind or even take a real nap."

Kallie looked at the stairs leading to the flat above the botanica that Belladonna rented from Divinity. As blissful as a nap sounded, Kallie didn't want to sleep until she knew Layne's condition and had a chance to talk with her aunt about *loups-garous*, *loas*, and exorcisms. But a shower, on the other hand . . .

Tapping a finger against her lips, Kallie mentally reviewed recent sleepovers and decided that, yup, she'd left clothes at the apartment on several occasions. If she was wrong, she could always roll up a pair of Belladonna's jeans or wear one of her tunics as a minidress.

"I like that idea, Bell. Wanna do a coin toss to see who showers first?"

"How about rock-paper-scissors?"

"Sure."

Kallie leaned forward between the seats, shivering as her side brushed Layne's leather-jacketed shoulder. She tried not to think about skin-on-skin contact. Tried not to imagine the feel of him—all hard muscle and heat— beneath her hands.

The heat pooling in her belly and points south told her that she'd failed.

Belladonna's gaze met Kallie's, then shifted over to Layne. A knowing smile slinked across her lips. "Maybe he's going to need a sponge bath," she said, her eyes returning to Kallie's.

The mental images Belladonna's suggestion conjured set Kallie's blood ablaze and put coherent thought on pause. Heat suffused her body in a tingling rush. Glaring at Belladonna, she growled, "Pure evil."

She yawned. "Stating the obvious, girl."

Once her racing pulse had calmed down and her temperature had dipped below the steam threshold, Kallie said, "Okay. Ready."

"On three," Belladonna instructed, counting down, and thumping her fist against her palm.

Kallie's scissors won over Belladonna's paper, so she eyed her friend suspiciously. "Did you just *let* me win?"

"What? *Me*?" Belladonna shook her head, her blue and black curls swaying. "Hoodoo, please. Why would I do that? It's not like you've been rolling around in the mud or chasing judgmental chickens or going five rounds with death or anything." She flapped a hand at Kallie. "Get over yourself, girl."

Grinning, Kallie stretched across the seat and planted a kiss on Belladonna's cheek. "You're the best friend ever."

"Again, stating the obvious." But a pleased smile lit her face.

The mingled odors of wet pavement and eau de Dumpster swirled in when Belladonna opened the door and hopped out of the car. Just as she flipped the driver's seat forward so Kallie could climb out of the back, a low, husky voice said, "Where are we?"

Kallie twisted back around. Looking at Layne, she saw the same things she'd witnessed before—no color to his handsome face, pain-tightened features, dilated pupils. "At my *tante's* botanica," she replied. "She's meeting us here."

"I appreciate that," Layne said. "I prefer a hoodoo healer to a hospital. Thanks."

Kallie smiled. "Who doesn't?"

Pushing against the reclined seat with his elbows, Layne levered himself upright, and Kallie realized she was wrong about his face being *completely* drained of color as she watched him blanch, his fox tattoo stark against his suddenly bone-white skin. He squeezed his eyes shut and swallowed hard. His hands white-knuckled around the seat edge, holding on for dear life.

"Fuck," he whispered after a moment. "Yeah. Okay. I think I need a minute here." He slumped back down in the seat, eyes still closed, jaw tight.

Ducking her head down into the car, Belladonna eyed

him critically, then tsked. "Back at Doctor Heron's place, Augustine and Babette kept fighting over control of your body. I told those damned ghosts that they weren't helping the situation—namely, you."

Layne slivered open one eye and looked at Bella-donna. "Babette? Holy fuck. So *that's* my other passenger, the one Augustine's got snared in static. Shit."

"I thought it wasn't possible for a ghost to enter an already occupied Vessel," Kallie said.

"Me too. Ain't *supposed* to be possible," Layne replied, draping an arm over his eyes. A muscle flexed in his jaw. "But apparently that supposition's dead wrong. I don't know how long Augustine's gonna be able to keep her in the bubble."

Bubble? Kallie mused. So much she didn't know about Vessels, and so much she didn't know about this one in particular.

"Look, let's get you inside and lying down," Kallie said, reaching over to squeeze his forearm. His leather jacket creaked beneath her fingers. "Then we'll figure out how to exorcise Babette. I can always call McKenna—if neces-sary."

"Thanks, sunshine. I know how much that cost you. Especially since Kenn's no doubt still plotting your demise. By now, she must be up to plan W."

Kallie shrugged. "Like I said before, everyone needs a hobby—even leprechaun-sized nomads with a Darth Vader complex."

Layne snorted. "This is one hobby you *don't* want to encourage. But we can't do an exorcism until my head-ache's gone, anyway, so no point in calling her yet."

"She doesn't worry me. Let her give it her best shot."

"Famous last words, sunshine."

"We'll just see about that. Now hold still, okay? Me and Bell are coming around to get you."

"Christ on a corn tortilla," Layne muttered. "What's next? A wheelchair blanket and a can of Ensure?"

"Only if you ask me nicely. What flavor would you like?"

"Vanilla. Gonna drink it out of my belly button?"

Kallie paused, reignited heat flooding her body as she imagined doing just that, her tongue licking across Layne's vanilla-sweetened skin. Her mouth dried as all moisture raced south of the border.

"I'd call that asking nicely," Belladonna said, voice light and airy with mock innocence. "Wouldn't you, Shug?"

Sucking in a deep breath, Kallie banished all thought of her tongue and Layne's skin from her mind, banished the word that begged to slip from between her lips in response to the nomad's teasing question: *Yes.*

"Shut up," Kallie growled instead, cheeks burning. "Both of you."

It didn't help that both Belladonna and Layne chuckled in unison, like evil twins. But at least her desire—*desire*? How about grab-him-throw-him-down-tear-off-his-clothes-and-ride-him-for-all-he's-worth *lust*?— had cooled.

Kallie climbed out of the backseat, then walked around to the passenger door, relieved that she and Belladonna wouldn't have to haul Layne inside the botanica. She honestly didn't think she had the strength to carry him again, although she would've given it her damnedest.

Hell, she would've trotted over to the Beyond Roses

flower shop next door, if necessary, and politely asked the proprietor and main bouquet *artiste*, Arthur Dempsey, if she could borrow his muscular and often shirtless boy-friend, dark-eyed Cole.

Kallie had no doubt Arthur would've been agreeable. Especially once he'd gotten a look at the nomad his boy-friend needed to scoop up and carry. Probably would've directed the entire thing too, she mused.

Careful, Cole, he may be a nomad, but he's a human being. A lean and sexy human being. Carry him like one. Over the shoulder like a fireman—that's right. Now follow the ladies. They'll show you the way, darling.

And just like that, the lusty thoughts returned.

"What are you snickering about?" Belladonna asked as she joined Kallie at the passenger door.

"Just picturing Cole from next door carrying Layne inside for us."

"Are they both shirtless in this little imagining?" Bella-donna replied, voice dreamy. "Chests oiled? Rippling abs gleaming? Belts unbuckled?"

"Yup," Kallie said, pulling open Layne's door. "And that's just the start."

"Mmm-mmm-mmm," Belladonna purred. "Oh, I'd pay to see that."

But, Kallie reflected a split second later, it seemed that what Belladonna *wouldn't* pay to see was Layne suddenly leaning out of the car and dry-heaving onto the pavement in a very nonsexy, but undeniably nomad, manner.

Kallie gathered Layne's thick dreads in her hands and held them away from his face while Belladonna slapped her hands over her own mouth and back-pedaled a healthy distance across the parking lot.

After a few moments, Layne stopped trying to upend his stomach and lifted his head. He slumped against the door frame, sweat glistening on his forehead, eyes closed. Some color had returned—green.

"Well, that was seven degrees of awesome," he muttered.

Kallie knotted his dreads to keep them back in case he got sick again. She brushed the backs of her fingers against his heated face. He shivered beneath her touch. "You want to wait a bit before trying to stand up?" she asked gently.

"Just for a minute, yeah," he whispered.

"Let me know when you're ready." Kallie motioned for Belladonna to return. "Dry heaves and puking aren't contagious, Bell. And anyway, he's done." *For now.*

"I know they're not contagious," Belladonna replied indignantly, lowering her hands from her mouth, but remaining right where she was. "It's the whole monkey hear, monkey puke thing that's at issue."

"Ah. Then why are you still over there? There's nothing to hear—"

The botanica's back door creaked open, and Divinity stepped out, hands on the hips of her purple Gypsy skirt. "Dere y'all are. I was starting to wonder, me." A pause, then, "You girls need help with de nomad?"

Kallie shook her head. "No. He's just resting."

"Not anymore," Layne said, opening his eyes and glancing at Kallie. "I'm ready."

"Okay. Let's do this," Kallie murmured.

Kallie snugged a bracing arm around Layne's waist once he'd levered himself upright and helped him out of the car and onto his feet. He swayed, stumbling against

Kallie, but another arm looped around his waist from the other side, warm hand brushing against her own, and steadied him.

"Nomad, I don't care how good you look in wet boxers—or out of them," Belladonna grumbled, "you puke and y'all are on your own."

"Ain't you just an angel of mercy?" Layne replied.

Kallie looked up to see a smile twitch across his bloodless lips. She felt a smile pull at her own when he winked at her.

"Damn straight," Belladonna affirmed. "Now, move your fine ass."

Still holding the back door open, Divinity called, "Sometime dis century."

"Yes, ma'am," all three replied in unison. Then laughed.

TWENTY-FOUR

UNBROKEN TRUST

Divinity's consultation room at the back of the botanica held carved oak tray tables, an examination table, and two white-sheeted twin beds. Shelves lined the walls, displaying bottles full of potions and oils, jars brimming with roots and herbs and powders, dressed and undressed candles, along with medical and first aid supplies.

Kallie and Belladonna helped Layne over to the nearest pristine bed, Divinity and Gabrielle bringing up the rear.

"You need to undress, boy," Divinity ordered. "Yo' clothes be wet. De girls can take dem upstairs and toss dem into de washer."

"Wait," Kallie said, tugging at Layne's leather jacket. The metal studs jingled. "Let's get this off first." Once she'd removed his jacket, she helped him strip down to a pair of black boxers. Blue and purple and black bruises, along with road rash, peppered the skin along the right side of his body, bleeding into his tattoos.

"Ouch," Kallie sympathized.

"Socks too," Divinity said.

Layne pulled off his socks, then Kallie helped him ease down onto the bed, the crisp sheets crinkling beneath him and wafting the citrus-and-spice scent of Florida Water—lavender, lemon, jasmine, and cloves—into the air. He stretched out with a soft, pained sigh, then draped his arm over his eyes.

While Divinity covered Layne with a warm blanket, Kallie went over to the dimmer switch near the doorway and dialed down the light until it was just a dim night-light glow.

"Better?" she asked.

"Much. Thanks, sunshine." But the arm remained over his eyes.

"You go on upstairs and shower, Kallie," Divinity said. "You look like you been wallowing in a pigsty, you." She gave Belladonna the critical once-over also. "Mm-hmm. You ain't much better, girl."

Belladonna smoothed a hand over her damp, mud-spattered tunic. "Yes, ma'am." She glanced at Kallie. "You coming? You won first dibs on the shower."

"Yeah, I just want to make sure everything's all right first," Kallie said, returning to the bed and gathering up Layne's clothes. "You need anything?" she asked him.

"I'm good," Layne said. "You go."

"If by *good* you mean a head full of tiny men with sledgehammers banging at your skull from the inside," Kallie said, "then yeah, you're dandy."

Layne snorted, then seemed to regret it as even his new greenish cast drained from his face and more sweat popped up on his forehead. Kallie grabbed the trash can and held it next to the nomad's head while Belladonna scurried from the room, hands pressed against her ears.

Layne swallowed hard, then waved the trash can away. "False alarm."

"For de moment." Divinity joined Kallie beside the bed, a stoppered green glass bottle in her hands, and eyed Layne. She uncorked the bottle. A sweet aroma curled into the air—allspice, poppies, and cinnamon—along with the sharp odor of alcohol. "Drink dis. It'll take de edge off yo' pain and nausea."

Lowering his arm, Layne regarded the bottle dubiously. "But it won't put me out, right? I got a battle going on inside and I really need to keep conscious. I need to focus as much as possible."

Divinity drew herself up to her full, magically looming five-seven. "Who be de healer here, nomad? You or me?"

"Say 'You,'" Kallie stage-whispered.

A wry smile twisted up the corners of Layne's mouth. "That would be you, ma'am," he said, accepting the bottle and drinking from it until Divinity told him to stop.

"Now lie back down." Divinity took the bottle back from him and worked the cork back into its mouth. "And let me know when de pain starts to fade."

Murmuring his assent, Layne eased his head back onto the pillow and draped a muscle-sculpted arm over his eyes once more. With a satisfied nod, Divinity walked away, crossing the room to join Gabrielle at the worktable.

Kallie grasped Layne's hand, gave it a gentle squeeze. "I'll see you in a bit, okay?"

"Go on, sunshine," Layne replied, his words soft, slurred, his voice already drowsy. He squeezed her hand back. "I'll be here."

Kallie reluctantly released him, then hugged his damp, road-stained clothes against her chest and stalked over to her aunt's worktable. "Why the hell did you lie to him about the potion?" she hissed, arrowing a furious look at Divinity.

"Because de boy woulda argued wit' me and I ain't got time fo' dat kinda nonsense," Divinity replied in a low voice, grinding herbs with a pestle. Bundles of leaves and other plants rested on the table, awaiting their turn— bitterweed, boneset, devil's shoestrings.

"He said he needed to stay awake, needed to focus," Kallie reminded her in a strained whisper.

"No doubt he do," Divinity murmured. "But de pain in his head ain't making dat possible, so de more he struggles wit' it, de more he drains himself of strength and de ability to focus."

"She's right." Gabrielle, measuring ground herbs and roots into a pot of water on the table, glanced at Kallie. "Layne's going to lose his fight against Babette if he keeps sapping his will by struggling with his pain."

"If he's unconscious, are the ghosts inside of him unconscious too?" Kallie asked.

Divinity shrugged one shoulder. "Yo' guess is as good as mine as far as Vessels go. I know a little, but only a little."

Kallie looked over her shoulder at Layne. His chest rose and fell with an easy, untroubled rhythm. She wanted nothing more in that moment than to crawl under the blankets with him and sleep.

As if reading her mind, Divinity said, "Go upstairs, girl. Get cleaned up and catch some sleep. Nothing for you to do here. Not now, anyway. Go on. We'll talk later—about *everyt'ing*. I promise."

"But Jackson is still out there," Kallie said, voice husky. "He might be hurt, potioned, God knows what. How can I *sleep*?"

"If you don't, you ain't gonna be any good to yo' cousin

or anyone else," Divinity said. Voice gentling, she added, "Jackson is gonna need you at de top of yo' game, Kallie. Rest—for his sake, if not for yo' own. I'm gonna try de shells and see if I can get a fix on de boy."

Exhaustion smudged Kallie's thoughts. "Layne . . ."

"He be fine. I'll take care o' yo' nomad."

Kallie opened her mouth to protest, to say that Layne wasn't *her* nomad, that they'd known each other for just a couple of days and only kissed once—well, okay, and made out a little—but the denial dried up in her throat as she remembered how she'd fought to bring him back when his hex-poisoned heart had stopped, and how he'd fought for her, knives flashing in the moonlight as he sank them into Doctor Heron's chest.

Remembered the feel of his lips against hers.

A few days that felt like a lifetime.

Remembered looking into green eyes that whispered a promise of *always* and *again* into her heart. A promise that might now end—between the hurricane and the *loa*—before it truly began.

"You do that," Kallie said, voice rough. Then walked from the room.

In the end, Belladonna beat Kallie to the shower.

By the time she had climbed the outside stairs to Belladonna's apartment, her friend was stepping out of the steam-filled bathroom wrapped in a plush burgundy bath towel and rubbing her hair with another, smaller burgundy towel.

Tendrils of steam fragrant with the smells of Ivory soap, Listerine, and jasmine-and-honey shampoo curled into the hall.

"*Et tu*, Belladonna?" Kallie asked, walking into the hall and tossing Layne's clothes on top of the white Maytag.

Bending over and wrapping the towel around her hair with a deft twist, Belladonna said, "You were right about me throwing the rock-paper-scissors challenge." She straightened, patting her turban. "So I figured I'd make it up to you and do the right thing by taking the first shower."

"Magnanimous of you. I applaud your integrity. Did you leave any hot water?"

"Plenty. But I have a feeling you need a *cold* shower, not a—" Belladonna stopped talking. A vertical line creased the skin between her hazel eyes. Her amusement wisped away like shower steam. "What's wrong, Shug?"

"It's Jackson," Kallie said, finally giving vent to her fears. "The Baron mentioned that he smelled *loups-garous* at the grave, hinted that they might've taken him."

Belladonna's frown deepened. "*Loups-garous?* Seriously?"

Kallie nodded.

"But why? Why would werewolves dig up and nab Jacks?"

"I don't know." Kallie sighed. She tugged her fingers through her tangled, mud-stiff hair. *Yikes. I really need to hit the shower.*

Belladonna leaned one bare brown shoulder against the bathroom doorjamb. "Do you think *loups-garous* exist, Shug? I mean, I hear rumors about them all the time, that they live in packs out on some of the bayous, but . . ."

"When I was little I used to believe in *loups-garous*, and Jacks and I would—" The words died in Kallie's throat as memory finally unfolded and drew her gaze inward.

*She and Jacks race through the night-cooled grass and underneath the old oak's thick twisted branches chasing fireflies—*mouches à feu*—and capturing them in one of his mama's—Tante Lucia's—jam jars. When Jacks looks at Kallie, grinning, his mischievous eyes glow with a soft green light. Faerie dust and fireflies and summer moonlight.*

"Wanna hear a secret? But you gotta swear never to tell."

"Promise. Cross my heart and hope to die."

Jacks flops down into the dew-glistening grass, then rolls over so he's looking up at the stars jeweling the black velvet sky. He folds his arms behind his head.

"My papa be loup-garou," *he announces proudly.* "That means werewolf."

"Are you one too?"

"Kinda. I'm a half blood. I won't do a big Change into a real wolf, but I'll do a little Change, me, and be a two-legged wolf someday."

"I wish I could be a wolf. I'd howl all night and eat up the people I don't like." *Kallie plops onto the grass beside him. She holds up the jar of fireflies, traces their soft light against the glass with one finger.* "Does Nonc Nicolas eat people?"

"No," *her cousin snorts.* "But Papa could if he wanted to, him. He changes into a wolf, a big black one, and chases me around the yard and gives me rides on his back and stuff."

"What about your mama? She a loo gah-roo too?"

"Nope. Just a hoodoo like your mama."

"How did your papa become a werewolf? Did one bite him?"

"*C'est ça couillon,*" Jackson scoffs, making their three-month-age difference sound like a chasm years wide. "It don't work like that."

Kallie stops tracing light and turns her head to glare at her cousin. "Hey, don't call me names, booger-brain. It ain't nice."

Jackson looks at her, his eyes still glowing faerie-dust green. "Big baby. Now who's calling names?"

"Ain't no baby and you had it coming."

"Nuh-uh."

"Uh-huh. Did so."

Jackson grins, his teeth flashing white in the darkness, and returns his fairie-dust gaze to the sky. "I guess," he allows. "But Papa wasn't bitten or nothing. He was born *loup-garou* in a town fulla *loups-garous* called Le Nique."

"*Le Nique,*" Kallie repeats, trying out the sound.

"We used to go there all the time when I was real little, but then we stopped."

"Why?"

"Dunno."

Kallie holds up the jar. "Wanna let them go now?"

"Sure, we can always catch them again, us."

Kallie unscrews the jar lid, tosses the fireflies into the night, and they wing away in zigzaggy paths of pulsing light.

"Remember, you can't tell anyone about this, you. Papa says that people be afraid of *loups-garous.* That if people find us, they will kill us—all of us. Even baby Junalee. So this has gotta stay secret, okay?"

She feels his gaze on her face and turns her head to look at him. She sees a desperate trust in his glowing green eyes. A trust she'd never break, no matter how many names he called her.

"*I'll never tell. Not Mama. Not Papa. No one. Ever.*"

And she hadn't. At six years old, she'd kept Jackson's secret; and as she'd grown older and that night of fireflies and wolf whispers had grown dimmer, she'd come to believe that Jackson's words had been a little kid's make-believe fable, one she'd been eager to share in during a time in their lives when anything was possible: swamp monsters, giants, dragons, and *loups-garous*.

After all, their mamas had already showed them that magic was real.

Kallie's heart pounded hard and fast, stole her breath. Maybe it had never been *make-believe*. Maybe Jackson had told her the *truth* that long-ago summer night.

But then, why had he never mentioned it again? Never again breathed the word—*loup-garou*?

"Shug?" Belladonna repeated. "You fall asleep standing up and with your eyes open? Talk to me, girl."

"Le Nique," Kallie said as the resurrected memory receded once more. "Ever heard of it? It's a place, a town."

Belladonna considered, then shook her turbaned head. "Nope. Why?"

"I think—thanks to the goddamned Baron—I might have a lead on Jackson." Hope flickered to life, a soft firefly glow. "I gotta talk to Gabr—dammit!—*Divinity* and see what—"

"No, uh-uh, you don't," Belladonna said, stepping forward and grabbing Kallie by the arms. "Here's a list of the only things you *gotta* do: get in the shower, eat something, and catch some sleep. It doesn't have to be in that order, but each thing on that list will be done. If you want to help Jackson and Layne and the rest of Louisiana, then you need to take care of *yourself* first." Belladonna's voice dropped into a dangerous purr. "You hearing me, Shug?"

"Yeah, I am, but—"

A warning light sparked in Belladonna's eyes, a challenging *Don't even think about crossing me, I will ruin your day* gleam. "I *said*," she purred again, "you hearing me, Shug?"

Survival instinct kicked in and Kallie gave the only answer she could. "Yeah, yeah, I'm hearing you."

Belladonna looked her over, then released Kallie's arms and folded her own over her towel-draped chest with an imperious ease that Divinity would've envied. "Mmm-hmm. That's right. Now, get your fanny in the shower."

TWENTY-FIVE

BICYCLE CARDS AND COCKLESHELLS

Divinity finished cleaning the last of the gravel from the abraded road rash stretching along Layne's right side from rib cage to hip—as though his jacket and T-shirt had rucked up as he'd slid down the road. She daubed a salve smelling of lavender, beeswax, and astringent comfrey onto his cleansed skin, then stepped back so Gabrielle could bandage gauze over the rawest sections.

"I t'ink dat's it," Divinity said, wiping her fingers on the white cotton towel draped over her shoulder. "No broken bones, no internal injuries, just one serious knock to de noggin. He be one lucky nomad, him."

"That he is," Gabrielle agreed. "Good thing he was wearing a helmet. Even though nomads are exempt from helmet laws, they seem to be pretty good about protecting their skulls."

Carrying the basin of blood-pinked water over to the sink, Divinity snorted. "Dat was major foolishness, de federal government making dat treaty with de clans. Dey should hafta abide by de same laws we do."

Gabrielle gave a chuckle devoid of humor. "That's funny coming from an identity thief."

Jaw tight, Divinity emptied the basin in the sink, set it on the counter, then turned around to face the mambo, arms crossed over her chest. Gabrielle's red-scarfed head was bent over her task, her hands smoothing and taping squares of gauze intermittently along Layne's side.

"You were in Haiti. And I had need, me."

"So you've said. You were protecting your niece. I understand all that."

"Den what do you want from me?"

Gabrielle straightened, then swiveled around, her fingers squeezing around gauze pads and medical tape, her expression composed, her eyes full of icicles. "An apology, to start."

Divinity met the mambo's cold gaze and lifted her chin. "I already gave you one. But if you want anudder—"

Gabrielle's composure gave way to indignation. "You did not. You *never* apologized. In fact, you said you had no regrets."

"I be t'inking yo' ears be fulla cotton, 'cuz I *know* I told you—" An old-fashioned *bring-bring* ringtone from the pocket of her skirt cut off Divinity's scathing retort.

Holding Gabrielle's narrowed-eye glare as well as serving up one of her own, Divinity pulled out her cell. "*Oui?*"

"I couldn't reach you at home," Addie greeted, her voice wound pigtail tight. "But I didn't think you'd be at the botanica, what with all the mishaps. Finally dawned on me to try your cell."

"Well, I *am* at de botanica," Divinity said, "taking care o' someone who took himself a bad tumble. What news you got?"

Addie drew in a deep breath, then said, "It's been

confirmed. The wards have become storm magnets and they're luring Hurricane Evelyn to the Louisiana shore like those sailor-luring nymphs who tried to snare Odysseus."

"But didn't de ward hoodoos undo de wards? I t'ought dat had been decided—"

"They tried," Addie said in a near whisper. "The wards refused to be undone."

Divinity's blood turned to ice in her veins. "Sweet Jesus."

"We're having a meeting here at my place at ten tonight—as many hoodoos, conjurers, voodooists, and voodooiennes as I can round up—to see if we-all can't come up with a solution before Evelyn drops in on us. Are you and Kallie going to need a ride? I'm sure I can find someone traveling through your neck of the woods to pick you up. Oh! And could you let Kallie's friend know too? The mambo-in-training?"

Divinity's thoughts returned to her missing nephew. *He's out dere alone, maybe hurt, maybe trapped, and he ain't got no hope but me and Kallie.*

As much as Divinity wanted to help Addie and the others, as much as she wanted to keep the hurricane from devastating the unprotected coastline, as much as she wanted to restore magic to its natural rhythms, blood came first. It always would.

"I'd like to come," she said finally, "but have me a patient to tend to, plus I have t'ings I need to take care of—t'ings dat won't wait. Kallie and Belladonna are still at dat carnival o' fools down in New Orleans," she lied, "so I ain't expecting dem back until tomorrow. But"— she paused and gave a frowning but listening Gabrielle an inquiring look, a lift of the eyebrows—"I'm sending a friend in my place in de meantime, a mambo from Lafayette by way of Haiti."

A muscle ticked in the mambo's jaw, but she nodded.

"Oh," Addie replied, her tone somewhat surprised. "All right. But if anything changes—"

"Den we'll be dere as soon as we can," Divinity assured her.

After the call ended, Divinity filled Gabrielle in on the wards and the meeting. The mambo looked shaken. "Bon Dieu," she whispered. "And they're sure? About the wards?"

"So Addie said."

Gabrielle nodded, then put the crushed gauze pads and medical tape down on the bedside table. Turning, she drew the blankets up over Layne. She sat down in the rocker angled beside the bed, closed her eyes, and rocked, furrows creasing her brow as though she were deep in thought—or praying.

We can use all de prayers we can get—provided dey don't backfire too.

Divinity crossed to the shaded window facing the street. With a tug at the bottom of the shade, she rolled it up to the window's midway point.

Rain poured again, falling hard from a ragged gray sky, filling the gutters with leaf-littered streams and puddling on the pavement and sidewalks. Cars—few and far between—shushed along the glistening street. Even with an apartment as buffer between the botanica and the building's roof, she heard the steady drum of rain against the shingles.

She scrutinized the people hurrying along the

sidewalks in front of the storefronts across the street—
Irene's Café, Rouses Market, Bayou Cyprés Noir Phar-
macy, and, for what was truly ailing you, the Hair of the
Dog Tavern—relief trickling through her when she didn't
see anyone who looked out of place like a goggle-eye
perch in a banana tree.

One thing Divinity knew for certain, her sister hadn't
acted alone; knew Sophie had lacked the strength to
remove a soul and replace it with a *loa*—and a wild one at
that—all by her lonesome.

Thing was, Divinity had no idea who her sister's partners in crime were. Or where they were. She'd intended
to keep Kallie hidden from them as long as possible—
preferably forever. But now she felt time slipping away
from her.

*I will never forgive you, Sophie. Nor will I ever under-
stand why you did it. What you hoped to gain.*

With a sigh that gusted up from the far reaches of her
soul, Divinity drew the shade back down and walked over
to her worktable. She'd never felt older or more tired.

She reached into the pocket of her skirt and pulled
out the unfinished poppet with its purple button eyes,
then placed it carefully on the table among the leaves and
herbs. The air was redolent with the smells of sage and
sulfur and bitterweed.

Divinity stroked the brown yarn hair between her fingers,
smoothing it, remembering with a sharp pang brushing the
thick, dark waves of Kallie's hair when she was younger and
how it had flowed like silk through her fingers.

*Back when I was first getting to know her, my sister's
daughter, dis wounded and angry fourteen-year-old girl, dis
violet-eyed stranger. My Kallie.*

Divinity's chest tightened. She drew in a deep breath, her fingers resting against the poppet as though for comfort, and considered her options one more time—which, with the magic misfires, had become extremely limited.

Her original plan to bind Kallie and, hopefully, the *loa* to the poppet, chaining both to her will, now seemed impossible without the necessary spells to weave the binding.

Another option would be to potion Kallie up and keep her unconscious until a method to remove the *loa* without harming her could be figured out. *If* such a method existed.

Of course, the option Divinity hated to even entertain— Kallie's death—would be a surefire way to remove the *loa*, since it would refuse to remain in a lifeless body. But right now, without the proper tricks to bind and contain the *loa*, killing Kallie would be senseless. At the moment, for better or worse, the *loa* was at least contained inside her niece's flesh like the ghosts were inside of the nomad.

Divinity stiffened. *Sweet Jesus.* Spinning around, she regarded Layne, a new possibility wheeling through her mind.

The question was, would it work? A Vessel housed the dead and, as far as Divinity understood, the *loa* inside Kallie wasn't one of the *Gédé*, wasn't the spirit of someone who had once lived, then died.

It was an elemental spirit. One born of darkness and strife and cruel intent. A black heart *loa*.

Divinity padded across the room, stopping beside the nomad's bed. She studied his relaxed and sleeping face— a handsome one, for true, with its sharp cheekbones and lips curved for kissing.

He was designed by nature to take spirits in, then send them on. Could he do the same with a living *loa*? Tendrils of hope threaded through Divinity.

She glanced over her shoulder at the poppet lying on the table. She might have to risk a binding spell if the nomad couldn't take in the *loa*. Maybe if she reversed the spell—made it a freedom trick instead of a binding one—it would work.

As soon as de nomad wakes up, we gonna have a nice long chat, us.

Now to look for Jackson while Kallie rested. Divinity went to the front of the store to fetch her cards and shells. She had every hope a reading, a divination, would be accurate, since it wasn't accomplished by magic or spell or potion.

It was accomplished by intuition.

A knowing that glittered liked stars in heart and mind.

Once in the consultation room again, Divinity sat down at her worktable. She consecrated the cockleshells with blood and herbs, lit a candle and offered up prayers to the saints, then went to work.

Boy, where are you?

TWENTY-SIX

EVERYTHING SHE LOVES

Belladonna had been right. Not that Kallie had any intention of telling her so.

The hot shower had sluiced away her exhaustion, easing her taut muscles, and Belladonna's flowery shampoo and conditioner had her hair smelling of jasmine and honey instead of swamp mud.

With a bowl of Cap'n Crunch in her tummy, she felt more alert, and dressed in a pair of black leather shorts and a black tank top that hit her midriff—the only things of hers she'd been able to ferret out of Belladonna's closet—she'd even stretched out on the sofa while running Layne's clothes through the washer and dryer.

But she hadn't slept. Not after watching the news on TV.

HURRICANE EVELYN NOW APPROACHING CATEGORY FOUR WITH WIND SPEEDS OF 130 MPH.

With a new projected trajectory indicating that the storm was headed for the Louisiana coast, Kallie had a niggling suspicion that the wards *were* acting as beacons and/or magnets for the hurricane, guiding it straight to them. She also thought of Jackson howling in the wind, fists clenched and grieving, and the cereal she'd eaten turned to stone in her belly.

She texted him another message, hoping against hope that he would see it, wishing her messages to be a beacon for him, a night-light in the darkness.

HOLD ON WE'RE GONNA FIND U.

Eyes burning, Kallie decided to place a quick call to Lord Augustine's assistant at the Prestige and check on Dallas's condition. Maybe she'd get some good news there.

When Felicity answered, even though their conversation was brief, Kallie received the good news she was hoping for—Dallas's recovery was proceeding at an amazing pace.

"I suspect the magic snafus might be responsible for it," Felicity said, her normally smooth British tones clipped and rushed. "Just as they are for the change in the hurricane wards—I need to start evacuating the guests."

"You've heard about that, then," Kallie said, surprised.

"Indeed," Felicity replied, her voice tinged with amusement. "The Hecatean Alliance has a wide information network. Magic *is* our business, after all. And with its current state of disarray, we've certainly had our hands full here, what with the carnival."

Thinking of all the magic practitioners attending the annual May Madness fest in News Orleans, Kallie could only imagine. *Yikes.*

"Yeah, we've been having problems here too," Kallie said. "My aunt thinks it's due to a hex laid down by Doctor Heron. But . . ."

"But you disagree?" Felicity asked quietly. "What do you believe is causing it?"

"I don't know," Kallie lied, unable to give voice to her suspicions—or at least not to a woman she barely knew. "I hope we find out soon."

"As do I," Felicity murmured. "I'm afraid I really must go, Ms. Rivière. It seems that a contingent of wands, dolls, and chalices have taken over the dealer's room."

Kallie blinked. Yikes again.

"But I'm sure Mr. Brûler would be very happy to hear from you." Giving Kallie Dallas's room number in the med center and a polite farewell, Felicity ended the conversation.

When Kallie heard Dallas's voice on the other end of the line, low and little rough like after a hard night of drinking, she said, "I'm sorry I punched you, Dallas. You were right all along and if you'd—"

"Whoa. Stop right there. Who the hell is this?"

Kallie paused, wondering if there was something Felicity hadn't told her about the root doctor's condition or if this was some aftereffect of whatever pain meds he'd been given; but before she could say anything, he continued speaking.

"'Cause this sure as hell can't be Kallie. The word *sorry* ain't in her vocabulary."

"Goddammit, Dal, I'm trying to apologize here."

"Must be under a spell, then," he teased. "You okay, hun?" he asked, all humor vanishing from his voice. "I heard about what happened, about Doctor Heron, and your goddamned aunt too."

"*Me?*" Kallie protested. "I'm fine. I ain't the one lying in a hospital bed full of transfused blood. How the hell are *you?*"

"Worried," he admitted. "I been watching the news

about the hurricane. They're saying that landfall might be near Houma and might be as soon as thirty-six hours. They're gonna evacuate me to a hospital in Baton Rouge. Just to be on the safe side."

Kallie puzzled over his sudden switch in subject. "I'm glad. I'll breathe a little easier knowing you're farther inland." She paused a beat, then tackled the elephant in the airwaves. "Dal, about what Divinity did—"

"Don't wanna talk about it," he said, cutting her off, voice flat. "Not yet. And I plan to talk to *her* first—whoever she claims to be—when I do."

Kallie couldn't blame Dallas. Divinity had lied to him too. And her lie had slashed a knife across his throat. "I hear you, *cher*," she said softly.

"I know you do, hun."

Kallie told Dallas about the tainted wards, but not about Jackson. Knowing how fond the root doctor was of her wayward cousin, she worried that he'd try to haul himself out of his hospital bed to aid in the search.

In many ways, she, Jackson, and their aunt *were* Dallas's family.

"Y'all keep safe, y'hear?" Dallas said. "If the problem with the wards doesn't get fixed, this blowdown is gonna be a motherfucker."

Kallie's gut knotted. "I know. You keep safe too. I'll talk to you later."

She stared at the ceiling for a long moment after the conversation ended, heart pounding, Felicity's words rolling along the edge of her thoughts like a hurricane warning at the bottom of a newscast.

What do you believe is causing it?

The raucous and nerve-jarring buzz of the dryer

brought Kallie to her feet. Hoping the damned thing hadn't awakened Belladonna, she hurried down the hall. A quick glance into Belladonna's room revealed her friend facedown and still drooling on her pillow. A smile twitched across Kallie's lips.

Stopping in the doorway, she used her cell phone to snap a picture of Drooling Beauty. After checking the screen to make sure she'd captured the moment, Kallie continued on to the dryer.

But as she yanked Layne's warm jeans, socks, and black Inferno T-shirt out of the dryer, her thoughts returned to the storm and her gut feeling—despite Divinity's words to the contrary—that she, or rather the *loa* inside her, *was* somehow responsible for the magic misfires and the hurricane's rapid approach.

What do you believe is causing it?

Me.

Kallie couldn't help but wonder if this was what her mama had tried to unleash when she'd pulled the trigger nine years ago.

Sorry, baby. I ain't got a choice.

The old familiar anger seared the back of Kallie's throat. Bullshit. Bullshit. Bullshit. Gathering up Layne's clothes, pressing their lingering warmth against her chest, Kallie marched for the door, pondering her options.

One: Do nothing. Allow the hurricane to destroy cities, ecosystems, and lives—both human and animal—and devastate the Louisiana coast and economy. Oh, and the best part of this particular option? More hurricanes would follow Evelyn, since the goddamned wards would still be broken and broadcasting a Welcome! signal. The fun would continue nonstop.

Two: Summon Baron Samedi and hand herself over. Let him yank the *loa* out of her body and allow him to do whatever he needed to do to stop the hurricane, restore magic's natural flow, and save everyone and everything she loves—people and land. The cost? Her own life.

Three: Try to remove the *loa* herself. Of course, she would have less than thirty-six hours to accomplish it if she hoped to stop the hurricane. Otherwise, she'd have no choice but to summon the Baron. Provided he didn't find her first.

Kallie mentally exed out option number one, since it wasn't even in the running. *Do nothing. Yeah, right.* But before she did anything, she needed to find Jackson, pull him out of the fire Doctor Heron and a mistaken identity had tossed him into.

As she unlocked and opened the apartment's front door, a sleepy voice asked, "Where you off to, Shug?"

"I thought you were still droo—I mean, sleeping," Kallie replied, swiveling around, her hand still resting on the doorknob. "I'm running Layne's clothes downstairs and checking on his progress. You should go back to bed."

Belladonna eyed her dubiously. "Did you sleep?"

Kallie never even blinked. "Yup. And I plan to come back up to get a little more."

"Oh. Okay." Belladonna flapped a hand at her, dismissing her, then yawned. "Maybe another hour wouldn't hurt."

As Belladonna shuffled back to bed, Kallie quietly left the apartment and headed downstairs to the botanica.

TWENTY-SEVEN

FAMILY NEVER DOES

"How is he?" Kallie asked as she walked into the darkened consultation room, Layne's clothes in her arms.

"Resting," Gabrielle said with a smile. She sat in the rocker beside the bed.

"He took a nasty knock to de head, him," Divinity replied from where she sat at her worktable, her gaze focused on the table's surface. Candlelight flickered against her face, casting shadows. "But his helmet saved him from a broken skull. Concussion, bruises, and road rash from his spill, but boy will be living to ride anudder day."

Kallie exhaled in relief, a smile warming her lips. "Ça c'est bon."

"Mmm-hmm. Dat it is. I always heard dat nomads got t'ick ol' stubborn skulls. Must be true."

Kallie laughed, low in her throat. "Another good thing," she said, then amended, "Except when he's being man-stupid."

"Ain't you supposed to be sleeping?" Divinity asked, voice sharp. "I t'ought we had an understanding, girl."

"I know, I know." Kallie sighed. "But I couldn't

sleep. I kept thinking of Jackson and I was watching the news about the hurricane and . . ." She shrugged. "I just couldn't."

Divinity swiveled around on her stool and eyed Kallie in the dim light, arms folded underneath her breasts. "Mmm-hmmm." Her tone of voice suggested that she intended to do something about that particular little problem.

Kallie promised herself not to drink anything her *tante* offered. Resting the folded pile of clothes on the nightstand, she slowly sat down on the bed beside Layne, careful not to jostle the mattress and wake him.

Layne's face looked peaceful, the lines of pain that had tightened his features gone, his skin no longer chalk-white. He was half turned onto his side, facing the wall, one athletic arm draped along his hip, his long blond dreads trailing across the sheet and over his muscled bare shoulder.

Like a sleeping Greek god or an enchanted Viking warrior awaiting the kiss that would open his eyes. Heat pulsed in Kallie's veins.

Leaning forward, Kallie breathed in the sandalwood and sweet orange scent of Layne's thick, coiled hair. She also smelled sage and myrrh on his skin, mingled with something astringent.

"Comfrey?" she asked, glancing at Divinity. "A health wash?"

"Dat's right, along with salve for his abrasions."

Resisting the urge to press her lips against Layne's, Kallie reluctantly straightened and shifted her attention to her aunt. "Have you had time to do a reading? About Jackson?"

"Dat I did, me. Just finished one." Divinity nodded at the table.

Gabrielle stood. "If you don't need anything else, then I'll be heading to Crowley for this Addie Martin's conclave of local conjurers."

"A meeting?" Kallie asked, glancing from one woman to the next. "What kind of meeting?"

"A meeting to figure out how to fix de mess we all be in," Divinity replied, candle flame highlighting her grim expression. "Before it be too late." She inclined her head at the mambo. "Gabrielle's going in my place, since we got yo' cousin and yo' dreaming nomad to contend with."

Dread and guilt twisted through Kallie. "Yeah," she said, voice low. "We need to talk about that."

"Dat we do. But in due time, child." Divinity looked at Gabrielle. "You got de address and directions?"

"I do, yes." Gabrielle crossed to the doorway, cords whisking with each step, then she paused. "I'm heading home first. I've got my own place, my own people, to worry about. Once I have things squared away, I'll head over to Crowley. I'll let you know what happens, but I'm not coming back—not right away."

"Dat's understood," Divinity said. "I can't t'ank you enough for everyt'ing."

Gabrielle half turned and looked at Divinity, one hand on the threshold. Her face was composed, cold. But Kallie saw fire simmering in her eyes.

"We're not finished, you and me," she said. "We got stuff to work out. *Big* stuff."

Divinity met the mambo's gaze and held it. "True, dat. I ain't going nowhere. When dis nightmare be fixed and done, I'll take care of my debt to you."

With a curt nod, Gabrielle strode from the room and out the botanica's back door. A few moments later, Kallie heard the VW's engine start up.

"How do you plan to make it up to her for stealing her identity?" Kallie asked.

"I'll t'ink o' somet'ing," Divinity replied. Rising to her feet, she went to the rocker Gabrielle had just vacated and plunked down into it. "Go take a look at de reading. Tell me what you see."

"Okay." Easing up from the bed, Kallie padded over to the worktable. Perching on the stool, she studied the cards and shells arranged on top of the table. She smelled fragrant frankincense from the white votive candle placed at the head of the cards, its light dancing across their slick surfaces.

Seven rows of six cards each formed a square that was read from left to right, then from top to bottom, again going down from left to right. She scanned the layout—*so many goddamned spade cards*—several cards in particular capturing her attention.

> King of diamonds: *An older man or a green-eyed man with blond or red hair*
>
> Nine of spades: *Disappointment and failure, sorrow or tears*
>
> Eight of spades: *Controversy, conflict with others or even family members*
>
> King of spades: *Bad luck coming from a man*
>
> Queen of hearts: *A woman with blue or gray or hazel eyes*
>
> Jack of clubs: *A male child or a flirtatious person of either sex*

Jack of hearts: *A female child or a proposal of marriage; a promise*

Ace of spades: *A change of residence or unexpected, rapid events; death*

Queen of spades: *Bad luck coming from a woman*

Ace of hearts: *Home and environment*

An icy blade of fear pierced Kallie's heart when she realized that the ace of spades was nestled against both the queen and king of spades, altering the meanings of the cards.

A woman will die. A man will die.

With the queens of spades and hearts both in play, the doomed woman could either be dark-haired or one with blue, gray, or hazel eyes.

As for the doomed man . . . Kallie's gaze flicked from the king of spades to the king of diamonds. A dark-haired man or maybe a blond or red-haired man with green eyes. Her heart skipped a beat.

Blond. Green eyes. *Layne.*

"You stiffened up," Divinity said from the rocker. "I'm guessing you saw it. De reading be for Jackson, so de man and de woman marked fo' death be known to *him.* But de cards only show possibilities, child. Not certainties."

"I know," Kallie replied. Even so, the chill wouldn't leave her. So many of the women in Jackson's life possessed dark hair—as far as she knew, anyway—Belladonna, Divinity, herself, among them. And now she was determined to keep Layne as far away from Jackson as possible. Just in case.

"But did you notice de pair of jacks?"

Kallie nodded. "Yup." Separately, the cards meant one

thing, and another thing entirely as a pair. In this case, the two jacks indicated the return of what was lost or the return from a journey. "I think we're gonna find him, *Ti-tante*."

"Tell me what else you see."

Kallie's gaze flicked across the cards, piecing together meaning and connections. "The pair of aces indicates trickery from enemies—I think Cash and Kerry fall into that category. Jacks was forced from his home, betrayed, caught in conflict and facing failure and possibly death. And I think one of his captors is a woman."

"Mmm-hmm." Divinity's tone was noncommittal.

"But, except for the queen of hearts, I don't see anything here that we didn't already know." Kallie glanced at her aunt from over her shoulder, frustration kinking her muscles. "I don't see a single thing that points to *where* Jackson is."

"Keep looking. You ain't getting the whole picture."

Kallie sighed, knowing Divinity was right. Exhaustion blurred the sharp edge of her thinking, muffled her intuitive sense. She knew she needed sleep, but had too much on her mind and heart to keep her eyes closed.

Returning her attention to the table, Kallie caught a faint and bitter whiff of vervain from the Green Blood of the Earth potion her aunt had used to consecrate her shells before the reading.

To the right of the square of cards, five cockleshells rested on a straw mat marked with a cross shaped out of powdered egg shells. To the practiced eye, the apparently random positions of the shells revealed a potent pattern brimming with meaning.

Kallie's breath caught in her throat as she read that

pattern: *Strength. South. Fierce animals.* "This is talking about undeserved and unnecessary punishment and judgment from others," she said. "Says Jackson needs to do whatever's necessary to protect himself from it. That he might become someone's scapegoat."

Thinking of Doctor Heron, Kallie's jaw tightened.

"True, dat. It also mentions dat de boy needs to rely on his inner strength, dat if he hopes to survive, he can't allow himself to rest. He be in a fight fo' his life."

"Did the fifth shell land as negative or positive?" Kallie asked.

"Negative," Divinity replied, voice low.

Kallie's heart sank. "So he's in a bad way. Hurt."

"I been saying Psalms o' protection for yo' cousin. Trying to send him all de strength he needs to see him tru."

"Strength," Kallie murmured. "South. Fierce animals."

Sliding off the stool, she returned to the bed and sat down carefully so as not to disturb Layne's healing sleep. She looked at her aunt's gloom-shadowed face. "I think I might have a lead on Jackson. But which do we wanna discuss first—Jackson or what we're going to do with me . . . with the *loa.*"

Divinity's gaze slid past her to Layne, and something Kallie couldn't quite name rippled across her aunt's face—a sharp-planed grief, a stoic resolve, she couldn't be sure. But whatever it was, it left her uneasy.

"Let's start wit' yo' cousin," Divinity said finally. "What's dis lead?"

"You ever heard of a place called Le Nique?"

Divinity's chair rocked as she considered, frowning.

"*Oui*. I heard of Le Nique. It's about forty miles southeast, out toward Chacahoula."

"Southeast," Kallie whispered. *Strength. South. Fierce animals.* She was more sure now than ever. Certainty and hope blossomed within her.

"But de place ain't marked or nothing," Divinity added.

"Because it's hidden, right?" Kallie asked. "A *loup-garou* village."

Divinity tilted her head. "Dat's de rumor. What dis have to do with Jackson?"

Kallie held her aunt's gaze. "A long time ago, Jackson told me that *Nonc* Nicolas was a *loup-garou* and that he himself was a half blood. Told me they used to go to Le Nique all the time." As her aunt's mouth snapped open, an accusation in her eyes, Kallie held up a *Hold on, I ain't finished yet* hand. "He swore me to secrecy. We were little kids and I thought it was just a game. He never mentioned it again and I forgot all about it."

Divinity grunted, then looked away. The rocker moved faster, the runners creaking in a soothing rhythm against the hardwood. After a moment, she asked, "What brought up de memory now?"

"Baron Samedi. At the grave, he told me he smelled dogs and *loups-garous*."

"I wonder if dat's why Nicolas and Lucia divorced," Divinity mused, lifting her eyes to Kallie's. "I only met Nicolas a few times. *Beaucoup* earthy, dat man, wild and strong. Good-looking in a rugged way. Quiet and watchful. But de man loved to laugh. And he loved my sister, him." After a moment, she murmured, "*Loup-garou*. Coulda been, I suppose. Never met one."

Kallie stared at her aunt, caught off guard. She'd been positive that Divinity had been hiding the truth about Jackson the same way she'd hidden the truth from Kallie about her own past.

"*. . . a big wrong's been done to you.*"

Kallie had expected Divinity to flap an annoyed hand at her and snipe something along the lines of *Of course yo' cousin's a werewolf. What's de matter wit' you? You need to pay mo' attention to t'ings, girl.*

"Seriously? You didn't know?"

"Nope. Like I said, I only met Nicolas a few times."

"So it's possible Jackson told me the honest-to-God truth that night."

"What does yo' gut tell you?"

Kallie trailed a hand through her drying hair. Thought of two little kids lying in the grass on a sultry summer night, sharing secrets. "That he was telling the truth."

Which created an even greater mystery. Why had he never mentioned it again? And though Kallie was deeply grateful that they had, how had the *loups-garous* found and rescued him?

Another thought occurred to her, a dark and disconcerting possibility.

What if she was making a huge-ass mistake in assuming the *loups-garous* meant Jackson well?

"I need to find him," Kallie said, curling her hands into fists, stretching the skin taut over her knuckles. "I need to get back out there." But she kept other words unvoiced for fear that speaking them aloud would make them come true: *Before it's too late.*

Divinity sighed and rose to her feet. "I know. I keep t'inking of de boy too. I keep wondering what dis blowdown will trigger in him if we don't fix de wards before Evelyn reaches us."

"I've been thinking of that too," Kallie admitted softly.

Divinity went to her worktable. Grabbed the teakettle. "You want some tea? Me, I need a cup."

"Sure," Kallie lied, figuring refusal would only make her aunt resort to less obvious methods of sleep-trickery. "How come you only met *Nonc* Nicolas a few times? My folks used to take me to their place in Houma all the time, and Jackson and his sisters used to visit us all the time too. Until we moved to goddamned Shreveport."

And less than a year later, two gunshots and a whispered apology changed Kallie's life forever. And ended her father's.

Divinity filled the kettle in silence, then set it on one of the burners of the two-burner cooktop beside the table. She turned around to face Kallie, her back against the table, her arms crossed loosely over her chest. The dim lighting and cobwebby shadows made her face unreadable.

"Y'know," Kallie said, "I didn't even know I had another aunt until you arrived at the hospital in Shreveport to take me home. That was the first time I'd heard of you."

"I know. I planned it dat way."

"I hope to hell you don't think that statement alone is going to cut it."

A smile quirked at the corners of Divinity's mouth. "I don't."

"Do I have to pull the info out of you word by goddamned word?" Kallie growled. "What did you *mean* by that?"

"I had a falling-out a long time ago with my sisters, and no, de reason for dat ain't none o' yo' business. Suffice it to say dat your mama and *Tante* Lucia weren't talking to me no more. Course, to my mind, *I* wasn't talking to *dem*. But even so, I kept up with what was going on in deir lives. And yours—you kids, dat is. And dat's when I learned what yo' mama had done."

"How did you find out?"

Divinity shook her head, a familiar stubborn glint in her eyes—eyes that were more green than hazel in the dim light. "Dat be a story for anudder day, girl."

A muscle twitched in Kallie's jaw as she glared at her aunt. *Pick your battles. This one can wait.* "Fine," she grated. "Then what?"

Divinity shrugged. "Den I stole Gabrielle's identity and made a new life for myself because I knew de day would be coming when you would need me—a mysterious stranger with a false name who could hide you from dem dat would finish what yo' mama started."

A chill traced the length of Kallie's spine. "You saying Mama didn't act alone?"

"Mm-hmm. Dat's what I be saying."

"But who—"

"Now, dat I don't know, hun. I never did find out who Sophie had been working with, but I know for true dat she had help. I just wish I knew who. And why."

"So you think they're still looking for me—Mama's partners?"

Divinity snorted. "*Course* dey be looking for you. Dey go to all dat trouble to yank out yo' soul and stuff a *loa* inside? What you t'ink, girl?" She glanced at the kettle. "Ah, de water's hot."

Kallie waited while Divinity busied herself with pouring the hot water into mugs and steeping the tea. This newest bit of information stunned her. She'd always believed her mother had acted alone for reasons beyond her understanding. To learn that everything—her father's murder, her being shot, the soul-*loa* transfer—had been coolly planned and deliberate and a group effort left her feeling gutted, a fish twisting on a hook of brutal and inexplicable truth.

Dread coiled ever tighter in Kallie's chest as she listened to the rain thrumming against the roof in a hard, steady patter, heard gusts of wind hitting the windows.

The goddamned clock is counting down.

Divinity returned to the bed and handed Kallie a warm mug fragrant with strong black tea flavored with blueberries and what smelled like bergamot. "Drink all o' dat," she commanded.

"Thanks," Kallie said. She waited until her aunt had settled into the rocker, her own mug in hand, then widened her eyes and said, "Shit! I don't think I locked the back door when I came down. I'll go and—"

"No you won't, you," Divinity interrupted. "I'll take care of it. You just drink yo' tea." Setting her own mug on the bedside table beside the pads of gauze, Divinity rose to her feet, then strode from the room.

Kallie stood and quickly switched mugs, replacing her aunt's with her own. Another nap wouldn't hurt her, she thought, easing back down onto the bed and lifting the mug to her lips just as Divinity returned. Kallie sipped at the tea, feeling its warmth flow from her belly and into her bloodstream.

"De door was locked," Divinity said, settling into the rocker once more. "Yo' mind might be sleep-deprived, but yo' instincts still be working at least." She picked up her mug and took a swallow of tea.

"I was thinking I might try to talk to the *loa*," Kallie said, looking at her aunt from over the rim of her mug. "See if I can reason with her. I honestly have nothing to lose by trying."

Divinity stared at her, mug frozen in the air. "*Her?*" she questioned.

"Yeah, I've seen her in my mind's eye." *And reflected in the Baron's sunglasses*, but Kallie decided to keep that to herself. "Long cinnamon curls and café-au-lait skin, wearing a *vévé* that shows a heart bound in chains made of pale bones and surrounded by black *X*'s."

Divinity lowered her mug. "You sure, girl?"

"Positive. I saw her when I died. I think she was a horse then, a *talking* horse, an obnoxious one, actually, but that's all fuzzy and . . ." Suddenly light-headed, Kallie's words slowed to a stop as she lost her train of thought. Drowsiness swept over her in a heavy tide, weighing down her eyelids and blurring her thoughts.

"Goddammit," she whispered, struggling to focus on her aunt. "You tricked me."

"You tricked yo'self, child." Divinity was standing in front of her. She gently plucked the mug from Kallie's fingers and placed it on the bedside table. "You coulda kept de mug I gave you, but I knew you wouldn't. Headstrong, dat's you."

"I can't sleep . . . Jackson . . ."

"Dere's nothing you can do for him right now. Not with de shape you be in. You need rest and strength for what lies ahead. We both do. So curl up against yo' nomad and close yo' eyes."

"Goddammit," Kallie repeated. Hands guided her head down to the pillow. Lifted her legs onto the bed. "No . . ."

"Hush now and sleep."

As if by instinct, Kallie rolled over and pressed herself against Layne's warm body, drew herself in tight against his lean-muscled length. She tried to keep her eyes open, but failed, her eyelids heavy as steel. Her eyes closed.

As she slid into a velvet-soft darkness full of fireflies, she heard the wind rattling like a bad thief at the windows. Heard her aunt whispering, "Rest, *chère*. I'm gonna see you and Jackson tru dis nightmare. I ain't giving up on either of you. Family never does."

Sleep enfolded Kallie, and she surrendered.

TWENTY-EIGHT

BOUND TO ONE FORM

Slipping an arm behind the half blood's neck—*no, not just a half blood, this was Jackson, her long-lost nephew*—Angélique lifted his head. Heat radiated from his body in intense waves, a dangerous, Change-wrought heat that she knew would eventually result in either transformation or death.

But with First Change coming so late, the odds favored death.

"Fight," Angélique wished her nephew, then she repeated the words René had whispered earlier, "*Lâche pas.*"

She lifted the uncorked blue glass bottle containing the pain potion from the table's edge. The bitter scent of vervain prickled against her nostrils as she tipped the bottle against Jackson's lips. "Here, drink," she coaxed. "C'mon, Jackson."

But, lost to fever dreams and pain, eyes closed, he turned his face away from the bottle's cool touch and the temporary relief it would give him.

"Hold on, hun." Merlin cupped Jackson's burning face between his large hands and gently centered it again.

Then he pushed his thumb against the young man's chin to open his mouth. "I'd just upend the bottle if I was you," he said.

Liking her husband's advice, Angélique did just that. Tilting the bottle, she carefully poured the honey-sweetened liquid down her nephew's throat.

Jackson coughed, then swallowed convulsively, taking the potion. Angélique lowered his head back down onto the table, then eased her arm free as her husband cleaned dribbled potion from Jackson's face with a practiced swipe of his washrag.

Having managed to wrestle off Jackson's wet and muddy jeans—leaving him in navy blue boxer-briefs—Merlin resumed cleaning the dozens of cuts sliced into her nephew's limbs and torso, applying an antiseptic tincture containing cinnamon bark, clove oil, sweet clover, and myrrh, the pungent spicy-sweet odor filling the room.

"What the hell is taking René so long?"

"My guess would be that Jan and Ambrose went hunting or Outside to restock supplies, and he's waiting for them to get back," Angélique replied with a shrug. "They'll get here when they get here."

"It's a shame that the mind-to-mind thing y'all have doesn't work long-distance."

"A damned shame," Angélique agreed. She studied Jackson's still face, the bright roses of fever blooming on his cheeks, the muscles twitching and rippling beneath his skin. A heaviness settled like ash in her heart as she remembered the honey-eyed little boy so excited about his new duties as a big brother.

Why did Lucia bind her son to only one form? And why did that binding fail now?

"Why don't you let me finish up here while you go check on the twins and Moss?" Angélique asked.

Merlin never even looked up from his work. "You go, woman. Ain't nothing here I can't handle."

Feeling uneasy, Angélique shook her head. "You're wrong," she said softly. "You've never dealt with a First Change before, let alone a half blood's First Change, and one so late to boot. You've got no idea how careful you need to be."

Merlin looked at her then, indignation in his bicolored brown and blue eyes. "I'm *always* careful with my patients. And you know that I've treated *loups-garous* before, so—"

Angélique leaned across the examination table and pressed her fingers against her husband's lips, effectively closing them. "Of *him, cher.* You need to be careful of *him* so that he doesn't hurt *you.*"

Merlin's gaze dropped to the unconscious young man lying between them, then returned to Angélique, comprehension lighting his eyes. His warm lips moved against her fingers. "Oh."

Angélique felt a smile quirk up one corner of her mouth. "Yup. Oh." Sliding her fingers away from her husband's lips, she turned her palm up and nodded at the washrag he held. "Let me do this, and you tend to the munchkins, you. Make sure that Moss has survived."

Merlin snorted. "Trust me, Moss is egging them on. He's nothing but an overgrown cub, that one."

"For true." Angélique inclined her head at her waiting palm. Arched an eyebrow.

With a sigh, Merlin shook his head, a few of the beads at the ends of his short, thick braids clicking together with the movement, then reluctantly piled the washcloth in her hand. "You be careful too, hear?"

"I will," she promised him.

With a wink, Merlin turned and walked out of the room. As he headed into the kitchen, Angélique heard him calling, "Where's my babies? Where's my chubby little road riders? I don't see them. Did you gobble them up with the scrambled eggs, Moss?"

"Yup," Moss replied cheerfully. "And they was tasty, them."

"Here, Papa, here!" Ember and Chance shrieked happily in unison. "Papa!"

Smiling, Angélique bent to her task. By the time she'd finished cleaning Jackson's many wounds, a deep anger burned in her gut. Whoever had done this to him had intended, had *planned*, for him to suffer, long and slow and hard, his blood seeping into the earth.

And that blood loss worried her. Jackson would need every ounce of strength if he was to have any chance of surviving what she soon would no longer be able to stop with potions and drugs.

With the twins cleaned up and herded, giggling and shouting, into the playroom where Moss was keeping them company, Merlin strode into the room, a bowl of breakfast leftovers in one hand, a bowl of water in the other, and placed them in front of the watchful Siberian husky who lay at the examination table's head, her muzzle resting on her paws. Her nose twitched as she breathed in the tasty odors.

"Eat up," Merlin encouraged. "I have a feeling you've earned this and more."

The dog vaulted to her feet, but it wasn't the food that

held her attention. A low warning growl rumbled from her throat—an unnecessary warning, since Angélique had heard too.

René and the Alphas had *finally* arrived.

"They're here," she told Merlin. Trusting her keen senses, he just nodded.

"Sit, girl," Merlin said, snapping his fingers at the Siberian husky. "These are folks we're expecting."

The growling stopped, but the dog remained on alert. Ears pricked forward.

"Definitely got a mind of her own," Merlin said, voice amused.

"Hmm. So do you. Seems like I was right about that Siberian husky bloodline."

"Hush, woman."

Angélique snorted. "Like that's ever going to happen."

Hearing the door creak open in the living room, then snick shut again, Angélique counted three sets of quiet footsteps as René and the Alphas—her sister and brother-in-law—crossed to the back room in urgent strides.

"You sure it's him, *traiteur?*" Ambrose Bonaparte asked as he entered the room, his whiskey-smooth voice pitched low and tight.

"After all this time?" January added, following on his heels, and glancing at her sister with vivid jade-green eyes. Her glossy, snow-white hair had been twisted into a French plait that hung with precision between her shoulder blades.

"Positive," Angélique replied. "Take a look yourself." She stepped back from the table.

Ambrose stepped up beside Jackson in one long-legged stride, his six-foot frame dressed in rain-spattered black jeans and a faded blue workshirt whose rolled-up sleeves revealed sun-browned and muscle-corded arms. His intent amber eyes swept his nephew from head to foot. Studied the cuts. Lingered on the tattoo inked into his arm.

"*Mon Dieu*," Ambrose breathed, raking a hand through his shoulder-length chestnut waves. "It *is* him." Old grief shadowed his face. "He looks so much like Nicolas . . ."

"He was conscious for a little bit," Angélique said. "But he didn't know me."

"How could he?" January asked. "He was little more than a toddler the last time Nicolas brought him here." She joined Ambrose at the table. Their mingled scents—juniper, ripe apples, and damp cotton—washed over Angélique.

René lingered in the doorway, one hand touching the threshold, as if uncertain whether he should stay or not. Or, Angélique reflected, if he *wanted* to. She felt a twinge of understanding and sympathy. *He knows what's coming.*

"Moss is in the playroom with the twins," she said. "He might need a hand."

A smile brushed René's lips, but he shook his head, refusing the out she offered him, pretty much as Angélique had figured he would. He'd found Jackson and felt responsible for him.

Decision made, René leaned his shoulder against the threshold and folded his arms over his hard-muscled chest.

A muscle flexed in Ambrose's jaw. "René told me where and how Jackson was found. Do you know what was done to him?"

"It looks like someone went to a lot of trouble to make

him a true zombie," Merlin replied. "Ain't exactly sure why the trick failed, but we're gonna fix him with an uncrossing to make sure no trace of the hex remains."

"*Before* you send him to the cage," Angélique added quietly, "he needs all the help he can get."

Ambrose lifted his eyes to hers, looked at her from beneath his dark lashes. His nostrils flared. "That's wise," he said. "But I suggest you hurry. Your potions ain't gonna hold him long. See how he's twitching? He reeks of impending Change."

Angélique didn't need to look. She knew. Ambrose was right—time was running out and they needed to get Jackson over to the solid stone cottage they called the cage and shackle him in steel chains before it was too late.

Turning to her husband, Angélique instructed him to prepare an uncrossing bath while she readied her spell. Merlin nodded, then silently went to his worktable and set to work with his mortar and pestle. Just as Angélique started for her own worktable, her sister spoke.

"He's too old. He'll never survive. We should spare him the agony."

Angélique froze, not sure she'd heard right, then hoping she hadn't. Slowly, she swiveled back around. "You don't mean that. You *can't*. He deserves the chance."

"Thanks to his mother's binding, Jackson would've been better off if Gaspard had taken him along with the rest of his family." An odd blend of despair and icy fury washed across January's pale face. "He's finally returned to us and we're going to lose him again, just as quickly. Lucia murdered her own son."

"That remains to be seen," Ambrose growled. "Your sister's right—the boy deserves the chance his mama stole from him. No one's giving him the coup de grâce unless he fails. No one."

As Ambrose locked into a stare-down with his wife—amber eyes versus jade—Angélique felt the Alpha's powerful aura—primal and commanding and rooted in the deep, dark earth—sweep over her like an invisible wave. Tension stretched between the Alphas, thickened like cold molasses.

January finally ended it when she looked away. "A chance he'll have, then." Her cold gaze landed on Angélique. "Where is it?"

Angélique frowned. "Where's what?"

"The binding his mother marked him with."

"I didn't notice anything . . ."

January leaned over Jackson, sliding her hands over his nearly nude body, her fingertips searching for the scars that had chained him into one form and denied him the other. Ambrose's long, callused fingers searched alongside his wife's until he tugged down the waistband of Jackson's boxer-briefs and revealed a tiny series of crisscrossing scars on his left hip.

Angélique joined them in studying the age-whitened scars—a seemingly random arrangement that wasn't, but nothing that Jackson would've ever realized carried meaning beyond an old injury he no longer remembered.

Angélique noticed that her sister's thick, black claws now curved from the tips of her fingers, and before she could even blink, January slashed her claws across the scars, severing their pattern. Dark blood welled up on Jackson's skin.

"Great Mother," Angélique muttered, glaring at her sister. "I don't think that was necessary. He's been cut more than enough already and lost more blood than he can afford. Obviously, the binding no longer works."

"Now it won't for true," January replied unapologetically.

Angélique's pulse sped through her veins when Jackson's eyes flickered open and he looked around, his dilated honey-colored eyes glassy. He squinted against the light, then his attention locked onto Ambrose, expression puzzled. After a moment, his face smoothed, and he whispered, "Hey, *Nonc. Ça va bien? Comment les zaricos?*"

TWENTY-NINE

STRENGTH, SOUTH, FIERCE ANIMALS

Cielo let out a happy but anxious string of *whoo-whoo*s.

Daddy!

Still here, girl.

But given the familiar face above him, Jackson was pretty sure he was still dreaming, caught up in the fever's blistering and thought-warping heat, pain chewing on his bones with sharp little rat teeth.

For a moment, he thought he was back in the hurricane-rocked pickup, Jeanette clutched against his chest, his papa yanking open the door and reaching for Mama — and a different kind of pain pierced his heart.

No, ain't going there. No.

Then a rusty cog of a memory slipped into place and an image rolled through his mind: amber eyes. Chestnut hair falling in waves to his broad shoulders. The sharp smell of juniper and ashes. Teeth flashing white in a quick grin. Strong hands hoisting him into the air. Tossing him up into the sky.

"Ah, there he is, *mon neveu préféré. Comment les zaricos, eh?*"

"*Les zaricos est salés, Nonc* Ambro. I wanna keep flying. Throw me again!"

The memory faded and Jackson closed his eyes again, tasted honey and bitter herbs on his tongue and at the back of his throat, felt himself drifting above the fire while distant teeth nibbled on his muscles and bones.

Ice-cold fingers brushed against his forehead and Jackson sucked in a breath, inhaling the earthy and familiar scents of juniper and ashes, ripe apples and cinnamon. A husky voice—one from long-ago dreams—said, "*Les zaricos est salés, cher.* Jackson. Can you hear me?"

Jackson forced his eyes open again, squinting against the light. His uncle Ambrose still stood over him. Persistent dream, this. But—no harm in double-checking. "You real?" he croaked.

A sad smile brushed Ambrose's lips instead of the joyous grin that Jackson remembered. "*Oui*, boy, I'm real. Your *tante* January is here, so is *Tante* Angélique. You finally found your way home."

"Home?" Jackson looked past his uncle to the woman with the ivory hair standing beside him in a tight purple T-shirt over jeans. Remembered her mesmerizing eyes, the lullabies she would sing in Cajun. Remembered her white fur and fast paws. *Tante* January.

"I'm in Le Nique?" he whispered, feeling like he'd slipped in time. He saw shelves behind his uncle, stocked with jars and bottles of potions, powders, and salves like at his *tante*'s botanica, then realized he lay on a sheet-draped and padded examination table.

"Yes," a woman's voice said. "René and the others followed your dog and found you where you'd been buried. Do you remember any of that?"

"Cielo . . ." Jackson began, alarmed. A cold, wet nose nuzzled his hand, reassuring him.

Daddy.

"That her name?" the woman said. "She's fine. She's been fed and watered and she's refused to leave your side."

"Good girl, you," Jackson murmured, giving his fingers to Cielo's warm tongue. He felt himself falling toward the bonfire raging just beneath him. And shook himself.

Stay awake. You need to get a grip and figure out what's going on.

"Do you remember what happened to you?" the woman asked again.

Images flashed behind Jackson's eyes, stabbed at his thoughts—a desperate and brutal fight, an oily potion, a knife slicing into him, shovels, dirt. No air and bad memories and a woman's voice—all silver sea tones.

Might be too late for this little chien de maison.

Lâche pas, lâche pas.

"Musta pissed someone off royal, me," Jackson whispered. "Zombie-hex and a fucking grave."

"The hex didn't take, near as we can tell," the woman said. "But we plan to follow up with a cleansing, make sure you're uncrossed for true."

"C'est ça bon. Merci," Jackson rasped. Despite the potion he still tasted on his tongue, pain throbbed at his temples. Fire smoldered beneath his skin.

"Here's some water."

Jackson felt an arm slide beneath his shoulders and ease him up so he could drink from the glass someone pressed against his lips. He drank the cold water down in long, grateful gulps, icing his aching throat and cooling—for a moment—the fevered heat behind his eyes. When he finished the water, he was laid down again.

"Better?" the woman asked.

Jackson turned his head, following the sound of her voice to the other side of the table. A woman with warm, emerald-green eyes met his gaze. Her long hair was tied back, but a single auburn ringlet had escaped to frame her pretty face. He didn't recognize her at first, not until her lips curved into an encouraging smile. She'd been a freckle-faced teen when he'd last seen her—a lifetime ago.

"*Tante* Ange," he breathed.

She nodded, her smile widening, only to fade as concern flickered in her eyes. "Do you know what's happening to you? What comes next?"

Fear iced Jackson's spine. "'Next'? I thought you said the hex didn't take."

"It didn't," Angélique assured him. "That's not why you're hurting, not why you're fevered. Did your papa ever talk to you about your First Change?"

Jackson stared at her. "First Change?" he repeated, pulse racing through his veins. "Just that I ain't . . ."

The words turned to ash in Jackson's throat as the bonfire blaze snapped up from below and engulfed him. Pain wrenched at him as his muscles spasmed. His eyes snapped shut. Hands as cold as Arctic icebergs grasped his shoulders, pinned him down. His body twitched and thrummed—a live wire.

The spasm ended as abruptly as it had begun and Jackson gasped in relief. But the freezing hands remained on his shoulders, heavy as steel.

"We're running out of time," he heard his uncle say, voice wire-tight. "Jackson, can you hear me, boy?"

Light needled Jackson's eyes as he forced them open and met Ambrose's grim gaze. Realized the hands holding him belonged to his uncle. "*Oui, Nonc.*"

"*Bon.* Then I need you to listen close," Ambrose said. "I don't know what-all you remember, but you need to understand what's happening to you. Your papa was a *loup-garou* and you're a half blood. And you're going through your First Change."

Jackson's heart pounded wildly in his chest. "Change? No. I was told that some half bloods *never* Change and that I was one of those."

January stirred beside Ambrose. "Who told you that?" she asked. "Your mama? She lied to you, Jackson—"

"That doesn't matter," Ambrose cut in, slanting a dark look at his wife. "Not now. This ain't the time."

January shook her head, but said nothing more, her lips compressing into a thin, bitter line.

Fury shook Jackson. He aimed his heated gaze at his snowy-haired but youthful *tante.* "You ain't got no business saying my mother lied to me or to anyone else," he said, voice strained. "No business. None."

January met his furious regard, a wolfish and powerful light gleaming in her jade eyes, but no regret. Her lips parted, but before she could say anything, Ambrose spoke, his words sliding like a butter knife between them.

"Nicolas was just as responsible as Lucia in what happened to you and your sisters."

Jackson's heart clenched. He remembered Jeanette snuggled in his arms, Junalee's smile. Tried not to think of how they'd looked in the end. "My sisters?" He shifted his attention from January to his uncle. "No disrespect, *Nonc,* but what the hell are you talking about?"

Releasing Jackson's shoulders, Ambrose said, "Your papa never told your mama what a half blood faces during First Change until after Junalee had been born." He paused, trailing a long-fingered hand through his hair, his expression pensive. "I don't know whether it just never occurred to Nicolas that Lucia might want to know *before* they had kids or if he deliberately 'forgot' to tell her. He never told me."

Jackson felt sick as he remembered the late-night arguments between his folks when they thought the kids were sleeping. *Over us. The fights were over us.*

"In any case," Ambrose said, "your mama was so worried about what might happen to y'all during First Change that, after she learned the truth, she used her hoodoo to bind all you kids to one form—your human one. And she forbade your papa to ever bring you here again." He shook his head. "Nicolas was hurt and furious."

Jackson looked away from his uncle and stared at the timbered ceiling. He didn't want to believe what he was hearing, didn't want to believe that his mother *had* lied to him and buried a part of who he was.

Maybe if she'd lived, she woulda told me when I was older, allowed me to choose for myself . . .

"What happens during First Change?" Jackson asked from a throat gone tight. "I don't remember Papa ever having trouble during his Changes."

"It's different for half bloods," Ambrose admitted, voice low. "Far more difficult and dangerous. You'll be bound to the cycle of the moon, when we're not. If your human nature is too entrenched, you won't be able to accept the wolf. Your papa tried to help you by making sure you knew that the wolf was a natural part of who you are."

Until Mama changed all that and Papa stormed from

the house, his hands clenched into white-knuckled fists, hurt and fury glinting in his eyes.

Ain't gonna forgive you for dis, Lucia. Dey be my kids too. You t'ink I wouldn't guide dem tru de Change? Keep dem safe? Dis ain't done, woman. Not by a long shot.

Papa never lived in the house again.

"If your First Change is successful," Angélique told Jackson in a gentle voice, "then you'll Change during full moons—just like in the movies—but you won't be a full wolf, you'll be a hybrid wolf-man—*loup-homme*— with fangs and claws, heightened senses and strength, and the inherent need to run and hunt. But your heightened senses and strength will remain with you always, during all phases of the moon."

Jackson lowered his gaze from the ceiling and looked at Angélique. He felt his potion-distanced pain starting to return. "And what happens if my First Change is unsuccessful?"

"You could end up mindless and stuck in a monstrous wolf-man form," she replied, sympathy glinting in the green depths of her eyes. "Or lost to madness in two forms, or dead."

Jackson nodded, mouth almost too dry for speech. "Well, then. Need to make damned sure I succeed, me."

Angélique smiled, but looked away for just a split second, and he realized that she hadn't told him everything.

"Hey," Jackson said, "I need to know every—" Another spasm bit into his muscles. His teeth sliced into his lower lip and the copper-penny taste of blood trickled into his mouth. Pain snaked out from its hiding place and sank sharp teeth into him everywhere.

Angélique whispered into his ear as the spasm passed.

"All you need to know is this: Be a wolf, Jackson. Don't let your humanity Change you into a monster. Or end your life." Something pressed against his lips—the cool mouth of a glass bottle. "Drink."

Jackson did as she asked, gulping down another potion of thick honey and bitter herbs, then closed his eyes again, trying to make sense of everything he'd just been told. Trying to understand what he was facing, trying to prepare for it, but pain kept dashing his thoughts to pieces against a wicked reef.

"I've got his bath ready," a man said, a voice Jackson didn't recognize.

He opened his eyes and saw a black guy, his hair twisted into a bunch of short braids poking out in all directions and angles around his skull, dressed in jeans and a deep-blue T-shirt. He was standing beside the table with a large basin of steaming water in his hands.

Nomad, Jackson realized when he saw the little squirrel tat inked beneath his right eye. Then he noticed the man's eyes. One dark brown and one deepest blue. "Never seen that in a person before," he marveled, then clarified, "Your eyes. Is it a *loup-garou* trait?"

"Wouldn't know, since I'm human," the man said with a quick smile. "But I got a feeling they all *wish* it was a *loup-garou* trait."

Someone snorted.

"Be quick, Merlin," Ambrose growled. "We need to get Jackson to the cage *tout de suite*."

Before Jackson could question his uncle about what he meant by "the cage," he felt himself drifting away on a tide of fever and potion and distant pain, and his eyes fluttered shut.

Words from one of his favorite Keats poems curled through his mind, as though whispered into his ear by an older brother who'd shared the same grief, guiding him through the shoals of darkness he'd washed up against following Gaspard.

Darkling I listen; and, for many a time / I have been half in love with easeful Death / Call'd him soft names in many a musèd rhyme, / To take into the air my quiet breath; / Now more than ever seems it rich to die, / To cease upon the midnight with no pain . . .

To cease upon the midnight with no pain.

He'd *never* wanted to cease, he'd always been in love with life and laughter. But not to feel—that had been another matter. Not to remember the weight of a sister in his arms or the sight of her empty and staring eyes . . .

No. Oh, hell no. You can't afford to sleep, to drift. To peel scabs off half-healed wounds. You need to focus so you can survive what's coming. Change. First Change.

Jackson grabbed onto that thought and reeled himself up from the dark and soothing herb-soaked depths like a free diver following a weighted line to the ocean's light-glimmering surface. He forced his eyes open.

Merlin bent over him, a look of intense concentration on his face—as if praying—as he dipped a cloth into the steaming water and wrung it out. Jackson breathed in the odors of myrrh and minty hyssop and warm milk.

Jackson tried to lever himself up on his elbows. Merlin glanced at him, surprised, wet cloth in hand. "Help me up—*s'il vous plaît*," he said. "I need to take part in whatever's going on—all of it—since it's my life."

Merlin didn't even hesitate. He dropped the cloth back into the basin of water, then eased Jackson up into a sitting position with strong but wet hands. "Damn straight, man. It *is* your life."

The room spun and black spots peppered Jackson's vision, and for a moment, he thought he was going to pass out; but the nomad supported him with one hand between his shoulder blades, the other gripping his shoulder until the room steadied.

"*C'est ça bon*," Jackson murmured, gripping the table's edges for balance. He met Merlin's bicolored eyes. "Thanks."

"We got no time to waste," Ambrose reminded them. "Get this done."

"*Mais oui, Premier*," Angélique said in a respectful tone.

With a quick smile, the nomad wrung the cloth out again. "Close your eyes and try to envision a column of white light pouring in through the top of your skull and flowing like blood throughout your body, okay?"

Nodding, Jackson closed his eyes and did just that—or tried to, anyway. The potion's drugs and the fever kept chipping away at his concentration like chisels into ice.

He felt a wet cloth on his skin, trailing ice along his chest, his back, his limbs. Smelled smoky incense. Heard Angélique's soft voice chanting, "Spirits of the wilderness, sacred mother, fair and true, I appeal to you. Jackson Bonaparte has been crossed by evil and desires to be free of this negative and attacking energy . . ."

"Incoming," Merlin whispered into his ear.

Jackson opened his eyes, trying to puzzle out that cryptic comment, when the nomad upended the basin over his head and ended his speculation. Jackson gasped as the potioned and fragrant water cascaded over him—fever-morphed into an icy waterfall—streaming down his face, chest, and back. Soaking his hair. He shivered convulsively, his skin goosebumping, and pushed his wet hair back from his face.

Cielo watched him, tongue lolling, from where she sat beside the table, looking somehow amused.

Get-in-the-tub time, Daddy.

Angélique stepped past Merlin, a lit white candle in one hand—which she passed to the nomad—so she could anoint Jackson on the forehead, throat, heart, just above the belly button, and then, as he shifted uncomfortably beneath her light touch, on the crotch of his boxer-briefs with oil that smelled of sandalwood and patchouli and myrrh.

"Protection comes to you this day, negativity and evil no longer hold sway," Angélique chanted. Pacing back a step, she handed Merlin the bottle of oil and took back the candle. "So be it," she proclaimed, finishing her trick.

Jackson felt a strange energy pogo through the room like a hyperactive child freebasing sugar, then Cielo disappeared from view. Vanished. Jackson blinked. He was pretty sure either the fever or the drugs or both were fucking with his perceptions again, since Siberian huskies didn't possess cloaking devices.

"Did y'all see that?" Angélique said, her words slow and stunned and shaken. "The dog just went invisible."

Oh, she's gonna like that, Jackson reckoned. A soft *whoo* confirmed his opinion.

Voices clamored that they had, indeed, seen the dog go invisible, and what the hell just happened? And what had been that weird-ass energy that had bounced through the room just prior to the dog's vanishing?

Jackson closed his eyes, listening, as a burning tide of fever and reawakening pain swept over him. He swayed and his fingers tightened their grip on the edges of the table. The muscles in his right forearm spasmed, then quieted.

"We'll figure it out later." Ambrose's voice cut through all the perplexed and anxious chatter. "It's time to go. I'll carry Jackson."

"No." Jackson opened his eyes. "I'll walk. I might need some support," he admitted. "But I'm going on my own two feet. Ain't being carried, me."

Ambrose nodded, and Jackson could see that his response had pleased him. "*C'est bien.* We'll walk together."

Once Jackson had swung his legs around and slid off the table to the floor, Ambrose's steel-fingered hand locked around his biceps and kept him on his feet when his legs wobbled beneath him. Angélique draped a blanket over him for the walk outside.

With Angélique on one side and Ambrose on the other, Jackson walked slowly—more like tottered, he thought grimly—to the door, his muscles protesting each step. A tall, powerfully built man with tawny hair and beard stepped aside.

"*Bonne chance,*" he said.

Recognizing his voice, Jackson stopped. "René, right? I remember you. At the grave and in the pirogue. '*Lâche pas,*'" he said. "*Merci beaucoup.*"

René inclined his head, brown eyes glinting with an emotion Jackson couldn't name, then said, "And it still holds true, you. *Lâche pas.*"

Once outside, the small party—Jackson, Ambrose,

January, and Angélique—followed a well-trod dirt path past other swamp cottages and *cabanes* dripping with rain beneath a canopy of oaks and cypress. The air smelled of wet leaves, moss, and the bayou stretching beyond the houses and serving as their driveways.

Jackson sensed more than saw people watching from their windows and on their porches. The quiet was so pro-found—except for cicada buzz and bird trills—he heard only their own quiet footfalls. A cold dread nestled in his guts.

At the path's end, he saw a small stone cottage with narrow slits for windows near its roofline. *Must be the cage.* His dread deepened.

"It's tradition to have someone with you during First Change," Angélique said. "Someone to comfort and encourage and guide."

"Under normal circumstances, *oui*," January replied. "But not with such a late First Change . . . if he becomes a monster, a mindless wolf-man. Too dangerous."

Jackson stiffened at his *tante*'s words: *such a late First Change.* Did his age make a difference in his survival—his human nature too deeply rooted?

"He's my brother's son. *Mon neveu préféré.* I'll stay with him. See him through."

"Ambrose, no . . ." January sighed.

Sudden dizziness spun Jackson and he stumbled. His uncle kept a tight grip on him. "No shame if you don't have the strength to walk any farther, boy," he murmured.

"I'll make it," Jackson replied, feeling like he was com-ing unmoored and about to drift away again, a piece of flotsam on a dark tide.

He thought of Keats, dying of consumption at

twenty-five, trapped in a cramped little room on the Spanish Steps, listening to the sounds of life just outside his window and wanting to get up and walk out—yearning for it, but unable to. He'd never leave that room again. Not alive.

I have a choice and I can walk.

When they reached the cottage, Ambrose grabbed the thick stone door's iron ring and pulled it open, stone scraping against stone. Stale air smelling of straw and old blood and musky pheromones rushed out.

Angélique gently drew the blanket from Jackson's shoulders and draped it over her arm. "You can do this," she told him. "You came back to us for a reason and it wasn't to die." She brushed the backs of her fingers against his cheek, the touch of skin icy against his. "Whatever you do, don't give up."

"I won't," Jackson promised, a smile brushing his lips.

January said nothing. Instead, she embraced him tightly, then released him and walked away.

As Jackson stepped into the dark cottage, he heard the click of nails against stone. "Out, you," he said to his invisible dog. "You be a good girl and go with Angélique."

Angélique came over and patted the air, feeling for Cielo. Cielo's argumentative *whoo-whoo* gave her position away and the *traiteur* was able to grasp the Siberian husky's collar. With a reassuring smile at Jackson, she led Cielo away, which looked pretty damned odd—a woman walking hunched over, her fingers looped through an invisible collar.

"Over there," Ambrose said, pointing at the far wall. Steel glinted in the gray daylight shafting into the cottage. Chains.

Jackson nodded, mouth too dry for speech, and sat where his uncle had indicated. He closed his eyes and swallowed hard. Butterflies raged in his stomach. He felt cold stone underneath him, heard the clink of chains, felt their icy touch against his skin as Ambrose locked them around his wrists and wrapped them around his waist. He smelled straw and steel, his uncle's juniper scent.

"I'm here, boy," Ambrose said quietly. "You ain't alone, you."

And like a dog whistled to a bone, the pain capered over on eager paws. Seized him. Wrenched and pulled. Tore him apart. His body arched and contorted as his bones cracked and shifted.

The chains clanked as the links suddenly pulled taut.

Jackson screamed.

THIRTY

SHE BE A JINX

It was nearly midnight and the rain had stopped by the time the scarecrow finally wandered out of the sugarcane field. Wearing weather-beaten Goodwill clothes and her husband's old straw cowboy hat, the scarecrow tottered on stiff, straw-filled legs into the pale pool of light spilling into Addie Martin's front yard from the porch.

Addie watched from her front porch, hands on the hips of her bluebell-printed sundress, as the scarecrow—missing one black button eye—plowed straight into the palm tree near the cracked sidewalk leading up to the steps, bounced, then fell into a heap of faded cloth and straw on the lawn.

"One of your backfires?"

Addie nodded. "At least I think so." She glanced at the dark-haired man standing beside her wearing a short-sleeved white shirt and faded jeans, a root doctor up from Jeanerette to attend the hoodoo emergency meeting. "The result of a spell I fixed this morning for good health—of all things."

The root doctor—and now Addie's memory deftly supplied his name, John Blaine—shook his head. "Near as

I've been able to learn, it seems like everything started going to hell in a handbasket right around dawn."

"Sounds about right," Addie agreed. "The wards musta went haywire near that time too."

"Whatcha gonna do about *that*?" John nodded his head at her yard.

Addie sighed as the scarecrow heap twitched and rustled as though the straw were crawling with beetles, then pulled itself up onto its straw feet. Again.

"Ain't a whole helluva lot I *can* do without laying a few tricks," she said. "I thought about burning it. But I couldn't imagine what I'd do if it started screaming."

"Can't scream. Ain't got no vocal cords."

"Ain't got no bones neither, but it seems to be standing upright just fine without 'em." When the scarecrow wobbled back into the palm tree's trunk again, she amended, "Mostly."

The stomach-rumbling smells of a late, impromptu supper wafted out from the porch door: butter-grilled cheese sandwiches, dill pickles, potato salad, and sweet tea. Voices murmured from inside the house, caught in urgent conversation as they listened to the Weather Channel and discussed the nightmare they were facing.

Magic gone wrong, the wards playing siren to seaborne disaster, luring it in.

In all of Addie's twenty years of hoodooing, nothing like it had happened before.

Miraculous Mother, save us.

Addie eyed the scarecrow and wondered if shooting it full of buckshot and salt would do any good. She doubted it. Besides, it seemed incapable of doing much more than playing scarecrow bumper car with the palm tree. Harmless.

And she had a meeting to tend to. Fifteen hoodoos, conjurers, voodooists, and voodooiennes had traveled over to her place to discuss how to find the problem and, once found, how to solve it. Others had been too busy calming their communities and preparing for the blowdown.

It troubled her that her invitation to Gabrielle and her niece, Kallie, to join in the discussion and problem-solving session had been declined. Well. More or less. Addie replayed her most recent conversation with the blunt root worker.

"I'd like to come, but I have me a patient to tend to, plus I have t'ings I need to take care of—t'ings dat won't wait. Kallie and Belladonna are still at dat carnival o' fools down in New Orleans, so I ain't expecting dem back until tomorrow. But I'm sending a friend in my place in de meantime, a mambo from Lafayette by way of Haiti."

Addie had murmured her understanding, but the only thing running through her mind was: *What on earth could be more important than fixing the magic glitch and stopping the jinxed wards?*

Addie couldn't think of a single thing. And that made Gabrielle's absence all the more disturbing, despite the arrival of her mambo friend, Gabi—and *that* must make get-togethers fun, Gabrielle and Gabi—a slim, fiftyish woman with dark skin and hazel eyes more honey than green who'd arrived in an orange and ancient VW Bug.

Taking in a deep breath of air laced with the sweet scent of fresh-cut grass and wet lilac, Addie dropped her hands from her hips and silently gave the scarecrow her blessing.

Enjoy your short life, palm tree scrapes and all.

Addie glanced at John as she turned around. "Time to get back to work."

"If that's what you call talking ourselves in circles, then yup, time to get back to it," he agreed with a wink. The porch door creaked as he opened it and held it for her.

The hoodoo rootworkers, conjurers, and root doctors were gathered in the book-crammed living room, paper plates heaped with grilled cheese sandwiches and potato salad balanced on knees or resting on the coffee table as they gave their attention to Addie's new flat-screen TV. Addie and John silently joined them.

Across the bottom of the screen, the words HURRICANE WARNING MANDATORY EVACUATION kept scrolling past in a bright yellow banner.

Addie stood behind the plush microfiber sofa, gaze locked on the high-definition screen, her arms folded under her breasts, and discovered, despite the food's buttery, toasted aroma, that she had no appetite.

The talking heads on the Weather Channel kept up a grim patter about Hurricane Evelyn's continuing increase in wind speed and ferocity. Just yesterday, the system had been a tropical storm headed for Belize. Now it was a category five hurricane with wind speeds nearing 180 miles per hour. And building.

"This hurricane is a monster, Jim," one of the talking heads commented. "I've never seen one develop this fast before and it's setting new records all across the board. Size. Speed. Ferocity. It's not looking good."

"I agree, Greg. Any idea where it will make landfall and when?"

"As of now, its trajectory puts Hurricane Evelyn on a direct path to the Louisiana coast, with landfall expected—right now—anywhere between Houma and New Orleans. As for when—my estimate, based on its current forward speed, and keep in mind that keeps increasing as well—is tomorrow evening, maybe the following morning. Evelyn's outer rain bands accompanied by tropical storm force winds will reach us within a few hours if her present forward speed continues."

A short, stunned pause, then: "That doesn't give folks much time for evacuation."

"No, it sure doesn't, Greg. This could be the biggest and deadliest hurricane in a century."

And just like that, with a few words and a few satellite and radar images, a bad situation became infinitely worse.

HURRICANE EVELYN NOW A CATEGORY FIVE WITH WIND SPEEDS OF 180 MPH AND STILL INCREASING. EXPECTED TO MAKE LANDFALL IN 24–36 HOURS. MANDATORY EVACUATION IN THE FOLLOWING PARISHES: JEFFERSON, ST. BERNARD, PLAQUEMINES, ORLEANS, ST. TAMMANY, LAFOURCHE . . .

More than one person seated in Addie's living room murmured, "Dear God."

Amen, Addie added silently.

She felt just as grim as good ol' meteorologist Jim had sounded. She had a feeling that his prediction would be an understatement if she and the other conjurers couldn't figure out how to either fix the magical misfires or undo the wards. Both would be ideal, but . . .

"We're running out of time," someone else said— Auntie Dominique from Morgan City. "We've got to get those damned wards fixed before there ain't nothing or no one left to protect."

"Maybe if we petition the *loa,*" someone else said, and all eyes turned hopefully to the mambo in her red scarf.

Shaking her head, regret shadowing her face, Gabi set

her crust-littered paper plate on the coffee table. "Invocations seem to use the same kind of magical energy as spells."

"*Seem* to?" Addie asked. "How do you know?"

"An invocation I performed this morning to help a friend . . . well, let's just say it didn't go as I'd hoped."

"*Merde*," Auntie Dominique muttered.

"Okay, then. Let's hear more suggestions, y'all," John Blaine said from where he perched on an arm of the sofa. "Anything—no matter how stupid you think it might be."

"I can't think of anything that doesn't require using magic in some shape or another," Addie said. "But I don't think we're going to be able to fix or undo anything until we find out what caused this mess in the first place."

John swiveled around to look at Addie, then he looked past her, eyes widening in disbelief just as a cold gust of wind blew through the screen door, slamming it and scattering empty paper plates like autumn leaves throughout the living room. Everyone seated in front of Addie looked past her to the door. More than one mouth dropped open.

A spoon clattered to the floor.

"O mighty Baron," someone whispered, dropping to their knees. "Welcome."

Power, dark and muscular, snaked into the room along with the pungent scent of burning tobacco and hot-peppered rum and, inexplicably, rank swamp mud.

Mouth dry, heart pounding so hard she felt faint, Addie slowly turned around.

Baron Samedi stood just inside the porch door, his *cheval* a tall blond man in a black fedora, mud-flecked shades, a black suit, and skull face paint. He held a walking stick loosely in one hand.

"I happen to know de source of dis mess we all be facing, *loa and* mortals," the Baron said. "But I can't find her ever since *my* magic backfired and now she be hidden from me because it did."

"'She'?" Addie managed to say.

"*Oui*, she. Dis girl be a jinx. She be a true walking hex because o' de monster inside her," the Baron replied. "Maybe *I* can't find her, but *you* can. All of you. Find her *tout de suite*, do whatever it takes, den summon me, and together, we'll put an end to dis storm before it puts an end to all of you."

"Who do we need find?" Addie asked.

"Kallie Rivière."

As Addie stared at him in shock, her pulse reaching its own hurricane velocity, the Baron strolled into the living room and over to the chair Gabi sat in. The mambo stared at the *loa*, her hands clutching the arms of the chair, sweat glistening on her forehead.

The Baron thumped the end of his walking stick against the hardwood floor, then murmured, "But you know all about dat, ain't dat so, *ma belle*?" Leaning over, he brushed his painted skull grin against Gabi's lips. She paled. "It be time to share what you know, woman."

Stunned silence thickened the air as all eyes fixed on the red-scarfed mambo. A silence that soon prickled with suspicion and hostility.

"I also t'ink," the Baron said, straightening and thumping his walking stick against the floor again, "dat it be time you summon yo' godson—"

Gabi's eyes grew wide with dismay. "No, there's no need, I know right where Kallie is—she's at her aunt's botanica. Or she *was* when I left there."

But the Baron kept on talking as though the mambo had never opened her mouth. "—de demon wolf o' de bayou, Devlin Daniels—and put him on de hunt for luscious Kallie Rivière."

"Please, no, we can go to the botanica. There's no need to summon—"

"Hush, woman!"

The walking stick slammed into the floor and thunder cracked through the crowded room. Gabi pressed trembling hands against her mouth.

"Yo magics ain't gonna hold de girl. But de demon wolf's teeth will. Summon yo' godson." Turning, the Baron winked at Addie. "Now. Where be de rum?"

Fragrant smoke—frankincense, rosemary, and myrrh—drifted up from the large brazier Addie had provided, threading into air thick with tension and silence.

Gabrielle added another small handful of powdered frankincense to the brazier's glowing charcoals, the incense crackling as it burned. White and blue candles dressed with High John the Conqueror root oil stood at either side of the brazier, flames dancing behind the smoke.

Gabrielle felt the Baron's dark and coiled presence behind her, felt the weight of his sunglasses-hidden gaze. Felt each pair of wondering and accusing eyes. She drew in the spicy scent of hot-peppered rum too as she inhaled deeply and attempted to center herself, but her scattered thoughts—wild with worry and fear—refused to be corralled. So she stalled, fanning the smoke into the room and murmuring Psalms.

"Why standest thou afar off, O Lord? Why hidest thyself in times of trouble?"

The Baron laughed. "Because He be de smart one, *ma belle femme*. Now, get on with it."

Gabrielle nodded, her hands clenching into fists. The last thing she wanted was to bring any harm or trouble to Kallie—Bon Dieu knew the girl had more than her share already. And the thought of putting her grief-shadowed and savage godson onto the girl's scent made her feel sick.

Forgive me, Devlin. Forgive me, Kallie.

"Be merciful unto me, O Bon Dieu," she intoned, tracing patterns and sigils in the smoke, "be merciful unto me; for my soul trusteth in thee: yea, in the shadow of thy wings will I make my refuge, until these calamities be overpast."

"Amen," someone gathered in the room said, echoed by several other voices.

"Devlin Daniels, I call you, boy. Rise from the bayou's dreaming shadows, leave the hunt and attend me. Hear my voice, *mon filleul*. Step into the smoke and show yourself."

The sweet-smelling smoke thickened and a shadow took shape within it—hair of tangled smoke, gray ash eyes—*wary* eyes—lean-muscled build, a bare sculpted chest, the pecs crisscrossed with old scars, jeans over narrow hips, bare feet.

She never *could* get the boy to wear shoes.

Devlin Daniels's smoke avatar noted the *loa* standing behind Gabrielle and the wariness in his eyes increased. "Why you call me into de smoke, *ma marraine*?" His nostrils flared and his eyes narrowed. "And why de hell do I smell burning bindweed?"

Before Gabrielle could answer her godson's accusation, the Baron said, "Because we need to bind you to a cause, bayou wolf."

Devlin looked from the Baron to Gabrielle. "*Marraine?*" he asked, voice low.

Gabrielle nodded, folding her hands in front of her where Devlin could see them. "Baron Samedi's right. We need you to track someone." She moved her fingers discreetly in an old *loup-garou* sign language: *This girl is not to be harmed. She's an innocent and needs to be protected.* "Kallie Rivière, a hoodoo in Bayou Cyprés Noir."

Devlin blinked, indicating that he'd received her message.

"Yo' godmother isn't right about dat," the Baron said. "Dis girl be no innocent."

Gabrielle stiffened, her blood turning to ice. How had he seen her hands?

"Dis girl be responsible for de failure of de wards, for de hurricane bearing down on us at dis very moment. She be responsible fo' all manner of unpleasant t'ings. I command you to bring her down, boy."

The Baron stepped up beside Gabrielle and touched the end of his walking stick into the smoke. An image swirled into being beside Devlin's avatar—an image of Kallie wrought in smoke: long, wavy hair, slightly tilted eyes, gray instead of purple, a sultry smile on her lips, graceful limbs, firm curves packed into cutoffs and tank top.

Devlin's ashy eyes drank the image in.

The Baron instructed Devlin on where he might find Kallie—home or botanica. Then her image vanished when he dropped his walking stick back to the floor. Reaching inside his suit jacket, the Baron pulled out a length of purple cloth with a flourish.

A shirt, Gabrielle realized with a sinking feeling. A sleep shirt.

"I found dis on de girl's bed when I paid anudder visit to her home," the Baron said, extending the shirt toward Devlin.

Devlin's nostrils flared as he drew in Kallie's scent. Drew it in deep.

"Find her," the Baron said. "Rip into her tender throat. Taste her blood. Feast on her heart. You be bound and compelled, demon wolf of de bayou, not tru magic but tru de will of Baron Samedi, de lord of de dead, de gatekeeper between worlds."

With a powerful breath from his lungs, Baron Samedi blew away the smoke and Devlin vanished. Laughing, the Baron asked, "Who wants a drink befo' we hit de road for Bayou Cyprés Noir?"

Knees weak, Gabrielle sank into the nearest chair, closed her burning eyes, and struggled against the urge to weep.

THIRTY-ONE

BENEATH THE
WILLOW TREE

Bent beneath the hood of her 1970 Mach 1 Mustang— Oooh! I like this dream—*Kallie pours thick amber oil into the funnel angling up from the V-8 engine's fill hole. The low thunder of a motorcycle rumbles past, then drops down into a throaty idle as it stops in front of the Mustang.*

"Need me to take a look beneath the hood, sunshine?" Layne asks, voice low and sexy, lending layers of naughty meaning to each word and sending a bevy of scorching butterflies through Kallie's belly. "Check your fluid levels?"

Thinking of how he might do that—fingers, tongue, hot nomad dipstick—Kallie's pulse thunders through her veins.

"Bet you're good at lubing things up, road rider, but I think I've got this handled." Kallie ducks out from beneath the hood and turns around, wiping her hands against the seat of her cutoffs, and helpfully thrusting out her breasts, cupped in a snug black bra.

Hmmm. Seem to be missing my shirt. How convenient.

"Still," Kallie adds with a coy glance at Layne from beneath her lashes, "I wouldn't mind an expert opinion."

Swinging a leg over the seat of his road-dusted Harley,

Layne stands, a wicked smile playing across his lips as his green eyes take a slow pleasure cruise down her body—lingering on the bust she's busy displaying to its best advantage.

His tattooed and chiseled chest is bare beneath his leather jacket and snug leather pants cling to his thighs, his very masculine charms.

"I'll be glad to take a look," he says, sauntering over to join her at the Mustang.

His thick, honey-blond dreads swing against his slim waist with a sensuous life of their own—in slow motion, no less. And as she watches, his leather pants morph into a blue and black plaid kilt.

Belladonna—you and your damned romance novels with their hot, mouth-dropping covers have a lot to answer for.

Kallie's mouth goes dry as she imagines how his sandalwood- and sweet-orange-scented dreads might feel trailing and tickling against her breasts, her belly, not to mention points farther south.

When Layne reaches Kallie, he doesn't even pretend to look at the Mustang's engine; his heated gaze locks with hers instead. He doesn't hesitate. Without a word, he grabs her, one hand snagging in her hair, the other latching onto her waist, and yanks her against his hard body.

She smells musky desire and male sweat, tastes it as her mouth seeks his. His mouth closes over hers in a ravenous kiss. Grabbing his kilt-clad ass, Kallie kisses him back, hungrily thrusting her tongue between his lips to flick against his own. His arm snakes around her, leather jacket creaking and jingling, and pulls her closer still.

He devours her with his lips. Her breath catches in her

throat, a small moan, as she feels him growing hard against her belly. Remembering what she glimpsed beneath his wet boxers during the contest in New Orleans, her knees weaken.

His hand trails fire up the bare skin of her back so his fingers can oh-so-dexterously unfasten her bra. The straps slide down her shoulders, then Layne's road-rough hands are cupping her breasts, fondling them with an urgent and hungry need as his lips trace a molten path down along her throat to her stiffened nipple and—

—the dream shifts.

Kallie finds herself running through a night-blanketed forest, cold mud squelching between the toes of her bare feet, gray fingers of Spanish moss whispering soft against her face as she ducks beneath oak branches.

A cry cuts through the air, a horse's terrified scream. Kallie's heart drums against her ribs. Ahead, she hears the thunder of hooves trampling the earth, behind she detects the stealthy and measured tread of a predator.

She's caught between—racing toward one and fleeing the other.

And uncertain which is worse.

A huge weeping willow looms in her path, moonlight bleaching the cascading waterfall of pale leaves bone white. The slender, drooping branches rustle as though something crouches within the darkness beneath. Waiting.

A bird trills, a haunting sound. A nightingale.

Kallie slows to a stop, suddenly uncertain. Sweat plasters her short, black nightie against her breasts, her thighs. Beads her forehead.

Something thrashes beyond the willow branches. Hooves thud against the ground, the impact vibrating up through the soles of Kallie's muddy feet and up along her spine to the base of her skull.

Behind Kallie, something pads with steady and dreadful purpose. The hair rises on the back of her neck. The horse screams again, a wild and desperate sound. And Kallie moves, brushing aside the willow's slender branches as she dashes into the tree's shadowed shelter.

But what she sees beneath the willow brings her to a sudden and stumbling stop. Launches her heart into her throat.

A black cobweb entangles a purple-maned ebony horse in glistening, ropy tendrils. The horse's hooves slash frantically at the web, but the coils just re-form and loop even tighter around the struggling animal.

No, not an animal, not only or just a horse. A vévé depicting a heart bound in chains made of pale bones and surrounded by black X's hangs on a braided silver chain around the horse's muscular neck.

For a second, the scene flickers, and Kallie sees a young woman entangled in the black, sticky cobweb instead, a woman close to her own age with café-au-lait skin and long cinnamon curls, her curves caressed by a purple silk dress, the vévé tattooed into the smooth flesh just above and between her breasts.

The loa. Her loa.

Another flicker and the horse returns, rearing, hooves lifting, black eyes rolling wild. A dark and twisted energy pulsates out from the pythonesque web and into the night.

A whisper in the grass behind her, followed by a whiff of moon-washed fur and coppery blood, warns Kallie that something has launched itself into the air—all wicked fangs and claws and savage hunger.

She bolts forward, just as the horse's hooves slash down, headed straight for her chest with rib-splitting force.

Kallie jerked awake with a sharp gasp and found herself looking into pine-green eyes framed by long honey lashes. Concerned eyes. Layne lay on his back, his face turned toward hers, and that now-familiar sense of connection—heated and soothing—rippled through Kallie, wiping the last traces of the nightmare from her mind.

"Hey, sunshine. Bad dream?"

Snuggled up against the hard-muscled warmth of his boxers-clad body, the sandalwood scent of his dreads perfuming her nostrils, Kallie remembered the sizzling 'n' sexy earlier part of her dream.

And before she even knew what she was doing, before she allowed herself a second to think, Kallie cupped a hand against Layne's face and closed her mouth over his in a tender, exploring kiss. A soft *mmm* of surprise from him, the sound sliding down into a hum of pleasure that vibrated against her lips as he deepened the kiss, one hand reaching up to entwine itself in her long, thick hair.

His lips tasted of Divinity's potion, of allspice, poppies, and cinnamon and, faintly, of blood. Kallie trailed her fingers along his jaw, feeling the smooth glide of his slim sideburns. Fire, stoked and smoldering since the dream, since their first kiss in Augustine's office, flashed into white-hot flame. Pooled molten in her belly.

His arm snaking over her hip and pulling her even closer, Layne rolled over, then grunted in pain as his bandaged, road-rash-damaged side came into contact with the mattress. But it was Kallie who broke the kiss and shoved him onto his back again.

"You're hurt," she whispered breathlessly. "How's your head? You took one helluva knock."

"Ain't the first time, betcha it won't be the last," Layne replied, toying with a strand of her hair, green eyes amused. "But thanks to your aunt, I'm feeling a helluva lot better than I was when I got here." He studied Kallie's face, his amusement fading. "How did you find me, anyway? I mean, my trip to Chacahoula was spontaneous and I thought you were gonna get some sleep."

Kallie rolled over onto her belly, propped herself up on her forearms. "And I was," she said, looking at Layne, "but then I found my cousin's mojo bag lying in the yard, leather strap broken as though it had been ripped from his neck. And I knew something bad had happened to him."

A muscle worked in Layne's jaw. "Motherfucking Doctor Heron."

Kallie nodded, throat constricting. "Exactly." Speaking in low tones, she told him everything that had happened between the time he'd said good-bye to her at dawn and ridden away for New Orleans and the time she and Belladonna had helped him stagger through the botanica's back door, even sharing her blossoming belief that her missing cousin might be part *loup-garou*.

Layne listened without interruption, tension flickering across his face when she described discovering her cousin's grave, his eyes briefly squeezing shut in relief when he learned the grave was empty. And when she talked about *loups-garous*, his expression was thoughtful and full of speculation—not disbelief.

But given that Layne was a Vessel who housed the dead, not to mention being a nomad raised in a natural and pagan belief system where the supernatural was all part of the whole, Kallie wasn't surprised that talk of were-wolves hadn't triggered his *Stop feeding me bullshit* eye-rolling mechanism.

"Shit, Kallie, I left too soon," Layne said when she finished speaking, face hard. "I made a huge goddamned mistake in assuming that just because that bastard Heron was dead, you were safe. I shoulda made sure."

"My safety ain't your responsibility," Kallie said softly, holding Layne's gaze and trying to ignore the stubborn light suddenly glinting in their depths. "So knock off blaming yourself, okay? I can watch out for myself just fine."

"I know you can. Never said you couldn't," Layne replied. "But I refuse to take chances with your life, not when Gage paid for it with his own."

Guilt and sorrow pricked Kallie and she heard what he didn't say: *I lose you, I lose Gage all over again.*

"I shoulda made fucking sure," Layne repeated.

Kallie stared at him in exasperation. "So, what—you planning on following me around forever? Saving me from scraped knees and broken hearts?" A part of her thought that wouldn't be so bad, and that she could do a lot worse than having a hot and gorgeous nomad stalking her. Especially *this* hot and gorgeous nomad. "I don't need a goddamned babysitter."

Layne glared back at her. "Never said you did. All I want is for you to be safe."

Kallie returned his glare. "And I *was* safe. What happened with Cash and his cousin and with the Baron had nothing to do with Doctor Heron."

"Maybe not," Layne allowed, glare deepening. "But

being held hostage by shotgun-toting outlaws, then threat-ened with death by Baron Samedi, don't fall under the *I was safe* category in my book."

Kallie narrowed her eyes. "Really? Speaking of safe, how *did* you wind up wrecking your bike, anyway?"

The glare-a-thon ended when Layne's eyes widened, his focus shifting inward. "Shit. Maybe I saw your cousin. Does he drive a pickup? A Dodge Ram?"

Kallie's heart gave a hard pulse. "Yeah, he does."

Layne told her about the pickup that had blasted out of the driveway, steered by a guy with tawny hair and beard, practically taking the turn onto the road on two wheels, and of the Siberian husky and two wolves staring at him from the truck bed as he and his Harley were going down into the gravel.

"Cielo," Kallie breathed, hope awakening. She sat up. "That's Jackson's dog. Maybe he was in the back too, since he wasn't driving. And the wolves . . ."

"Just might be the *loups-garous* Baron Samedi men-tioned," Layne finished for her.

"The question is, if the man and wolves you saw are *loups-garous*, where did they take my cousin? Where the hell is Le Nique?"

Memory tugged, and Kallie dipped down into the past, heard herself asking that same question, but in a six-year-old's curious voice.

"How do you get to Le Nique? Does your papa drive or do you need magic?"

"Nope, no magic. We drive most o' the way, then we take a pirogue up Bayou Cocodrie or . . . wait . . . maybe it be Tiger Bayou. I don't 'member exactly . . ."

Cocodrie—alligator—and tiger.

Strength. South. Fierce animals.

"Holy shit," Kallie breathed. "I think I might know where to look for Jackson." Excitement curled through her. She believed both bayous were south of Bayou Cyprés Noir, but she'd need a map to locate them. She could check one, then the other. She'd bet anything both bayous were relatively close to Chacahoula—at least as far as running wolves were concerned.

She paused to look at the clock. It read 2:11 a.m. *Shit! I've been asleep nine or ten hours. Jackson . . .* "I need to get my ass goddamned moving. I need to find him before . . ." She allowed the sentence to trail off, unable to finish it, refusing to voice her fears.

"Hey, it's gonna be okay," Layne said. "You're gonna find him."

"I can't wait on you," Kallie said, looking into his eyes. "I wish I could, but—"

"Don't you worry about it, sunshine," Layne interrupted, brushing the backs of his fingers against her cheek. "You go find your cousin. That's the only thing that matters. I wanna help, but I got a fight on my hands here. I'm no good to you right now."

"*Merci*," she whispered.

"You just keep safe, okay?" Layne's hand trailed away from her face, then he squeezed his eyes shut. "Enough with the damned bell," he grated through his teeth. "I hear you. Hold on, just hold on for a moment."

Kallie realized Layne was having a conversation with Augustine. At least, she *hoped* it was Augustine. She couldn't imagine Layne having words even resembling civil to say to Babette St. Cyr. Couldn't imagine how it must feel to have the cold and bitter ghost of Doctor

Heron's murderous wife inside your body, nestled against your heart, and against your will.

An image from Kallie's nightmare flashed behind her eyes. *A black cobweb entangles a purple-maned ebony horse in glistening, ropy tendrils.* Repressing the urge to shiver, she reached for Layne's hand and laced her fingers through his, squeezed.

Looks like we're both carrying things inside that were forced upon us.

Opening his eyes, Layne looked at her. She noticed sweat gleaming at his hairline. "Gotta go, Kallie. Babette's starting to break free."

"Anything I can do?"

Layne closed his eyes again. "See if your aunt can find someone who can handle ghost exorcisms. Augustine knows how to banish . . ." His words trailed off as though he'd fallen asleep midsentence, but the tension in his body and in the line of his jaw declared otherwise.

Kallie trailed a hand through her hair, wondering if Divinity had any experience exorcising body-snatching ghosts, or if she knew of anyone who could. Since Layne's ex was two-plus hours away in New Orleans, Kallie didn't see a point in trying to contact McKenna.

"You're awake," Belladonna's welcome voice stage-whispered from the doorway. "It's about time. I was beginning to think Layne's coma was contagious."

"One—Layne ain't in a coma, and two—goddamned Divinity potioned me," Kallie said as she swiveled around on the bed. "But I think I might have a lead on where Jackson might be. Something I remembered him saying. You ever heard of Bayou Cocodrie or Tiger Bayou?"

Belladonna stood in the doorway, a blue plaid bathrobe

belted around her tall, slender frame and fuzzy blue kitty slippers on her feet. "I've heard of Bayou Cocodrie," she replied. "I've got a map in the car, Shug. When do you want to go?"

"Now."

Holding a *Shush* finger against her lips, Belladonna glanced over her shoulder into the heart of the botanica.

Kallie held her breath and listened. She heard the low murmur of voices, male and female, heard the clump of boots against hardwood, heard low laughter. She frowned.

They weren't alone.

Had Gabrielle returned from the meeting with a few of the hoodoos in tow?

Releasing her breath, Kallie watched as Belladonna lowered the finger from her lips and shuffled into the room in her fuzzy blue kitty slippers and over to the bed, bringing the clean scent of Ivory soap and jasmine-and-honey shampoo along with her.

"Nomads," she whispered, sweeping an appreciate gaze over Layne's boxers-clad form, then plopping down on the mattress. "The pixie, in particular."

Kallie stiffened. "McKenna? She's *here*?" She darted a quick glance at Layne, but his expression of closed-eyes concentration remained unchanged as he dealt with the ghosts he carried inside. Belladonna's words hadn't been heard.

Belladonna nodded. "Yup, she arrived several hours ago with a couple of nomad buddies, soaked to the skin, and about as friendly as a possum cornered in a blackberry bush."

"Did she see—"

"Oh, she *saw*, all right. She kept insisting." Belladonna

dropped her voice into a rough brogue that sounded more gangsterland New Jersey than Scotland and quoted, "'Where is he? Wha has tha' sodding swamp witch done wit' him?'"

"'Done with him'?" Kallie said indignantly. "What makes the woman think I'd do anything with him?"

Belladonna's eyebrows arched toward her hairline.

"Well, besides *that*, I mean. I sure as hell don't mean the man any harm."

"Mmm-hmm. And I think that's the problem. But you haven't heard the best part. So your aunt led Leprechaun Girl back here so she could see for herself that Layne was alive and snoozing and"—a cat-hoarding-the-tuna smile played across Belladonna's lips—"Shug, you shoulda seen the steam pouring out of the woman's ears when she saw you snuggled up against Layne, all nice and cozy."

"I can just imagine," Kallie muttered. "Well, whether we like it or not, we're probably going to need the woman to exorcise Babette from Layne, so maybe it's just as well that she's here."

"Well, tha' makes me feel so mooch better, tha' it does. Tae be needed by the likes of you," said a voice with a genuine Scottish brogue, rolling and full of brambles.

"Speaking of the pixie-leprechaun-devil . . ." Belladonna mumbled.

McKenna marched into the room in black jeans and a tight leather jacket, boot heels tapping against the hardwood floor, a mocking smile on her lips to match the mocking words. She stopped at the foot of the bed and Kallie caught a whiff of wet leather and body-warmed amber.

She met the pint-sized nomad's scornful gaze and offered her a praline-sweet smile. "Goody. 'Cuz making *you* feel better is my *raison d'être*, after all."

"Aye, right," McKenna scoffed. "Well, at least ye have clothes on this time."

"I had clothes on *last* time. In fact, I was wearing clothes *every* time."

"If ye reckon bra and tiny skivvies tae be clothes, then aye, ye were clothed—stripper-style. And most likely clothed by accident."

As Kallie and McKenna tried to murder each other with increasingly strained and saccharine *Die bitch die* smiles, Belladonna piped up with, "Speaking of tiny skivvies, I think that's what you both should wear during your inevitable cage fight. We can even call your sure-to-be-epic battle the Die-You in the Bayou. Sell tickets."

McKenna blinked—breaking the death match—then joined Kallie in staring at her best friend. A triumphant smile curved the mambo-in-training's lips.

"Bell, what the—"

Belladonna arched an eyebrow. "You think the two of you could maybe focus on what Layne needs instead of picking each other apart?"

And yet another reason in an endless list of reasons why Belladonna was her best friend, Kallie reflected. *She always manages to redirect my attention to what's truly important. Not that I plan to tell her so. I'm worried she'll poof-turn into the Cheshire Cat if I do.*

"Yeah," Kallie agreed. "I can do that."

"Aye," the pixie-nomad growled. Leather creaked as she folded her arms over her chest. She shot Kallie a look, one that said, *For now.* Then McKenna's dark eyes shifted from Kallie to Layne. Worry glimmered in their depths. "How's he doing, anyway?"

"He's doing better." Kallie kept her fingers firmly folded through Layne's.

"Thanks to yer aunt," McKenna agreed. Her gaze shifted to Kallie and it was easy to read what she hadn't said: *But no thanks to you.*

"Pixie, please," Belladonna purred, voice a low and dangerous swipe of the claws. "*We're* the ones who found him. *We're* the ones who hauled his fine nomad ass off the ground, into the car, and brought him back here"—she paused to eye-molest Layne before adding—"every hard-muscled inch of him."

"Aye," McKenna growled. "So ye did." She seemed to choke on any other words she might've added, like, *Thank you* or *I appreciate you rescuing my ex-husband's fine nomad ass.* Instead, she said, "I ken tha' he has another ghost in the cargo hold."

Kallie nodded. "Yeah, he does. Babette St. Cyr stowed away while he was unconscious. That's why he needs an exorcism as soon as possible."

Another voice entered the conversation, speaking in a posh British accent from Layne's lips, "That he does, Ms. Rivière. In fact, we need to commence with the exorcism immediately. Mrs. St. Cyr is about to break free."

Layne—or rather, Kallie realized, Layne with Augustine at the controls—eased himself up into a sitting position on the bed. One honey-blond eyebrow arched up as he regarded their linked hands. "Going steady, are we?" he murmured, gently unthreading his fingers from hers.

Kallie felt a smile tug at her lips. "Only because *you* insisted."

"I'd like tae speak wit' Layne," McKenna demanded.

Layne-Augustine shook his head, a look of annoyance passing over his face as he felt Layne's dreads sweeping across his back. "Damned things," he muttered before saying, "Not possible, Ms. Blue. Valin has been secured in his so-called Fortress of Solitude at the moment, hopefully safe from any memory meshing or unraveling due to contact with Mrs. St. Cyr. If he were to—" He stopped speaking abruptly. His gaze turned inward for a moment, then a muscle jumped in his jaw.

"Augustine?" Kallie asked, muscles tensing.

Layne-Augustine shuddered, then said, voice grim. "May I suggest we hurry?"

THIRTY-TWO

HOODOO POSSE

While she waited for Belladonna to get dressed so they could start the search for Le Nique and Jackson, Kallie helped Divinity gather the candles, incense, and sea salt that McKenna had requested for the exorcism.

The fierce leprechaun of a nomad was kneeling in front of the rocker, dark brows knitted together in concentration as she drew chalk symbols—spoked wheels, suns, and other runic patterns—on the wood floor.

The other two nomads, Maverick and Jude—a guy with an action hero's impossibly ripped physique and a gal with ash-blonde hair and a gymnast's light-footed grace—propped themselves against the wall nearest the consultation room's doorway and snickered like two schoolgirls whenever Layne-Augustine spoke.

Seems the sound of a upper-crust British voice coming from their clan brother's mouth is the equivalent of a stand-up routine, Kallie mused.

Dressed in the freshly laundered jeans and Inferno tee, Layne-Augustine sat in the rocker beside the bed and strapped on his flame-painted scooter boots, dreads snaking over his shoulders to the floor. He'd winced as he'd bent over and Kallie figured he'd felt the painful pull of the road rash stretching along his right side.

"You okay?" she asked, bending to set the candles, incense brazier, and jar of salt down beside McKenna to join the fragrant incense, charcoal, and sand her aunt had already deposited. Straightening, she pushed her hair back from her face.

"I am indeed, all considered," he replied, ignoring the snickers shadowing his words. "No nausea, no dizziness, headache down to a dull roar. My considerable thanks to your aunt."

"Well, now, I didn't do it fo' *you*," Divinity said, parking her hands on her hips and leveling her gaze on Layne-Augustine. "I did it fo' *Layne*, so him, he be welcome. Now as for you—yo' foolish Hecatean Alliance is gonna bring nothing but—"

"Hey, will the magic misfires affect an exorcism?" Kallie hastily interrupted before her aunt could wind her anti-HA diatribe up to full swing. "Gabrielle's invocation to Baron Samedi went south in a big way."

"Dat be a good question," Divinity agreed. "Could end up inviting possession instead o' ending one."

The sound of the chalk scraping across the floor stopped. McKenna looked up, expression uneasy. She glanced over her shoulder at Divinity. "Ye never mentioned a spiritual invocation going bad," she said, "just spells."

"Musta slipped my mind," Divinity said, shaking her head. She quickly filled the nomad in on what had happened following Gabrielle's invocation to petition the Baron for Jackson's life.

"Shite." McKenna raked chalk-dusted fingers through

her black hair, leaving pale smudges in her angled anime-hero locks. "Shite!"

"This might pose a problem," Layne-Augustine mused, stroking his chin. "But we need to do something, and soon." He looked at McKenna. "Does an exorcism involve magic and incantations or a ritual of mental focus, individual power, and will?"

Kallie noticed that Maverick and Jude had corralled their snickers—for the moment, anyway—switching to a respectful silence.

"It involves the latter, aye," McKenna said, voice low. "So this still might work."

Divinity frowned. "It be de same way fo' an invocation—focus, power, and will. But it still went wrong."

"Shite," McKenna muttered.

"Maybe it wasn't the invocation itself that went wrong," Kallie said, her pulse drumming in time with the possibilities racing through her mind. "Maybe it was the fact that Gabrielle was summoning a *magical* being."

Layne-Augustine's green eyes lit up, cool and considering. "Yes. That makes sense, given the circumstances. Fortunately, Babette St. Cyr is *not* a magical being, just a dead one. I say we proceed. As soon as you're ready to begin the ritual, I'll exit Valin's body." Strain showed on his face—Layne's face. Sweat beaded his forehead. "We're almost out of time."

McKenna nodded. "Aye. Someone tie him to the chair."

"I've got rope and a roll of duct tape out in my pack," Maverick said, shoving himself away from the wall, leather jacket creaking.

"We've got duct tape here," Kallie said, glancing at her aunt. "In the supply closet, I think."

"Dat we do," Divinity confirmed.

"Are ropes or duct tape going to hold him if Babette takes over?" Belladonna asked as she walked into the room, her woodsy patchouli perfume preceding her. She was wearing black cords, a short-sleeved blouse the purple-blue of ripe blueberries, and square-heeled black boots. The strap of her black leather bag was looped around one shoulder and across her chest.

McKenna snorted. "They'll hold. We're dealing with a ghost using a man's brawn, not the bloody Incredible Hulk."

Kallie chewed on her lower lip, troubled by one thought, one she decided to voice. "Once Babette's out, what's to stop her from jumping back inside of Layne?"

"A ghost forced out by exorcism cannae return tae tha' particular Vessel ever again," McKenna replied. "It's as though the Vessel becomes poisonous or radioactive to the ghost, or maybe the exorcism just seals the Vessel against the evicted ghost's energy." She shrugged, a frown on her lips. "I dinnae ken why. Wish I did."

A measure of relief trickled through Kallie. "If it works that well, I'm surprised you don't perform an exorcism every time Layne gets possessed."

McKenna snorted in utter disdain. "Tha' shows how little ye ken about Vessels."

Kallie's hands clenched into fists. "Then enlighten me."

"From what Valin told me, an exorcism isn't particular," Layne-Augustine smoothly interjected before the pixie could reply. "His spirit could also be evicted along with that of the ghost."

A chill brushed against Kallie's spine. "Meaning his body would be forever closed to him too?"

"Aye," McKenna growled. "But there's another reason I dinnae perform exorcisms each time a ghost jumps into Layne's body. Sometimes the bloody fool *offers* himself so a ghost can say their farewells to loved ones or reveal who their killer was if they've been murdered."

Kallie could picture that, Layne offering himself to lost souls, giving them a chance to find their bearings, to adjust, before traveling on to the realm of the dead or heaven or wherever they were destined to go.

"I don't think that makes Layne a fool," Kallie said. "I think it makes him a man of compassion and heart. A man who accepts what he is."

"Then that makes *ye* a bigger fool than he is. And when he no longer remembers ye, then ye'll know why." Still kneeling in front of the rocker, McKenna began arranging the candles—white and purple and black—around the chalked symbols, the conversation clearly finished.

When he no longer remembers ye . . .

Kallie stared at McKenna as she filled the brazier with sand before topping it with a circular piece of charcoal for the incense. Whatever the hostile little nomad had meant by that, Kallie would just have to find out later.

"You ready to go, Shug?" Belladonna asked.

"Just about."

Inclining his topknotted head respectfully toward Divinity, Maverick asked, "Where's the supply closet, ma'am?"

"I'll show you," Kallie replied, and started forward. Divinity stopped her with a hand to her shoulder.

"I'll show de boy," she murmured. "You girls get going, you. Find yo' cousin. Bring him back befo' dis blowdown hits."

Kallie nodded, anxiety and dread a cold knot in her belly, a knot that had been growing larger with every passing minute since she'd learned that Evelyn had powered into a category five storm and was less than thirty-six hours away, maybe even less than twenty-four.

And if I'm—I mean, if the loa *inside of me is—the reason for the tainted wards, the hurricane? What then? The goddamned storm is winnowing away time.*

Drawing in a calming breath, Kallie decided that once she had Jackson home safe and hopefully sound, she'd do whatever was necessary to blunt the hurricane's devastating fury. Her mouth dried as she pondered the odds of her survival, then she shoved the thought and her fears aside. Not now. Plenty of time to be scared later.

"We'll bring him back," she promised her aunt.

"And yo'selves too." Divinity's stern-eyed gaze skipped from Kallie to Belladonna, then back.

"Yes, ma'am," Kallie and Belladonna replied in unison.

Divinity nodded, then eyed Maverick's tall, powerful form. A hint of approval glinted in her hazel eyes. "Mmm-hmmm. Now, you look like a man—unlike those shotgun-waving boys. Let's get you some duct tape."

"Uh, yes, ma'am." A bemused smile on his lips, the red-haired nomad followed Divinity out of the room and into the botanica proper.

Not caring what McKenna thought, Kallie carefully sidestepped the chalk symbols and went to the rocking chair. As Layne-Augustine looked up at her, she bent and pressed her lips against his in a tender kiss.

"Pass that onto Layne," she whispered. "Keep safe, y'hear?"

"I shall endeavor to do my best—on both counts," Layne-Augustine replied, voice dry as sun-bleached kindling. "The first presents an interesting challenge, but one I accept."

Smiling, Kallie straightened and turned; then, without looking at Layne's prickly ex, she crossed the room and joined Belladonna at the doorway. Belladonna arched an eyebrow. "You know that wasn't Layne you were kissing, right?"

"Yup. Augustine's supposed to pass the kiss along."

"Oh. Ooooh!" Kallie saw a dreamy smile curve Belladonna's lips as she swiveled around and led the way into the botanica. "Another thing I'd love to see."

"Wicked, through and through."

"Singing to the choir, Shug."

Just as they reached the back door, Kallie thought she heard the thunk of a car door slamming shut out in the parking lot, quickly followed by the thunks of several more. The frantic hammering of a fist against the other side of the door told her she'd been right.

"Who'd be here so late?" Belladonna puzzled.

Good question. Inner alarms blaring, Kallie lifted herself up on her toes and peered through the door's spyhole. She exhaled in relief when she saw Gabrielle and Addie, who was wearing a bright blue rain slicker, along with several people behind them that she didn't recognize.

"Who out dere knocking at dis hour?"

Kallie glanced over her shoulder at her aunt as she twisted the door's dead bolt open. "Gabrielle, and it looks like she brought the hoodoo meeting with her."

Divinity stood at the sales counter, Maverick beside her, a roll of duct tape in his hand. "Den let 'em in, girl. Maybe dey got some good news for us."

Kallie hoped so, but the distressed expression she'd seen on the mambo's face suggested otherwise. She finished unlocking the door and swung it open. The warm, humid night poured in, smelling of rain, wet concrete, and ozone.

"Hey," she greeted as the mambo and the others—and she counted ten in addition to Gabrielle and Addie—stepped inside, most pausing to wipe their feet on the doormat, and filtered into the botanica. "I'm surprised y'all came out here instead of just calling."

"Hey yourself, Kallie. I thought you and Belladonna weren't due back from New Orleans until tomorrow," Addie said, shooting a look at Divinity.

Kallie remained quiet, uncertain of what her aunt had told Addie.

"De blowdown brought dem home early," Divinity said.

"Uh-huh. No doubt," Addie replied, tone dubious.

"What be de word?" Divinity asked. "Y'all find a way to fix t'ings?"

Gabrielle glanced at her, and Kallie was startled by the look of guilt in her pale green eyes. But the word the mambo's lips soundlessly shaped filled her with skin-tingling dread.

Run.

Kallie had no idea why Gabrielle would be telling her to hightail it, but she knew there had to be a good reason. Better to go now and find out the why behind it later—from a safe place.

Nudging Belladonna's shoulder with her own and capturing her friend's attention, Kallie mouthed, *Let's go now.* Belladonna nodded, the question in her autumn-dappled eyes remaining unvoiced. But before they could step out the still-open door, one last hoodoo—a middle-aged man in a hooded yellow rain slicker and rubber boots—strode inside, kicking the door shut behind him.

"Baron Samedi will be here soon," he said, voice grim, "and he'd be damned unhappy if you weren't here when he arrived."

Kallie's heart sank. Gabrielle's warning was no longer a mystery.

The sound of crinkling plastic, followed by a bone-chilling *shuh-shunk*, drew Kallie's attention away from the door and the man in front of it.

Addie had pulled a shotgun out from inside her rain slicker and chambered a round. She leveled the weapon at Divinity and Maverick. "Everyone keep still and we won't have any problems. We're only here for the girl. Nomad, put any guns or knives or deadly whatnot on the floor."

Maverick's ginger brows slanted down in a scowl. His free hand knotted into a large, fight-scarred fist. Kallie wasn't sure he would comply with Addie's request until Jude stepped into the doorway and said quietly, "It's squatter business, Mav. Ain't got nothing to do with us."

"Might be squatter business," Maverick said, "but this woman tended to an injured clan brother, and we've been enjoying her hospitality as well. So that makes it *our* business too."

"Aye. He's right," McKenna growled from behind Jude. Kallie could well imagine what it had cost the leprechaun to say those words. "Put down yer weapons, both of ye."

"Addie Martin, what de hell do you t'ink you be

doing?" Divinity demanded, eyes narrowed, knuckles against her lavender-skirted hips.

"Ending the problem, fixing the wards, and saving Louisiana from Evelyn," she replied, regret and anger both edging her voice. "We're doing what you couldn't: the right thing, no matter how hard."

"And what would dis right t'ing be? Dis t'ing dat you couldn't discuss wit' me? Dis t'ing you felt you needed to accomplish by force, you?"

"Sacrificing your niece," Addie replied. "And removing the *loa* she carries."

Kallie felt someone move up behind her, felt body heat and coiled tension, smelled sweat and desperation. But before she could step aside or whirl away, the cold steel edge of a knife pressed against her throat. Kallie's pulse thundered in her ears.

Divinity's hands slid away from her hips, her face pale. "Addie, no. No."

"You gave us no other choice," Addie replied, her words husky.

Sorry, baby. I ain't got a choice.

A dizzying sense of déjà vu whirled through Kallie. History was about to repeat itself. She swallowed hard and felt the knife scrape against her flesh. Blood trickled warm down her neck. She wasn't about to offer herself up as a sacrificial lamb, not with Jackson still out there, not with those she loved in danger because of her.

An image from Kallie's dream flared behind her eyes—the horse fighting to free itself from the poisonous black snare—and doubt simmered in the back of her mind.

What if the *loa* wasn't the cause?

Divinity seemed to have the same thought. "Listen to

me," she said urgently. "I believe de problem be because Doctor Heron—"

"Laid a hex on your doorstep," Addie cut in. "I know. Gabi told us. But Baron Samedi believes otherwise."

Divinity's gaze cut over to the mambo, fury blazing in her eyes. "Seems she done told you all manner of t'ings. So, dis be how you get back at me for stealing yo' name?"

Several people, including Addie, appeared confused by Divinity's statement.

"Dat's right," Divinity said, lifting her chin. "My true name be Divinity Santiago and I stole de damned woman's identity—to protect my niece from her *maman*. I tol' Gabrielle dat I would make t'ings right, but it seems like my word ain't good enough for her."

The mambo looked at Divinity, expression dismayed. "No, that wasn't it. I didn't want this. I was forced—" She stopped talking, a wave of despair washing over her face. She shook her head.

But Divinity's glare only deepened. "Forced, my fanny. You can't trust her. Dere ain't no *loa* inside my girl. She's just trying to get back at me. Vindictive, her."

"No," Addie said, "The Baron told us—"

"A being *she* summoned," Divinity scoffed. "A being warped by tainted magic, a being dat probably ain't even de true Baron Samedi."

"Addie . . ." someone said, uneasy. "What if she's telling the truth?"

"You saw the Baron," Addie replied. "Felt his power. Heard him. Why would the *loa* of death and resurrection lie? Now, this woman"—she paused to direct everyone's attention to Divinity—"clearly lies. And has for years.

Stole an identity. She'd say *anything* to save her niece. Hell, who among us wouldn't for our own kin?"

"True, dat," someone muttered.

"We all knew this wouldn't be easy," Addie said. "But we also knew it was necessary."

"Maybe you and the Baron are right about the *loa*, Addie," Kallie said, speaking quietly to keep from earning herself another nick from the knife. "And if you are, I won't fight you. But I need to find my cousin first. Need to bring him home. Let me do that, then I'm all yours."

"Kallie, no!" Divinity and Belladonna protested practically in unison.

Addie looked at Kallie, face bleak, eyes hollowed. "The Baron thought you'd say something like that. So he gave me a message to pass on to you: 'You be all mine *now*, Kallie Rivière. And as for yo' cousin—don't worry yo' pretty little head, *jolie*. We be finding him soon enough.'"

"Goddammit, Addie," Kallie pleaded, her hands curling into fists. "Don't do this. Let me find Jackson—"

Addie turned her face away from Kallie, a muscle twitching in her jaw. "John," she called to a member of her posse. "Fetch the duct tape from the nomad and let's get everyone in the back room. Let's get this damned thing done."

THIRTY-THREE

AN OLD GRUDGE

Maverick and Jude never made it to the consultation room. Addie ordered the pair of glowering nomads to be triple taped at wrists and ankles, then locked in the supply closet as a safety precaution.

McKenna spared herself the same treatment with the words "I have an exorcism tae finish—a Vessel with a hostile spirit aboard."

"Never met a Vessel," Addie commented, voice intrigued. "All right, then."

The first thing Kallie noticed once they'd been herded into the room was that although Layne-Augustine still sat in the rocker, he now wore his leather jacket. She also noticed that his Glock rested on the floor in front of his boots.

When a member of the hoodoo posse—skilled in hoodoo, but utterly inexperienced in subterfuge and hostage taking—picked up the gun, then moved away without bothering to search the nomad for additional deadly items, Kallie felt hope blossom within her.

He still had his knives.

But given the strain on Layne's handsome face, the

tension in his body language, Kallie suspected that Augustine's hold over Babette was wearing thin. She wondered how long he could hold out. She had a feeling he was wondering the same thing.

The dark-haired root doctor in his early forties named John moved from person to person in the crowded room, carefully binding everyone's wrists and just as carefully avoiding their gazes, while Addie and her shotgun kept an eye on the proceedings. Once Kallie's wrists had been taped together, the knife was removed from her throat, and she could finally breathe a little easier.

Divinity was perched on the edge of Layne's former bed, Belladonna beside her, her duct-taped hands in her lap, her back stiff, a fierce and bitter fire burning in her eyes as she stared at Gabrielle.

McKenna knelt on the floor, wrists bound, with what looked like a slim willow branch inlaid with delicate curls and twists of silver clutched in one hand—her kosh, she'd called it. A wand she would use as a focus for her will and energies when she performed the exorcism.

Addie stood in the center of the consultation room beside the chalked symbols and burning candles on the floor. Tiny flames danced reflected along the barrel of her shotgun. The sweet smell of candle wax mingled with the musky earth tones of the incense wafting up from the brazier.

"I need tae begin the exorcism," McKenna said, looking up at Addie. "Before his control slips."

Addie studied Layne-Augustine for a long moment. Sweat beaded the nomad's face. She nodded. "Okay, yeah. Go ahead and get started."

Layne's head cocked to one side, a tight smile curving

his lips as Augusine's chessboard-assessing gaze shifted to Gabrielle.

Kallie wondered what the Brit had up his duct-taped sleeves. No illusion would work right in magic's currently twisted stream. No time for smoke and mirrors. But . . . Her pulse picked up speed as she considered the foremost tool of any illusionist—misdirection.

"So *you're* Gabi, Doctor Heron's sweetheart," Layne-Augustine said in posh tones. "Gabrielle LaRue—the woman clever enough, ruthless enough, to poison his clients and put him in prison when he refused to leave his wife." He winked. "Hell hath no fury, indeed. Kudos."

"What? No," Gabrielle said, startled. She stared at the nomad. "I never—" Her words were cut off as the man she directed them to suddenly stiffened, then slumped in the rocker, his eyes rolling up white.

Uh-oh, Kallie thought.

"Holy Mother," McKenna muttered. She started chanting rapidly in a flowing language that Kallie didn't recognize, a language the pixieish nomad spoke with ease and authority.

Layne straightened in the rocking chair and scanned the room, his icy green gaze coming to rest on Gabrielle. A chill crawled over Kallie's skin when she saw Babette looking out through Layne's eyes. She wondered if Augustine was still inside or if he'd bailed.

Layne-Babette rose to his feet awkwardly as Babette adjusted to the feel of a physical body after a ten-year absence. "Of course *you* never," he said without a British accent or Layne's easy tones. "It was *me*. I was the clever one, you husband-stealing, home-wrecking whore. And I taught you both a well-deserved lesson."

Layne-Babette lurched forward, kicking aside McKenna's candles and brazier, and spilling melted wax and hot incense across the floor, as he shuffled after Gabrielle, bound hands extended zombie-style.

"Shite!" McKenna scooted away from the wax and embers. Swiveling around on her knees, she resumed her melodious and exotic chant, her kosh aimed at Layne-Babette's back.

"Sit back down!" Addie commanded, following Layne-Babette with the shotgun.

"It be de hostile spirit inside o' him," Divinity said. "Seems she holds an old grudge against Gabrielle." She tsked. "No surprise dere. De exorcism will take care o' de problem. Now, aim de gun at de floor befo' you accidentally shoot someone."

Flustered, Addie did just that. "John, grab the girl and let's wait for the Baron in the other room."

"Okay," the root doctor replied, ripping his fascinated gaze away from the slow-motion chase and heading for Kallie.

Gabrielle stepped backward until she stood just in front of Kallie. Reaching back with one surreptitious hand, the mambo tapped something against her knuckles. A glance down revealed a folded pocketknife. Kallie's heart gave a little leap. Grabbing the knife, she tucked it against her palm.

"Run," she whispered, before saying in a loud, contemptuous voice, "The only lesson you taught, Babette, was how to hate. Your poor daughter is dead because you poisoned her heart and soul as surely as you poisoned your husband's potions."

Kallie whirled and shouldered her way past the

surprised—and distracted—hoodoo standing behind her and raced into the botanica, arrowing herself at the back door.

"Stop her!" Addie shrieked. The thud of multiple pairs of feet pounding against the hardwood floor behind her goosed Kallie even faster toward the door, flooded her veins with adrenaline. Her heart thundered in her chest.

Slamming up against the exit, Kallie unlocked the dead bolt with a quick flip of her fingers, then threw the door open. The pungent scent of hot-peppered rum and dark tobacco curled inside. Baron Samedi stood in the doorway, dapper as ever in shades, a black fedora, and a fine-cut suit, a smoldering cigar clenched between his teeth.

Kallie fell back, her breath caught in her throat.

"Toldja I wouldn't be forgetting you, darlin'," Cash-Samedi drawled. "You or your damned cousin."

But Kallie noticed he wasn't looking at her, the Baron's head was swiveling and cocking from side to side like a blind man's, as if he couldn't see her and was waiting for her to betray herself with sound or scent.

Her thoughts flew back to their encounter in the grave and the Baron's abrupt disappearance—and the unhappy black hen's equally abrupt appearance—when he'd worked a trick to compel the *loa* inside of her.

Am I hidden from him somehow? Blocked by a magic snafu?

Kallie backed away as quietly as possible, knowing the cause was lost as Addie's hoodoo posse slowly surrounded her. She fumbled the pocketknife's blade open.

The Baron stepped into the botanica and shut the

door. He blew a plume of blue-gray tobacco-fragrant smoke in her direction, then grinned. "I hear yo' heart, *jolie femme*. I also see a circle o' people. I bet a certain purple-eyed hoodoo be in de center."

"C'mon, now," John Blaine said, reaching for her. "This is hard enough, no need to make it any harder—"

Kallie sank the knife tip into the back of his hand, then pulled it back out—a snake strike minus the venom. With a sharp cry of pain, the root doctor jumped away from her, his bleeding hand held against his chest.

"She's got a goddamned knife!" he cried.

A whiff of tobacco and rum, then the Baron stood a few feet in front of her, his head cocked as he tried to figure her exact location. Kallie shifted to the side, but one of the hoodoos took hold of one of the Baron's hands and directed it toward her.

"She's right there."

Before Kallie could shift again, the Baron's hand clamped onto her shoulder. Electricity thrummed through her at the contact, shocking her senses and short-circuiting her control over her body. She heard a *tunk* as the pocketknife tumbled from her numbed fingers to the floor.

She tried to speak, to wrench free, but her body was no longer her own.

"Ah, dere you be, *ma belle*," the Baron murmured. And Kallie wasn't sure if he was speaking to her or the *loa*. He reached a hand into her chest.

Pain exploded through Kallie like a nuke made of ice—cold and razor-sharp and devastating—as the Baron's fingers closed around something inside of her and yanked.

Kallie tried to scream, but couldn't. The pain had stolen her voice.

Augustine watched, amused, as Gabrielle LaRue evaded Babette St. Cyr's shambling attack, easily stepping away from Valin-St. Cyr's outstretched hands.

One advantage to being recently deceased, I know how to use a body and move it, it's still a natural and automatic action. For Mrs. St. Cyr, however, it seems to be quite the opposite.

Powerful and positive energy charged the room's atmosphere as the little nomad *shuvani* continued her exorcism chant—*sounds like an intriguing blend of Gaelic and Romany*—following Valin's stumbling progress around the room with her slim, silver-inlaid kosh.

The woman with the shotgun and her accomplices all chased after the fleeing Kallie Rivière, leaving her aunt free to hop down from the bed and hurry to her worktable—the lovely Belladonna Brown right behind her.

"You found a poppet bearing your name at Jean-Julien's shop, didn't you?" Valin-St. Cyr said in sly tones. "And you thought he'd tricked you into bed."

Gabrielle paused in front of the empty rocker and looked at the slowly pursuing nomad, comprehension glittering in her eyes. "That was you too," she said. "You planted the poppet where you knew I'd find it. I accused Jean-Julien of toying with me. And broke off our relationship." She shook her head in disgust. "I underestimated you."

"That you did. You should've never taken up with *my* husband."

"You're right," Gabrielle said softly. "I shouldn't have. I was young, foolish, and believed myself in love. I wronged you and I apologize for that."

The nomad staggered to a halt. "You what?"

"Apologize. Jean-Julien was a married man with a child on the way. Taking up with him was wrong. I'm sorry for all the pain I caused you."

McKenna finished her chant and pointed her energy-quivering kosh at Valin's leather-jacketed back, allowing it to channel her will in a concentrated beam of power. Valin's body went rigid as though struck by lightning, the muscles in his neck cording, his dreads coiling up into the electrified air.

Even in his ghostly shape, Augustine detected the strong odor of ozone.

A dark mist sieved out of Valin's body, coalescing into Babette St. Cyr's form. She stared at Gabrielle, the sheen of tears on her face, but whether from rage or grief, Augustine couldn't tell. Valin collapsed bonelessly to the floor, a marionette with broken strings.

"Shit," he groaned. "That did *not* feel good."

With a soft sigh of relief, McKenna lowered her kosh to her side, perspiration glistening on her forehead. Sitting on her heels, she closed her eyes.

Augustine watched as Babette St. Cyr rippled over to Gabrielle and touched a hand to the woman's hair. Gabrielle shivered convulsively and wrapped her arms around herself as though she'd felt a cold draft.

"I will *never* forgive you," Babette said.

"And I ain't forgiving you," Valin growled, rising up on his hands and knees, gaze locked on the late Babette's inky, swirling form. "And neither will they."

Babette's attention shifted from Gabrielle to Valin. Her eyes narrowed. "'They'?"

"The spirits of those you poisoned," Valin replied. "They're waiting Beyond. Been waiting a long time. All I gotta do is let them in."

Babette flowed over to Valin, her eyes electric with fury. "You're talking shit, boy. You can't do no such thing."

"Watch me."

Power radiated from the nomad, setting the ghostly ether ablaze with a blinding white light. Squinting, Augustine averted his face from the source of that cold and dangerous brilliance—Valin himself—fear prickling along his figurative spine.

Electricity crackled through the air. Augustine caught a glimpse of an ethereal gate pinwheeling open near the ceiling and breathing ice into the room.

"Sweet Jesus."

"Hellfire!"

"For Gage."

From within the gate's jet-black and icicled mouth, Augustine heard a low, multivoiced sigh, followed by *<At long last.>*

Babette screamed in terror as a gray and silent tide rushed in and enveloped her. The tide shimmered, wavered, then vanished, leaving behind the fading echo of Babette St. Cyr's scream.

"Sweet Jesus," Kallie's aunt repeated, voice stunned.

"Well done, luv," McKenna murmured. "Our Gage has been avenged."

"Doesn't feel that way," Valin whispered.

Augustine stared at the nomad. *I had no idea he*

possessed power of that magnitude. I wonder if he knows his limits, his strengths. Could be interesting finding out.

"Aye, luv, I ken what ye mean, but give it time," McKenna sympathized.

"Seems justice *does* exist after all," Augustine murmured, sauntering over to Valin's body and sieving into him with a small contented sigh.

The nomad struggled up to his knees, then grabbed ahold of the bedpost to pull himself upright. *<Kallie . . .>*

<Very possibly in need of your help,> Augustine informed him, surrounding himself with a security bubble. *<Baron Samedi was coming for her.>*

<Shit. Shit. Shit!> Valin ran for the door.

THIRTY-FOUR

BOUND BY THE BARON

Head throbbing at his temples and behind his eyes, Layne raced to the doorway, pulling a blade free from inside his jacket. But what he saw as he loped into the botanica iced his blood and made him grab a second blade.

Kallie, her long, espresso-dark hair veiling her face dangled limp and lifeless in the grasp of a white guy in fedora, suit, and shades along with a skull-painted face.

The white guy—Baron Samedi, Layne assumed, never having seen the *loa* before—was busy hauling something out from within the swamp beauty, a struggling female shape, black and glistening, and giving the *loa* the fight of his existence.

A small circle of people near the pair had backed a healthy distance away, their faces drained of color, expressions shaken.

Cold fingers clenched around Layne's heart. Adrenaline fueled his muscles, stretched out his long stride. With Kallie's soul removed and hidden, he had a suspicion that the *loa* planted inside of her had taken her soul's place in more ways than one, and without the *loa*, she might die.

He couldn't lose her. He *refused* to lose her. Not after

having fought so hard to keep her alive and to give Gage's loss some kind of meaning. He didn't know if stainless steel had any effect on *loas* or not, but he was about to find out.

Layne heard someone running just behind him and figured it had to be a friend, since everyone else stood around Kallie and the Baron.

Shoving past a pair of chalk-faced onlookers, Layne brought both blades up for a double-sided stick to the Baron's throat, just as the *loa* gasped in horror and tossed Kallie aside. The female-shaped *loa* disappeared inside Kallie once more.

"By Bon Dieu's holy cock, I be hexed," the Baron cried, trying to shake a cobweb of darkness from the hand he'd plunged into Kallie's chest. "De damned girl be right. It ain't de *loa*. It be—" He and his *cheval* vanished in a stinky and sulphurous puff of black smoke before he finished speaking.

Layne skidded to a stop on the hardwood floor beside Kallie's crumpled body, then dropped to his knees. He brushed her hair away from her face and touched shaking fingers to her throat. He sucked in a rough breath when he felt a slow, steady pulse beneath his fingertips.

"Virgin Mary in a leaky boat," he said. "Stay with us, sunshine."

"Is she okay?" Belladonna asked, her voice tight with fear.

"She's alive," Layne said, resheathing his knives, then scooping Kallie into his arms. "But I don't know about okay." Cradling her unconscious body against his chest, he rose easily to his feet and turned around.

Divinity, McKenna, and Gabrielle had followed him

and Belladonna into the botanica and they now stood alongside the frightened-looking hoodoo crew.

"Dear God. What went wrong?" the woman with the shotgun asked. "Where did the Baron go?"

"He mentioned a hex," someone else replied. "What do we do now?"

"He said it wasn't de *loa* inside Kallie, so you all be fools," Divinity snapped. "And as for what we do now, we figure out how to break a hex without using magic." She looked at Layne, lines of worry bracketing her mouth. "Take my girl to de back so I can look her over."

"No," Gabrielle said, resting a hand on Divinity's arm. "You can't. She's still in danger and she needs to get out of here before it finds her."

Divinity's eyes narrowed. She jerked her arm free of the mambo's touch. "What else have you done, woman? What kind o' danger be looking for Kallie?"

Sorrow and guilt shadowed Gabrielle's eyes. "You ever heard of the demon wolf of the bayou, Devlin Daniels?"

"Dat I have. A *loup-garou*, ain't he? One with powers beyond dose of other *loups-garous* because he was conceived in de crossroads, his daddy a *diable* posing as Papa Legba?"

Gabrielle nodded. "Close enough. He's my godson. And the Baron forced me to summon him to hunt Kallie down."

"Hellfire," Belladonna breathed.

"Den call him off," Divinity insisted. "If he be yo' godson, make him listen."

"I can't," Gabrielle choked. "The Baron bound him to the hunt and to Kallie. The binding only ends when Devlin finds her."

First *loas* and now *loups-garous*. Layne didn't like the sound of that one bit. "Do I need a goddamned silver bullet to put him down?" he growled.

"Silver's not necessary," Gabrielle said, and Layne had the distinct feeling she wasn't telling him the whole truth. "Regular bullets affect him. Devlin didn't ask for this any more than Kallie did. He's lost so much already. He can be reasoned with. Don't kill my boy—please."

"Ain't making any promises," Layne replied. "Not where Kallie's life is concerned."

Gabrielle nodded, jaw tight. "Then you'd better go. Maybe he'll lose her trail. Maybe I can convince the Baron to unbind him."

"We'll take my car," Belladonna said. "Continue the search for Jackson."

McKenna stepped past the mambo and Layne saw his Glock in her hand. She slipped it into his jacket pocket, then yanked one of his dreads. Layne winced. "Dammit, Kenn."

"You're a man-stupid idiot," McKenna said, her brows slashed down over her dark, fierce eyes. "But do what ye need to, luv. We'll take care o' things here. Ye just come back safe."

Surprised by her words, Layne bent and kissed her forehead. "Thanks, buttercup."

"Aye, and I'm sure I'll sodding regret this," she muttered.

Layne carried Kallie to the back door and followed Belladonna to her car. For a split second, he thought he saw a canine-shaped shadow disappear behind the Dumpster and he moved a little faster, his heart drumming against his ribs.

He didn't breathe easy until he had Kallie and himself in Belladonna's car with Kallie reclining in the front passenger seat this time and himself folded into the back. The dark-haired hoodoo stirred and murmured something he couldn't quite catch, but didn't wake up. Since her face remained relaxed and peaceful, Layne had a gut feeling that Kallie was okay—despite the Baron's actions.

"Where we headed?" he asked as Belladonna started up the Dodge Dart.

She glanced tenderly at her unconscious friend. "Bayou Cocodrie."

THIRTY-FIVE

DEMON WOLF

Kallie was pretty damned sure they were being followed.

Ever since they had left Belladonna's car parked on a gravel back road a few miles outside of Gibson and had hiked into the rain-wet woods, following the dark and tree-lined banks of the bayou, Kallie had caught glimpses of stealthy movement from the corners of her eyes. Imagined she heard the soft pad of paws beneath every gust of wind rattling through the trees and palmetto bushes.

She wrapped her fingers tighter around the hilt of the knife she'd borrowed from Layne after he and Bell had told her about Gabrielle's godson when she'd awakened—with little memory of her encounter with the Baron other than pain and ice and a haunting sense of emptiness—about forty miles outside Bayou Cyprés Noir.

A chill crawled up Kallie's spine. *Demon wolf.* She'd first heard the legend of Devlin Daniels a couple of years after she'd come to live with her *tante*.

If a person be evil or wicked or just plain bad and leave misery and grief in deir wake, den one night, de demon wolf will come for dem and he'll rip deir black hearts from outta deir chests. He be de voice of dark retribution, him. Now, be good and eat yo' peas, girl.

Since when does not eating peas equal dark retribution, huh?

Mebbe de peas don't, but yo' sass certainly qualifies. Now tais-toi, you, and eat.

But Kallie had never believed the story to be true or that the legend himself would turn out to be the godson of a mambo she'd met only a couple of days before.

Wind whipped through the trees and Kallie's hair, rustling leaves, fluttering Spanish moss, and rippling across the bayou's dark surface. Tree branches creaked. She smelled impending rain mixed in with the odors of moss and mud and decaying vegetation.

Layne walked just ahead of her and Belladonna on the spongy, rain-saturated trail, his dreads knotted behind him and out of the way, his posture alert, coiled for action. His wary gaze scanned the shadows.

"You sure we're going the right way, Shug?" Belladonna asked in hushed tones.

Her question nudged at the knot of anxiety lodged in Kallie's chest, amplified the countdown timer ticking away at the back of her mind. "Ain't sure, no," she finally replied. "Just following my intuition. What does *your* intuition say?"

"That your intuition is right. It's also telling me I should've broken in these boots before going on a long slog through a swamp. How far have we gone? Five, ten miles? My feet are *killing* me."

"One mile, Bell. Maybe two. And what the hell are you doing in new boots?"

"Breaking them in, apparently," Belladonna said with a sigh.

Kallie glanced at her friend. Belladonna clutched a borrowed knife in her right hand and held it half lifted, Norman Bates style. "What method of knife fighting you planning to use there, Bell?" she teased.

"A reliable method known as shriek-slash-and-run."

"Might save time if you skip the shriek and go straight to the slash."

"The shriek is essential, Shug. It stuns the attacker, making the slash much more effective."

"Less chatter, ladies," Layne said in a low voice. "Trying to listen for the approach of fanged death here."

"Right. Sorry," Belladonna whispered.

A sudden fork of lightning split the sky and bleached the land bone white. In that brief, stark-still frame, Kallie thought she saw distant rooflines through the trees. A hunter's encampment or a hidden village?

But just as the night returned and thunder grumbled low, Kallie's heart leapt into her throat when she spotted a sleek canine shape with gleaming eyes weaving among the oaks and willows and cypress, before disappearing into the underbrush.

She knew Layne had seen it too when he slipped his Glock from the pocket of his leather jacket and carefully chambered a round. "Keep close," he murmured.

"Hey," Belladonna whispered. "I think I see lights." She pointed to a spot up the trail and across the bayou with her knife. "Over there. Look. There must be a bridge."

Grabbing Belladonna's arm, Kallie maneuvered her quietly protesting friend—*What the hell?*—around to her other side, placing herself between Belladonna and the night-drenched trees.

And whatever they hid from view.

Not for the first time, Kallie wished she could lay down a protection trick. But Belladonna was right—she saw the soft and steady glow of faraway light, like a lamp illuminating a window, through swaying branches. Hope curled through her. Maybe it *was* Jackson's fairy-fable Le Nique.

From within the wooded darkness looming beside them, a twig snapped with a sharp crack. A very *deliberate* sound. Layne stopped and swiveled in one fluid motion, swinging the Glock up in a two-handed grip.

Then, as lightning blazed across the sky, the demon wolf made its move.

So did Layne.

He squeezed off two rounds just as the dark, wolfish shape bulleted out from beneath a broad-leaved palmetto and launched itself at the nomad. The shots rolled like thunder through the night.

Kallie caught a blurred glimpse of black fur, bared and glistening fangs, and glowing silver eyes. Then the wolf hit Layne with a solid, bone-rattling impact, knocking them both to the ground, and a desperate determination burned through her.

It's me he wants. Me he'll chase down. He'll ignore Layne and Bell. All I hafta do is run. Two people have already died for me. I refuse to let anyone else.

Kallie whirled, adrenaline speeding her reflexes, fine-tuning her senses, and shoved Belladonna aside just as the mambo-in-training rushed up, knife in hand, to help Layne. Belladonna stumbled, then slipped on the wet grass and fell, sliding down the bank toward the water, shock blanking her face.

Sorry, Bell.

As Kallie pivoted back around, her heart skipped a beat

when she saw Layne throw both arms up to protect his throat from the wolf's darting, snapping muzzle. Stepping forward, she punched her blade between the *loup-garou's* ribs. "Let him be, you goddamned *fi' de garce!*" she yelled. "You want me, then you gotta goddamned catch me."

With a savage snarl, the demon wolf leapt off of Layne, silver eyes lit with a devilish flame and fixed on her. Kallie spun and raced into the woods. Behind her, she heard Layne screaming, "No! Kallie! NO!"

She ran, dodging tree trunks and ducking under low branches, trying to avoid ankle-snagging vines and ankle-breaking rodent holes. Lightning flared, revealing her surroundings for a split second, then plunging her into darkness once more.

She ran, lungs burning, heart pounding, aware of the demon wolf loping behind her. Nipping at her heels. Remembering his breathtaking speed, she wondered why he was just playing with her, why he didn't bring her down.

Spanish moss caressed her cheek as she pelted beneath a thick, twisted oak branch, and the dream she'd had just before she'd awakened snuggled up against Layne's warmth poured into her mind.

She finds herself running through a night-blanketed forest, cold mud squelching between the toes of her bare feet, gray fingers of Spanish moss whispering soft against her face as she ducks beneath oak branches.

A cry cuts through the air, a horse's terrified scream. Kallie's heart drums against her ribs. Ahead, she hears the thunder of hooves trampling the earth, behind she detects the stealthy and measured tread of a predator.

She's caught between—racing toward one and fleeing the other.

And uncertain which is worse.

Maybe it was time to stop running altogether and make a stand.

A side-stitch knifed Kallie's ribs and she gasped. Besides, maybe the damned wolf wasn't tiring of this game, but *she* sure as hell was. Slowing her frantic pace, she came to a stumbling halt, one hand pressed against her aching side. She bent over, panting, her borrowed and bloodied blade still clutched in her hand.

I really need to jog more. Of course, that might not matter pretty soon.

The demon wolf padded to a stop several yards from Kallie. He stared at her with intent silver eyes—a hunter's implacable regard—and she smelled smoky fur, wolf musk, and the coppery tang of blood.

"I know your name, Devlin Daniels, and I know your godmother," Kallie said, straightening. "I also know it was the Baron who put you on my trail. All I ask is that you leave my friends and family in peace and give me the time to find my cousin. He's—"

Her words jammed up in her throat and her eyes widened when the wolf's fur began to ripple, to pour *inward.* Odd cracking and popping sounds percolated through the air—like someone snapping kindling for a campfire or splitting open walnuts—as the wolf's body rearranged itself with a fast and flowing grace.

Kallie blinked. The wolf had Changed into a crouching man.

A very nude man, one with a sculpted and lean-muscled build and wild good looks. Long, tangled black hair tumbled past his shoulders. Scars white with age furrowed both pecs. Blood smeared his side—her knife. Black claws curved from his long fingers. And he regarded her with lambent eyes the color of ashes—still the hunter's implacable stare.

He rose from the leaf- and vine-cluttered ground with a natural fluidity, unself-conscious of his nudity, and Kallie's gaze drifted helplessly south. She felt her pulse pick up speed as she realized that he would've done very well in the wet boxers contest—might've even given Layne some real competition.

Dear God. I'm as bad as Belladonna.

Hearing a low growl, Kallie jerked her gaze up and met Devlin's intent and somewhat amused regard. She lifted her chin, cheeks flaming.

"I know yo' name too, Kallie Rivière," Devlin said in a low voice. "And *ma marraine* told me dat you be an innocent, no matter what de Baron say, and dat you ain't to be harmed, but protected instead."

"And what did the Baron say?"

"Dat you be responsible for de failure of de wards, for de coming hurricane—among udder t'ings." Devlin padded forward, closing the distance between them. "He commanded me to bring you down."

A chill touched Kallie's spine, goosebumping her skin. "And is that what you're going to do?" She smelled him, a deeply earthy aroma—musk and blood and vetiver grass, masculine.

"Not yet. Not until I get de truth. See if you be de evil t'ing dat de Baron claims you to be or not."

"What if I am?" Kallie asked, heart drumming. She wondered if he was as fast in human form as he was on four paws. But remembering how quickly he'd Changed, she knew she wouldn't outrun him for long.

"Den I eat yo' heart."

Kallie swallowed hard. "And how do you find the truth?"

"I gotta look inside." Devlin tapped one black claw against his temple, then against his scarred chest above his heart. "It be de only way."

"But what if you can't find the truth? What if it's hidden even from me?"

"You know de answer to dat, you. Heart. Eaten."

Kallie curled her fingers around her blade, but she never got a chance to use it, let alone lift it. Before she even realized he'd moved, Devlin stood behind her, both steel-muscled arms locked across her chest—one just above her breasts, the other beneath. The claws of one hand raked into the skin above her heart. Blood oozed hot into her cleavage.

Pulse thundering in her ears, Kallie struggled to bring up the knife, to twist free, but her body refused to move. The blade dropped from her nerveless fingers. She felt a strange pressure behind her eyes, in her mind. Panic capered through her. Her mouth dried.

"It be all right," Devlin whispered into her ear. "Just relax, you. Dat's just me holding yo' mind and body still so you don't hurt yo'self while I look inside for de truth. Dis way I can see everyt'ing. Ain't no hiding."

Kallie tried to close her eyes, but couldn't. The pressure in her mind built and built until, at last, everything faded away in a soft gray haze.

Layne stumbled forward, nearly falling into what looked like a thorned blackberry bush when Belladonna crashed into him after his sudden stop, then bounced away like a flipper-smacked pinball.

"Oof! Nomad, what the hell?"

"We've got company, cupcake."

Layne studied the man who'd stepped out from among the Spanish-moss-draped cypress and into his path. He wore a white tee and jeans and stood taller than Layne by a couple of inches, with a well-muscled and powerful build. Tawny hair and beard. Empty hands. And his body language was as motionless as that of a hunting dog on point. His nostrils flared.

Looks like he's trying to catch our scent. The hair prickled on the back of Layne's neck as a very real possibility occurred to him—especially given the way the man's eyes held captured light.

Might be loup-garou.

The man's gaze slid from Layne to the Glock in his hand to Belladonna, then back to Layne. "What y'all doing out here dis late?" he asked. "And shooting a gun, no less. Dis be private property, not an all-night shooting range. What you be shooting at?"

"A wolf," Belladonna volunteered. "The demon wolf of the bayou in particular. He's chasing down our friend."

The man scowled, rubbed a hand over his beard. "You sure?" he asked, completely unfazed by talk of demon wolves. "Devlin Daniels be hunting *here*?"

And knowing the wolf's name explained why.

"Yeah, we're fucking sure," Layne growled.

The man's scowl deepened. "Dis ain't his territory. He knows better too."

"Sounds like a problem between the two of you," Layne said. "Good luck working it out. Now, if you don't mind, we need to continue—"

The man shook his head. "Like I said, dis be private

property. You both wait here. I'll go after yo' friend." He half turned, then paused. "I hate to say it, but if Devlin Daniels be hunting yo' friend, he probably already caught her."

"That's only because you don't know Kallie."

Sympathy flickered in the man's eyes. "Y'all wait here," he ordered. Then he turned and loped away into the darkness.

"You waiting?" Belladonna asked.

"Hell no."

"Mmm-hmm. I didn't think so. Me either."

Layne trotted after the man, Belladonna running beside him.

The gray haze drifted away like morning mist on a sunny day. Kallie blinked. She tasted copper on her tongue, while the earthy smell of vetiver filled her nostrils. She felt strong arms around her and thought of Layne, felt herself reclining against him. Imagined they were still snuggled warm together on the bed in her aunt's botanica.

"I found de problem," a voice said. A voice that, with its Cajun accent, definitely wasn't Layne's.

Kallie's heart launched itself into her throat as she remembered who the voice belonged to. *Black wolf. Demon wolf. Man with tangled black hair. Devlin Daniels.* She shoved at his arms, nearly tumbling face-first onto the ground when he released her. She crawled away for several yards before rising to her knees and turning around.

He was, of course, still nude, but artfully posed. His long hair shadowed his face, but not his lambent eyes. He seemed to look into her. Knowing he'd been rifling through her mind, her memories, Kallie felt stripped naked and vulnerable. Lifting her chin, she forced herself to meet his gaze.

"I found de problem," Devlin repeated.

"The *loa*," Kallie said as her heart slowed its frantic pace. "I know."

Devlin shook his head. "De *loa* yo' *maman* planted inside you ain't de original problem, but it be a *part* of de problem."

Kallie frowned. "Original? You mean there's more than one problem?"

"It be de black dust you took in from Doctor Heron. De hex you sucked down when you unzipped de man's soul."

Devlin's words rocked Kallie like a high-pressure blast of cold water. Her thoughts flipped backward.

"Don't do it, child," her aunt says. *"It ain't yo' place."*

The black dust coating St. Cyr's soul ripples, then flows backward and down, back into Kallie's waiting palm. The root doctor's spirit unravels inch by inch, molecule by molecule, until the air is empty.

"De black dust captured de *loa*," Devlin continued, "webbed her up like a fat fly in a spider web and it feeds on her power, using it to magnify its own. Dat be the cause of all de magical mishaps. And dat why you be a living hex, Kallie Rivière—a breathing jinx."

"Bon Dieu," Kallie whispered in horror, sitting back on her heels. *What the hell have I done?* "How do I fix it? *Can* I fix it?" Lightning strobed across the restless sky and she looked up, then added, "Before it's too late?"

Devlin tilted his head as though listening to something she couldn't quite hear and Kallie caught a glimpse of one delicately pointed ear. "Almost time to leave," he murmured, before focusing on her again. "When you reach Le Nique, ask for de *traiteur* and her *shuvano* mate. Den ask dem about de sacred fire. Dat be de only way you can fix what you done."

Kallie's heart gave a hard pulse. "Am I heading the right way?"

A smile touched Devlin's lips. "*Oui.* You practically right on top of it."

Eyes closing in relief, Kallie drew in a deep breath as hope unfolded within her. Maybe she wouldn't need to give up her life to keep the hurricane from devouring all that she loved.

Warm and callused hands gripped her arms and pulled her to her feet. Devlin's earthy odor swept over her. Her eyes flew open and she looked into his ash-colored gaze.

"Let go," she growled.

She tried to jerk free, but the demon wolf wasn't having it. A wild and primal fear fluttered up her spine. She imagined his claws ripping into her flesh. Tearing out her heart. Imagined him devouring it. She struggled to break free—twisting, kicking, knuckling punches.

But he simply held her at arm's length and let her flail away like a tantruming child refusing to go to bed, until she wore herself out. "You done?" he asked when she went limp.

"For now," Kallie panted.

Devlin pulled her close, then leaned in, his cheek next to hers, but not quite touching. He inhaled. "I've got yo' scent," he said, nostrils flaring. "I can find you anywhere. Anytime. Yo' heart be mine, Kallie Rivière, hoodoo woman."

Kallie wasn't sure how he meant that, exactly—literally

or figuratively, but either prospect terrified her. Devlin released her, and she stumbled back a step as he dropped into a crouch and began to Change.

His transformation to wolf happened just as swiftly as his Change to human. Pops and cracks snapped into the air like sparks from a burning log as joints, tendons, and bones rearranged themselves, altered shape. Black fur covered flesh with a wind-ruffling-the-grass sound.

From within the shadowed darkness beneath the oaks and cypress, Kallie heard growls and snarls, then three wolves darted out of the trees to skirmish with the demon wolf. A few quick snapping feints, then Devlin whirled and raced off into the woods and the night. The other wolves chased after him, leaving Kallie alone.

Lightning strobed across the sky, chased by a ground-rattling boom of thunder.

Muscles trembling, she dropped to her knees on the soft leaf- and grass-padded ground and sucked in a shaky breath. "Shit," she whispered, shoving her hands through her hair.

"You must be Kallie," a man's deep voice said from behind her. "Guess de nomad was right."

Kallie spun around on her knees. A tall, tawny-haired man in a tight white T-shirt and jeans stood barefoot underneath an old oak. He studied her with a wild animal's watchful and unwavering gaze. Like a wolf. Like Devlin.

Skin prickling, she jumped to her feet. "Layne. Where is he? Is he all right?"

The man shrugged. "He be fine, far as I know. He and de girl been following me. But dey t'ink I don't know dat." He paused, eying Kallie's chest, nostrils flaring. "You be bleeding."

Kallie glanced down. Four bloody scratches marred the top of her left breast. And stinging pain kicked in the second she realized Devlin had left his mark on her. "Shit."

The thud of running feet pulled Kallie's eyes up. Layne pelted out from beneath a willow's moss-draped branches, Belladonna a couple of steps behind him. Relief washed across the nomad's handsome face, then quickly vanished. A muscle in his jaw flexed and his blond brows slanted down over a furious glare. Belladonna folded her arms over her chest.

Uh-oh.

Layne stalked over to Kallie in two long-legged strides and grabbed her by the shoulders in a steel-fingered grip as though he intended to shake her. "Are you hurt?" he asked harshly.

"Just scratches."

"What the *hell* were you thinking? You ever pull a stunt like that again, woman, I'm gonna put you over my knee and paddle your ass."

Belladonna snorted. "Paddle her ass? *That's* a punishment? Nomad, please."

"Shut up, Bell," Kallie and Layne said at the same time.

Layne's grip shifted from Kallie's shoulders, then he wrapped her up in a tight-muscled hug and pulled her against him. "You scared the crap outta me, sunshine."

"Is that what I smell?" Kallie teased.

"No, that would be Belladonna."

"Mmm-hmm. Laugh it up, road rider," Belladonna purred. "You just went to the top of my payback-is-a-bitch list."

Laughing, Kallie relaxed into Layne's embrace, her cheek against his leather-jacketed chest. Listened to the hard beat of his heart. Tried to keep the moment, knowing it couldn't last. Magic was still in flux and a hurricane raged only hours away.

When you reach Le Nique, ask for de traiteur and her shuvano mate. Den ask dem about de sacred fire.

Kallie reluctantly freed herself from Layne's arms. "Hey," she called to the man in the white T-shirt. "What's your name?"

"René," he replied.

"I need to find a place called Le Nique," she said. "I'm looking for my cousin Jackson Bonaparte, and for a *traiteur* and her *shuvano*."

René shook his head. "Can't help you, *je regrette*." He turned to walk away.

"Wait! I'm the reason the hurricane wards turned into magnets. The reason magic ain't working right. And I desperately need the help of your *traiteur* and her mate."

Kallie heard Belladonna's breath catch in her throat.

René swiveled back around and regarded her for a long moment, then nodded. "Follow me."

THIRTY-SIX

LE NIQUE

Wolves had followed their slow progress down the bayou, melting in and out of the inky darkness beneath the palmettos and cypress and weeping willows as if pawed extensions of the night, their eyes luminous with storm light.

Kallie climbed out of the gently rocking pirogue and onto the weathered cypress dock connecting to stairs that led up to the raised cottage's front porch. The cool scent of fresh mint from the cottage's window boxes sweetened the air.

From what she'd seen of Le Nique from René's boat, stone piers lifted each cottage and *cabane* a good six or eight feet above the ground. Plywood slabs already covered most windows in anticipation of Evelyn's landfall.

Tree branches swayed and creaked in another gust of wind. Rain finally fell, dimpling the bayou's dark surface. Wolves gathered, watching intently as Belladonna, then Layne, hopped from the pirogue and joined Kallie on the dock.

Layne gave Kallie's shoulder a quick squeeze and she looked up at him. "Give me a minute," he murmured, then strode past her, stopping at the dock's midway point. His cluster of knotted-back dreads hid most of the orange-tailed fox and other clan markings painted on the back of his rain-beaded leather jacket.

Lightning flared—one, twice, a double strike. Thunder rumbled.

Layne dropped down to one knee on the gray-planked dock and lowered his head respectfully beneath the lupine gaze of the *loups-garous*, his hands palms-out at his sides. "Fox clan," he said, quietly identifying himself. "And we know about being hunted. We know about living Outside. Your secrets are safe."

Kallie's heart double-thumped against her chest as several wolves—gray and russet and black—stiff-legged over to him, fur spiked.

Layne inclined his head toward Kallie and Belladonna. "We've come seeking help. We ain't here to cause trouble."

Kallie held her breath, her fingernails biting into her palms as she watched the *loups-garous* circle Layne.

Layne remained still as the *loups-garous* checked him over, sniffing his dreads, his face, his body, nosing at his clothes. He looked up and made brief eye contact with each before dropping his gaze again. One nipped the back of Layne's leather jacket, then tugged at it, a low growl vibrating into the air.

"You need to leave yo' gun, Fox Clan," René said, stepping onto the dock.

"Not a problem," Layne replied in an easy drawl. "I'm gonna do just that." Reaching for the Glock tucked into his jeans at the small of his back, he pulled the gun free, then rested it carefully on the weathered planks.

René bent and scooped it up. Slipped it into the front of his jeans. Layne rose to his feet and the wolf sentries escorted him to the base of the cypress stairs before loping away. He waited there for Kallie and Belladonna, shadows masking his face as he scanned the area, automatically searching for any threat, any danger—inbred nomad survival trait, Kallie realized.

Kallie released her breath in a relieved exhalation. "Goddamn."

"Nomad's lucky they didn't pee on him or use him as a chew toy."

Kallie laughed, then nodded. "You might be right."

"I don't know about you," Belladonna said in a low voice as they went to join Layne at the foot of the stairs, "but it worries me that our guide hasn't even said if Jackson's actually here and, if he is, whether he's okay or not."

"Me too," Kallie admitted. Doubt had settled in, like dark silt. What if she'd been wrong about Jackson being in Le Nique? What if Baron Samedi had lied about the *loup-garou* scent in the grave? And worst of all—what if she'd finally found her cousin, only to arrive too late? Her nails bit even deeper into her palms.

Kallie parked herself beside Layne. Gave him a measuring look, one he returned. "Did you know what you were doing?"

"Nope. Flying by the seat of my pants. Just felt like the right thing."

"Then you've got good instincts. Even better, you *listen* to them."

A lazy smile curled across Layne's lips. "Thanks, sunshine, but I know several people who would disagree with you on that."

Kallie would bet that Layne's ex-wife led the list. "No doubt. But *she's* wrong."

"Y'all wait here," René said, striding past the three of them, then trotting up the stairs to the porch. He rapped his knuckles against the door lightly before opening it and disappearing inside.

The door opened again a moment later, spilling soft light onto the porch. A woman stepped out wearing a purple silk robe, her auburn hair sleep-tangled and tumbling past her shoulders. She was followed by an athletically muscled black man in blue-striped pajama bottoms carrying a lit Coleman lantern. He closed the door firmly behind him. René remained inside.

Must be the traiteur *and her mate, the man Devlin Daniels named to be a* shuvano, *a nomad healer and conjurer like McKenna.* The lateness of the hour hit Kallie when she took in their nightwear. *Pajamas and robes, shit—it must be 4, maybe heading on 5 a.m.*

"C'mon up out of the rain," the woman said. Light flickered across the porch as the man rested the lantern on the railing. Her lambent gaze skipped over all three of them, taking careful note of each before settling on Kallie. "I understand you're looking for someone—among other things."

"My cousin, ma'am, Jackson Bonaparte," Kallie said as she climbed the cypress stairs to the porch, flanked on either side by Belladonna and Layne, then stopped a couple of yards from the waiting pair. "My apologies for showing up at your door so late."

"And what makes you think you'll find him here?" the *shuvano* asked. Swirling Celtic-style clan tats were blue-inked into his dark skin, covering his torso and swooping across his shoulders and down his arms.

"*Loups-garous* rescued him from a grave in Chaca-houla," Kallie replied, "and I've got reason to believe he was brought here to Le Nique because his papa was *loup-garou*."

The Coleman lantern emitted a steady hiss, loud in the sudden silence. The pungent odor of kerosene mixed uneasily with the mint from the window boxes.

"Are you Kallie?" the *traiteur* asked.

Tension unspooled from Kallie's muscles, unknotted her fists. "*Oui*, I am. Jackson's just a couple of months older than me, but—"

"He used to brag about being older," the woman finished with a smile. "Said it made him the boss of you—when he was little. Before he stopped coming to Le Nique."

Kallie laughed in relief. "That's Jackson, all right. You *do* know him."

From inside the cottage, Kallie heard the faint click of claws against wood, the jingle of a metal collar, then a familiar and pulse-quickening *whoo-whoo*. Excitement spilled through her like wine.

"Cielo! Bell, that's Cielo."

"The Siberian husky I saw in the back of the truck?" Layne asked.

"Yup. That it is," Belladonna said. "I'd know that *whoo*-ing anywhere."

A long string of *whoo-whoo-whoos* sounded behind the door as Cielo launched into a long Siberian-husky-style explanation of events.

"That's my cousin's dog, so he *must* be here," Kallie said. "Where is he? Is he okay? I'd like to see him." Her heart fell when she saw the look the *traiteur* exchanged with her husband, an uneasy blend of reluctance and apprehension that spelled nothing but bad news. "What is it? What's wrong?"

The woman shook her head, auburn locks brushing against her silk-draped shoulders. "We've got a few other things to discuss first. René said you claimed to be the reason magic is ricocheting and the reason Evelyn's headed for Louisiana, that you told him you needed help from a *traiteur* and her *shuvano* mate. That would be us—I'm Angélique Boudreau and this is my husband, Merlin Mississippi."

Kallie quickly introduced Belladonna and Layne. Merlin and Layne acknowledged each other with friendly nods, Merlin's short twists of bead-locked braids jabbing out in all directions around his skull like a multiple-armed star.

"Fox," Layne stated.

"Squirrel," Merlin answered. "Welcome, *drom-prala.*"

"Road brother," Layne translated before Kallie could ask.

Meeting and holding Angélique's eyes, Kallie said, "René's right on all counts. And I'll explain everything, tell you anything you want to know, but I need to see Jackson first. I *need* to know that he's okay." Tension returned, ratcheted her muscles wire-tight. She looked from Angélique to Merlin, then back. "*Is* he okay?"

"No, he's not okay, Kallie," Angélique said in a soft voice. "But he's still alive."

Kallie nodded, not trusting her voice. Still alive was good. Still alive suggested he could remain that way. But if he needed more than potions and salves? If he needed a healing or uncrossing trick?

"What's his condition?" Belladonna asked for her. "Maybe we can help."

"Can you help a half blood *loup-garou* enduring his First Change?" Stark and furious emotions tightened Angélique's features. "A Change made even more dangerous because it comes years later than it should've? A Change made impossible because his mama carved a spell into his flesh binding him to just one form—a spell that suddenly ended?"

A horrifying thought occurred to Kallie. She felt sick. She glanced at Belladonna and saw the same realization in her eyes. "Because of me," she whispered. "Because of the goddamned black dust and the *loa*."

"Now, hold on, Shug—" Belladonna began.

"Ain't your fault," Layne said, stepping in front of Kallie and gripping her shoulders. "Doctor Heron—"

"Mighta laid down the hex, but *I'm* the one who took it back inside of me when I unraveled that *fi' de garce*'s goddamned soul." Kallie twisted free of Layne's tight-fingered grip, walked away from the comfort he offered. She locked eyes with Angélique. "Take me to Jacks. I'll tell you everything, just let me see my cousin."

The *traiteur* regarded her for several moments, radiating a strong, steady energy—a healer's deep river aura. Then she nodded. "Fair enough."

THIRTY-SEVEN

DARKLING I LISTEN

Wolves loped along either side of the path leading to the small stone cottage beneath the old, twisted oak, raindrops pearling their fur in the slackening downfall, a *loup-garou* escort.

Kallie noticed that their eyes either shimmered silver or emitted a pale green, absinthe glow—like Jackson's had that long-ago summer night, seemingly glittering with green fairy dust. Had he already been enchanted, trapped into one form even then?

"He'll be okay," Belladonna soothed, as though reading her mind. "Jacks was bayou born and raised, so he's bayou tough. He survived that bastard Doctor Heron. We'll get him through this."

But Kallie was afraid all the bayou-born toughness in the world wouldn't be enough to counter the double-whammy of magic gone bad and a mother's broken binding. All the same, Kallie nodded. "Damn straight."

Angélique led the way while Merlin, now dressed in jeans, a blue tee, and scooter boots, followed a few yards behind his wife, his Coleman lantern lighting the way for those lacking preternatural sight—like himself.

The jingling of Cielo's collar told Kallie that the invisible stealth husky—thanks to the goddamned magic snafus—still padded beside her. She had a feeling, after Cielo's prancing, *whoo*ing greeting, that the dog was very pleased with her new condition.

A fierce rush of wind kicked Kallie's damp hair over her face, pushed at her back. Tree limbs creaked ominously. She smelled brine and ozone and wet fur.

"Wind's picking up," Belladonna commented.

"Yup," Layne replied, voice tight. "Ain't Evelyn supposed to be twenty or thirty hours out?"

"The wards could be doing more than just summoning her, they could be hurrying her along too," Kallie said, giving voice to a grim possibility.

"Virgin Mary in a leaky boat. There's a fucking cheery thought."

They drew to a stop in front of the cottage and Angélique grabbed hold of the iron ring in the stone door's center. She glanced at Kallie from over her shoulder. "Remember," she said. "He ain't gonna look the same."

Kallie nodded, throat tight.

The muscles in the *traiteur*'s arms corded and stone scraped against stone as she pulled the heavy door open. Heated air reeking of wild and wounded animals, dark and musky, rife with the odors of blood and straw and piss, washed over Kallie, tugged at her breath.

Releasing the ring, Angélique stepped back. "She's here, Ambrose."

"Send her in," a male voice replied, low and just a little weary.

The quick click of claws against stone and her jingling collar indicated that Cielo had already dashed inside.

"Dog too, apparently," the male said in dry tones.

Angélique's eyes flashed silver beneath Merlin's lantern. "Kin only," she reminded, her gaze skipping from Belladonna to Layne. Both nodded their understanding.

"We'll be right here, Shug," Belladonna said, slipping a companionable arm around Layne's leather-jacketed waist. "Give Jacks my love and tell him to get his fine ass feeling better. Wait. Is it a *furry* ass now?"

Kallie tried to smile, but felt her effort falter. "I'll tell him," she managed. Heart pounding, scared of what she'd find, she stepped into the cottage. The stone door thunked shut behind her, cutting off all light. She stood, blinking, waiting for her eyes to adjust, and for her heart to calm.

"He's over here, girl." The speaker's eyes glinted green in the thin light trickling in through the window slit from the dying night outside. "I'm Ambrose Bonaparte, Nicolas's *frère* and Jackson's *nonc*. I understand you're a cousin on his mama's side."

"That I am," Kallie replied. "His only cousin on that side of the family."

Making out a man-sized shape sitting against the north wall beside a darker, wolf-shaped form, Kallie hurried across the straw-strewn floor. A soft sigh, followed by a jingle, told her that Cielo had lain down near her Daddy.

Kallie knelt beside the dark-furred wolf lying on its side on the cold stone. "Jackson," she whispered, heart clenching. She studied him, struggling with the change in him—fur and paws and fangs. Her hand shook as she reached out and gently touched her cousin's side. Thick, warm fur greeted her fingertips.

Their shared long-ago summer night of fireflies and

wolf whispers pulsed through her mind. And Kallie drew on its magical possibilities as she remembered Jackson's pride that night.

"I won't do a big Change into a real wolf, but I'll do a little Change, me, and be a two-legged wolf someday."

"I wish I could be a wolf. I'd howl all night and eat up the people I don't like."

"He surprised me," Ambrose said quietly. "Him, he did something I ain't never seen a half blood do before—transform to full wolf."

Something in his voice made Kallie look up and meet Ambrose's lambent gaze. She felt a sharp pang as she realized how much he looked like her long-dead uncle. "Is that bad? I know he didn't expect to, but . . ."

"Normally, I'd say it was a damned good thing, an amazing and wondrous thing," Ambrose replied, "a thing to be proud of. But in this case . . ." He shook his head. "First Change ain't done, ain't a success, until transformation is made, then reversed." His attention returned to Jackson. A muscle played in his jaw. "He's had so much going against him: the late Change, all the blood he'd lost, exhaustion." His voice roughened. "Me, I don't believe he has the strength to Change back—not from full wolf."

"You giving up on him?" Kallie bristled, eyes burning. "'Cuz I ain't."

"Ain't giving up, girl. Just being realistic. Boy's done wrung out. If Change had happened at any other time, maybe . . ."

Wind moaned through the windows slits—an eerie chorus of ghosts.

"Then feed him, pour potions into him, have the *traiteur* work on him!"

"We've done all that and more," Ambrose said, and his gentle tone scared her even more than the slow, labored rise and fall of Jackson's chest beneath her fingers. "He's got nothing left to give."

Kallie shook her head, blinking away tears.

Don't do it, child. It ain't yo' place.

If she'd listened to Divinity and had allowed Doctor Heron's black-oiled soul to escape into the night, then the trick *Tante* Lucia—for whatever goddamned reason—had fixed to keep her son in one form would still be working, and Jackson wouldn't be dying.

But she *hadn't* listened. And guess what? Divinity had been right. What she'd done had been wrong, no matter how she justified it. In the end, she'd been no better than Doctor Heron himself.

"Jackson, hey, *cher*," Kallie said, stroking her hand along her cousin's side. "I ain't gonna let you give up. I know you're tired, but you gotta fight through it, just like you taught me how to box, how to aim my anger through my fists and into the bag."

Jackson's muscles twitched underneath Kallie's hand. His eyelids fluttered open and he looked at her with eyes that held a faint and dimming absinthe-green glow. His muzzle worked, like he was trying to talk, but the only sound he made was a combination gargle-*whoo*. She furiously blinked away more tears.

Cielo gave a soft answering *whoo*.

"I know a way to fix all this," Kallie said, voice husky. "But you've got to keep fighting, *cher*, until I can. I promised *Ti-tante* that I'd bring you home safe and sound and you know I can't break a promise—so don't make me kick your scrawny ass."

Jackson offered up another gargling attempt at speech, then swiped at the floor with one paw. *Okay*.

"*C'est ça bon*," Kallie said, her throat so tight it ached with each word. She bent, wrapped her arms around her cousin's neck, and rested her face against his, breathed in his sour/musky odor of blood and fur and too much pain. Whispered, "'Give me women, wine and snuff / Until I cry out "hold, enough!" / You may do so sans objection / Till the day of resurrection: / For, bless my beard, they aye shall be / My beloved Trinity.'"

Releasing Jackson, Kallie sat up. "I'm holding you to that, Jackson Bonaparte. You keep goddamned fighting. You wanna give up, you hafta be actually able to say 'hold, enough!' before I'll ever let you go."

Jumping to her feet, she strode across the floor, straw crunching under her boots, and hammered her fist against the stone door. She felt Ambrose's gaze on her back.

She could only hope that she'd told Jackson the truth about knowing how to fix things. What if Devlin Daniels was wrong? When the door shuddered, then scraped open, and Kallie stepped out, she found herself facing a woman she didn't recognize, instead of Angélique.

The woman looked to be a youthful forty with a narrow-hipped and boyish figure, her wind-tossed hair a spill of alabaster silk. But her eyes were her most arresting feature: a deep jade green like a depthless Caribbean sea at twilight.

Angélique and Merlin stood beside her—though the *shuvano* dimmed his lantern to spare the sensitive *loup-garou* eyes. "Kallie, this is January, Ambrose's wife, and the other half of our Alpha pair," the *traiteur* said.

"So, you're Kallie Rivière, Jackson's human cousin,"

January said, folding her arms beneath her small bust and studying her with those Caribbean eyes. Kallie tried not to bristle at the disdain threading through the word *human*. "Who marked you?"

Kallie glanced down at the bloodied claw scrapes scoring the tender flesh near the scooped neckline of her tank top.

Yo' heart be mine, Kallie Rivière, hoodoo woman.

Kallie quickly shoved aside the uncomfortable memory. "Devlin Daniels," she said. "He's also the one who told me to seek out Angélique and Merlin—although he didn't give any names."

"Devlin? *He* sent you?" Surprise flickered across the Alpha's face. Her gaze, now uneasy, returned to the claw marks on Kallie's chest. "And claimed you," she murmured, almost to herself.

Kallie stiffened. "The hell he did." She felt Layne stir beside her, felt his gaze. "Forget about that. It's what he *told* me that's important—that I'm the cause behind everything that's gone wrong since yesterday morning."

"Dat's what I been saying all along," a familiar voice said from the shadows beneath the oak tree. "Dis girl be a walking jinx, a living hex."

THIRTY-EIGHT

DEADLINE

"Jesus in a cracker tin," Layne muttered. "Just what we need."

A cold brick of dread dropped into Kallie's stomach when she saw Baron Samedi stroll into view, still wearing his Cash suit, and twirling his walking stick in one white-gloved hand. He sauntered to a stop beside January, his sunglasses-hidden gaze looking everywhere but at Kallie. The sharp smell of hot-peppered rum spiced the air.

He still can't see me. That's one good thing.

"Y'all don't understand—the magic ricochets have affected the Baron too," Kallie said. "And his *cheval* hates—"

"One thieving, betraying, sorry-ass sonuvabitch named Jackson Bonaparte who's just run outta time," the Baron said in Cash's voice, then laughed. "And I ain't a fucking *cheval* at the moment, darlin'."

Kallie's hands clenched into fists. "I know how to fix this. I need a little time—"

"Sorry. Time's up."

"We'll just see about that," Kallie promised, stepping in front of the *loa*. "Give me the time I need to set things right or I'll let *my loa* come out and play a few hexing games."

Of course, the last part was pure bluff, since she didn't even know how to contact her *loa*, let alone release her, but the Samedi-Cash didn't know that—hopefully.

Thunder boomed, shaking the ground and launching Kallie's heart into her throat. Baron Samedi seemed to stretch up into the cloud-roiling sky as though rising on stilts, his Armani suit jacket flapping in the wind, and his skull-painted face scowling down on her. Her blood turned to ice.

"Holy shit," Layne whispered.

"Agreed," Belladonna said.

"Who you t'ink you be talking to, little hoodoo? Mebbe I can't see you 'cuz o' yo' tricks, but I can close de gates between de world of de living and de realm of de dead and leave you wandering forever in de Between Places."

"I was talking to your *cheval*, Baron, not to you," Kallie said, mouth dry. "I never intended those words for *you*. All I'm asking for is the chance to restore things to their proper natures, the chance to save my cousin's life and—"

The Baron's voice rumbled across the night sky and vibrated up from the ground, echoing within her. "Kallie Rivière, you got ten hours to restore t'ings to deir proper natures. If you don't get it done in dat time, I'm sending yo' cousin to de realm of de dead—if he ain't had the good sense to die before den—and I will find a way to strip dat *loa* from yo' luscious body and leave you empty in de Between Places."

Baron Samedi vanished in a retina-searing flash of

forked lightning. The pungent scent of ozone and peppered rum saturated the air.

Kallie looked away, blinking and shaken. Instead of getting Cash to back off from his quest to kill Jackson, all she'd succeeded in doing was pissing off the *loa* of death and resurrection and earning herself a deadline. Never a good thing.

"Hellfire," Belladonna said. "Oh, Shug, ten hours . . ."

"Start talking, girl," January commanded. Wind whipped her hair across her face and her eyes glowed between the white strands.

Shoving her trembling hands into the pockets of her shorts, Kallie did just that. She told January and Angélique and Merlin everything. And she watched their expressions shift from disbelieving, to shocked, to horrified as she told them about Doctor Heron and his black dust and the tragic case of mistaken identity, about the *loa* her mother had replaced her soul with, about what Devlin had found inside of her.

It be de black dust you took in from Doctor Heron. De hex you sucked down when you unzipped de man's soul. It captured de loa, webbed her up like a fat fly in a spiderweb and it feeds on her power, using it to magnify its own. Dat be de cause of all de magical mishaps.

"Great Mother," Angélique whispered, her face stunned. Sympathy glimmered in her eyes. "You're caught in a nightmare."

"I think that sums it up, yup," Kallie replied. "Devlin told me to ask y'all about the sacred fire, that it was the only way to fix things."

Merlin's eyes widened. He whistled low and long, then said, "Holy goddamn. The sacred fire. Yeah, yeah, that could definitely work. The sacred fire is a very powerful and transformative energy, yeah. But . . ."

"But what?" Kallie asked. "I'll do whatever it takes."

"Excuse me," Belladonna said. "But we're talking sex magic, right?"

Kallie stared at her. "We are?"

"Yup," Merlin agreed. "But the sacred fire ain't magic, per se—which is a good thing, given all the problems we're having with magic."

"Then what is it?" Kallie asked.

"It's a ritual of prolonged, very intense sex," Merlin replied, meeting her gaze, and Kallie noticed for the first time that his eyes were two different colors, one blue and one brown—much like Cielo's, but with deeper, richer shades. "And by *prolonged*, I'm talking hours, not days. Though that's been done too, with some *amazing* results."

Kallie blinked. *Days?* She wanted to ask if the people involved had survived their marathon of intense sex, but decided that if they hadn't, they'd most likely died sweaty and exhausted, but very happy. "And this ritual creates the sacred fire?"

Merlin nodded. "Yup. Raw sexual energy heightened by connection on all levels—physical, spiritual, mental—by the couple performing. The sacred fire is powerful, a positive and life-affirming energy that will burn to ash anything dark or destructive within you and your partner—or around you."

Belladonna leaned in and cupped a hand around Kallie's ear. "Sounds like a fancy way of saying you fuck away the black dust," she whispered. "Where do I sign up to get hexed?"

Kallie whapped Belladonna's shoulder. "Evil."

"But," Merlin said pointedly, recapturing Kallie's attention, "there's still a problem. Like I said, the energy generated is way fucking powerful, and that kind of light and heat lures all manner of things—good and bad—to a couple completely vulnerable in the throes of sex."

"And now, thanks to the magic snafus," Angélique said, "we can't use normal protective measures, such as wards or protective circles."

Kallie nodded, her stomach sinking. "What other options do we have? I hafta do this, I hafta try, at least."

"If we had more trained *shuvanos* or *traiteurs* here, then we might have a chance," Merlin said thoughtfully. "We could become living wards, surrounding you with positive energy and channeled white light, instead of magic. Use chants. Drums."

"I could help," Belladonna volunteered. "I'm a voodooienne."

Hope surged renewed through Kallie as a possibility bloomed bright. "Would hoodoos and voodoos work too?"

A light glinted in Merlin's eyes. "Definitely. But we ain't got much time to round a bunch of people up—"

"Wait, hold on," January cut in, slashing her hands through the air in front of her. Once she had everyone's attention, she continued in a quiet but forceful voice. "As unhappy as I am to have Outsiders in Le Nique"—her narrowed gaze slashed across Kallie, Belladonna, and Layne—"and as much as I wish to avoid admitting more, I realize the situation gives me little choice. But I have conditions that need to be met so I can keep my pack safe."

"*Mais oui*," Kallie said. "Anything."

The Alpha's conditions were simple: only those trained in magic and healing would be allowed—no friends or other tagalongs. René and a few other *loups-garous* of his choice would meet the incoming conjurers near Morgan City, some twenty miles distant, blindfold them, then bring them to Le Nique.

"If they refuse the blindfold, they will be left behind," January finished.

"Fair enough," Kallie said. "Give me just a minute."

She slipped her cell phone from her pocket, then walked up the path until she caught a signal. "We found Jackson," she said when her aunt answered.

"Praise Bon Dieu," Divinity breathed. "Is de boy okay?"

Kallie thought of the slow, labored rise and fall of her cousin's chest beneath her fingertips and her throat tightened. "For now," she lied. "Look, we need help. Are Addie and her posse still there?"

"*Oui*, we been hashing t'ings out, us. What you need, child?"

Drawing in a quick breath, Kallie told her, passing along the Alpha's instructions.

"We be dere, girl. Don't you worry. I'll let dem know dey have an opportunity to make up for deir earlier foolishness."

"*Merci, Ti-tante.*"

When Kallie returned to the stone cottage, she told January, "They've agreed."

"Then I'll get René on his way." The Alpha's eyes unfocused, her gaze seeming to turn inward, and remembering how Devlin had delved into her mind, Kallie suspected the *loup-garou* was using telepathy to contact René.

A moment later, January slanted a glance at Angélique.

"He's taking Jubilee and Dorian with him, and Moss will keep an eye on your sleeping cubs in the meantime."

The *traiteur* smiled. "Good."

"You have children?" Kallie asked.

"Double handful," Merlin replied, pride in his voice. "Twins, a boy and girl."

And, Kallie thought, sympathy prickling through her as she glanced at the stone cottage behind the *shuvano*, half bloods.

"Who's gonna be your partner in the ritual?" Angélique asked. She flicked a speculative glance toward Layne. "If it's going to be too awkward to do it with your nomad friend, I'm sure I can round up volunteers. Merlin is skilled in sex magic and rituals—one of his specialties, actually. You couldn't ask for better."

"Thanks, hun," Merlin replied, smiling at Angélique.

Kallie's cheeks flamed. She looked up at Layne. His best friend had died in her bed and that was something she wasn't sure either of them could get past just yet. Or, in Layne's case, ever. No matter how much she wanted Layne, being together like this *would* be awkward, especially with everything that hung in the balance. But hopping into the sack for a long, boisterous round of ritual sex with a stranger would be even more so.

"I'll understand if you say no," Kallie said. "Please don't feel—"

Bending, Layne brushed his lips against hers and stopped her words. "Ain't saying no, Kallie," he murmured. His dreads lifted into the wind, pale tendrils against the fading night.

She touched her fingers to his face. Saw the grief and guilt he buried in the depths of his eyes. "*Merci, cher.*"

"Let's get going," Angélique said. "There's a lot we need to do to get you two ready and—" She stopped talking and her gaze turned inward, as though she was listening to something only she could hear. Kallie noticed that January had the same introspective expression.

"*Mon Dieu*," Angélique said a moment later, expression dismayed. "According to what René just heard on TV, landfall is in *fifteen* hours, not twenty or thirty. And Evelyn is still a category five."

Dread folded through Kallie. If Evelyn landed as a five, nothing would be left in her wake. Reaching for Layne's hand, she met Angélique's glowing eyes and said, "Then tell us what we need to do."

THIRTY-NINE

CONSECRATION

Kallie rose shivering from her cold, sea-salt-charged bath, the water's cinnamon, cloves, and neroli fragrance clinging to her wet body and hair, and stepped out of the tin tub and onto a plush towel resting on the consultation room's hardwood floor. The wolf-clawed skin above her left breast stung and ached from the salt water.

"Ready," she said, through nearly chattering teeth.

It turned out that the first things Kallie and Layne needed to do before they could begin to spark a fire between them hot enough to incinerate the black dust in a column of molten flame—and thus save magic, Jackson, Louisiana, and her own existence—were to be ritually bathed, smudged, and anointed.

Angélique had led Kallie and Belladonna back to the cottage she shared with her husband, while Merlin had ushered Layne to a raised *cabane* the *loups-garous* used for seasonal ceremonies and celebrations when the weather refused to allow such to be performed outside beneath the moon.

"There's a lot more to this than just fucking, bro," Merlin tells Layne as they walk away. *"A helluva lot more."*

While the bathwater dried on Kallie's goosebumping skin, Belladonna moved behind her and began to gently towel-dry her hair. The pungent aroma of cedar and juniper and cypress curled into the air from the brazier Angélique held.

The *traiteur* stepped in front of Kallie, using a peacock feather fan to wave the smoke over her nude body, taking care that the fragrant smoke touched every part of Kallie, beginning with her feet.

Consecrating her. Blessing her. Purifying her.

Despite the fact that she was chock-full of a dead root doctor's poisonous black dust, not to mention a hex-webbed *loa*—thanks to the same black dust and her mama.

As Belladonna and Angélique murmured prayers of protection, Kallie hugged her arms over her breasts and breathed in the smoke, suspecting Layne was going through the same process.

As much as she'd been longing to tumble the nomad into bed, this wasn't the same thing. Their joining would be deliberate, a means to an end—a delicious and pleasurable means, sure—but not a spontaneous moment of mutual passion.

And once again, as though reading her mind, Belladonna murmured, "Wonder if Layne is feeling like a virgin bride being prepared for a randy groom too?"

Picturing that, Kallie laughed, and some of tension unwound from her muscles. Belladonna's lips curved into a satisfied smile.

Angélique finished with the smudging and returned the fan and brazier to her worktable. "We're almost done," she said, picking up a small blue bottle and carrying it over to Kallie. "When we get to the *cabane*, Merlin will have a potion for you—an aphrodisiac to awaken and alter your consciousness so you can channel the fire, the pure blazing energy, you and your nomad will be creating."

"What do I need to do?" Kallie asked.

"For the most part, just what comes naturally when left alone with a handsome naked man," Angélique replied with a smile. "Once you two get busy, let the energy build, let it flow through you, between you. Abandon yourself to it, even as you direct it. The main thing—and this is what takes the longest, probably all of the time the Baron allotted you—will be opening one another's chakras. Each chakra needs to be opened in turn, a sevenfold path to the sacred fire."

"Does it need to be done slowly?"

"Yes. It needs to be kindled, fed, developed into a holy bonfire within you both. Too fast, too soon, and it dies, a tiny flame. And the black dust will remain."

Kallie smelled rose and lavender and frankincense as Angélique anointed her chakra points with the oil at the crown of her head, between her eyebrows, on her throat, her sternum, her navel, then—with a gentle touch—just above her crotch.

"I'll let you get the last one, *chère*." Angélique handed Kallie the bottle.

With a drop of aromatic oil glistening on her fingertip, Kallie anointed the most intimate part of her anatomy. Heat rushed into her cheeks as she thought of Layne touching her in the same place. Tasting her. Exploring.

"Not sure I'm going to need the aphrodisiac," she muttered, giving the bottle of oil back to the *traiteur*.

"It's not just for intensifying desire," Angélique reminded her, a knowing glint in her emerald eyes.

"You're going to need endurance and strength to get through this ritual. Here." She handed Kallie a red silk bathrobe and a pair of slippers for the walk outside. "Are you on birth control?"

"Yup."

"But this will be your first time with Layne, right?"

"Yeah," Kallie answered softly, belting on the robe. "The first time." And a far cry from her fantasy of a broken-down car and a helpful nomad in a kilt.

Angélique filled the robe's pocket with a double handful of foil-wrapped condoms. "So you don't know where that boy has been. You can never be too safe."

"Am I going to need this many?"

Angélique shrugged. "Young man. Revved up on a passion potion. Hours to open your chakras and awaken the fire. Most likely. Better too many than not enough."

Kallie nodded. "For true."

Belladonna pulled her into a quick hug. "I know you can do this, Shug. Forget about everything except Layne. Just focus on each other. And ravish the bejesus out of that nomad."

"Evil," Kallie declared, planting a kiss on Belladonna's cheek before slipping free of her embrace. "Thanks, Bell."

"Ah," the *traiteur* murmured. "René's back, and the hoodoos—including your aunt—are waiting at the *cabane*. Time for us to go."

Kallie followed Angélique out of the cottage and into the gray, windy dawn, her heart and belly full of butterflies.

Only eight hours remained until the Baron's deadline. Thirteen till landfall.

The *cabane*'s black-painted interior was supposed to represent outside, Layne reflected, as he stepped from the tin tub's cinnamon- and cloves-fragrant water—road rash stinging and burning all along his right side—and onto a braided rug.

Curving up from the cypress wood floor, across the north wall, and trailing across the ceiling, then down again, the moon had been painted in all its phases surrounded by soft blue-white stars, transforming the black room into a night sky brimming with a simple promise: *everything has a season, a place.*

Now that Divinity's potion had worn off, pain throbbed at the back of Layne's head, echoing with a dull ache between his eyes. Something he'd told Merlin about in case it could affect the ritual, and the *shuvano* had assured him that he'd be given a potion later.

"You been with this girl before?" Merlin asked as he smudged Layne's wet body with smoke redolent of a deep wood forest—cedar and cypress and juniper.

Cupping his hands, Layne drew the pungent smoke over his face and head. "No," he admitted. "Not yet. It's . . . complicated."

His thoughts flipped back to the botanica and Kallie's sudden kiss, her lips soft and insistent, her warm and curvy body pressed up against his, remembered the silken feel of her thick tresses entangled in his fingers, remembered the intense heat, the thought-blanking desire that had swept through him.

Remembered Gage sprawled bloody and lifeless in her bed. Sharp-edged sorrow and guilt pierced him. He quickly shoved the image aside. "But I don't deny that I want her. That I care about her. When I look into her eyes . . ." Layne shook his head, his dreads sweeping against his bare skin.

"Funny, ain't it," Merlin drawled, "how the most natural thing in the world between two people can become the most complicated when we allow our heads to lead us instead of following our hearts and bodies. Arms out to the sides, bro."

Stretching out his arms so the smoke could caress the skin beneath, Layne said, "So is that how a nomad *shuvano* wound up living in a hidden *loup-garou* village? By following his heart and body?"

"To make a long story short—yup. But my love life ain't what we're here to discuss, now, is it, *drom-prala*?"

"No, *shuvano*. But there's something else I need to tell you—I'm a Vessel and I have a ghost on board."

Merlin whistled. "I *knew* I sensed something different about you. Holy shit. A Vessel. Oh. You can put your arms down now." Finished with the smudging, he carried the brazier back to the kitchenette worktable tucked up against the west wall. "Your ghost is gonna hafta disembark. The sacred fire might not harm him or her, but then again it might. I just don't know for sure."

"That's what I was wondering."

Merlin returned with a jar of salve and bandages. "Sit," he said, nodding his head at a low stool.

Layne did as directed and, as the *shuvano* tended to the raw abrasions on his skin, he turned his attention inward, summoned Augustine from his safety bubble, and explained the reason for the upcoming sacred fire ritual, including the Brit's imminent need to depart.

<*Look, you helped me out with Babette, so I ain't gonna desert you,*> Layne promised. <*I'll get you back to New Orleans and Felicity. Then you split. Agreed?*>

<A gentlemanly gesture, Valin. Agreed.>

Layne felt a moment's disorientation, the moon-etched *cabane* spinning around him, his heart pounding hard and fast, as Augustine sieved out of his body, leaving Layne feeling strangely lighter.

As the spinning slowed to a halt, Layne felt a tap on his shoulder. Heard Merlin's irritated voice. "You listening to me? These are goddamned important instructions, road rider."

"Apologies, *shuvano*," Layne murmured. "I'm listening."

"You need to open her chakras slow, one by one," Merlin repeated. "And she needs to be opening yours. Restrain yourself from just jumping her bones, 'cuz building the fire's gonna take a *long* time. Each orgasm, each time one of you comes, adds more fuel, more intensity, to that fire. Now stand up."

Layne rose to his feet, fresh gauze crinkling against his side, and turned to face the *shuvano*, who continued to instruct him in a low voice as he anointed him with oil smelling of lavender, rose, and frankincense at each chakra point, handing Layne the bottle of oil so he could finish.

"Looks like the cold-water effect has worn off," Merlin said with a grin. He handed Layne his boxers and a glass. "I added a few things to your aphrodisiac to help with your headache, so drink up. Your girl will be here soon. I'm gonna go out and get the hoodoos organized."

Layne swallowed the potion down in two long gulps, catching a hint of bitterness underneath its strawberry-wine sweetness, then pulled on his boxers. Thinking of Kallie, of lying next to her skin to skin, trailing his fingers down her bare back, he felt himself stir. Then his heart kicked against his ribs and his hands went cold.

They *had* to get this right.

Everything depended upon it. Including Kallie's life.

Dawn smudged the horizon a tropical-punch pink, a color soon swallowed by bruised and sullen clouds as Kallie walked with Angélique to the *cabane*.

Divinity and Gabrielle waited beside Merlin on the lantern-lit porch, as did a third, smaller figure. The muscles in Kallie's shoulders knotted as she recognized McKenna. Given the circumstances, she hadn't expected the nomad to accompany the others, and now she wondered how much information her aunt had shared with everyone.

Maybe the woman's simply a glutton for punishment.

Just as Kallie was about to follow Angélique up the steps, she caught a glimpse of movement from the corner of her eye. Pausing, she turned to look, and the claw marks on her chest throbbed and ached anew when she saw a lean silhouette with long, wild hair and glowing ash eyes watching from within the gloom-veiled trees.

Devlin Daniels.

But when Kallie looked again, she saw nothing—no silhouette, no ashy eyes—just darkness. She studied the shadowed depths, deciding she'd been wrong, the Le Nique *loups-garous* would never have allowed him so close, judging by their previous reaction to his presence. She couldn't help but wonder why he wasn't welcome.

Taking a deep breath of air heavy with the smells of the bayou—fish, cattails, and waterlogged cypress—and fighting to keep her robe down in a sudden gust of rain-sprinkled wind, Kallie climbed up to the porch.

Divinity enfolded her in a tight hug smelling of her herbs, comfrey and sage, before releasing her and stepping back. She tsked. Folded her arms over her bosom. "Funny how you left out de part about you pissing off de Baron in our conversation, you," she said.

"I didn't want you getting all worked up," Kallie replied. "Besides, I was trying to scare off Cash, not insult the Baron, but it went all wrong."

"There's a surprise," McKenna muttered.

Divinity's eyes narrowed. "Well, *mais oui*, ain't nothing to get worked up over, now, is dere? It ain't like Jackson will lose his life or dat you will be left wandering in de Between Places or nothing if t'ings go wrong again."

"Ain't gonna let that happen," Kallie said, returning her aunt's glare and lifting her chin. She hoped, anyway. The butterflies returned.

Divinity's expression softened. "No, I know you ain't, Kallie-girl."

"So how do we want to do this?" Gabrielle asked. "Take one-hour shifts?"

"Yeah, that'd be best." Merlin handed Kallie a glass, urging her to drink the contents with a nod of his head as he returned his attention to the Outsiders. "Five people at a time—one at the north side of the *cabane*, one each east and west, two on the south end—so we can form a pentagram."

"Dat sounds right," Divinity said, Gabrielle and McKenna murmuring their agreement as well.

Kallie drank the potion down, tasting strawberry wine and oranges, nutmeg, and bitter wormwood among its ingredients. Given her empty stomach, the wine went straight to her head in a dizzying rush.

Angélique took the empty glass from her hand. "Me and Merlin will be inside the *cabane* with you from time to time," she said quietly, "in case either of you need guidance or water or more potion."

Kallie nodded, even though heat flooded her cheeks.

"Or even a muscle cramp massaged away," Merlin added, with a serious expression. "Trust me, in a ritual this prolonged, it happens."

"You'll be given as much privacy as possible," Angélique reassured her. "And you'll be treated with gentleness and respect whenever one of you happens to need us. But you'll be so focused on what you're doing and what you're undergoing, you won't even notice us."

Somehow, Kallie doubted that.

"Ye need tae remember tha' this isn't a romantic encounter," McKenna said, her tone full of a teacher's cool poise, "but a ritual tha' will benefit us all. "

Looking into the nomad pixie's dark eyes and seeing a deep-rooted grief, a bitter fury, Kallie realized that McKenna wasn't here because she was a glutton for punishment or a jealous ex-wife determined to sabotage her ex-husband's romantic entanglements—at least, not now.

She'd joined the hoodoo circle of protection because she loved Layne enough to lay aside her injured pride, her wounded heart, to ensure his safety during a potentially dangerous ritual.

All right, goddammit, maybe the woman ain't all bad.

Kallie gave McKenna a grudging nod. One that the nomad didn't return. "Just don't screw this up," she growled instead.

And I did say maybe.

Squaring back her shoulders, Kallie glanced at Angélique. "I'm ready."

"*Ça c'est bon*," the *traiteur* said, going over to the *cabane*'s door and pushing it open. The soft and wavering light of many candles spilled onto the porch.

"We'll be out here, keeping you safe, child," Divinity promised.

"*Merci bien*." Kallie stepped over the threshold, Angélique and Merlin right behind her.

FORTY

THE SACRED FIRE

Layne was waiting for her inside the night-sky-painted *cabane*. Clad only in his blue boxers, he stood beside a low bed that looked like little more than a sheet-covered mattress carried in from somewhere else and placed in the middle of the floor.

The sight of him in the flickering shadows of the candlelit room—long and lean and muscle-cut, his unknotted dreads coiling to his waist—flooded Kallie with a heat that she saw reflected in his green eyes. Her pulse quickened.

Angélique and Merlin led her across the cypress plank floor to the bed. Once Kallie was standing in front of Layne, he clasped both of her hands within his own, his thumbs rubbing across her knuckles, a soothing motion for them both, she suspected.

"Hey, sunshine," he greeted.

"Hey back, and here I am without a bucket of water," she teased in an effort to calm her nerves. "Y'know, in my dream, you were wearing a kilt."

"A kilt, huh? In *my* dream, you were wearing a coin bra and a hip scarf. Not that I'm complaining."

Kallie felt a smile curve her lips. Felt her nervousness fade. "Me either."

Merlin leaned over the bed and pulled back its rose-and lavender-scented sheets while chanting, "Upon this bed, you shall burn, your passion a pyre of all-consuming light, lip to lip, and hip to hip. Her breath shall be his breath; his desire shall be her desire; her pleasure shall be his pleasure. Entwined together, a single pulsing heart, he and she shall create the sacred."

"By the forest Mother, let it be," Angélique murmured. Separating Layne and Kallie's hands, she led them to the consecrated bed and sat them down upon it.

"We're going to go now and leave you to it," Angélique said. "We'll be back each hour to check on you to see if you need anything."

Layne nodded as though it was the most natural thing in the world to have people wandering in and out during sex. And, for all Kallie knew, in the nomad world it was.

"Remember," Angélique said as she and her husband headed for the door. "Each chakra in turn." The door closed with a solid *thunk* behind the *traiteur* and her *shuvano*.

Hour One

From outside, Kallie heard the rhythmic throb of drums begin, an earthy beat tapped out with fingertips and palms and the hard heels of hands.

"Kallie." Low and husky and compelling.

She looked into Layne's eyes—potion-dilated pupils surrounded by a pine-green corona—and her nervousness faded as that familiar electric shock of connection once more arced like mad-scientist lightning down her spine, between her legs.

Kallie cupped Layne's face, bringing it down to her and lacing her arms around his neck. She closed her eyes as he kissed her, his lips warm and tender and passionate upon hers, his hands on her hips. She tasted the aphrodisiac on his tongue—strawberry wine and oranges—and deepened the kiss with a soft and hungry moan.

Merlin's potion unfurled within her, igniting like napalm in her veins, tracing along her nerves, pounding in time with the drums thumping beyond the *cabane*'s walls.

Kallie burned, a single flame stretching up into the moon-painted night.

With one hand on her hip, the fingers of the other entangled in her hair, Layne lifted Kallie up and onto his lap. She felt him grow hard and taut underneath her. Heat pulsed in her belly, pooled between her legs. His mouth devoured hers in a searing and breath-stealing kiss.

She wanted more of him. All of him. Now.

Opening her eyes, Kallie curled Layne's dreads around her fingers. Then she twisted off his lap, pulling him down with her, still kissing, and on top of her. She pushed at his boxers, kneaded his firm ass, his erection like heated steel against her belly.

Layne's hot, rough hands were everywhere—unbelting her robe, trailing up the inside of her thigh, cupping her breast. She felt the sensuous kiss of air against her tingling skin as he opened her robe.

Then his mouth left hers, sliding hot, wet kisses down along her throat, before closing around her stiffened nipple and sucking. Kallie gasped, arched her back. He kissed a path from her breast to her belly, his tongue darting into her belly button, his dreads snaking across her soft skin. She shivered as molten heat flared in points just south of his exploring mouth.

Ah, but Layne's fingers—his fingers whispered up the insides of her thighs, then in between. Kallie moaned—a moan he echoed—as he slipped first one, then two fingers inside of her, stroking carefully, rhythmically, as his mouth continued its journey south.

Layne paused, then carefully scooted Kallie down to the edge of the bed. She watched as he slid off the bed to kneel between her legs, his dreads slithering like silk across her thighs, his eyes darkening as he drank in the sight of her.

Sliding his free hand underneath her ass, he lifted her to his mouth. At the first hot, swirling touch of his tongue, Kallie came in a sudden intense rush, arching herself against his mouth, demanding *more-more-more* as pleasure throbbed through her in tight circles, intensifying her arousal instead of quenching it.

Layne answered her demand, her scorching need, with his talented tongue and clever fingers, and Kallie cried out as another orgasm rocked her, and felt something open deep within her, unfolding like the petals of a flower.

Fire braided around the base of her spine in molten coils.

Angélique's instructions returned: *Each chakra needs to be opened in turn, a sevenfold path to the sacred fire.*

"Goddamn," Kallie panted. "There's one. Chakra, I mean."

Layne kissed the insides of Kallie's thighs, and she shivered, still aching with renewed—*no, make that still burning*—need as he kissed his way back up her body, pausing to suckle first one nipple, then the other, before brushing his lips against hers.

"Good," he whispered.

She felt Layne's erection rock-hard against her. Liquid heat rippled through her belly. Cupping his face, Kallie kissed him thoroughly, tasting herself on his tongue. She reached down with one hand and pushed impatiently at the waistband of his boxers.

"Off," she murmured against his lips, snapping the elastic.

Layne rolled onto his back, lifted his hips, then shoved off his boxers. Tossed them to the floor. Kallie's breath caught in her throat as she took in the sight of him—gorgeous and pagan, all wild masculinity—and the knotwork dragon inked into his very hard length, its tail curling up toward his flat abs.

What she'd glimpsed beneath the material of his wet boxers during the contest hadn't been an illusion or a lie. She reached for him, sliding the palm of her hand along his tattooed length, reveling in the feel of him—warm smooth velvet over steel—pleasure coiling into her belly at the sound of his indrawn breath.

Leaving her robe on the bed like a fallen red rose, Kallie straddled Layne on her hands and knees, playing adventurer, discovering the new world of his lean-muscled body, tracing the contours of his tattoos with fingers and lips and tongue—tasting male musk and cinnamon and cloves on his skin—and claiming her territory.

Sensation and the slow-building throb of pleasure blurred Kallie's thoughts, made it difficult to focus beyond the feel of Layne's skin, his taste, the musky scent of his manhood, the sound of his ragged breathing and low moans.

His fingers entwined in her long, thick hair and his breath caught in his throat as he released, muscles cording. "Holy shit," he gasped. "Does it feel like fire curling around your spine?"

"Mmm-hmm," Kallie murmured against his belly. She kissed her way to his nipples, tracing the concentric circles inked around both hardened nubs with her tongue. Then it was her turn to gasp as his fingers found her, exploring once more, and claiming the role of bold adventurer.

Hour Two

As Kallie played with Layne, he played back, cupping her breasts with his road-callused hands, sucking her nipples, his erection straining against her—demanding she give herself.

A foil package crinkled beneath Kallie's knee, reminding her of the treasure trove tucked into the pocket of her robe. She tore the package open with her teeth. Carefully unrolled the condom over Layne's breathtaking length.

Kallie eased herself onto Layne, bit by bit, his hands on her hips. She was so aroused, she felt only a little pain, but in a good way, a pain that quickly faded. Layne groaned low in his throat. As she rocked down, he thrust up to meet her, and they both cried out in pleasure.

Kallie looked into Layne's eyes as he drove into her and the electric shock of connection crackled between them once more. Saw his eyes widen and knew he felt it too. Pleasure fluttered in heated waves through her belly and something wheeled open within her again—a chakra blossom—and another strand of fire braided itself around the base of her spine.

Layne's arms wrapped around Kallie and he rolled her onto her back with him still buried deep inside of her. Panting, she laced her legs around his waist and met him thrust for thrust. Another sudden and intense orgasm rippled through her in powerful waves. And it was only the beginning.

Hour Four

Something besides the wind plucked at Belladonna's hair. Something dark and hungry and hoping to break her concentration as she stood in front of the *cabane*, one point of the protective human pentagram's five. But she ignored it and kept her eyes closed while she chanted prayers of protection to Saint Joseph, Saint Michael, and Papa Legba.

Belladonna didn't need to see the shadows and shades to know they were there. She felt them. Smelled them—mildew and rot and emptiness—as they tested each human ward guarding the pair joined together inside the *cabane*, irresistibly drawn like flesh-hungry piranhas to the life force Kallie and Layne were busy generating.

If the errant spirits broke through the ring of light that she and the other hoodoos had encircled the *cabane* with, nothing but shells would remain of Kallie and Layne.

"Gracious Saint Joseph, protect me and my friends and all present from evil," Belladonna prayed in a near-whisper. She continued to visualize channeling pure, white light down through the top of her head and into her veins, flooding her body with a radiance that she linked with that of the other two-legged wards.

"Jesus Christ! Something just touched my ass!"

Belladonna felt the circle of light waver. She opened her eyes and slanted a glance at the tall, skinny root doctor from Houma who stood at the *cabane*'s left front corner — with her on the right as the pentagram's bottom two points.

"Lucky you," she drawled. "Now keep focused, keep praying."

Nodding, jaw tight, the root doctor closed his eyes and resumed his quiet prayers. Above them both, branches creaked and groaned as wind tore through the trees in another savage gust. Rattled at doors and shutters like an angry and locked-out husband.

Belladonna shivered and shut her eyes again. *Hurry, Kallie*, she prayed.

Hour Six

Caught in Layne's embrace, Kallie became aware that someone else moved around them, speaking in soft and soothing tones. A damp cloth cooled her bliss-fevered forehead. Someone pressed a cup against her lips and she parted them. Water poured down her parched throat, followed by more strawberry-wine-flavored potion. Someone else kneaded fragrant oils into her weary muscles.

Then she and Layne were alone, joined lip to lip and hip to hip, their sweat-slick bodies sliding together once more.

Hour Eight

Drums pounded and pulsed, the bayou's dark, primal heart. Time spun away.

Kallie clung to Layne in exhaustion, her arms laced around his neck, as he sat in the room's only chair with her astride him, the thrust of his hips an urgent and steady beat. He kissed her, one hand cupped against her face.

Layne's final chakra had irised open some time ago in a breath-stealing explosion of ecstasy, but Kallie's remained stubbornly closed. And she was terrified they wouldn't be able to coax it open in time.

She'd lost count of the number of orgasms that had swept her body—each more intense than the last. But even though her body practically vibrated with electric pleasure, quivering at Layne's every touch, the taste of his lips, the feel of him inside her, her weary mind kept slipping into a near dream state—no, make that a near *nightmare* state—every time she was about to scale that last peak.

Like now. Pleasure looped around her, drew tight, then unraveled as her treacherous and dreaming-while-awake mind splashed an ugly image across the darkness behind her eyes.

Mama pulls the gun's trigger and the side of Papa's head explodes in a spray of blood and bone. He slumps down in his chair, a bottle of Abita still in his hand, his purple eyes wide and blank.

Kallie stands in her bedroom doorway, frozen. Mama turns and faces her, aims the gun carefully between her shaking hands. Her hands shake, but her face is still, resigned.

"I can't," Kallie mumbled in frustration against Layne's lips.

Layne's rhythm slowed, but he didn't stop, just eased into a gentle rocking motion. He brushed Kallie's hair back from her face. "What's wrong, Kall? You need me to do something different?"

She shook her head. "It just keeps slipping away from me. Why won't it open, goddammit? I'm pretty sure we're almost out of time . . ."

"You're exhausted, we both are, and you're feeling the pressure. We're almost there, sunshine. Don't give up on me now."

"I *ain't* giving up, goddammit. I'm just"—Kallie's breath caught as his hands cupped her ass and lifted her up to the tip of his erection, then dropped her down again—"trying to figure out why all of a sudden I can't . . ."

"Can't what?" Layne murmured, easing her up with agonizing slowness. He caught her stiff and swollen nipple with his lips and sucked it into his mouth.

"God," Kallie whispered. She was caught between his wet mouth and his hard, gliding length—a willing prisoner—as he lifted her up, then down, then up again.

Liquid heat pooled in her belly, ignited like napalm. She moaned.

But darkness seeped in at the edges of Kallie's vision like floodwater under a door, and another memory unscrolled through her mind.

Gage lies on his belly in her bed, his face turned to the side. Blood masks his fine features, glitters in his black curls. All color has drained from his espresso-brown skin. His empty, unblinking eyes tell her that he is dead.

Kallie forced the image away, but it was too late—the memory demolished her slow-building pleasure like a wrecking ball. She stiffened in Layne's embrace. Buried her face against his shoulder. Desperation burned through her. "Dammit."

"You need to tell me what's going on, Kallie," Layne said quietly.

"Memories," she replied, throat tight. "Of my father, of Gage . . . it's like I'm dreaming with my eyes open. I can't seem to control it."

"Too tired or too haunted," Layne said. His fingers traced heated trails along her back, her hips. Kallie shivered. "I know about haunted. And I know what to do. Hold on, beautiful. When I stand up, wrap those legs around me."

Layne rose from the chair, still inside of her, and lowered Kallie to the floor in one fluid move. He moved up along her body, his dreads snaking along over her belly, her breasts, teasing her nipples, then he flipped her legs over his shoulders and drove in deep. Kallie arched her back and gasped.

"The best way to forget about being haunted"— Layne's hands found hers and pinned them together above her head—"is to fuck."

Heated flutters rippled through her belly. "But that's what we've been doing for hours."

"No it ain't. We've been performing a ritual, exploring, playing. I'm talking about down-and-dirty, no-time-for-thought, primal fucking."

And before Kallie could say another word, Layne pounded into her with a savage and demanding urgency that blanked her mind of thought, erased all words. Her wrists bound together in his steel grip, she was once again his willing prisoner. Heat shimmered through her belly. She arched up to meet his thrusts, and pleasure shuddered through her in a molten wave.

Moaning, Kallie looked into Layne's eyes as the orgasm racked her body and suddenly saw a galaxy of tender and passionate possibilities in the unguarded depths of his green eyes.

Traveling the road with him and his clan, teaching hoodoo to their son . . .

Staying in Bayou Cyprés Noir, a cottage of their own, his Harley in the yard . . .

Him traveling, her staying, and the hot, sweaty acrobatic nights whenever he returned . . .

Layne drove into her, hard and fast, whispering her name as he came, pulsing inside of her. And triggered by his, another orgasm spiraled through her. Kallie gasped, and the last reluctant chakra pinwheeled open inside of her, clearing the way for the energy she and Layne had created with each kiss, each touch, every joining.

The snake of feminine fire looped at the base of Kallie's spine uncoiled and shot up in a blazing path of energy through her opened chakras to merge with the molten column of Layne's rising masculine fire.

Something writhed and twisted at Kallie's core, trying to escape, sank fangs into her heart. She cried out in pain. She felt something dark and oily swirling along her spine, only to disintegrate in the white-hot river of energy rushing through her.

Incandescent light starred out from between her and Layne, spiking into them both with a heated radiance, enveloping them.

Sacred fire swallowed the *cabane*.

Outside, thunder rumbled, drowning out the drums, and a voice boomed, "Time be up, Kallie Rivière."

Belladonna, on her third shift in the protective circle, and wearing a borrowed yellow rain slicker against the storm, stared in wonder as brilliant white light shafted out from around the *cabane*'s door seams and from around the edges of the plywood nailed over the windows, illuminating the afternoon's gloom in thin stripes.

"Hellfire," she breathed.

A voice rolled in on the thunder. The Baron's. "Time be up, Kallie Rivière."

"Not yet it isn't!" Belladonna cried.

The *cabane* shuddered as though rocked by a small explosion, then the door was blasted off its hinges and the plywood blown from the windows as blinding light shafted from the *cabane*'s interior.

Shielding her eyes with the edge of her hand, Belladonna twisted away from the light. Power pealed through Le Nique like a wedding bell. The smell of brimstone curled thick into the air—spent magic.

Belladonna's heart gave a little leap. "She did it. I knew she would."

Over by the stone cottage, wolves lifted their voices in an eerie howl.

A sheet draped around her body, Kallie staggered into the doorway, panic on her face. She looked in the direction of the howling wolves. "Jackson," she whispered, and stumbled down the steps.

"Shug, wait!" Belladonna chased after her.

FORTY-ONE

TO THEIR
PROPER NATURES

The wolves ringing the stone cottage stopped howling and their multitoned, primal song dropped away to be replaced by the wind's rising voice. Kallie pulled to a stop in front of the cottage, her bare feet sliding in the rain-slick grass.

A cold hand spider-walked up her spine. The heavy stone door stood wide open. Storm-thinned daylight trickled inside. Her heart contracted. Was she too late?

Time be up, Kallie Rivière.

She heard footsteps squelching to a stop beside her. "Hold on, already," Belladonna said, grabbing hold of Kallie's arm. "I'm coming with you."

"Me too." Layne joined them, clad only in his jeans, earning himself a look of appreciation from Belladonna.

Flashing a grateful smile at both of them, Kallie walked into the cottage. The musky wounded-animal smell had faded underneath the fresh air. Jackson lay curled on the straw-littered floor, eyes closed, his bare skin a pale smudge in the cottage's shadows.

In human form again. His Change finally complete. But he was so still.

Holding on to her improvised sheet sarong, Kallie

hurried across the straw to her cousin, kneeling beside him. Just as she reached a hand toward him to brush the hair from his face, she became aware that someone besides Ambrose waited in the cottage. She smelled hot peppers and rum.

Kallie swiveled around on her knees, pulse pounding, and looked up into Baron Samedi's skull-painted face—or rather, *Cash*'s skull-painted face. She realized there was something different about him, something she couldn't put her finger on. Exhaustion buzzed through her, blurred her thoughts. Only adrenaline kept her more or less upright.

"Jackson's safe," she insisted. "I restored things to their proper natures." Doubt wormed through her. "Didn't I?"

"Dat you did, *ma jolie*," the Baron replied, sliding a gloved finger along the brim of his top hat. And Kallie realized that the fedora and Armani suit had been replaced by the Baron's traditional top hat and tuxedo. "Everyt'ing be where it belongs. Except my *cheval*."

"And my cousin?"

"You made de deadline, little hoodoo. Barely. So yo' cousin lives and you get to keep de *loa*—until such time as you find yo' soul, dat is."

"Then what happens to the *loa*?" Kallie asked.

The Baron shrugged. "Ain't none o' yo' business, little hoodoo," he said. "Now, as for dis *cheval*, I t'ink I'll take him back to where I found him."

Kallie thought about how well that would go—the Baron depositing Cash like an empty bottle at her aunt's house. "A better idea would be to take him to his cousin, Kerry. He's been worried that Cash was changed into a black hen."

At worst, Kerry would faint at the Baron and Cash's sudden arrival and the hen would cluck disapprovingly.

"Dat be a fine idea." The Baron thumped his walking stick against the floor. Then slid it between his legs and waggled it back and forth suggestively. "If not for my beautiful Maman Brigitte . . ." Grinning, he vanished in a puff of cigar smoke—even though he hadn't been smoking one.

Kallie sat back on her heels, exhaling in relief.

"I can see there's never a dull moment around you," Ambrose drawled, an undertone of amused irritation threaded through his voice.

"Then you haven't been shopping with her," Belladonna said. "Girl buys the first thing she sees. Doesn't try things on. Doesn't compare. Doesn't even squeal when she scores a tasty item—like these boots," she extended her foot. "Knockoffs, sure, but you'd never know it. Trust me. She offers *plenty* of dull moments."

"Thanks, Bell," Kallie growled.

"Don't mention it, Shug."

Ambrose blinked. "Poor Jackson," he murmured.

Kallie swung around to face Jackson again. Leaning over, she smoothed his tangled espresso locks back from his face. Although dried blood smeared his lips and one cheek, he looked peaceful.

"When I heard the wolf song," she said, "I thought that maybe he had . . ." She let the words trail off, reluctant to say them aloud even now.

"That was a song of celebration," Ambrose replied. "First Change successfully completed."

"I was right about his fine ass," Belladonna murmured approvingly.

"He's my cousin, Bell. My *cousin*. Quit looking at his ass."

"She can look," a soft voice slurred, "as long as I get to look at hers too."

"Deal," Belladonna replied.

Kallie looked into Jackson's sleepy, honey-colored eyes, saw the smile brushing his lips, hinting at wickedness. He reached up and grasped her hand, folded his bloodstained fingers through hers.

"I ain't had enough yet, short stuff," he said. "*Merci beaucoup*, Kallie."

"*Tais-toi*. Just go back to sleep." Tears stung her eyes. Happy tears, this time. Tears she didn't bother to blink away. She squeezed his hand.

"Bossy, you," Jackson said, eyes shuttering closed again.

The click of claws on stone and the jingling of her collar announced Cielo's arrival. The Siberian husky—no longer the stealth variety—trotted over to Jackson and deposited a freshly killed squirrel near his head. Nudged it toward him with her muzzle.

"Dog, please." Belladonna's nose wrinkled in disgust. "You can't be serious."

Cielo looked from the squirrel to Jackson, then back to the squirrel.

"Gah," Belladonna declared.

"Um . . . good girl, but Daddy's sleeping," Kallie said. "He'll eat later, okay?"

Tongue lolling as if in agreement, Cielo sat and waited.

As Kallie watched Jackson sleep, wondering if she had the energy to climb to her feet, she became aware of an irregular *thunk-thunk* against the roof—like tree branches pushed by the wind—became aware of drumming rain. Her heart contracted. The hurricane was still on its way.

"Divinity needs to contact the ward hoodoos and make sure the wards are working," Kallie said, twisting around to look up at Belladonna. "Evelyn's still on the way. How long till landfall?"

Belladonna opened her mouth, but it was Divinity's voice that answered as the hoodoo walked into the cottage. "About five hours, *chère*. And I contacted the ward hoodoos the moment I saw yo' light shafting tru de village. We be hoping it ain't too late for de wards to slow Evelyn down, steal some of her punch."

"I think y'all will be riding the storm out here," Ambrose said.

"True, dat," Divinity said, joining Kallie. "Boy looks like a mess, but he be alive, t'anks to you and yo' nomad. And you both look dead on yo' feet."

Ambrose knelt and draped a blanket over Jackson, then gathered him into his arms. "Let's get y'all over to my home, get ready for the blowdown."

Releasing Jackson's hand, Kallie rose to her feet. Her vision grayed and a high-pitched humming filled her ears. The cottage's dim interior spun.

Kallie felt herself falling, then felt strong arms snapping around her. She caught a whiff of musk and sweet orange and knew the arms belonged to Layne.

"I'm surprised de girl stayed conscious dis long," she heard her aunt say.

Then nothing as Kallie tumbled into a dreamless dark.

FORTY-TWO

EVELYN

The eerie shrieks of a thousand furious cats shredded the dark and yanked Kallie up from sleep. She stared at the unfamiliar ceiling above her, heart pounding, struggling to remember where and when and what—until the wind's steady howl sank in.

Le Nique. Blowdown. Evelyn had arrived.

Rain machine-gunned the house. The roof creaked and groaned.

Kallie sat up, pushing a quilt off her legs. She realized she still wore the sheet she'd grabbed from the *cabane* and that she was on a bed in a darkened room that smelled faintly of ripe apples. Layne slept on his back beside her, his face turned away toward the plywood-protected windows. Beyond them, Evelyn raged.

Kallie slid off the bed and stood, then gasped. Every muscle in her body ached and she was sore in some very tender places. She glanced over her shoulder at Layne. And no wonder. A marathon eight hours.

Her cheeks heated as a tide of emotions—embarrassment, affection, uncertainty, yearning—washed over her. It was a ritual, she reminded herself, a necessity. Not a romantic hookup. Not even a date. Still, she couldn't stop herself from turning around, leaning over the bed, and trailing a finger along one pale dread.

When Kallie straightened, she noticed her clothes resting in a neat pile on the nightstand. Removing her sheet-sarong, she dressed quickly. At the door, she paused to give Layne one last look, then slipped from the room.

Clad in a white tee and jeans, Jackson sat hunched forward on the sofa in the front room, his body knotted, his fisted hands braced between his knees. Shadows and soft light from the lantern on the end table flickered across his face. The bottom edge of his tattoo peeked out from beneath his right sleeve.

> *Gone, but never forgotten*
> *Nicolas & Lucia Bonaparte*
> *Junalee & Jeanette, my angels*
> *Je t'aime toujours*

A pang of sympathy cut through Kallie. She suspected that the hurricane outside had nothing on the blowdown of grief and rage and survivor's guilt Evelyn had resurrected within her cousin.

"Hey, Jacks," she said.

He looked at her, his eyes glowing a pale absinthe green in the lantern light. "Hey back," he replied, rising to his feet as she crossed the room to join him, a smile on his lips. *"Comment ça va?"*

"Ça va bien. How about you?"

"Never better, short stuff. Thanks to you." Jackson wrapped Kallie up in a tight hug. As always, he smelled of the sea—brine and surf and wet sand—a soothing, familiar scent. "*Ti-tante* said that you and Bell never stopped searching for me, never gave up."

"You'd do the same for me," Kallie said, looking up into his honey-eyed gaze.

He grinned. "In a fucking heartbeat."

"What happened to you—the Change—was all my fault," she said, throat constricting. "If you'd . . . if anything had . . ."

"Bullshit. It was my mother's fault, Kall, not yours. All you did was set me free."

"And nearly killed you in the process!"

"Again, wasn't your fault, *chère*. Ti-tante told me what happened." He chewed on his lower lip as though mulling over the words he'd just spoken. "Or most of it, anyway. She told me that we-all needed to have a long talk when we got home."

"Understatement," Kallie muttered. She wondered how her cousin would react to the news of his aunt's new identity—correction: *original* identity.

Kallie reached up and pushed Jackson's dark hair back from his face. No pointed ears like Devlin Daniels's. "How did it feel?" she asked. "Changing."

Releasing her, Jackson stepped back a pace. "You know when you get a tattoo, how it hurts like holy hell as the needle pierces your skin over and over until your brain kicks out the endorphins and everything goes numb and you're riding an awesome endorphin high?"

"No, actually, but I've heard that's how it works," Kallie replied.

"You didn't pick up any tats while in N'awlins?"

"Nope. But was that how Changing felt?"

"Oh, hell, no. Changing hurt like a motherfucker."

Kallie whapped his shoulder. "While I'm really sorry to hear that—I'm relieved to note that you're still a god-damned brat."

Jackson snorted. "I coulda told you that."

Kallie hesitated for a moment before saying, "Y'know, it took me a while to remember what you'd told me when we were little—about your papa being a *loup-garou*. It'd been so long, I'd forgotten about it. How come you never mentioned it again?"

With a low sigh, Jackson sank back down onto the sofa. "After Papa moved out of the house and Mama told us that we'd never Change, that it wasn't in us, I was so disappointed"—he shrugged—"that I didn't want to talk about it. For a while, I even thought Papa had left *because* we couldn't Change." A muscle flexed in his jaw. "I know different now."

Kallie sat beside him. "How you doing with all of this? You've had a ton of shit dumped on your plate in the last forty-eight hours."

One dark eyebrow quirked up. "So have you," he pointed out. "Me, I'm fine."

Kallie knew better, but she let the lie pass. She looked around the shadowed room to where Belladonna and Divinity sat at a lantern-lit table playing cards with Ambrose and January—Go Fish, given Belladonna's polite request for Divinity's twos and her aunt's crowed, gleeful response. An anxious *whoo* from beneath the table and the gleam of lambent eyes revealed Cielo's huddled presence.

"Where's everyone else?" Kallie asked.

"Gabrielle left fo' Lafayette right after de magic fix," Divinity replied. "Some o' de udder hoodoos left about den too; a few stayed to ride out de storm. Dat little nomad, McKenna, she be over at Angélique and Merlin's place. Me, I invited her to come here, but she refused." She glanced at Ambrose. "Gimme all o' yo' fives."

The Alpha sighed. Plucking two cards from his hand, he gave them to Divinity. "Never play cards with a hoo-doo," he grumbled.

"Mmm-hmm," Divinity affirmed.

Kallie could understand McKenna's refusal. Could imagine how she would feel in the *shuvani*'s place if an ex-husband she still loved had just spent eight sweaty, passion-drenched hours in the sack with a woman she despised.

"How long was I asleep?" Kallie asked. "And when did Evelyn make landfall?"

"Almost six hours, Shug, for sleep," Belladonna answered, "two hours since landfall. It's a little past midnight. I thought maybe you'd just snooze through the whole thing."

The house shuddered in a fierce blast of wind, the rain's nonstop staccato hammering sounding like a herd of cows tap-dancing on the roof. Something thudded hard against the side of the house.

"Not me. But it looks like Layne might," Kallie said. "For some reason I thought he'd be a light sleeper, since he's a nomad and all—"

"I potioned him," Divinity explained. "His head was hurting again. The sleep will do him good."

"It will," Kallie agreed.

A heavy crash from outside jarred the house. Cielo backed farther into the shadows under the table. Jackson jumped to his feet.

"Just a tree, boy," Ambrose commented. "It missed us, otherwise the wind would be whipsawing through here, tearing everything apart."

"Gonna check." Tension edged Jackson's voice. He winced as he headed for the kitchen and the back door at its end, his stride as slow and stiff as that of an arthritic old man.

Bet he hurts everywhere. Muscles. Joints. Tendons. Even his skin and teeth.

But it was Jackson's haunted heart that worried Kallie the most.

She rose from the sofa and hurried after her cousin, catching up with him at the back door as he was lifting up the wooden bar barricading the door. Kallie blinked. Seemed that *loups-garous* didn't believe in locks, just slabs of wood to keep doors shut during blowdowns.

The wind wrenched the door from Jackson's grasp and slammed it open against the counter. Falling in horizontal sheets, rain slashed into the kitchen, slicked the floor tiles. The din outside was deafening—a monstrous roar. Things thumped and snapped and twanged in the pitch-black darkness beyond.

Wind blasted into the kitchen, sucking at Kallie's breath and yanking at her hair. "Close the door!" she shouted over the noise. "You can't see nothing anyway!"

Jackson grabbed the doorjambs and braced himself. "I wanna see if the water's rising. I'll grab a lantern."

"Even if it is, the house is on pilings. The water can't reach us. Forget the goddamned lantern and close the goddamned door!"

Rain needled Kallie's face, stung her eyes. She spun

away from the door and Evelyn's savage maw. Wind grabbed at her, shoved.

"Our house was on pilings too," Jackson yelled, trying to be heard over the storm. "Ten feet up, remember? And it wasn't enough. Not even close. Gaspard's storm surge turned out to be eighteen fucking feet. We never had a chance."

Kallie's heart drummed against her ribs. Those were the first words he'd ever spoken about what had happened during that awful day nine years ago. She turned back around to face him. Jackson was struggling to wrestle the door shut, fighting the wind, the muscles cording in his arms and neck. Kallie joined him, and it took all of their combined strength to close the door.

Panting, Jackson dropped the thick wood bar back into place. He was soaked to the skin, his white tee rendered transparent by the rain and clinging to his chest and flat belly. He shoved his wet hair back from his face. Behind him, the shrieking wind pounded at the door, rattling it in its frame.

"Tell me," Kallie said softly, pushing back her own wet tresses. "What happened that day, *cher*? How come y'all didn't get out in time?"

Jackson stared at her for a long moment, his back against the shuddering door. Water dripped from his face. A muscle in his jaw snapped taut. "We were only supposed to get the edge of the storm," he said, his tone flat. "But Gaspard shifted course from Texas to Louisiana. We didn't find out until it was too late. When Mama realized what was happening, she loaded us into the pickup."

Jackson slid down the door to sit on the rain-puddled floor and wrapped his arms around his upraised knees. He continued speaking, and tears stung Kallie's eyes as she sat down beside him and listened to his heartbreaking mono-tone words.

The pile-driving wind refuses to allow Papa to open the truck's door, so Papa pulls them from the truck through the driver's-side window after Mama manages to it roll down. Jackson is lifted out last. He scoops Jeanette up and she locks her arms around his neck in a near stranglehold and scissors her legs around her waist. He feels her trembling against him.

"Tout va bien," he promises her. "Everything's gonna be okay, p'tite. Just hold on tight."

"It's too late to drive outta here!" Papa yells, gathering Junalee into his arms. "Head back to the house!"

They race back home through horizontal sheets of rain and caterwauling wind, fighting to keep upright every step of the way. Once inside, Jackson coaxes his baby sister into releasing her death grip around his neck and eases her onto the sofa.

Even though it is still daylight, Mama busies herself with lighting lanterns and handing out flashlights. With the windows boarded up against the storm, the house is full of shadows and gloom. The girls sit huddled together on the sofa, eyes wide and faces pale as things thump and thud against the roof and exterior walls.

Jackson fetches Monopoly out of the hall closet and sets the game up on the coffee table. Papa claims the top hat, and Mama the iron. It takes some coaxing, but finally Junalee picks the thimble and Jeanette the dog, leaving Jackson the roadster.

They're in the middle of the second game — Junalee has hotels on Boardwalk and Park Place — when the sound of splintering wood and screeching nails from overhead suggest that parts of the roof are being peeled away. Jackson's heart launches into a frantic rhythm.

Everyone looks up.

"What's that, Papa?" Jeanette asks in a small voice.

Papa rises to his feet, his gaze on the ceiling. "Just the wind, p'tite."

Something large crashes against the outside wall and the house sways as though no longer anchored to the pilings or the foundation, then shifts. Cracks zigzag along the walls, the ceiling. Plaster dusts the hardwood.

Jackson stands and reaches for Jeanette. The house is starting to disintegrate beneath the howling wind's ferocious onslaught. Just as he scoops his baby sister into his arms, the front door slams open and a brown wall of churning water a good eight feet high surges into the house, knocking Jackson off his feet and sucking him and Jeanette under.

In the dark, tumultuous water Jackson can't tell up from down. Debris and furniture swirl along in the briny tide, crashing into him with bruising force. Arms locked around his sister, he kicks upward—or at least what he hopes is upward—and breaches the water's surface.

He has a split second to realize that the house has vanished before something massive—maybe an uprooted oak—smashes into him. Pain knifes his ribs. His vision grays. By the time the tree sweeps past him, Jackson realizes his arms are empty.

Jeanette is gone.

"I lost her," Jackson said, voice low and tight. "I let go. She was counting on me to keep her safe and somehow I let go."

"No, that's bullshit," Kallie said fiercely, blinking back

tears. "You *never* let her go. She was ripped from your arms, but you didn't let go."

Jackson met her gaze and held it. "You don't know that."

"Neither do you," Kallie retorted.

"Yeah, I do. I was there."

"Doesn't mean you know what happened."

"Christ," Jackson muttered. "Let's just drop it."

A sharp, splintering crack cut through the wind's howl, followed by a hard thump. Another tree, Kallie figured— or part of one, anyway. "The wards must be working," she said, "because this sure as hell ain't a category five storm."

Jackson nodded. "It ain't."

"Oh, wait. Speaking of wards." Kallie pulled Jackson's mojo bag from the pocket of her shorts and handed it to him. "I found this in the yard. That's when I knew something bad had happened to you."

"*Merci*, Kall." Jackson knotted the leather strap around his neck, then tucked the small red flannel bag into the neck of his T-shirt. The woodsy scents of dog rose and sandalwood curled into the air. He draped a companionable arm across Kallie's shoulders and she snuggled in against him.

"You're wet," she complained.

"Whiner." After a moment, he said, "Thanks for not giving up on me."

Kallie looked at him and smiled. "Family never does."

FORTY-THREE

AFTERMATH

Sitting in the porch swing at home, cold glass of iced tea in one hand and a PBJ sandwich in the other, Kallie watched Jackson trot down the steps and return to work clearing the yard of tree branches and other debris left by the hurricane.

He swiveled around, shading his eyes against the sun with the edge of his hand, and looked at Kallie. "You gonna laze about like some bonbon-eating hoodoo diva or are you gonna get your ass back down here?"

"Whiner," Kallie said. "I'll be there in a minute. I need to finish my sandwich. Some of us actually chew our food instead of inhaling it."

"Chewing is overrated."

"Said the wolf. Go away."

Puckering his lips and patting his ass—very clear message—Jackson grabbed the wheelbarrow and rolled it across the yard to what remained of a young dogwood tree.

"He took de news pretty well," Divinity commented.

Kallie agreed. In fact, her cousin hadn't seemed fazed at all by Divinity's new identity or by her theft of

Gabrielle's. Had taken the revelation of Kallie's missing soul and the *loa* nestled in its place equally in stride.

"You did what you had to, *Ti-tante*," Jackson had said. "And you did it for us—for Kallie in particular. Ain't gonna get no complaints from me."

"Well, he *is* a pirate," Kallie murmured. She shifted her attention to her aunt, met her gaze. "But he's right, y'know. Everything you did—right or wrong—you did for us. You took us in, cared for us, and educated us. And we both appreciate that more than we can say."

Surprise flickered in Divinity's eyes. "You be feeling all right, girl?"

"Fine. I'm feeling fine," Kallie said. "I've just had time to think about the value of family, about what's important and what isn't. I wish you would've told me about the *loa* from the start, wish you would've trusted me with the truth. But trust shouldn't be an issue now, right?"

"Shouldn't be," Divinity agreed.

Kallie's eyes narrowed as she realized her aunt hadn't actually answered the question. Placing her empty tea glass on the porch railing, she was about to point that little lapse out when she heard the low rumble of a motorcycle thundering up the dirt drive. And, yup, it looked like Belladonna's Dodge Dart was right behind him.

Kallie smiled. Layne's Harley had survived both wreck and storm. The wards had managed to diminish Evelyn's ferocity from a catastrophic category five to a category one by the time she made landfall near Houma. After that, she had weakened even more. The damage to land and property had been minimal—all things considered.

It'd been a goddamned close call.

"We're gonna continue with this later," Kallie said.

"*Mais oui*," Divinity replied, then flapped a hand at her. "Shoo."

Kallie pulled off her work gloves, tossed them onto the porch railing, then went to meet the pair stopping in front of the house. Belladonna was there to pick her up so they could fetch Dallas from the hospital in Baton Rouge and bring him to Bayou Cyprés Noir to finish his recuperation.

Layne was there to say good-bye.

Kallie drew in a deep breath of clean, storm-scrubbed air, hoping it would help ease the ache in her heart. She wasn't sure if what she felt for the sexy nomad was love or gratitude or hot-blooded lust. Or even a combination of the three—especially after their impassioned hours together.

One thing she'd never forget—the feel of his body against hers, a perfect fit.

She knew she cared for Layne—a lot. And she knew he would always be welcome in her bed. But she couldn't ask him to stay any more than he could ask her to ride with him.

At least, not yet.

Belladonna slid out of her car, her slim frame draped in a purple minidress, black tights, and platform boots. Kallie pursed her lips. Had Belladonna mistaken their trip to Baton Rouge to pick up a certain grumpy and restless root doctor for an audition gig on *America's Next Top Model*?

As if reading her mind—again—Belladonna winked. "Thought I'd give Dallas something to think about other than his anger at Divinity. Distract him."

"That'll do the trick, hun," Jackson said, admiration

glinting in his eyes. He circled a finger in the air. "Twirl around."

With a coy smile, Belladonna did just that, her skirt lifting just enough to entice.

Kallie rolled her eyes. The pair had been flirting shamelessly ever since Le Nique, even though they'd known each other for years. Maybe it was the wolf musk. . . .

"Hey, sunshine," Layne said as Kallie stopped beside his Harley, a warm smile curving his lips. He swung his leg over the Harley and stood. Closed the small distance between them. The backs of his fingers brushed her cheek. Kallie looked up into his eyes, and a shock rippled through her, as always.

"What are your plans after Gage's cremation?" she asked, fingering one of his honey-blond dreads.

"Going to New Orleans to unload Augustine."

"And after that?"

"Dunno. You got something in mind?"

"I was wondering if you'd go to Shreveport with me. I think it's time I got a few answers from my mother—like where the hell she hid my soul."

Layne's road-rough hands cupped Kallie's face. Then his head dipped and his lips—warm and firm—kissed hers. His kiss tasted of coffee and peppermint schnapps and bitter grief, and she knew it was Gage he was thinking of.

"When do you want to go?" Layne asked against her lips when the kiss ended.

"How about in four days? Will that be enough time?"

"I'll meet you here in four days, then, sunshine."

Kallie smiled. "It's a date, *cher.*"

Another quick kiss, then Layne lifted his head. His dread slithered free of her grasp, taking the scent of sandalwood and orange blossom with it. "See you then." He straddled his Harley, gunned the engine.

Kallie watched him ride away up the dirt road and felt a sharp pang as she wondered if she would always be watching him ride away.

"You ready to go, Shug?" Belladonna asked. "I don't want Dallas to think we've forgotten about him."

"He should know better," Kallie said as she walked around to the Dodge Dart's passenger door. "Family never does."

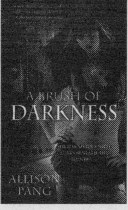